THE DAWN OF THE SACRED

THE MAWOAKIN CONSPIRACY

BY
MORRISON FULLER

To my wife and step-daughter,
for your endless patience and support,
and to my late mother,
who always carried a song in her heart.

PROLOGUE
The YAYAPTI

"It happened long ago, far across the Great Sea to the east," Tiam began. "Mawoi burst out of the frozen marshes in the Land of Many Rivers and his Great Light blossomed in the sky."

"The sun!" her little boy squeaked, making her giggle.

"Yes, Atura."

On a short bedside table, a beeswax candle flickered in her teal eyes and illuminated her son's small bedchamber in a soft yellow glow. Above the table and centered in the eastern wall, a window opened to the dark jungle outside and the swirling gray clouds of an approaching storm. Tiam did her best to ignore the storm and gazed down upon her firstborn son who snuggled himself tighter against her hip with a big smile on his perfect face.

"The wicked Frost Spirit, Sikulka, ruled over the many rivers before we Itabayiti emerged from the reeds, but Mawoi banished him to his mountain peaks."

She spoke softly, taking her time recounting her son's favorite bedtime story, the Yayapti, the story of their people. He liked to hear the whole story in one sitting and not just in bits and pieces like his father, Abensu, preferred to stretch out over several nights. Suddenly, a flash of lightning startled them, followed by a low rumble of angry thunder and the first plops of raindrops on the palm fronds outside. Atura threw his thin arms around her bulging pregnant belly and buried his face in her tunic.

"There, there," she said with a sigh, running her fingers through his thick black hair.

Atura was born under a new moon in the heart of the rainy season nearly two and a half years earlier. He arrived early with pale skin and an adorable tuft of dark-brown hair on his steaming head. Like his mother, he was instantly curious and vocal, but Atura was also easily frightened like his father. Abensu was in the other room waiting for her, but Tiam wasn't ready to join him. She rubbed her son's shivering arms and kissed his forehead, and then she forced herself to look out through the window to the ominous sky beyond.

The evening was starting exactly like the Eternal One had said it would – *A second son twists the sky, while Ora churns around him.* Tiam recalled the vision as clearly as if she had been the one to have it, but then she quickly closed her eyes again and reminded herself the vision hadn't come to her. There was still a chance, however small, it wasn't intended for her. Shaking the thought from her mind, she returned her gaze to her boy who was now looking back up at her. Dim firelight from the fire basin in the other room reflected in his worried, pale-green eyes, making them sparkle like sunlight on the sea.

"Mawoi's great light radiated over the frigid reeds," she said, "and he vowed his warmth would never again diminish. As the rivers melted, we Itabayiti used bone hooks and line made from strips of reeds to fish along the sandy banks, and we sharpened our stone-tipped spears on river rock."

"Why, itaba?" Atura asked his mother.

"Well, we had to defend ourselves from the dangerous creatures who drank from the cool waters of the many rivers," she replied. "It is said that some of those ferocious beasts had long sharp fangs and arms the size of tree trunks." Tiam walked her fingers up his arm, tickling him and making him giggle. "The *nani* walked on their fists in large packs, and the meanest of them had shimmering gray hair on their backs. One strike from a nani could crush you, or even someone as big as your baba," she said, referring to his father. "During the dry season, when the water was shallow enough to walk across, all sorts of creatures came to the many rivers. That was when we stopped fishing and took up our spears."

"Kanu!" Atura shouted, anticipating the next part in the story. There was another crackle of thunder, and the rain grew louder.

"It is said that Boynay, the Rain Spirit, became angry one day and caused the rivers to overflow and the marshes to flood." Tiam hovered over her boy like a cloud, wiggling her fingers like rain. "The deluge was so sudden and fierce, it forced the Itabayiti to climb the few remaining kiosay trees before the riverbank washed away. It was *then* that Kanu, the Great Serpent, came up from the deep, dark waters and spoke to them."

She dropped the tone of her voice to a deep growling hiss. "*I am lonely*, Kanu said. *I want children of my own, but I am old, and my body is tired.* The Itabayiti could do nothing but listen as the floodwaters continued to rise. *I will teach you to make reed boats in my image*, Kanu said, *that you might navigate these waters as I do and bring back offerings for me.*"

"Kanu bad?" Atura asked.

Tiam shrugged. "Maybe, but the Great Serpent was true to her word, and she taught us how to build fantastic reed boats we call *canuti*. Each canuti has a head, a slender neck, a wide belly like your itaba, and a long slender tail that curves upward."

"*Ca-noo-tee!*" Her boy enunciated the word perfectly.

"The offspring of Kanu," she added, but then grimaced from a sharp pain in her stomach.

He watched her with concern, but Tiam held up her hand to let him know she was alright. She then took several long, controlled breaths, and waited for the pain to subside. After a tense moment, a warm wave of relief washed over her, and she continued the story.

"We Itabayiti became great navigators of the many rivers, and it wasn't long before our canuti were stained blood-red and Kanu had grown fat." She rubbed her belly for emphasis, making her boy giggle again. "But one warm night after the waters finally receded, the Amunti arrived in the Land of Many Rivers."

"Oh no!" her boy exclaimed.

"They were like us, but covered in long, coarse hair." She ran her fingers through his hair again, making it stick straight up. "Like the hair of a howling kugo, but with sand-colored skin underneath. It's said, they also spoke a strange tongue that was choppy and forced through jagged yellow teeth. Fortunately, the Amunti weren't hostile toward the Itabayiti, but they did have a deep hatred for Kanu."

Tiam dropped the tone of her voice again, "*Pick up your spears and destroy them*, the Great Serpent pleaded, but the Itabayiti refused. They were exhausted by Kanu's unquenchable hunger and didn't want to get involved." She set Atura upright, so that she could look into his eyes. "The Great Serpent hissed, *Cowards!* And then, without our protection, the Amunti descended upon Kanu and carved her up into four pieces. *Baga, avenge me!* she cried with her dying breath, and that was the last we heard from the Great Serpent."

Just then, a strong gust of wind blew in through the open window, pelting their exposed skin with rain as if by a handful of pebbles. Atura shielded his face, while his mother set him on the bed and quickly closed the shutters. When she finished latching them in place, she slowly sat beside her boy, slightly out of breath, but trying not to show it.

"Baby?" he asked, rubbing his wet arms.

"Not yet," she replied, forcing a smile.

"When?"

"Babies come from Ora, the Birthplace of Life," Tiam explained. "Your itaba is a gateway to Ora, and itabati were once revered and cherished. It's said, we Itabayiti were once ruled by a line of great itabati, starting with Obya. When Obya passed on to be with the ancestors, her name became the title bestowed upon her oldest daughter, Dukya." She watched her boy nodding along as if understanding completely, which made Tiam smile. "Now, when your brother arrives, your baba..."

"*Bruh-ver?*" Atura interrupted her.

"Yes," she answered, tickling him again. "When your brother arrives, your baba will blow a lungful of air over him until he stops crying. This imparts the breath of life, or Great Spirit, to him on behalf of Yucahu."

Tiam took a deep breath and started to blow over her son, but then she felt another surge of pain. She quickly looked at the rattling shutters to distract herself, counting the rainwater dripping onto the stone floor and attempting to control her breathing once more. She fussed with her tunic belt, which she suddenly realized was unbearably tight. When she finally got the belt into a position that was reasonably comfortable, her thoughts returned to the vision – *and Kayki sinks beneath his feet...*

"Where was I?" she abruptly asked, attempting to subvert her intrusive thoughts. "Oh, yes. Without Kanu, it was important to keep the knowledge of building canuti alive by training every child from the moment they can walk." She looked at her boy. "You've been to the reed yard, haven't you?" she asked, and Atura nodded. "Did you know we also measure everything by them?" He shook his head. "One reed is almost three arm lengths." Tiam gestured with her arms outstretched. "When you're half-a-reed tall, you'll begin training to harness Maroha, the Wind Spirit, and tame

Niama, the Water Spirit. Children who do not cry at birth, do not receive the breath of life, and are denied this training. Then they are handed over to the araco to be trained in their ways."

"Why?" he asked.

Tiam raised her eyebrows just as Abensu entered the room. "Ah – your baba will tell you when you're older."

"Tell him what?" Abensu asked, pensively. Her husband was a tall man, fit and thin, with dark cocoa skin, and a strong jaw beneath his short and neatly kempt black beard.

"About the *ayr-co*," their son answered, struggling with the pronunciation of the word.

"Oh. Of course, Atu." He tousled their boy's hair and then turned to Tiam with pity in his jungle-green eyes. "My love, we need to get you..."

She thrust her hand in his face, silencing him. "I will be ready, when I am ready," she said firmly. "I want to finish the Yayapti and tuck Atura into bed first."

Abensu sighed and feigned a smile. "Of course, my love. But please..." he paused, looking at her finger nervously tracing around her large belly. "Try to skip a bit – for me?"

"No!" Atura protested, but Tiam laid her hand on his little shoulder.

"I will," she conceded.

"Very well. Tayokun, Atu," he said. Abensu then kissed his son on the cheek and left.

"Tay-kun, baba!" Atura called after him, saying goodnight.

Another crack of thunder boomed outside, causing Atura to quickly hide beneath the covers. Tiam calmly adjusted herself on the edge of the bed, watching the shutters continue to rattle and the rainwater pool on the floor.

"When the beasts came to the many rivers," she said, returning to the story, "Itabayiti women were protected by the men and kept safe in their huts. It is said, in the middle of the hottest and stickiest night anyone could remember, a cry rang out and everyone rushed to a thatched hut and the wailing child inside."

"*Maboti*," Atura whispered, and his mother nodded.

"The wailing child pointed to a hole torn in the wall of the hut where he said a growling shadow had taken his itaba. They searched and searched but never found her. The following night, one of the araco wandered into the river to cool off and was never seen again. The third night, a newly appointed guard went missing after relieving himself in the tree line." Her boy snickered but she continued, her tone growing more ominous. "The Itabayiti panicked, loaded their canuti, and sailed until the dry season came and the river turned to dust beneath them."

Just then, the shutters burst open, and a wall of stinging rain drenched the room. Tiam immediately jumped up from the bed and forced them closed. She set the latch but could see the howling wind would simply blow them open again. Not knowing what else to do, she took the belt from her tunic, looped it around the latch, and then tied it into a knot.

"There," she said, slowly pulling her hand away from the shutter; they remained closed but rattled louder in protest.

"What happens?" Atura asked, wiping rainwater from his cheeks.

Tiam brushed herself off and gently sat back down, relieved to no longer be wearing her belt, but now her irritation shifted to her soaking wet tunic that was sticking to her skin. And then the baby started kicking – *while Ora churns around him...*

"*Itaba,*" Atura whined.

"Yes, my little moon," she said through a forced smile. "Umm...that night, after Mawoi went to sleep in the Durali, beyond the jungle, the Itabayiti remained awake and huddled together around the last kiosay tree. They were scared to follow Mawoi to sleep, but the journey had been hard, and it wasn't long before the heat closed their eyes for them." She leaned over and ran her palm across Atura's eyes, which instantly closed, and then Tiam continued at a whisper. "All were soon sound asleep, except for Obya Tabay and her oldest son, Yaya.

"They talked softly in the hollowed-out section at the base of the tree. when Yaya suddenly noticed the jungle had fallen silent. Wearily, he stepped out from the hollow to investigate. Only a reed away, he instantly saw a shadowy figure staring back at him. He quickly rubbed his eyes and looked again, but he had been mistaken. There wasn't one shadowy figure but five, six, seven, and then he stopped counting at eight and screamed..."

"*Rudu,*" Atura mumbled, his tired eyes still closed.

"Yes. At the call for alarm, the rest of the Itabayiti woke up to see the Amunti emerging from the jungle. A spear zipped past Yaya's ear, through the opening of the tree, and into Obya Tabay. Yaya rushed to his itaba's side, yanked the spear free, and quickly scooped her up into his sturdy arms. He charged out of the kiosay tree and ran toward the sleeping sun in the Durali. Behind him, the Itabayiti and the Amunti collided in combat."

Tiam paused to lift her feet out of the deepening pool of rainwater covering the floor. She could now clearly see the knuckle-deep water trailing off through the doorway of her son's room and into the rest of their residence, where the firelight danced across the ripples – *and Kayki sinks beneath his feet...*

"*Itaba!*" her boy said through a big yawn, snapping her back to the moment.

"Before long, Yaya noticed a great number of Itabayiti running alongside him. It's said, he recognized they were faster than the Amunti, who had always relied on stealth when tracking their prey. Though he doubted they could have escaped Maboti, the Dark Shadow, Yaya was certain they could outrun the Amunti.

"They fled until Mawoi was high overhead. Bright beams of sunlight pierced the dense jungle canopy and illuminated the underbrush far below. When Yaya found a safe place to stop, he gently laid his itaba down on the damp jungle floor and spoke to her, but she did not respond. The Great Spirit had already left her body. As he looked around, breathing heavily, he saw his fellow Itabayiti were bowing toward him."

"Why?" Atura asked, struggling to stay awake.

Tiam raised her eyebrows and pursed her lips, but she stopped herself from answering his question. "There was no time to think!" she blurted out. "Suddenly, a rustling from a thick patch of omabu shrubs not far away alerted the others. They quickly surrounded Yaya and Tabay with their spears pointing outward. So, he kissed his itaba's cool forehead, got to his feet, and charged into the jungle in the direction they had been traveling, realizing he was still carrying the Amunti spear. After a moment, the rest of the Itabayiti followed him.

"Broad wet leaves the size of turtle shells slapped at their thighs as they ran, ducking and dodging under and around tree branches and thick hanging vines. After three more days and nights of running without rest, the Itabayiti found themselves on the edge of an endless sea. The Bocoa, the

Great Sea, stretched out before them. And there along the rocky shore grew the biggest and strongest reeds the Itabayiti had ever seen.

"Even though they hadn't rested in days, they built four canuti before Mawoi's great light sank into the sea. Yaya believed the only way to save our people and escape Maboti and the ravenous Amunti was to do what we Itabayiti do best. So, that night, instead of following Mawoi to sleep, they sailed out across the Great Sea.

"Once the sail lines were tied off and the rest of our people fell asleep, Yaya stood alone at the tiller to welcome the darkness, watching our ancestors dot the sky like sparks from a thousand fires. Suddenly, he noticed something he had never seen before. From behind a swirling mass of dark clouds, a white light appeared. It was too small and dim to be Mawoi, but much bigger than the ancestors."

"*Koo-ra-ka*," her sleepy boy mumbled.

"That's right," she replied. "Kuraka, the Moon Spirit, appeared out of the clouds and has watched over us ever since. But that wasn't the only spectacular thing Yaya witnessed that night," she continued. "As Kuraka passed overhead, Yaya saw a colorful river of light, as if the embers of those thousand fires had been spread from one edge of the void to the other by a giant hand. This smoldering river followed Kuraka, illuminating the canuti and flickering across the gentle waves of the Bocoa. The more Yaya watched, the more there was to marvel at. Large clumps of our ancestors swirled around great bonefires – where we burn the dead to release the Great Spirit. Others silently shot across the void with long white tails like the Great Serpent. I will show you some other night, my little moon."

"Yay!" He yawned an even bigger yawn than before.

"Yaya was mesmerized and wanted to share what he had seen with the rest of the Itabayiti, but by morning the clouds had spread across the entire sky and the waves climbed high above their sails. The enormous waves crashed back down upon the canuti, knocking anything not tied down and anyone with a weak grip into the turbulent waters."

"*Yoo-ra-ca*," Atura said, and his mother nodded.

"Yes, but the Itabayiti had never come across Yuraca before," she told him. "Yaya battled the Storm Spirit not knowing who he was, and helplessly watched as the Itabayiti were flung into the water one by one. Soon, the waves were so high and the pouring rain so thick, he lost all sense of direction. In desperation, Yaya prayed to the spirit of his itaba to guide him, and that was when the light from a single ancestor pierced the canopy of clouds.

"Determined to follow the light, Yaya pointed their canuti directly at it, but the storm instantly blew him back around. After many attempts, he discovered that if he kept the light on his right, the ancestor would follow alongside them, and Maroha would fill their sail."

Tiam abruptly stopped talking when she noticed how quiet the storm outside had become. The shutters were no longer rattling, and she couldn't hear the wind or a single raindrop – *and Hurassa consumes the fields, and Sikulka returns from his peaks, and the gateway to Ora will close forever...* She shivered and shook the vision from her mind.

"Itaba?" Atura rubbed his tired eyes.

She resumed her controlled breathing and thought the Eternal One's vision might have been wrong. It wasn't likely, she had to admit, but as the sound of buzzing insects and the nighttime jungle filled the room once more, a glimmer of hope began to form in her mind.

"*Itaba!*" she heard her son moan.

"Alright, my little moon. Where was I?" she asked.

"Tabay," he muttered.

"Of course. Yaya concluded the bright ancestor must have been Tabay, but his joy was shattered when Mawoi rose from the waters once again to reveal the other canuti were gone. Yaya feared he was destined to wander the Great Sea alone until he heard a faint cry behind him. There, bobbing in the gentle rolling waves like a family of sea turtles, were his fellow Itabayiti. After he pulled them out of the dark waters, he told them all that had happened, and together they named the smoldering river Mayu, and started tracking Kuraka across the night's sky. They counted twenty-nine different phases. And then, after forty days and nights, the Itabayiti spotted land."

"*Id-ba-kan!*" Atura shouted.

"That's right, Itabacan," Tiam said. "They found eleven islands surrounding a much larger twelfth island. There were massive flocks of squawking birds in the sky, chacu and crabs and other creatures on shore, and every kind of fish imaginable swimming in and around brightly colored rocks beneath the surface of the shallow water. They named the largest island in the center Itabaca, and the surrounding eleven islands are called what?" she asked her boy.

"Conaca, Pacca...umm...*Ba-ca?*"

"Ba-*ha*-ca," Tiam helped him. "Remember, many of the islands are named for their most abundant resource." Atura gave her a confused look. "Hatca was infested with large red crabs. Niamca has many freshwater springs. Chacu are raised and trained on Chacuca."

"Why's baba call them *boar?*" he asked.

Tiam giggled, "Because your baba spends too much time with Yaya Amnu, who hates chacu and calls them his great pain!" She tickled Atura's belly, making her boy squeal like a baby boar. "So, Yapaca you know, is flat and where we used to live. Sparkflies once covered Coyaca at night, but now it's where we grow our vegetables. Tell me, what grows on Hamaca?"

"Cotton!"

"Good. And what about Amaca?"

Atura thought for a moment and then said, "Twees?"

She giggled again. "Close enough. Yes, Amaca is densely forested, but it is also where the lesini train in their craft. They are our healers and move from island to island collecting the ingredients they need. Lastly, there's Risca, which has bubbling pools of bitumen that we use for what?"

"Ca-noo-tee!"

"Yes. It helps seal and protect them from the salty water of the Bocoa. Now, because it was Yaya who had rescued everyone, and it was his mother who guided them safely across the Bocoa, the Itabayiti made Yaya their ruler for life. We now refer to him as the Biyaya, the first Yaya, and he ruled for fifteen years. After he went to be with the ancestors, it was proclaimed the name Yaya would be passed down to every ruler of Itabacan."

"How long?" Atura asked.

"Oh – umm," Tiam stumbled over her words. His question caught her off guard. "Well, for nearly a thousand years, I guess. In that time, we Itabayiti created the liquid stone, cibmani, which we pour into molds to form the walls of our homes and the great wall that protects us from Yuraca. We built the Pyramid of Mayu for the araco to observe our ancestors, and at the foot of the pyramid, the plaza hosts our festivals, and the almec courts our almec matches. Spirit temples stand atop the highest point of every island..."

"Kayki!"

"Yes, the Earth Spirit resides in the Temple of Kayki here on our island." Tiam heard her husband sloshing his way through the ankle-deep water toward them. "We have fresh water pumped through covered channels to every home, and our waste and flood water feed into ditches, which then travel to cleansing stations near the harbor."

"Two Grand Gateways straddle the wide waterways between the island of Chacuca and Niamca to the east, and Yapaca to the west," Abensu said, leaning in Atura's doorway. "Our fishing canuti exit through the Gate of Kuraka and return to Itabacan Sound through the Gate of Mawoi. And..." He paused for effect as he sloshed the rest of the way to the foot of his son's bed. "On top of Mount Otaba, the Yaya's Palace glistens like a sun-bleached conch shell overlooking all of Itabacan."

"Wow." Atura's mouth fell open.

"You know, Yaya Amnu is my friend and I'm sure he'll invite us up to the palace one day soon," Abensu added. He turned to Tiam as if wanting to say something, but only smiled at her before turning around and slowly sloshing back the way he came.

"I'm ready," she said, stopping him. "It's time." She slipped her feet into the cool water covering the floor and stood looking down on her firstborn. "Tayokun, my little moon."

"Tay-kun, itaba!" he replied.

Tiam tucked her boy tightly into his reed bed, kissed his forehead, and smiled as he turned over beneath the blanket, closed his eyes, and was soon asleep. She picked up the flickering candle and walked with Abensu into the dining area, which was bright and warm thanks to a blazing fire in a copper-lined basin in the northeast corner. They turned left, their bare feet still sloshing through the water, and walked past a long wooden table in the center of the room covered with the fresh flowers she had gathered earlier that day. After several paces, they turned left again to enter their bedchamber. Suddenly, the air pressure in the residence increased and the howling wind returned, thrusting the back door of the residence open and blowing out the candle in her hand.

Tiam looked up at her husband. "Did the storm not already pass over us?" she asked.

"It did, my love," he answered, rushing to close the door. Once it was secured, he returned to escort her through the doorway and into the bedchamber. "But we only remain in Yuraca's gentle heart for so long."

Tiam's mind was racing as fast as her heart was pounding. She barely noticed Abensu lift her dripping feet out of the water and place them on the bed, where she now lay facing the doorway into the other room and the flickering firelight within. Sweat gathered on her brow and cascaded down into her eyes, but she didn't have the strength to clear it away. She could only let it pool there before allowing it to run down her cheeks. She heard the rain pick back up and the shutters over the window in their bedchamber start to rattle. There was a squeaking noise beside her, and she suddenly noticed Lesini Nun sitting in a wooden chair folding a stack of towels. The elder lesini was staring at her with her dagger-like azure eyes. And then the pain returned – *A second son twists the sky, while Ora churns around him. Kayki sinks beneath his feet...*

She grabbed Abensu's hand. "We must name him..." she started to say, but the pain was excruciating.

"Take it easy, my love," he whispered, petting her hand. "Breathe."

"No!" Tiam shook her head. "Promise me – you must name him *AN-KI.*"

"We'll discuss it later, my..."

"ABENSU!" she screamed, and then she saw the expected shock on his face. Tiam tried to catch her breath, glaring at him as he started to object, but then Abensu quietly nodded his head. "Promise me," she demanded.

"Alright, my love," he wisely conceded. "I promise."

"Thank you," she smiled at him through her pain, and then Tiam reclined her head and closed her eyes.

It was time. She couldn't delay her destiny any longer. As she struggled to control her breathing, feeling her second son squirm within her belly, her thoughts returned to the Eternal One's vision – *and Hurassa consumes the fields, Sikulka returns from his peaks, and the gateway to Ora will close forever.*

PART ONE
The Sons of ABENSU

CHAPTER ONE
The Frayed Thread

Morning light trickled through the cracks in the jungle canopy on the island of Conaca, making all of the foliage glisten and sparkle. Cuckoos, echo birds, and other winged creatures fluttered about and chattered to one another in chirps and whistles, while hutias, spiny rats, and all the flightless critters scurried about in the dense underbrush. A family of howler monkeys whooped and barked back and forth, playing noisily on the winding roots of a kapok tree, eating the leaves, flowers, and berries scattered about on the ground.

Conaca was the northernmost island of the twelve that made up Itabacan, and it was the home of Chief of Wares Abensu and his two sons, Atu and Anki. Their island featured two hills of near equal size, one on the southeastern half and the other on the northwestern half, where the chief's residence sat alongside their attendants' quarters and the Temple of Kayki. A wide clay deposit separated the hills and ran the width of the island, providing all of the materials for Abensu and his waki artisans to make Itabacan's ceramic bowls, plates, and other wares.

When it rained, the clay pits flooded, and a drainage pool was dug near the southwestern edge to collect the excess rainwater, which instantly became Anki and Atu's favorite place to play. It was a typical morning after a late-night thunderstorm. The clay pits had flooded, the drainage pool was full of mucky rainwater, and the sons of Abensu were competing to see which of them was better at slithering like a snake.

Anki pushed past his older brother and slid down the slick clay embankment first, his bottom bouncing on the bumpy surface before he splashed into the light-brown water with a squeal of joy. Atu came down immediately after him but slithered into the pool next to his brother without so much as a ripple.

"Not fair," Anki complained, spitting out a stream of gritty water. "You're too small to make a splash!"

"I am as the Great Spirit made me," Atu replied arrogantly. Anki rolled his eyes and watched his brother climb onto a floating log and balance himself by waving his thin arms. "I bet I'm better at being a turtle too!" Atu challenged him.

Anki glared at his brother wiggling around on his belly like a beached whitefish. His brother knew he was too big to balance on the floating log, and so Anki kicked the log instead, sending it spinning away and his brother splashing face first into the water. Anki laughed so hard, he failed to notice his brother swim up behind him until he got a mouthful of wet clay.

"Gross!" he shouted, sticking out his tongue and letting the slop drip off.

Atu laughed as he waded over to the edge of the pool and started gathering blades of dune grass. His nasal laugh got on Anki's nerves.

"Here," Atu said. "If you can't balance like a turtle, maybe you can eat like one!" He handed Anki a fistful of grass and then howled with laughter, sounding like a pack of baby hutia squealing for their mother.

Atu was older than him by nearly three years, but shorter by a hand, thin, and with a light complexion that made Atu blend in with the clay. His pale-green eyes stuck out like two baby frogs, and he had a fluffy bush of brown hair on top of his head that he kept slick on the sides with olluli sap. His brother was endlessly teased by their friends, especially when Anki wasn't around to defend him, but Anki knew Atu was incredibly patient and conniving, and he would take his revenge when he thought his victim would least expect it.

Anki, on the other hand, had dark cocoa skin, a muscular build, and their father's strong jawline. He tried to mimic his brother's hair style, but the olluli sap wouldn't stick to his thick, oily black hair. His brother's friends avoided confronting Anki because of his size, but also because they knew he didn't know when to quit. He was told he had a bad temper and was impatient. They called him a *yaduka*, a spirit thief, because it was believed that a child whose mother died in birth had stolen the Great Spirit from her. The Itabayiti often avoided waking the yaduka within and would tip-toe around and try to not upset them. For some reason, Anki's brother never tiptoed, but stomped, especially when no one else was around.

"Come on, Anki! Eat your morning meal!" Atu pressured him. Anki quietly fumed but defiantly took a bite of the dune grass and started chewing. "Aww, good little turtle! Happy turtle!" Atu continued mocking him.

Anki suddenly spit the wad of half-chewed dune grass into his brother's face, making Atu shriek and shove him backward. Anki slipped and bumped his elbow on the log, and the tears instantly welled up in his forest-green eyes. He stood there a moment, sniffling, just before he lost control and charged his brother, himself screeching like a giant hutia.

The lively jungle fell silent as the sons of Abensu wrestled in the waist-deep clay pool. Dead leaves clung to their backs and arms, and the mucky water sloshed over the edges, churned up by the two boys trying to outmaneuver one another. Anki was pretty sure Atu laughed first, but it was contagious, and he soon started giggling as well. In an instant, they were no longer snakes, or turtles, or even angry brothers, but the legendary wrestlers Matas the White and Biam the Strong. They became so focused on their wrestling moves they failed to notice their father approach.

"Boys!" their father shouted, his tall and lanky frame casting a thin shadow over the murky water. Atu and Anki immediately stopped mid-hold and looked up at him with their wet clay-covered faces. "Get out of the pit, get cleaned up, and put some clothes on! You're going to be late for your lessons!"

"Yes, baba!" the boys replied in unison.

They scrambled out of the slippery pit, sprinted down the shelly path, hooked right at the clay ovens, and then raced each other up the slope toward the chief's residence at the top of the hill. Wet leaves, twigs, and bits of clay dripped off their bodies as they ran, giggling all the way.

Knowing their father was already upset with them, the boys worked quickly to rinse off the filth from the clay pool, taking turns standing in the cibmani bath and pouring freshwater over themselves from a ceramic jug. The water made a gurgling sound as it ran between Anki's feet, into the stone channel, and then outside through a fist-sized hole at the base of the wall. He was born in the chief's residence and had never lived anywhere else, but Atu said he remembered when they used to live on the island of

Yapaca and had to walk down to the docks to bathe in the shallows alongside their neighbors. He said freshwater and indoor baths were the best things about being the son of a council member, but Anki thought he liked not having neighbors at all.

They quickly towel-dried before dressing in their favorite cotton tunics. Atu wore his new green one, while Anki wore an old, faded-brown one. Each of them wrapped a boarhide belt tightly around their waists, slipped back on their wet sandals, and then raced each other out into the shelly yard in front of the residence where they jumped on the boar-drawn cart behind their father.

Conaca's harbor was on the southwest shore and had little protection against Yuraca's powerful storms. Anki's father told him, over many hundreds of years, the cibmani docks had taken a beating, and were now cracked, had shifted, and became a huge annoyance for him and every ferryman that had to use them. His father had recently tried to get the Yaya to approve repairs, but he was told more important projects were on the horizon and to wait another year. It was then not surprising when his father brought them to a stop beside a hitching post and flung the reins around it. Anki was actually relieved, because it beat having to unharness the boar, drag the cart over the uneven, bumpy docks, and waste time loading them onto the ferry. He giggled when the boar snorted and instantly laid down in the sand, as if relieved to be left behind.

"Taycoay, Abensu!" the ferryman welcomed them. "Heading to your lessons, are we boys?" His name was Haro, and he had copper-colored skin, a full black beard, a shiny bald head, and his left cheek twitched when he talked. He wore strings of multi-colored shells around his wrists, which he looped over the tiller, so he didn't have to hold it all the time.

"Taycoay, Haro," Abensu replied with the customary greeting. The ferry rocked and sloshed against the dock as they climbed on. "Boys?" Abensu glared at his sons.

"Taycoay, Haro," the boys said, one right after the other. Neither one of them cared to look at Haro and his creepy, twitching cheek, and deep-brown, muddy eyes.

"Taycoay, boys! Hold on, we're shoving off!" he said. Using a long oar, Haro pushed the canuti out of the slip, away from the crooked dock, and into the sound with a great splash.

Nestled right in the middle of all the islands was Itabacan Sound. It was nearly four times the size of the big, main island of Itabaca and remained blessedly calm most of the year. All manner of seabirds squawked overhead, flying from island to island, and the water below was crystal-clear, allowing them to easily see from top to bottom and all the sea life in-between. While the center couldn't be more than ten reeds deep, it was only about three reeds deep directly between the islands, which was why they called it the shallows.

"I am red, round like an almec ball, and spikey," Atu suddenly said, peering over the side of the ferry into the water.

"That's easy! You're a yellowfish." Anki didn't wait to see if he was right. "My turn!" He and his brother liked to play a game where one of them described the opposite of a fish they could see and the other had to guess what it was.

"Good luck!" Atu said, crossing his pale arms. "That's all that's down there."

Anki took a moment to study his options, but quickly saw what he was looking for. "Oh, I am yellow, and skinny, and have flat teeth!" he said excitedly.

Atu thought for a moment and then guessed, "Whitefish?"

"Nice guess!" he said, his eyes beaming.

"No way!" Atu rushed to Anki's side of the canuti, rocking the little reed boat.

"Easy, boys!" Haro said, adjusting his footing to rebalance the canuti.

His brother quickly searched the shimmering water and said, "There's no whitefish."

"Yeah, there is – it's right there," Anki pointed.

"That's a manati!"

Anki quickly looked again. "No, it isn't. That's a whitefish!"

"Baba, remind Anki that there are no whitefish in the sound anymore," Atu said, proudly returning to his side of the ferry.

Anki turned to his father, who only shrugged his shoulders, not liking to get involved if he could help it. Anki knew there hadn't been any whitefish in the sound for several hundred years, but the creature did look a lot like a whitefish. He started to feel embarrassed and could hear his brother quietly snickering behind him.

"It's a manati," Haro interjected. Anki looked back at him in time to see the ferryman wink at his father. Actually, the wink might have just been Haro's twitching face. "But, once you dice them up," the ferryman continued, "their meat is white and tasty!"

"See," Atu said and leaned back with his hands behind his head.

"Oh," Anki sighed. "It's a stupid game, anyway," he muttered under his breath.

They traveled the rest of the short trip in peaceful silence. Anki watched the manati swim alongside them, and he listened to the waves lap against the sides of the canuti and the gentle breeze whispering in his ear. When he looked up, he could see Mount Otaba as a dark, blurry smudge of green on the horizon, like a giant palm frond sticking up out of the water. He knew somewhere on top of that smudge was the Yaya's Palace, but he had never been there. His father said Yaya Amnu was his friend and would invite them for evening meal one day, but his father had been saying that for as long as Anki could remember.

The mountain dominated the northern half of the island of Itabaca but plunged sharply toward the center where the Grand Plaza and Pyramid of Mayu were. Anki had been to the plaza plenty of times for festivals and almec matches. Almec was created hundreds of years ago and named after Yaya Almec who had ruled at the time and built the first ball court. It was played by hitting a ball the size of a coconut through stone hoops with a clay mitt. The ball they made out of a mixture of sap from the olluli tree and the white flowers that grew on the vines of Pacca. Anki loved to watch almec, but he didn't like playing it, because he wasn't coordinated enough to strike the ball and make it go where he wanted it to go. He preferred wrestling, even though he wasn't very good at that either.

Soon enough, they came within eyesight of Itabaca's massive harbor, which Anki guessed was about half the size of the island of Conaca. He was told the harbor could accommodate a thousand canuti, and that looked just about right to him. Actually, from the side, the island looked like it had immense steps leading down from the base of Mount Otaba – the plaza on the top step, then the village of Badhan, then the Temple of Yucahu, and then Itabaca Harbor stretching across the southwestern shoreline. Anki suddenly realized the wall wrapping around the island kind of looked like the straps of a sandal, which made the mountain a leg, the steps the bridge of the foot, and the docks were the toes. He giggled at himself for being so clever and wondered if anyone else had ever thought of that before.

As they got closer, he was able to make out one of the two lighthouses built just inside the wall. It rose twice as high as the wall itself above the docks on the southernmost end closest to Anki. He knew the matching one hovered over the other end, but it was just out of sight. When seen together, Anki had always thought the lighthouses looked like giant uca birds keeping watch with their glowing eyes. He imagined them shining down on the rocky coastline during a stormy night. As he did, he realized the ferry was close enough for him to see all of the different reed boats at the docks. There must have been a hundred of them, and even more were crowding around the harbor waiting to get in. Anki saw that Haro had positioned them in line with the other ferries, so Anki decided to pass the time by counting all of the reed boats he could see.

There were about forty fishing canuti, which were thin and had two arms reaching out from their sides gripping small carved logs they called cano. He easily recognized the transport canuti, because they came to Conaca a lot. They were long and wide and had a mast at both the head and the tail, making them easy to spot. He counted twenty transports. Anki wasn't sure about the dredging and towing canuti, because both were stubby and had a lot of oars, but he counted twelve of them. There were still dozens more he was trying to identify when the ferry pulled into the slip, squeaking against the slick cibmani dock.

The boys immediately leapt off the ferry and waited for their father.

"Thank you, Haro," Abensu said, giving the pristine dock a dirty look.

"All in a day's work," the ferryman said. "Have fun at your lessons, boys!" Then Haro turned to welcome his next passengers with a twitchy smile.

Anki tried to push his way through the multitude of workers moving about on the docks, but there were simply too many of them. They bumped into one another, frantically going in different directions, and the noise and smell surrounding him was nauseating. He could hear the harbor vendors yelling over the crowd, peddling their goods, and then he could smell them too. Suddenly, his father grabbed his hand and pushed through the wall of people toward the grand Steps of Ajan, the only entrance to the interior of the island. Anki looked back to see Atu trailing behind them, weaving through the crowd like a nimble reed bending with the wind.

The Steps of Ajan were as wide as the clay pits on Conaca were long and featured interlocking identical cibmani blocks, each two hands tall, half-a-reed deep, and a reed wide. They had once been highly polished and well maintained but were now worn down by hundreds of years of use. Many were chipped and cracked, and Anki had tripped and skinned his shin on them plenty of times.

Slithering up the outside of the wall to the right of the stairs was a carved stone snake the size of which Anki had only ever imagined. Carved on the opposite side and charging down the left wall was a pack of wild boar. The snake he knew was supposed to represent Kanu, but he wasn't exactly sure what all of the boar represented. At the top of the seventy-two steps, the spirit shrine to Bitabay, the First Mother, welcomed everyone, standing several reeds tall on the western corner of the first terrace.

A smooth stone street in front of the statue stretched east toward Badhan and in the opposite direction northwest toward the training docks, which was Atu's destination. On the right, a second street branched off near the head of the stone snake and casually wrapped around the inside of the wall toward one of the lighthouses. The street continued from there to the Temple of Yucahu and then the reed yard beyond, which was where Anki would be spending the rest of his day. But his father kept a firm grip on Anki's hand and dragged him with his brother to the left.

They arrived at the training docks just as Bocoani Numila was hurriedly herding the shoats onto a training canuti. Anki knew sailors in training were called shoats, but he wasn't sure why, because that was what they also called baby boar.

"Taycoay, Numila!" his father called out, still several paces away.

"Ah, taycoay, Abensu," Numila replied coldly.

The coani were the navigators of the canuti, while the bocoani was appointed by the Yaya as the navigator above all navigators. Numila was the youngest bocoani there had ever been and his pride in this fact was always on full display. He was shorter than most men, which was especially noticeable when he was standing next to someone as tall as Anki's father, but Numila always stood upright with his muscular shoulders thrown back and his chest puffed out. He styled his hair like the other coani, using a long braid to wrap around the rest of his fluffy hair on top of his head to form a knot called a ga'an. He wore a polished boarhide tunic that hung from just his left shoulder and held tight at his hips by two boarhide straps, which was quite unique.

"You're late," Numila said, tossing a bundle of rope to one of the other shoats, a boy Anki recognized as Hamsi. "We don't wrestle Maroha and bend her to our will by being late. We must be both reed and – what is it, shoats?" he called over his freckled right shoulder.

"Rudder!" the shoats responded.

"That's right," he said, looking at Anki's brother. "Rudder, Atu. I wasn't appointed bocoani because I was late and weak." He turned to their father. "Look at your boy, Abensu. Have you ever seen such a scrawny, and pale, and *late* boy?"

Anki didn't understand what *reed and rudder* had to do with being late, but he couldn't' help but giggle at the bocoani being a jerk to Atu. His father, on the other hand, didn't seem to find any of this funny. Anki watched him force a smile, before leaning in real close to the bocoani's freckled face.

"I understand, Numila," his father sneered, causing Numila to nervously back away. "I promise, he won't be late again."

Numila appeared momentarily threatened, but he quickly found his pride and scoffed, "I'm sure he won't." With that, he turned and started climbing onto the canuti. He paused, his back turned, and added with a sigh, "Well, are you going to come and join the other shoats?"

Atu hurriedly ran down the dock and leapt up onto the canuti with his friends.

"Thank you, Bocoani Numila," his father said, but the bocoani didn't reply.

Still maintaining a tight grip on Anki's hand, his father quickly led him back up the dock and down the street to the top of the Steps of Ajan, where he stopped and knelt down.

"You know the way to the reed yard, correct?" he asked and Anki nodded, watching the workers coming up the docks, then up the steps, and then walking past them. There weren't nearly as many workers as there had been earlier, but they seemed to be just as noisy. "Good," his father said. "I have to get back to Conaca to finish the ceremonial plates for the Day of Biyaya." He tousled Anki's hair. "Taycoay, son, and be mindful of your temper."

"Taycoay, baba," Anki replied.

He watched his father bound down the steps with his long legs, dodging people left and right, and then he saw his father hop onto a different ferry from before. He could just barely see the ferryman was Oboco, possibly the oldest ferryman in Itabacan, who slowly pushed off the dock. He knew his father would undoubtedly be bored to death by the ferryman's weird stories. Oboco once talked to Anki and his brother nonstop the entire trip back to Conaca about possessed mothers who eat their children. Anki laughed aloud to himself at the memory and how absurd it had seemed, but then it started to make him sad, knowing he didn't have a mother to get possessed and eat him. He instantly recognized this was also an absurd thing to get upset about, shook it from his head, and continued walking toward the reed yard.

He took his time following the street southeast, winding past the lighthouse and drifting slightly uphill to the base of the Temple of Yucahu. He paused for a moment to admire the temple. It was the largest of all the temples and sat on an earthen mound that rose high above the inner wall to overlook the sound. Mighty stone pillars supported an overturned boat-shaped roof that jutted out in the front and curved downward toward the ground. He could see there were enormous wooden doors designed to look like sails tucked back between the pillars. Acrid black smoke billowed up from flickering torches in two stone torch basins on either side of the doors, leaving a wash of soot on them and the walls. Anki guessed they were using sponge torches, which were soaked in a combination of boar fat and palm oil. Sponges burned a lot longer than the wooden torches commonly used around Itabacan, but they also released that horrible, suffocating black smoke.

He continued past the temple, wondering what it must be like to be an akin and spend an entire lifetime devoted to keeping one of the spirits appeased. Kayki was the Earth Spirit who gave of herself the clay that could be molded into anything and hardened in the ovens. It then made sense to Anki that the Kayakin appeased her with clay figurines. But he had no idea what the Yucaakin could be doing to appease the Great Spirit. *Did they breathe on his shrine?*

The street descended slightly and turned to the northeast. On his left, the jungle was dense and foreboding and Anki could see it flowed up the hill toward Mount Otaba like a great green blanket of palms rippling in the wind. After he had walked what he thought must be nearly the entire length of Conaca, there came a doorway built into the inner wall on his right that led to a set of stairs. He hurried down the stairs to a rock-enclosed beach like he had done plenty of times before.

Until he was Atu's age and old enough to learn how to harness the wind and tame the water, Anki was expected to learn how to build canuti. The reed yard was just ahead, and he could see several rows of stone buildings on the left. These joined thatched-roof huts in the back that were partially tucked into the jungle at the base of the mountain. A long row of stone baths led back down to the rocky shore on the other side, and in the middle was an open dirt field where the other students were sitting and listening to Instructor Jokimbi. Beyond the students, farther up the shore behind a low stone wall, he could see the shallows and a bog of tall green reeds swaying into the distance.

Jokimbi was already instructing the others but acknowledged Anki approaching and gestured for him to take a seat without skipping a beat. Anki knew Jokimbi had yet to earn coani status, but he maintained a long, tight braid over his left ear just in case. His arms and legs were speckled with tiny brown freckles, and Jokimbi had a graying, fist-sized tuft of hair directly in the center of his head. Otherwise, he was just about the most average Itabayiti Anki had ever met. There was nothing even remotely interesting about him, except for maybe how bored they all got when he talked.

"After the bog, we will move on to the baths. Are there any questions at this point?" Jokimbi asked and Anki raised his hand. "Besides Anki, we'll catch you up later."

A little girl sitting near the front raised her hand. She had black hair in tight braids with small white flowers set into them, and she wore a bright-red tunic trimmed in gold thread and held tight on the side with a matching gold belt. Anki had never seen the girl before and couldn't help but be fascinated by her hair and the color of her tunic. It made him wish he had not worn his old, faded brown one.

"Kina Wani, you have a question?" Jokimbi pointed to the girl.

Still trying to find a place to sit, Anki spotted his friend Biacoya and sat next to him. Biacoya's family lived on the island of Pacca, which was the next island south of Conaca. His father was Chief of Vines Tambu, who was responsible for making all of the rope in Itabacan. Biacoya was slightly shorter than Anki, but so were most of the other boys. He had a perfectly round head with an equally round sponge of hair on top, big ears that stuck out on the sides, and chubby cheeks that made him look like a puffer fish. He was Anki's best friend and, if they weren't in lessons or doing chores at home, they were together and probably causing mischief.

"Who's that?" he asked Biacoya.

"Who?" Biacoya replied, clearly trying to listen to what the girl was saying.

"The new girl?"

"She's not new."

"But I've never seen her."

Biacoya turned to him without taking his eyes off the girl, "She just doesn't come all the time – kind of like you."

"Why doesn't she come all the time?" he asked.

The girl stopped talking and Jokimbi smiled, "Of course, Kina Wani, we understand completely, but in order to answer your question I must start the lesson. Alright, everyone, get up and let's head over to the shallows."

Anki knew what *wani* meant, because he had heard his father use it before when talking about the Yaya's wife, but he wasn't sure why Jokimbi would use it to refer to a little girl.

"She's the Yaya's daughter," Biacoya said, as if reading Anki's mind. Biacoya then stood and held out his hand.

"Oh," Anki said, pulling himself up with Biacoya's help.

Besides Biacoya, Anki's second best friend was Luculati, the son of Boagur Gudugu, the chief of the agur warriors who lived on the southernmost island of Chacuca. They protected the Grand Gateways and raised Itabacan's boar. Anki suspected Luculati might be part boar, because he had a thick, rounded chest, broad shoulders, and skinny little legs. To top it off, his hair hadn't grown much since he was a baby and looked like a piece of picked-at yatak bread.

"Hey, Anki! Late again, huh?" Luculati said, getting Anki into a headlock and rubbing his knuckles across his scalp.

Anki pushed him off, smiling. "Quit, Lucu. I was only late because of Atu."

"He's a dope," Lucu said.

"And a skinny little pelican!" Biacoya laughed.

Anki punched Biacoya in the arm. Calling his brother a dope was one thing, but making fun of how the Great Spirit had made Atu was crossing the line – only he was allowed to do that.

"Boys." Jokimbi gave them a stern look as he passed them on his way to the reed bog.

They all sloshed into the shallow water as well, quickly becoming surrounded by tall green reeds that would one day become canuti, and gathered around a thick patch where Jokimbi was waiting. Anki saw the new girl was looking at him and he quickly turned away, his face becoming as red as her tunic.

"Remember, the reeds are rooted just below the waterline, so you will need to cut them free without damaging the roots," Jokimbi instructed.

"Why?" a girl named Sheka asked.

Sheka was taller than the other girls, but that was only because she had extremely long legs like those of the white-tailed brocket on the island of Amaca. Unlike most of the other girls, Sheka's hair was split at the front and formed into two thick braids, which were then wrapped around her head and tied in the back. She was easily the smartest girl Anki had ever met, and her sea-green eyes were hypnotizing. Any time he, Biacoya, or Luculati devised a plan to let loose a snake in the bog, or put frogs in the reed baths, Sheka would either foil their plans or had already committed the prank and was already in the process of convincing Jokimbi to blame Anki and his friends. She was a worthy adversary, and he respected her greatly.

Anki didn't hear what Jokimbi said to Sheka, but she seemed satisfied and winked at him as she glided through the water and disappeared behind some of the other students.

Jokimbi held up a curved stone blade. "This is your chaak, and it is curved so you can have more control over what you're cutting," he explained. "Lewa is passing them out now. Please, be careful. They are sharp!"

An older girl, Lewa wore a plain tan tunic and entered the bog carrying a reed basket full of chaak blades. Her hair was parted in the middle and put into braids that dangled over her shoulders like rope. She was the younger sister of Olari, one of the waki diggers that worked in the clay pits for Anki's father, and he had played almec with her before in front of the Temple of Kayki while she waited for Olari to be done for the day. He watched the other children slosh loudly over to Lewa to get their chaaks first, and then he did the same.

"Now, you snake your left hand around a group of reeds and gently pull them toward you," Jokimbi said, demonstrating. A few children watched, but most just grabbed handfuls of reeds and yanked them. "Gently!" He raised his voice. "Now, with the reeds *gently* grouped and pulled toward you, you will see there, near the waterline, that darker colored area at the bottom of the reed?"

Anki watched with Biacoya, paying close attention to the instructions, mostly because they both had noticed Kina was also paying close attention. Luculati was already hacking away at the reeds with Sheka and a few others, bits of green and yellow fibers covering their arms and legs, but Jokimbi hadn't noticed them.

"Next, you take your chaak and in one quick, sturdy motion, cut the reeds toward you." Jokimbi's blade sliced through the reeds smoothly, and he stood holding a neatly cut bundle over his head. "There, now you try." Jokimbi looked around and saw only Anki, Biacoya, and Kina were watching, while all the other children were shredding the reeds to pieces around them. "Children!" he shouted; his eyes wide in frustration. "Nawuni, Luculati...ugh! You other boys over there, stop what you are doing!"

Anki and Biacoya giggled, and Anki noticed Kina was giggling too. They both noticed her at the same time, but Biacoya was first to slosh over to where their instructor had been. Like a seasoned professional, he snaked his hand around the reeds, pulled, sliced, and tossed bundle after bundle to Anki and Kina.

"Well done, Biacoya!" Jokimbi said with pride, wrestling the chaaks away from two boys Anki didn't know. One had short spikey hair like a yellowfish, and the other was as bald as Haro and had a droopy eye.

He turned back to see Kina and Biacoya smiling at one another. Not to be outdone, he shooed Biacoya away and started stretching his cutting arm behind his back, making a big show out of it. He then snaked his pulling arm around the reeds and pulled, but he pulled too hard, and the reeds bent and broke.

"Gently, Anki!" Jokimbi shouted and splashed over to demonstrate again, but Anki was too embarrassed. He dropped his chaak in the shallow water and ran out of the reed bog, splashing the other children as he went. Jokimbi sighed and gestured to Lewa to go after him, before corralling the other children and explaining the cutting process once more.

Anki slumped against the low stone wall near the soaking baths, out of sight from the other children, pulled his knees up against his chest and buried his head in his arms.

"You alright?" he heard Lewa ask, her wet sandals squishing closer to him.

Anki sniffled. "What do you think?"

"I think you got embarrassed in front of your friends and ran away."

"Shows what you know!" he snorted. He knew he was being rude, but he didn't care. And then he heard her sit next to him and felt her cheek press against his head.

"I can hear your thoughts, you know?" she said with a sigh.

"What?" Anki pulled his head away. "That's a dumb thing to say," he mumbled.

"No! I can hear your thoughts," she said again. "But it's dark in there."

"No! It's not." Anki scooted away, but Lewa scooted with him.

"Sure is." She laid her cheek back down on his head. "Oooh, but I hear something else, someone's voice!"

"No, you don't! Stop bothering me," he said, but he was starting to calm down.

"Yes, that's what it is! I thought I recognized that voice."

"What? You do not." He raised his head, revealing streaks of tears on his cheeks and snot on his lip.

Lewa wiped the tears away with her thumb and smiled. "I did, until I lost contact!" She nudged him with her elbow.

Anki smiled, wiping the snot off his lip with his forearm. He wasn't sure where this was going, but he was definitely intrigued. He liked imagining things. Anki recalled when they were playing almec, Lewa had a pretty good imagination. "Who was it? What did they say?" he asked her.

"It was the voice of a woman I once met," she answered. "She was very kind to me and helped me pick flowers in the public gardens on Yapaca."

"That's where you live," he scoffed.

"Yes, and she lived on Yapaca too with her husband and a little boy named Atura."

"Wait – that's my brother's name." Anki was becoming less interested now. This was not very imaginative at all. "Baba doesn't like to call him that though," he explained, "because itaba used to, and Atu hates it for the same reason."

"I know," she said and nudged him with her elbow again.

"You knew my itaba?" Anki was skeptical. "She gave her Great Spirit to me when I was born."

"Nonsense," Lewa said. "She went to be with our ancestors just like everyone else, but I did hear a little spark of her in there for sure!"

Anki put his chin on his knees. This was not turning out to be a fun, imaginative conversation, but he did like to hear stories about his mother. "Baba tells me I'm a lot like her," he admitted. "It's so hard. I sometimes can't help getting upset."

"I know. It's alright to be upset, but you don't have to let the Dark Shadow consume you. Listen for her spark and you'll be just fine," she encouraged him. "Did you know my itaba died the same night as yours?" Anki shook his head. "She was fishing with my baba when Yuraca took both of them."

"That's sad," Anki said and leaned his head against Lewa's shoulder. He had no idea Lewa had lost both her mother and father.

"It was sad," she said, "and I was upset for a very long time, but my big brother took me to the temple, and we prayed to Ma'an together." She put her arm around him. "You know Olari, don't know?"

"Yeah, I once saw him get into a fight with a giant mole he accidentally dug up." Anki suddenly jumped to his feet and pretended he was swinging a shovel around like a club, battling the ferocious mole like he had seen Lewa's brother do.

Lewa laughed and stood as well, but then they both heard Jokimbi talking and the approaching children. "Come on," she said. "Let's learn how to make the strongest canuti ever, and maybe Yuraca will never take anyone's baba or itaba ever again."

Anki smiled, but then he paused, looking at her proffered hand. "What did my itaba say?"

"She said to be patient," Lewa smiled. "Delicate reeds, like delicate flowers, are like the delicate threads of our lives, woven by Orlil one at a time."

"She said all that?" he asked and Lewa nodded vigorously.

"Each moment is just a small part of the story. It would be a shame to allow one frayed thread to unravel the whole thing."

Anki smiled. He liked how that sounded and thought it might have been something his mother would say. He took her hand but immediately let go, seeing the rest of the students walk up to them. "Thank you," he said, acting like nothing had happened. "I feel much better now."

Lewa giggled, "Don't mention it."

"Alright, these are the soaking baths," Jokimbi said. "Nawuni, you can set those bundles down here next to me." He pointed to the ground in front of the baths and then turned to Lewa and Anki. "Are you ready to join the lesson?"

"Yes, I am," Anki nodded.

"Good. Lewa, can you bring the rest of the bundles up from the shallows?" Jokimbi asked and Lewa nodded.

Biacoya knocked Anki's elbow with his and grinned at him. He knew what it meant and bumped his friend's elbow right back. Biacoya was often the first to console Anki when he got too worked up, and probably would have instead of Lewa, had Biacoya not been distracted by that girl. Just then, Kina walked up next to them, but she was looking at Anki.

"I broke all the reads too," she whispered to him. "It's a good thing my baba is the Yaya!"

"You said it," Anki joked, nervously. There was something about the girl that made him feel giggly, like his stomach was being tickled from the inside.

Handing one bundle to Jokimbi, Lewa returned and set the other reed bundles in front of the baths alongside the stack Nawuni had dropped.

"Thank you, Lewa." Jokimbi held up the bundle for everyone to see. "We take the reeds and put them in the baths for six notches." Lewa held up the candle-timer, but then she looked at the sky, set down the timer, and quickly ran toward the first building on the other side of the reed yard. Just then, the sun suddenly emerged from behind a cloud and Jokimbi had to shield his eyes with his hand. "Ah, maybe we won't need the candle-timer after all," he said.

Anki recognized the device lying on the ground, because his father used them when firing the clay to avoid cracking and uneven finishes. The candle-timer was just like a regular beeswax candle, but it had twelve evenly spaced notches carved into it. The cibmani sundial, on the other hand, had been designed to attach at the end of the bath and glide around the edge on an indented channel. It made a horrible crunching sound as it grinded around, but Lewa was instructed to add palm oil to make it smoother, which she carried with her as she returned slightly out of breath.

"As you can see," Jokimbi continued. "The sun is now beating down on us, so we will be using the sundial today – Mawoi be merciful." Jokimbi ordered the children to line up with their own bundles of reeds ready to be laid in the water. He watched the shadow on the sundial cross a long notch in the stone. "Amoc, go ahead, but make sure to submerge them all the way," Jokimbi instructed the bald boy with the droopy eye. "Ah, very good. Next!" He pushed the heavy device around the bath with a *cruuuunch!* "Lewa, please," he said, but Lewa was already pouring the oil. "Thank you, next!"

Anki was last in line. He noticed Sheka had not gone ahead of him, and was obviously not behind him, so he called over to Biacoya. "Hey, where's Sheka?"

Biacoya's eyes got really big. "Oh no!"

Just then, Jokimbi jumped back from the sundial waving at the air around his face and holding his nose. Several of the children were backing away too, and then someone started shrieking, "*Wasps!*"

And then there were wasps swarming all around the reed baths, the sundial, and then they went after the gourd of palm oil. Lewa screamed and dropped the gourd, which broke apart on the ground. Wasps converged on the oil, causing Lewa to run away in a panic.

Anki started laughing. He seemed to be far enough away to where the wasps weren't interested in him. He turned to see Biacoya bent over in laughter as well, and then they both looked for Luculati. They spotted him lying on the ground and batting at the vicious creatures, which made them laugh even harder. "Did you?" he asked and Biacoya shook his head.

It then dawned on them at the same time. "Sheka!" they said in unison.

CHAPTER TWO

A Reed's Width Away

"When Itabacan's stunning harbors were first built," Bocoani Numila was saying, "Yaya Atan brought together a council of all the coani to settle once and for all their conflicting sailing terms." Atu watched him pace back and forth in front of them, but he paused when he noticed Kachi's boney hand raised high in the air. "What is it, Kachi?"

"Don't you mean, Yaya Ajan?" Kachi asked, arrogantly.

"Ajan, Atan, doesn't matter," the bocoani snapped with a wave of his hand. "Now, originally fashioned after the Great Serpent, canuti were intended to go up and down the many rivers. Basic directions like left and right were sufficient for this purpose, but once they were out on the Great Sea," Numila chuckled, "with massive waves tossing their reed boats no bigger than this training canuti – tossing them around in circles with no land in sight. Each coani quickly invented his own preferred terminology. Unsurprisingly, they all came up with different terms and no one could understand each other." He pointed to Joba's raised hand. "Yes, Joba?"

"Were there no *girl* coani?" she asked, eliciting a snicker from Atu and the other shoats.

"You sound like my wife," Numila snorted. "But the answer is, no. Not back then."

Atu watched Joba, expecting her to become uncomfortable, but she didn't. She was the daughter of Suga and Mugan Galo. Her father was the overseer of the wildlife, lakes, and the forest on the island of Amaca, but Atu wasn't exactly sure where the mugan title had come from. All he knew was that Suga and Galo had a beautiful, defiant, and intelligent daughter, and Atu liked her a lot. Her long black hair was wrapped up on top of her head like a bird's nest and held in place with two sticks, but Atu had no idea how it stayed so neat. He was jealous of her smooth ebony skin and long legs, like two olluli trees stripped of their bark. She was kind, thoughtful, never once late for lessons, and everyone knew Joba had already been promised to an araco named Draha.

Numila waited for her to reply and when she didn't, the bocoani continued. "As tribute to the Biyaya's legacy, the council decided every term must relate to the canuti as if it were sailing toward Itabacan."

Atu had been listening to Bocoani Numila drone on for what seemed like forever. They hadn't even left the harbor, and the sun was turning Atu's pale skin an ugly shade of pink. He looked up at the little ribbon attached to the sail near the top of the mast. Without any wind, it dangled like a dead worm. He sighed and plucked at the front of his tunic, trying his best to vent the heat trapped within. He would give anything for just one puff of wind.

"When facing the head, we refer to the right side of the canuti as *kona*, because Conaca is the northernmost island. And when it's the left side, we say *chok*, after the southernmost island, Chacuca. Is all of that clear?" Numila paused, but none of the shoats responded. Atu guessed it was because they were all too busy imagining what it must be like to actually be sailing. "Good," the bocoani continued. "Now, being that there are no giant snakes in Itabacan, our canuti are now fashioned after the mighty chacu we love so much."

There wasn't a trace of irony in the bocoani's voice and Atu had to roll his eyes — the chacu *we* love so much? Atu hated the boar for many reasons. First, they smelled horrible. Second, one of the boar that pulled his father's cart had bitten Atu on the arm when he was just a little boy. He could still feel its hot, stinky breath on his face from when he raised his arm to block the attack. And then there was the yuca leaf paste the lesini applied afterward, which burned like hot oil on his skin. He never trusted the lesini again either.

On the subject of the lesini, Atu had no idea why anyone would want to be one. They drifted from island to island gathering leaves, bark, bug legs, feathers, and all sorts of other random things, and were expected to heal people along the way. Even if they were allowed to take the ferry late at night, which would otherwise be reserved for official council business, Atu would still not be interested, because then he would have to listen to old Oboco ramble on about the Great Light being a giant eyeball, or something really weird like that. If he had to put up with that nonsense, then he definitely didn't want to be a lesini. Besides, he had no idea how anyone became a lesini in the first place. He remembered his mother telling him the lesini prayed at the Temple of Osani on the island of Amaca, but that was when he was, like, two years old. And...

He paused mid-thought when he realized the bocoani was staring right at him.

"Atu, I asked what you thought we called this..." Numila stomped on the canuti beneath his sandaled foot and pointed down. "Hmm? What is this?"

All of the other shoats' heads snapped back to look at him. Atu nervously said, "The belly?" Nearly all of them groaned, but Numila was looking up at the wiggling worm.

The bocoani raised an eyebrow and mumbled, "Umm – the belly, that's – that's right."

Of course it was right. They had all learned about the different parts of the canuti when they were younger and first learned how to build the reed boats. Atu started listing off the various parts of the canuti in his head. Each bundle of reeds is bound with rope to other bundles to form a rib, and then the ribs were bound together to form cages, and then two cages were bound together to form the chest, and the chest was...no, wait, belly wasn't right!

"Pay attention, Atu!" Tunku said, pushing past him to get to the tiller.

"What?" Atu pressed himself against the tailrib and out of the way.

Tunku was a grumpy boy who took everything personally, but he was neither big enough nor strong enough to vent his grumpiness on any of the other boys except Atu, which he did frequently. For some reason, Tunku thought he should start a coani braid, even though he was much too young to do so, and his braiding skills were awful. The hand-long bundle of loosely braided hair just hung there on the side of his head like a boar's tail.

"Atu, I *said* you're our scrounger," Numila was now in Atu's face. "Secure the gourds and run them up the mast and grab an oar." The bocoani turned and continued with his orders. "Kachi, stow the docking line and then you'll be on the chok-line. Joba, grab an oar and then you'll be on the kona-line. Hamsi, grab an oar and then take second tiller. Demican, put those muscles to work on the anchor and then grab an oar. Alright, we have to get out of the sound and into the beautiful Bocoa, but we're not going to make it if you shoats don't move faster! We must be both reed and...*what?*"

"Rudder!" the shoats shouted.

With everyone busily doing their jobs, the canuti slowly crawled away from the dock, out of the harbor, and into the sound. Joba and Demican were the stroke-oarsmen and sat nearest the tail, while Hamsi was the kona-oarsman and Atu the chok-oarsman. Numila remained at the head shouting for them to row in unison, but it was surprisingly harder than Atu imagined. The oars may have all been the same size, but their arms weren't. After they had rowed a bit farther into the sound, the wiggling worm became like a possessed festival dancer, snapping back and forth until it suddenly pointed south and stiffened.

"Stow oars, and ready the sail!" Numila yelled.

Atu was surprised to see Bocoani Numila so happy. It was obvious he hated teaching, but Atu hadn't realized just how much the bocoani loved sailing until that moment.

"Yes, Bocoani!" Kachi sprang to life, untied the chok-line from the midrib, wrapped it around his wrist, and hopped from foot to foot awaiting Numila's next instructions. Atu found it very difficult to stow the oars around Kachi, clearly enjoying himself and bouncing around like a spiny rat.

As the only son of Chief of Sanitation Kasim, Kachi seemed to always have something to prove. It wasn't surprising to Atu. Sanitation workers were often called kudi behind their backs, which was a hateful term typically reserved for the beggars that wandered the dark alleyways of Itabacan's villages. It didn't help that Kachi was only a little over a reed tall and just as skinny, adding to his rat-like appearance. He also slicked his hair back on the sides with olluli sap like Atu, revealing a scar above his right ear where his hair no longer grew. Atu was pretty sure Kachi had never explained how he got the scar, but Atu also didn't care to know either.

Annoyed, Atu glanced over at Joba, silently gliding across the canuti gathering oars and stowing them in fitted notches just below the oar-ports. She was like the white-tailed brocket Atu and his brother had seen prancing around the forested island of Amaca, but with deep orange eyes like glowing embers and the most adorable little nose. She was also taller than most of the girls he knew, and effortlessly and gracefully untied the kona-line from the midrib and held it firmly in her long, thin fingers. She suddenly looked at him, but Atu quickly looked away.

He noticed Kachi was no longer blocking the oar-ports, allowing Atu to finally slam the second oar into its notch. Once again annoyed, he plopped down behind Demican who was calmly sitting behind the mast. He looked back at Hamsi crouched next to Tunku at the tiller and made a silly face at him. Hamsi laughed, looked up at Tunku, and then rolled his eyes back at Atu.

Hamsi was the only son of Madiri, one of Itabacan's best navigators, but he didn't have any of his father's natural sailing abilities. He was of average height, but had chubby arms and legs, which reminded Atu of the clay figurines Olari sometimes made, which were also very similar to the ones the Kayakin offered in the temple. Hamsi's tight oily curls on top of his head glistened like sea moss, which perfectly complimented his muddy-green eyes.

The canuti was gaining speed and cutting through the water, sending a salty but delightful mist over their faces. Unfortunately for Atu, most of the relieving mist hit Demican since he was so much bigger than Atu and sitting right in front of him.

"What did Tunku say to you?" Demican suddenly asked without turning around.

"Nothing, he was just being a jerk," Atu replied, wiping sweat from his forehead.

Demican was the youngest of four brothers, all of whom were giants among the Itabayiti. He was a veritable tree. Actually, one time, Hamsi dared Atu to climb a palm to steal some honey from a beehive, but Atu asked if he could just climb Demican instead. That way, if the bees attacked, at least Demican could run and Atu could ride on his shoulders. Hamsi agreed, Demican agreed, and they all enjoyed fresh honeycomb that day.

"A numbskull in the morning," Demican said, "and then Tunku will be singing up a storm later in the day, acting like everyone's best friend."

Atu laughed, "True."

He knew Tunku's father was the former Chief of Gardens, but he died when Tunku was young. The new chief, Tamna, and his wife heard about the situation and offered to raise Tunku. Atu's father told him they only did it because they had no children of their own at the time, and the wife always wanted a son, but no one really knew the couple's reasoning for adopting Tunku. Whatever it may be, Tunku remained a son of a council member and a big pain in Atu's side! Of course, he always wondered what had become of Tunku's mother, so he asked.

"What became of his itaba?"

"She's a lesini," Demican answered. "At least, that's what I heard. Heartbroken after his baba died and abandoned him. My brother said he met her once on Niamca and that she sang while she scavenged for click-bugs near the springs."

"A singing lesini?" Atu asked. He'd never heard of a signing lesini.

"He said she had a pleasant enough voice too."

"Probably why Tunku tries to sing all the time," Atu said. "He remembers hearing her."

Demican laughed. "*Tries* is an important word, my friend."

Atu laughed as well, and then he remembered something. "My baba once told me Tunku could have an ararun," he said. "Ya know? Because of his itbaba."

The Itabayiti believed the Great Spirit could be tainted by events in a person's life, causing the spirit to wander instead of going up to join their ancestors in Mayu. They called these lost spirits ararun. Like the yaduka, if a body wasn't placed on a bonefire to release the spirit quick enough and someone happened to touch it without going through the proper ritual, the ararun could latch onto them and remain there forever.

"Maybe," Demican said. "Or maybe he's just weird."

They both laughed again until their laughter faded into the glorious wind blowing over their sun-kissed bodies. The rhythmic whooshing the canuti made as it rode the waves thoroughly quieted the entire crew. Soon they could hear the bustling docks of Yapaca off their kona side. Atu couldn't believe how excited he was they were finally fast on their way toward the Gate of Kuraka and the Great Sea beyond. He had never been outside of Itabacan before. His father told him a story once about mysterious creatures that lived in the deep waters of the Great Sea. He said there were sharks the size of the largest canuti, lizards that could eat a man whole, and gigantic manati with long necks that craned over the boats and chomped at the masts. His father told him the bocoani took them to an island called Sanaca, where wild boar walked on their hind legs and had long claws that were curved like tusks.

At the time, his father's stories seemed ridiculous and Atu thought they had to have been made up. But then they passed beneath the enormous Gate of Kuraka and Atu saw for the first time the unimaginable vastness of the Bocoa stretched out before them as far as his young eyes could see. *Maybe baba was telling the truth all along*, he decided.

The canuti suddenly lurched forward into the trough of an immense wave. Atu noticed all the sounds he had evidently been ignoring instantly disappeared and there was almost complete and total silence.

"Bring her a single notch to chok, Tunku," Bocoani Numila calmly ordered, his voice carrying across the canuti as if he had been shouting.

"Yes, Bocoani!" Tunku did shout, irritating the other shoats.

"Welcome to the Trough of Tranquility," Numila added, as Tunku pushed the tiller away from himself. The canuti turned slightly, just before it began to climb, and climb, and climb. Up and up the wave they climbed, and it looked to Atu like they were going to sail straight up into Ma'an, the Great Sky. And then, as quickly as it had gone, they crested the wave and the roar of the Bocoa came flooding back. The canuti slapped back down hard on the water again, sending a shower of salty seawater over the entire crew and Atu's morning meal out of his mouth over the chok-side tailrib. It was absolutely thrilling!

"Well done, Tunku!" Numila exclaimed.

They all applauded as the reed boat settled back into a rhythmic whooshing and plowed through the water once again toward the southeast. Atu's stomach seemed to settle as well, and then Joba brought him a gourd of water to wash the vomit out of his mouth.

As he grabbed for it, their hands overlapped, skin touching skin, but she didn't pull away. He looked up into her fiery-brown eyes, which flashed like gemstones in the midday sun. In that moment, all of the Bocoa faded away and the creaking reed boat and salty air dissipated like waking from sleeptime. Only Joba's beautiful face remained real and present. She smiled at him, at Atu, briefly, and as she slowly looked away and stood to leave, the crashing waves and nausea instantly returned. At which point, he almost vomited a second time into the water gourd. It was a very peculiar but amazing moment, and Atu found it hard to focus the rest of the day.

She went back to her position on the chok-line, glancing back at him now and then from across the canuti. She appeared to enjoy the attention, and nothing else seemed to matter anymore to him but giving her that attention. The exhilaration of riding the Bocoa's tremendous waves didn't do it for him any longer. The constant splashes of mist that had once felt so cool on his hot skin became aggravating, as they temporarily blinded him and prevented him from seeing her. He wasn't sure what any of their flirting might mean. It was all new to him. His best friend, Demican, didn't have any sisters, and Hamsi was an only child. The only other girl Atu regularly had contact with was Lewa, but Hamsi threatened to gut Atu like a fish if he ever showed any interest in her, and so he never did.

For quite a while, the bocoani had them sailing in immense figure-eights. The shoats took turns manning the sails and the tiller until everyone rotated through each position twice. Atu went out of his way to pass closer to Joba, much more than was necessary or convenient each time they switched positions, earning the glaring indignation of the bocoani but he didn't say anything. When Numila taught them a sailing song he had made up, Atu mouthed the words and pretended to sing along, trying to listen to Joba sing. Unfortunately, as Demican predicted, Tunku came to life and screeched over everyone.

Thankfully, the singing eventually faded, but there was still daylight remaining, and Bocoani Numila insisted all of the shoats rotate through their positions a third time. Atu wasn't excited about it, because he liked sitting behind the mast, but then he realized the rotation put Joba on tiller and him second tiller. The thought of getting to be so close to her, even if it meant sitting at her feet, made Atu glow with joy. While everyone moved from position to position, Numila decided to tell them about the Gusiti, the Golden People, who were discovered by Bocoani Tiktali many generations before.

"They're short, like Kachi," the bocoani said, making the other shoats laugh. "Yucahu hasn't blessed them with cibmani, or crops, or even tunics."

Atu liked the sound of that. He thought wearing nothing was a much better idea than his stupid tunic. It was drenched with sweat and seawater, but he was still unbearably hot. He purposefully brushed against Joba's leg as he sat and whispered an apology to her, but she didn't look at him. Her focus was on the tiller handoff with Demican, but Atu thought he might have seen her ebony cheeks redden a little. Of course, they could also be redder because the Great Light had been bearing down on them all day.

"Actually," Numila continued, "the Gusiti wear loincloths made from woven grass and skirts from furry hides they call tulu." The bocoani stopped pacing and held up his hands. "I don't know what tulu is, so don't ask me. Now, the Gusiti are said to survive by hunting and gathering in the dense forests of their land..."

"Why are they called the Golden People?" Tunku interrupted him, hoisting the water gourds back up the mast.

Bocoani Numila glared at him. "Because, when they were first discovered, their skin was painted with golden dust."

"Why?" Tunku asked.

Atu could almost see the boiling irritation in Numila's dark, tree bark-like eyes.

"Will you, please, stop asking questions," he demanded through clenched teeth. "Focus on what you're doing – you're spilling freshwater all over the spine!"

SPINE, that's right! Atu couldn't believe he had said belly earlier when he knew they stood on the spine of the canuti. He was wondering why no one had said anything about his mistake all day, but then Joba suddenly elbowed him in the back.

"Hey!" Atu reflexively shouted, attracting the attention of the entire crew. He didn't know what to do and looked up at Joba for direction, but she didn't dare look back down at him. "Uh – we should go see the Gusiti now!" he said with a timid little smirk.

"Unfortunately, the Gusiti lands are a fourteen-day journey west," Bocoani Numila explained immediately. "Yuraca prevented us from making that trip last year, but maybe Yaya Amnu will approve another attempt after the season has passed."

Embarrassing disaster averted, Atu adjusted himself so that he could lean against the chok-side tailrib and potentially avoid getting elbowed again. He glanced up a Joba, who's fiery eyes remained straight forward, but she had a mischievous smile on her pretty face.

"Why doesn't he send one now?" Hamsi asked, struggling with the kona-line. "Baba told me the whitefish haven't been as plentiful as they use to be, and he thinks we might have better luck farther west."

"Your baba," Numila scoffed, "is a funny man." The bocoani's words appeared to crush Hamsi, who hung his head shamefully. "Anyway, that's enough talk about whitefish and the Gusiti," Numila said, abruptly cutting the conversation short with a clap of his hands. "Joba, bring us round to chok," he ordered and Joba did as she was told. The canuti turned and bounced on the crossing waves, and Atu watched Bocoani Numila scan the faces of his students with his dark eyes. They paused on Atu for an uncomfortably long time, but then the bocoani pivoted back to Hamsi and smiled. "Son of Madiri, let's see what you got!"

Atu breathed a sigh of relief. He didn't care one way or the other about whitefish or people covered in gold dust and was beginning to care less and less about sailing. After also losing his midmeal over the tailrib, he was ready to give up exploring the vast Bocoa altogether. The one good thing to happen all day was when Joba kindly brought him that gourd of water. But it was time to head back to Itabacan, Joba was promised to Draha, and there was nothing Atu could do about it.

Hamsi nervously relieved Joba who then quickly ran over to the kona-line.

"Atu, take the chok-line from Kachi," Numila ordered, making additional changes. "Tunku, you're useless as a scrounger. Go sit second tiller. Demican, remain behind the mast – keep an eye on all the rest of these shoats! Kachi can be our scrounger. Hopefully he won't spill any of our freshwater!" A tail wind started to pick up from the southwest, making the wiggling worm at the top of the mast suddenly point directly toward Itabacan. "Perfect!" the bocoani exclaimed.

The wind actually felt nice, and it meant they could really pick up some speed and charge triumphantly into Itabacan Sound. Atu busily adjusted the chok-line, going back over the day in his mind and smiling at all the flirting he and Joba had been doing, but then something strange happened. He felt a bump through his feet. It had to have come from something hitting the chest of the canuti, but he wasn't positive. A moment later it happened again, but this second bump was much more powerful. Atu quickly looked at Joba and her terrified face told him she felt it too.

"Bocoani!" he shouted.

"Yes, Atu." Numila was standing at the head of the canuti, which was raised in the water due to their speed, and Atu doubted he had even felt the bump.

"Uh – something is bumping against the chest of the canuti."

"I felt it too, twice," Joba added, raising her hand. Demican then raised his hand as well, followed by Kachi.

"What?" Numila's eyes grew very big in his head, and then everyone but Hamsi rushed to look over the ribs of the canuti.

"What's going on?" Hamsi asked, struggling to keep the speeding canuti straight.

"Keep her steady, Hamsi!" Numila shouted, peering over the side. And then he must have seen something, because the bocoani shot upright and instantly backed away from the headrib.

WHAM! The canuti lifted out of the water and crashed back down on its kona-cage. Joba ricocheted off the spine, but her tight grip on the kona-line kept her from being thrown into the sea. Atu rode it out, tightly gripping the chok-line and tucking himself against the midrib, his eyes wide open and watching everyone and everything. Hamsi held onto the tiller for dear life, pulling it toward himself in the process, while Tunku anchored himself on Hamsi's legs. But scrawny Kachi was flung into the air and would have been lost to the sea, if Demican hadn't grabbed his tunic belt with one hand and the mast with the other, saving the Chief of Sanitation's son.

Bocoani Numila landed on his back in the wedge of the neck where the spine meets the head. "Niama, be merciful!" he shouted, and then he popped back up on his feet. Atu watched him quickly re-tie his braid around the ga'an on top of his head and get his bearings. "Whatever hit us pushed us off course," the bocoani mumbled to himself.

Off course? Atu looked over the midrib at the Grand Gateways approaching rapidly. He quickly determined, as he assumed the bocoani had as well, if they didn't turn immediately, they were going to miss the Gate of Mawoi and smash into the great wall!

And then Numila started shouting orders like a crazed howler monkey, which the Itabayiti called kugoan, but Atu and his friends shortened to just kugo.

"Bring us round to chok!" Numila hollered over the wind and waves crashing over the canuti. Hamsi pushed the tiller away from himself as hard as he could, and Joba loosened the kona-line, but the chok-line kept slipping through Atu's wet, clammy, trembling hands. "Atu, tighten that line or we're going to be smashed to pieces!"

"I'm trying!" Atu's knuckles were white, and his palms were burning.

"We're not *trying* to sail here, Atu, if you haven't noticed!" Numila yelled.

Atu had both feet braced against the midrib with the line running up between his legs and around both of his clenched fists. His baked salmon-colored body hovered there over the spine of the reed boat, but he was just not strong enough to rein in the sail.

"Atu!" Numila hollered again. He must have seen Atu giving it his all, because then the bocoani said, "Demican, get over there and help Atu!"

"Will do, Bocoani!"

Atu heard Numila's order, but he was still genuinely surprised when the massive boy cradled Atu in his left arm as if he were a newborn baby and simultaneously helped pull the chok-line tight with his right hand. The sail caught the wind and popped in the other direction, and then the canuti immediately cut hard to chok, slipping through the Gate of Mawoi a reed's width away from being shattered against the stone wall.

CHAPTER THREE

The Cave on the Cliff

Kina had been stung by a wasp before and it always hurt, but her mother was embarrassing her. She was making too big of a deal over the tiny little welts on her arm, and Kina could tell her father was growing tired of her mother's abrasiveness, because his responses were increasingly curt. When he dismissed the lesini and the palace attendants, she knew he had heard enough.

"You are the Yaya. She is your daughter. You must do something about this!" her mother demanded.

Unana Wani was a short and stout woman with a bulbous behind, thick legs, and the feet of a maniku, which were large rodent-like creatures with long hairless tails and pointy snouts. Kina's mother wore her hair in the fashion of all wani mothers. Three long, tight braids ran from her hairline, over her head, and all the way down to her hips where they were held in place with shells. Her braids swayed side to side whenever she walked, and the shells clacked together – *clack-clack-clack*. Unana imposed herself in every space, first with her booming voice, the clacking of her braids, and then her physical presence. She was commonly the life and then the death of festivals, and Kina's father worshiped her.

The Yaya wore one of his numerous different traditional sleeveless robes over his usual white tunic. Each one was a variation of the same design, trimmed in gold thread, and featured colorful embroidered images corresponding to the seasons or certain ceremonies. After the Gusiti were discovered, their gold powder was brought back, mixed with olluli sap, and used to coat the cotton before it was made into thread. Spools of golden thread were as rare as the largest gems, but there was a stockpile in the palace specifically for the Yaya's tunics and robes. The robe he wore now was sea-green with the black embroidered outline of a whitefish on the back and rippling waves stretching outward around the robe like a spider's web. Unana, on the other hand, had a different tunic for every day of the year and only her boarhide belt matched her husband's, as all marriage belts did.

Kina's father shut the doors to their private chambers behind the lesini and attendants, and then he turned to his frantic wife. In his deep-brown eyes, Kina could see the love her father had for her mother. To him, she was Bitabay, the First Mother, the guiding star in his world, but Kina knew her mother had a bad habit of making him appear weak in front of others.

"Well?" her mother asked, her hands on her round hips and tapping her tiny foot.

"Enough, Unana. Let us toss the matter up to children being children." His voice was stern but understanding. Kina's father had been the Yaya her entire life, but she had never known him to raise his voice in front of her. Her mother, on the other hand, loved to push her father to his limits.

"Reckless children assaulted your daughter, and an incompetent instructor allowed it to happen. You think that's enough?!"

Kina's father replied by only raising his eyebrows and looking at her mother with cold, fierce eyes. Then he sat down on the lounge chair at the foot of their bed, and Kina quickly scooched down the bed toward him cradling her lumpy arm.

"Ugh!" her mother huffed and threw up her hands. She turned to Kina. "Tell your baba the boys' names."

Kina squirmed. "I – I'm not sure the boys did anything..."

"Nonsense, of course it was the boys. Let me guess; Biacoya and Luculati?"

"Lucu got stung more than me," she answered honestly.

"Ahh – well, it was Anki then!"

"Alright!" He stood. "When I say enough, I mean *enough!*" he shouted, and then he turned to Kina and smiled. "My little obsidian gem, would you go to your room and let your itaba and I be alone for now?"

Kina nodded and scooted off the bed. "Yes, baba."

As she left her parents' chambers, Kina watched her mother become very still, clasp her hands around her stomach, and sit down quietly on the lounge chair, and then Kina closed the door. There was a lot of daylight left before prayers, evening meal, and then sleeptime, and Kina had plans to take advantage of every bit of it.

Outside of her parents' bedchamber a hallway ran to the left and right, east and west, and a wide corridor stretched north in front of her to the palace reception hall where the Yaya's throne stood atop a wide dais. If she turned west, the first and only door on the right was her room, just before a dead-end. Actually, it wasn't really a dead-end. Kina remembered being shown a secret passage there once, but she didn't know how to open it or where it went. If she turned east, there was a door on the left she had never opened, but then the hallway bent to the north and continued on behind the dais at the eastern end of the reception hall to a private entrance in the northeast corner of the palace. The Yaya often used this entrance to attend council meetings in the rotunda at the north end of the palace, and there was a raised walkway connecting the buildings for this purpose.

Kina didn't want to bump into any of the attendants, or adulu guards, or council members, and the quickest way to get out of the palace unseen was the northeast entrance. The only problem was she would either have to go through the Council Rotunda or jump off the raised walkway that was about two-reeds above the jungle floor. Of course, she had dropped from this height plenty of times and it was better than having to explain herself to council members or the adulu.

She went right, around the corner, up the steps past the secret door to the dais, and into the east hallway. This hallway always creeped her out because it was very dark, the stone floor was usually damp, and she was certain there were all sorts of bugs and icky things in there with her. Just ahead, she could see there were no adulu at the door of the northeast entrance, so Kina dashed to the door, shuffled to a stop, and pressed her ear against the cool wood. There was only the sound of the wind through the jungle canopy on the other side. She slowly opened the door, saw there was no one outside on the walkway, slipped out, and then closed the door behind her.

The sky was clear, and the sun was still shining somewhere on the other side of the palace in the western sky, but the wind was severe, and Kina had to keep her head down below the stone wall to avoid it stinging her face. She thought she would be used to it by now, having lived in the palace at the top of Mount Otaba her entire life, but it still stung. Kina crawled down the stairs to the walkway and then looked up into the rotunda – two adulu were standing on either side of the doorway in their crimson tunics and boarhide belts, spears in hand, but their backs were to her.

"Baga," Kina whispered. She slowly backed up, took a deep breath, and stood. The wind smacked her in the face and almost knocked her off her feet, but she grabbed the wall and pulled herself forward to look over the edge.

Because the Yaya's Palace had to be built on top of Mount Otaba, and later renovations had to extend it over the side of the mountain, the drop from the raised walkway was just a little scary, but Kina had done it before. After one last look to ensure the adulu hadn't noticed her, she threw one leg over the wall, then the other leg, and then dangled by her hands as the wind tugged at her. She looked down, aimed, took another deep breath, and then let go, allowing her body to crumple into a ball as she hit the ground. After she rolled to a stop, she remained lying there a moment to make sure nothing felt broken. Satisfied her arms and legs seemed to be intact, she popped up, brushed off the dirt, adjusted her tunic, and started walking around to the front of the mountain.

As she pushed through the underbrush onto the cibmani stone street and into the fading light of day, there was a rustling in the orange-and-pink-leaved omabu shrubs on the other side. "Biacoya?" Kina called for him – at least, she hoped it was him.

They had made plans to meet at the third turn in the street from the top when Mawoi touched the western wall. But now she realized the angle from the palace at the top of the mountain would have differed greatly from the bottom, which meant she could have missed him entirely. She also worried the incident with the wasps had kept him away, as it had just nearly done for her. It was also a long walk up the mountain and... There was suddenly more movement in the shrubs and Kina stopped walking, not knowing what to do, standing alone out in the open.

"Kina!" Biacoya suddenly shouted, jumping up from behind the shrubs. "I swear, I thought you were a howler coming to eat me!"

Kina nearly died. "A *kugo?!*" she asked, angrily stomping her sandaled foot, but her anxiety instantly gave way to laughter. "A howling kugo that knows your name? That just happened to arrive at the exact time and place that we agreed to meet?"

"Well, when you say it like that," he stammered, apologetically.

She sighed, punched him in the arm, and then said with a smile, "Come on, it's this way." And then Kina started running northwest through the underbrush.

"Hey, wait up!" he hollered, scrambling to catch up to her.

Daylight faded rapidly in the jungle beneath the thick canopy and Kina didn't want to waste it. Birds cawed and chattered to each other, smaller creatures scurried about on the jungle floor, no doubt fleeing from them, and she could hear Biacoya wheezing above it all.

"Slow down!" he called, but she didn't reply.

The little jerk had scared her, and Kina was in her element now. She knew this jungle better than anyone. She would have no problem navigating it blindfolded and in the middle of one of Yuraca's biggest storms, even if it were the worst storm in the history of Itabacan. She glided around a fallen tree limb and hollered over her shoulder, "We're almost there!"

"Almost – where?" Biacoya asked between heaving breaths, and then she heard him crash into the tree limb. "Oww!"

Kina smiled. It helped that the particular trail they were on she had personally widened over the past several years, making it less likely to be obstructed by fallen branches and more visible during the day and night. Of course, that didn't help her friend who had never been on the trail before, but she was pretty sure Biacoya could handle it.

The jungle started thinning out the closer they got to the Otaba Cliffs, opening up to the sunset and flooding the trail with light. Kina came to a stop at a bend in the trail a reed away from the edge of the cliffs. She caught her breath and took a moment to admire the beauty of Mawoi's final flicker before sinking off to sleep. It was called the Otaba Cliffs because the entire western face of the mountain had sheared off at some point in the distant past, leaving behind one immensely tall flat rockface stacked on top of another, cascading all the way down from where Kina stood to the Yaya's private docks at the base of the mountain.

"There – you are," she heard Biacoya shout, a half-dozen paces back down the trail.

She looked out to the orangish-red line that split the Great Sea from the Great Sky far beyond the western wall like a thread of fire, and in the middle was the upper half of the Great Light – now just a small yellow bump on the horizon. From there, the colors of the sky gradually faded from an almost white to pale-azure, deep purple over their heads, and finally to total black darkness toward the east.

"Whoa!" Biacoya exclaimed, quickly coming up alongside her.

"Hey!" Kina yelled and immediately grabbed his arm with both hands. She used his momentum to swing the boy around her and back onto the trail, him screaming all the way, and her yelling, "Cllliiiiifff!"

He skidded to a stop facing the interior of the jungle, with Kina now being the one wheezing and out of breath. "You – I just saved you. You – big – dummy!"

"Whoa," he said again, a bit less excitement in his voice.

"Yeah," she laughed. "Whoa is right!" They stood there a moment, catching their breath, like two boar that had just finished pulling a heavy cart. "Come on," she said, patting him on the back. Kina then continued north up the trail to the short but broad mouth of a cave. She paused and looked over at him. "This way."

Biacoya hesitated. "We're going in there?"

"Just, come on. Trust me!" she told him.

Her voice echoed down through the mouth of the cave, beckoning her forward. Kina didn't wait for Biacoya. She knew he would follow her, just like she had known he would follow her into the jungle. Boys were dumb like that, or so her mother told her.

"Hey!" She heard him yell, still outside on the trail. "Wait for me!"

Kina slowed down, not wanting to lose him entirely. Like the jungle outside, she knew the cave on the cliffs very well and, if she didn't proceed with care, Biacoya would certainly get hurt. "This way!" she hollered, listening to her small voice expand rapidly before slowly repeating in dissipating waves both behind her and directly in front her.

After a moment, she heard his reply, "I'm coming! Baga, it's dark!"

The narrow pathway ahead bent to the left and dropped slightly toward the floor of a large cavern, but it also shot right and into a small chamber where scorpions fed on swarms of insects, which in turn were feeding on a massive pile of bat droppings. It was the most icky area of the entire cave and it would not be good for him to wander that way. "When you get to the bend," she hollered, but let the echo dissipate before adding,

"Go left!" She continued on ahead, half jogging, half sliding down into the large cavern.

"Sure!" came his echoing reply.

Kina ran her hand along the slick wall of the cavern on her left until she felt the crack she was feeling for, and then she quickly knelt down to restart the little fire she had built and reused numerous times over the years. At the base of the rock wall, she found the sparker. Sparkers were made of two hand length cibmani sticks attached at one end by a copper hinge. Inset in their other ends were a shiny silvery-gold rock and a dull grayish-brown rock, each about the size of a thumb. When the two stones were struck together, they would emit a spark. The one Kina held in her delicate hand she had borrowed from the palace kitchen. Beside the sparker she found the pile of dry sticks she intended to use for the fire. Once she had some of the sticks arranged as best she could in the dark, she squeezed the sparker – *clack!*

"Uh – Kina?" Biacoya called to her. The nearness of his voice told her he was at or near the bend.

"Yeah, I'm here," she replied.

Clack!

"Uh – there's a weird noise over here."

Clack!

"It's just the bugs and the bats. Ignore it and come *left!*"

Clack!

"Uh – alright. What're you doing? What's making that clacking sound?"

Clack-whoosh!

The little fire ignited, instantly burning up stick after stick, but Kina kept piling them on until the fire started to sustain itself.

"Hey," he said, moving toward the light. "Who taught you to make fire? My baba said he won't teach me because he's afraid I'll burn the jungle down."

"I don't blame him. You and fire? It's probably a good idea you *never* learn." Kina smoothly pushed the sparker back behind her into her shadow and out of sight.

The flickering light from the fire revealed a massive cavern. Flames danced across hundreds of stalactites hanging from the ceiling, moist and shimmering, which dripped into pools of sparkling water below. A rhythmic *pwink-pwink* sound echoed in all directions farther into the darkness and also back out the way they came where the sound of the crashing waves remained faint in the distance.

"This is awesome!" Biacoya exclaimed.

"It is, isn't it?" Kina sat down next to her little fire.

"How did you find this place?" he asked.

Kina scooted back and leaned against the rock wall and said, "Several years ago – I think I was six or seven – I was playing on one of my baba's carts when the chacu got startled and ran down the mountain." She paused to toss a few more stick onto the fire. "I remember how crazy fast those hairy things were running, because when they made that third turn, I went flying out. You know the omabu shrubs you were hiding behind?"

"The orange and pink ones?"

"Yeah, well, the pedals were green and yellow then, but that's where I landed."

"Whoa!" Biacoya sat down next to her, still looking around the cave. "Something like that happened to me once, but the cart ran over my leg and the lesini had to stitch my thigh back together." He bent over and lifted his tunic so Kina could see his scar.

She saw it and smiled, "That's a neat scar! Did it hurt?"

"Nah, just hated not being able to walk for a mawa," he said, trying to act tough.

"I didn't get hurt from the fall, just disoriented," she said. "I wandered around in the jungle until I found this cave."

Since the Yayapti, the Itabayiti divided a kuranan into twenty-nine days. The first fourteen were called the *sumawa*, when Kuraka was growing and becoming full on the fourteenth day. The second fourteen were called the *samawa*, when Kuraka shrank and became *Hekura*, the sleeping moon, on the twenty-ninth day. Without the Moon Spirit's protection against Maboti, they avoided going outside at night during Hekura. *Well*, Kina thought, *they used to avoid going outside at night.*

"My baba says life is all scars and broken bones," Biacoya continued. "But Yucahu holds our bodies together, so his spirit doesn't escape." He stopped talking and Kina watched him stand up to look at the walls of the cave.

"I stayed here for two days," she added.

"Two days?! No one came looking for you?" Biacoya seemed shocked.

She shrugged, "They said they did, but no one ever came here. On the third day, I walked out on my own, found my way back through the jungle to the street, and then was picked up by one of the palace attendants."

"And you never told anyone where you had been for two days?"

"It didn't seem necessary. Besides, I've had this all to myself until now," she said and Biacoya smiled, still checking out the cave.

Beneath the wet sheen of the brownish gray stone, there were streaks of black here and there which increased farther back into the darkness. Kina quietly watched him admire the strange markings on the rock wall, the very markings she wanted him to see and the reason she brought him to her cave. Of all the other children she knew, Kina was most interested in Anki and Biacoya because she had heard about some of their adventures. Specifically, she heard they had explored a small cave on the island of Pacca where Biacoya lived.

"What's this?" he asked, pointing to a section of the rock wall that stretched far up toward the stalactites and was smooth and flat like the cibmani walls.

To Kina, the strange markings on this particular portion of the cave wall looked like the outlines of hands — a lot of hands, like, dozens upon dozens of overlapping hands. She stood and brushed the cave grime from her tunic. "I don't know. I call it Sutak'balo."

"Uh – what's that?"

"The hand of the Great Preparer," she said and walked over to where Biacoya was standing. He looked at her confusedly. "The Preparer of Children? Revered by all attendants?"

His bright-brown eyes flashed orange in the firelight. "Oh, right, the son of Yucahu. I think our attendants have mentioned him before."

"It's fine, if you don't know what I'm talking about," she said with a smile. "Of course, I don't think Sutak personally made these — I mean, I guess he could have. I think he inspired someone to make them, but I don't think that someone was Itabayiti."

Biacoya held up his hand to one of the markings. "They're huge!" He then tried to put both of his hands in just one handprint and was shocked to find they fit.

"Yeah," Kina said. "Whoever made them had to be enormous!"

He rubbed one of the outlines with his finger. "It looks like ash."

"Maybe."

"Like, if they had put their hand here," he said, demonstrating, "and then threw ash against their hand and the wall."

"That's what I was thinking," she said. "Have...you ever seen anything like this?"

She was hoping he had. She hoped the cave she heard about on Pacca also had these strange markings, because then she could compare them and maybe figure out who or what had made them. Suddenly, before Biacoya could answer her question, a sound from deeper in the cave startled both of them.

"Wha-what was that?" he stammered.

"I-I'm not sure." Kina replied. And then there was another sound, a lower sound, like the hefty breathing of an exhausted boar. Kina started backing up slowly, grabbing the neckline of Biacoya's tunic and pulling him with her. "We should leave." The breathing seemed labored, arrhythmic, and was getting louder, closer.

"Run!" Biacoya shouted, and they did.

They ran past the flickering light of the little fire, around the narrow corner, and back into the foreboding darkness of the beginning of the cave. The sun had fully set and only a faint whisper of moonlight told them they were headed in the right direction. Kina made sure to put her arms out and slow down to prevent them from accidentally racing off the edge of the cliffs. She was instantly glad she did, because Biacoya bumped into her right arm just as they emerged from the mouth of the cave, causing him to slip and kick a few pebbles over the edge.

"Whoa! Thanks!" he said, and then they heard the weird breathing again, but this time it was right behind them in the pitch-black of the mouth of the cave.

"Ahhh!" they both screamed and darted into the jungle.

Kina was in front of Biacoya and looked back over her shoulder frequently to make sure he was still behind her – he was, and right on her heels. They ran and ran, the sounds of the jungle around them completely ignored until they erupted from the jungle onto the street, stopped, and listened. First, the sound of the wind came back, then the insects, then the hooting of an uca bird, but there was thankfully nothing else. Relieved, they collapsed onto their backs in the middle of the street.

"What," Biacoya started, out of breath, "was – that?"

Kina sat up. "I don't know."

They remained on the street listening to the sounds of the island just long enough to catch their breath and then Biacoya sat up as well. "I better go, my baba is going to be mad enough as it is," he said.

"Me too." Kina stood and dusted herself off again. "Will you do me a favor and not tell anyone about this place? It's kind of my secret place – *our* secret place now."

"Are you crazy? I'm never going back in there again!" Biacoya stood up as well. "You shouldn't either." Kina smiled and nodded. "Good," he said. "Well, Tayokun, Kina Wani." Biacoya waved goodbye, spun around, and then started down the long and winding street toward the base of the mountain alone in the dark.

"Tayokun, Biacoya," she called after him with a deep sigh. "Boys are weird," she said quietly to herself.

Kina felt bad. She didn't have many friends, and with the wasp incident, the infrequent opportunities she did have to be around other children were in jeopardy. And now Biacoya had gotten scared and wasn't likely to ever come back again. Maybe, she thought, maybe she could figure out a way to remain after lessons longer, so her friends didn't have to come all the way up the mountain. She continued to ponder her situation as she walked up the moonlit street, noticing one of her fingernails had chipped. She picked at it. Night had come and she didn't like to walk through the dark jungle if she didn't have to, no matter how well she might know it. Kina maneuvered her head so that she could peek through the tops of the trees to Kuraka's position in the sky. If she hurried, she would likely just make it in time for evening prayers at the spirit shrine of Yucahu before evening meal.

She liked listening to the insects trilling loudly, punctuated here and there by a spattered stirring in the underbrush and the occasional hooting of an uca. She was told the uca birds were vessels for their ancestors, so that they may watch over the darkness and warn the Itabayiti of Maboti's presence. But Kina didn't worry too much about it, because she wasn't sure she really believed in evil spirits anymore. She let the thought fall from her mind as she walked up to the palace grounds.

The palace grounds on top of Mount Otaba featured stables to the west, which also housed the palace guards, the adulu. Living quarters for the attendants were just to the right of the stables along the northern rim, and then the palace kitchen sat between the attendants' quarters and the Council Rotunda and the rest of the palace to the east. The first thing Kina noticed was a flicker of light in the rotunda, which could only mean a meeting was in session. She looked around. Other than the two adulu at the palace entrance there was no one else in sight. She quickly ran across the open yard to the omabu shrubs on the eastern side of the palace kitchen. The shrubs grew wild all over the island and varied in color depending on the time of year until they each dried up and tumbled away in the dry-season wind. Kina crouched behind the orange and pink flowers and thought about how she might listen in on the meeting.

Light poured out of the door to the kitchen which faced the western entrance to the rotunda, where two adulu stood watch with their spears. Kina knew her best and only approach would be to climb back up the Yaya's raised walkway. But then her mother suddenly came out of the double doors of the palace.

"Kina!" her mother hollered, squinting into the night. "It's time for prayers!"

"Baga," Kina said to herself. But then she thought, if she appeased her mother now, she would stop looking for her. They would have to wait on evening meal anyway because her father was in the meeting, which meant she wouldn't have to climb the raised walkway and could then sneak into the meeting through the palace. "Here, itaba!" She stood and waved.

"Oh, there you are!" Unana started down the palace steps toward her daughter, the shells in her braids clacking together. "Where have you been?"

Kina met her mother halfway. "Just out and about. Is it time for prayers?"

"Yes, it is. Oh, merciful Yucahu, look at your clothes – they're filthy! You will need a bath and a clean tunic before evening meal."

A bath meant Kina wouldn't have time to listen in on the council meeting. "But itaba-wani, wouldn't it be better for me to have my bath *after* evening meal?"

Her mother knew this trick. Kina knew her mother knew she was up to something, which was the best trick Kina had ever come up with. She followed her mother's eyes as she looked around the palace grounds. The stables were quiet, the attendants' quarters were quiet, the kitchen was bustling, but it was always bustling just before evening meal. And then her mother noticed the light coming from the Council Rotunda.

"You want to sneak into the council meeting, don't you?"

Kina shied away, "Wha-why would I want to do that?"

Her mother knelt down to where their faces were just a hand apart and whispered, "Because, I want to do that." And then she winked at Kina.

Kina's turquoise eyes got really big, and she had to stifle a squeal. She took her mother's hand and practically dragged her back into the palace, through the reception hall, up the dais steps, through the secret door behind her father's throne, into the east hallway, and to the backdoor of the northeast entrance. The door creaked slightly as Kina slowly opened it, careful not to get blasted by the wind again, and then she led her mother onto the raised walkway and into the night. From there, they could clearly hear a council member talking, but they would need to sneak up to the doorway in order to see who it was.

"You have to duck down or else they might see you," Kina told her. "And itaba, you must quiet your hair!"

Her mother snickered but complied, as they both ducked and silently went down the steps to peer up into the doorway. The adulu were there like they were before, and Kina could see the tops of a few council members' heads sitting on the stepped seating of the rotunda. She put a finger to her mouth, motioning for her mother to be quiet, and her mother nodded and did the same.

Slowly, deliberately, and in complete silence, she climbed the three steps up to the landing before the doorway. They were still in shadow but now they could almost see the entire council chamber and all of the members. Her father, the Yaya, was sitting on his stone throne against the north section of the curved wall with a bored expression on his face, and there were two adulu standing on either side of him. Kina then saw the man talking was Boyiti Macoca, the elected representative for the Itabayiti on the island of Yapaca, and he seemed terribly upset.

CHAPTER FOUR
A Remarkable Matter

Even in the waning moonlight, the Pyramid of Mayu was a marvel of Itabayiti engineering. It rose one hundred and eight steps from the western end of the Grand Plaza and was topped by the araco observatory, which itself had been made from a single mold of poured cibmani stone and added a further two reeds of height to the structure. Large stone bowls of fire the size of giant sea turtles adorned the ends of eight ramps lining the four stairways to the top of the pyramid, casting erratic shadows across their polished surfaces.

Draha had not gotten over how wonderful it felt to stand at the foot of the pyramid and know it was where he would get to spend the rest of his life. From the moment he was born, Draha and his twin sister, Tabba, were raised by Elder Sengri and the Cult of Mayu and trained to read the messages in the sky in the ways of the araco. He was a star gazer, an intercessor for the ancestors, and would one day be boaraco to the Yaya. As such, the sides of his head had been shaved every day since he was five, and the sponge of black hair on top of his head was neatly trimmed into a tall, smooth, unmoving rectangle.

He watched the firelight from the basins dance across the polished steps, equally bathed in moonlight, and held up one of his hands to compare. Unlike the gray stone structure, Draha's skin was like oiled palm wood. But when he placed his hand against the step, something wondrous happened. The colors blended and folded into one another, and if he squinted just slightly, his hand seemed to disappear before his eyes.

"What are you doing?" Boaraco Unsari asked, startling him. "The steps aren't going to magically climb themselves." He shook his head at him, lifted his dark, azure robe, and painfully raised one foot up onto the knee-high step. "Be useful, give me your arm."

"Yes, Boaraco," Draha said and rushed to Unsari's side.

Unsari had a chubby, clean-shaven face, and a similar but graying rectangle of neatly trimmed hair on top of his head. He was widely considered the most unpleasant man in all of Itabacan, but Draha knew he relished in his reputation. Unsari often said it was because he refused to entertain idiocy in any form, which was why the boaraco was as likely to insult someone as he was to just ignore them altogether. Shorter than most men, Unsari made up for his vertical limitations by ensuring his waistline was well nourished, but his weight also wrought havoc on his joints. Consequently, climbing the pyramid steps appeared to be incredibly painful for him.

Draha had one of his arms and was helping him up another step, when Boaraco Unsari suddenly looked at him and exaggeratedly sniffed the air. "Ah, you're at that age where you either need to bathe more regularly or wear a garland of fragrant flowers around your neck."

"Yes, Boaraco," he replied and then sniffed his own armpit. He didn't think he smelled that bad.

"Trust me, Drahoo. I'm old, I've smelled some horrendous things in my life, and you need a bath."

"Yes, Boaraco, but my name is Draha," he tried to correct him.

Unsari snapped at Draha with a frightening quickness that made him slip on the smooth step and nearly tumble down the pyramid. "It will never matter who *you* say you are, Drahoo," he said. "It will only matter if those who wield power agree with you. Do you wield power, Drahoo?" Unsari's tone was cold and menacing.

Draha stammered, "I–I, no, I don't believe so."

Unsari laughed. "Of course, you don't. At least, not yet." And then he turned, shook his arm free of Draha's hands, and continued up the pyramid steps with the speed of a younger man.

Draha didn't know what to think. One moment the boaraco would appear to be old and infirm, and the next he seemed healthier and more capable than most of the other araco. Draha wondered if it might all just be an act, some kind of performance, and he vowed to discover the truth one day as he continued up the steps behind him.

Originally, the araco observatory had been on top of Mount Otaba in the center of what were now the Yaya's palace grounds, but Yaya Ajan wanted his palace on the mountain instead. He moved the observatory to the top of the Pyramid of Mawoi and renamed it the Pyramid of Mayu, which Elder Sengri told Draha greatly angered the Cult of Mawoi. The three buildings that ran along the northern edge of the plaza that had once been the palace complex became the home of the araco, their attendants' quarters, and the lesson hall for the Cult of Mayu they called Mayu Hall.

Draha stopped climbing the steps before he reached the observatory at the top and turned to look out over Itabacan. The moon was partially obscured by clouds, but the crests of the waves sparkled just like the stars in the night sky he was about to study. Near the shore he could see the torches burning around the Temple of Yucahu where the Yucaakin gave offerings of fruits, flowers, and sometimes live sacrifices to the Great Spirit. Up the hill from the temple was a broad plain and the village of Badhan. The village was lively at all phases of the sun and moon, appearing as a patchwork of oddly shaped buildings of varying sizes and heights, separated by a massive spider's web of cibmani stone streets and shell-lined alleyways. The wider streets were partially lit by hanging torches, clearly distinguishable from the darker, crisscrossing narrow alleyways linking every dark corner and courtyard. There were noisy markets, public baths, apartments, bonefire pits, and the one and only Badhan Gardens.

The village of Badhan could be tame during the day, but also wild and treacherous at night. More than a few claimed to have seen Utuchu, the Wicked Weaver, gliding over her web in the darkness and snatching up any wandering children unfortunate enough to lose their way. Draha was raised in those streets and never saw or heard any such thing, but the Cult of Utuchu, on the other hand, was an ever-present menace. From what Draha had overheard in the markets, the cult believed they were doing the work of Utuchu and ridding her web of unwanted vermin. He knew the problem had been taken to Yaya Amnu, but it seemed the Yaya was more interested in planning the Day of Biyaya festival.

Elder Sengri told Draha and his sister that the festival was held every fifteen years and commemorated the fifteen-year rule of the Biyaya, the first Yaya. The Biyaya and the Itabayiti first settled on the island of Itabaca nearly a thousand years ago. The first village they also called Itabaca, hugged the Nitaba River, the only water source on the island. The river still flowed down from the eastern slope of Mount Otaba, but it used to split near the base of the mountain and run through the interior of the island. At that time, Itabaca consisted of thatch-roofed huts a reed tall arranged in a large circle around a central bonefire. As the years went by, the huts were reinforced with cibmani to become bohi and the village expanded outward. Years turned into decades and the river was dammed at the split, making it flow into the reed yard instead and creating more room for the village to grow.

As decades turned to centuries, the village circles of Karun and Bukun were added, but eventually all three villages overlapped, morphed, and it was hard to tell where one ended and the other began. Around five hundred years later, the village of Itabaca became overcrowded and people began migrating to the islands of Yapaca, Amaca, or Hatca, where they then established new villages. According to Sengri, only the acodu scribes remained in Itabaca, because they preferred the clay deposits of the old riverbed to form their tablets. The acodu eventually cleared the bonefire pit in the center of the village and built Acodu Hall where they were said to have displayed a great history of Itabacan on seventy-two enormous clay tablets.

Sengri also told them that those who remained in the cramped conditions of Karun and Bukun were painters, tanners, bakers, and artisans of all sorts, in addition to almec players, their attendants, and their outfitters. Before long, they started referring to themselves as residents of Badhan, which Draha thought might be a reference to the grinding stones the bakers used, but he honestly wasn't sure. Karun became the Caru Market, Bukun the Buku Market, and the vendors would get together during festivals to form the Badhan Market along the eastern edge between the village and the almec courts across the street. The people of Badhan mostly avoided what was once Itabaca, referring to it simply as Acodun.

"You'll never learn about what's up in the sky by staring at the ground," Boaraco Unsari snapped, startling Draha. "Now get in here, Drahoo!"

"Coming, Boaraco," he shouted, breaking his concentration. The boaraco must have had a very bad council meeting for him to already be this grumpy so early in the evening.

Walking into the observatory was like nothing Draha had ever experienced, and he had even been in the caves of Bahaca and bathed in the springs of Niamca. The shiny walls in the observatory were a little like the caves, but these were perfectly flat and polished to a high shine. Because the observatory had been formed by poured cibmani into a mold, all of the edges and corners were perfect right angles, and the ceiling was curved like an overturned canuti. It was rectangular, exactly two reeds wide by three reeds long, and featured six observation windows a hand tall and cut into the stone a reed off the ground. Additionally, drilled in a seemingly random pattern were exactly seventy-two holes called dwamu, or star ports, all over the walls around the observatory – just big enough for Draha to put his hand through.

"That's a good way to get your arm amputated," Unsari said, matter-of-factly.

"Amputated?!" He tried to pull his hand out of the dwamu, but it briefly got stuck and he had to wiggle it free.

"See, I told you. Before my time, they had to cut a man's arm clean off so they could remove the other half from the dwamu," Unsari said as he pulled the sekom from its niche over the western window. He held it up for Draha to see and then inserted the wedge into one of the star ports. "The sekom is a rod made out of reeds with a wooden wedge attached at one end. We insert it into one of the star ports to block the path of the light."

Unsari pointed out the features as he talked, but Draha was already trying to remember the next step of the lesson. "Making it easier to map the paths of our ancestors," he said with confidence.

Unsari tilted his head and shrugged. "You're almost there, Drahoo. But look around – do you see any ancestor beams?"

Draha looked around. Some of the holes were lit up but there weren't any beams of light. "No, I guess not," he said.

"If you know the answer, it's not a guess, Drahoo. The answer is no. No, there aren't any beams of light or ancestors in the observatory." Unsari removed the sekom and put it back in its niche.

Tucked in the northwest corner of the observatory on the floor was a wooden stool, which Boaraco Unsari kicked away from the corner and sat on loudly, fuming in quiet irritation. Draha looked around for another stool but there wasn't one, so he sat on the cold stone floor.

"Who said you could sit?" Unsari smirked.

Draha quickly stood, dusted himself off, and then leaned against the southern wall. Boaraco Unsari was definitely in a sour mood, which meant the rest of the night was going to be brutal. But then he thought, maybe if the old man talked about what was bothering him, he might lighten up a bit and be more like his normal, slightly less abrasive self. He looked at the boaraco, his grumpy chin resting on his crossed arms over his large belly, and then Draha thought better of it.

"What is it, Drahoo?" Unsari asked.

"Nothing, Boaraco." He swallowed hard.

Unsari cleared his throat and said in a dry tone, "Nothing is not nothing, if your dwelling on it becomes *my* something." He waited for Draha to respond, staring at him with his old, wrinkled eyes.

Draha gulped. "Are there really seventy-two tablets hanging in Acodun?" he heard himself ask. It wasn't what he wanted to ask, but it came out of his mouth anyway.

"Acodun?" Unsari repeated him, and then stared out the window. "Aco-dooon..."

His voice trailed off and Draha got the feeling this was going to be one those times where Boaraco Unsari simply ignored him. "I mean," he tried to clarify, "Because there are seventy-two dwamu, and I heard there were also seventy-two..." He swallowed hard. "Umm...seventy-two tablets."

"Ah — so your question isn't about tablets or dwamu, but about the number itself," he said, still staring out the window.

"I guess..." Draha tried to stop the word from coming out of his mouth and failed. Unsari instantly glared at him. "I apologize, Boaraco," he quickly said. "What I mean to say is that Elder Sengri told us about the tablets, and he said they contain a history of the Itabayiti." Draha stopped talking, but the boaraco continued to silently glare at him. "I mean, we're not allowed — no one is allowed to enter Acodu Hall anymore, except for the boaraco, which is you. And I asked Elder Sengri why that was, but he said to ask you."

"Ask me?"

"Yes. I asked him about the tablets, and he said to ask you."

"Ask me what, Drahoo?" Unsari demanded, clearly getting more irritated with him. "You must formulate an idea or a quandary in your tiny mind, and then shape that idea or quandary into the precise words necessary to most adequately relate that idea or quandary to your listener.

51

Otherwise, what inevitably stumbles out of your mouth is more suitable for the ditches in the street than the ears on my head!"

"Forgive me, Boaraco," Draha begged him. "I won't ask any more questions. You seem to have come back from the council meeting more irritated than when you left, and I won't trouble you any longer." This could be it, Draha thought. This could be the moment Boaraco Unsari throws him off the top of the pyramid. He braced himself for the barrage of insults, but nothing happened. To his surprise, Unsari smiled, which was just as terrifying.

"Gladly," Unsari said, and then he leaned forward as if to tell Draha a secret. "Council meetings are, by definition, a trial of agonizing redundancy."

He must have sensed Draha's confusion, or maybe he had a lot of pent-up frustration, because Unsari immediately launched into a hate filled rant about the idiocy of the council members, the superfluous matters brought to it, and even the abominable seating. Boaraco Unsari used a lot of big words, some of which Draha had never heard before.

"The cold, unyielding stone benches are meant to be uncomfortable to encourage council members to either speak or be done with it, not for my backside to go numb and my legs to become like crab's legs in boiling water," Unsari complained.

Draha didn't respond except to nod along, especially when he had no idea what the boaraco was talking about. He knew Unsari loved an audience, and that it was best to allow him a little silent attentiveness.

"That was another thing! They call the floor the *round* because it is round and stepping into the round to speak, they call *Taking the Round*. What monumental absurdity! They couldn't have come up with something just a little less redundant. They might just as well have called it taking the floor, or to take a stand, or some other such nonsense!"

A fierce wind tore through the windows of the observatory, making Unsari tighten his robe around his belly. Draha felt it as well in his dark-azure tunic. He hadn't earned his robe yet and had been told to stop complaining about it. And then Unsari started to chuckle. It was a deep, guttural chuckle that vibrated his chest more than it made any sound, while Draha could only shiver.

"Boyiti Macoca almost lost his tunic to a gust of wind as he was speaking in the round. His hair was flapping about, but he couldn't focus on that, because his tunic blew up from below his belt and it took both hands to push it back down and tighten his belt again!" Unsari laughed and laughed, rocking back and forth on the poor little stool. "The Yaya nearly broke his wahas slamming it on the stone floor trying to bring order to the rotunda!"

Draha knew the wahas was a staff traditionally made of vines which symbolized the Yaya's authority. He vaguely remembered Elder Sengri saying it originated from an important spear, but Draha wasn't certain of that. He did know that, if it broke, some said the Yaya's authority broke with it. He laughed along with the boaraco and momentarily forgot his own strategy, but it was too late to bite his tongue. "What matter did Boyiti Macoca have?" he asked.

Unsari stopped laughing, adjusted his robe again, and then crossed his arms over his belly. "That is council business," he said, returning his grumpy chin to his grumpy arms.

Draha sighed, but there was another tactic he could try. He knew Unsari well enough to know that the boaraco despised Macoca. It wasn't that Unsari didn't like him as the boyiti or even as a council member, Unsari despised him for having the audacity to share the same Great Spirit as him. He wasn't sure why or what Macoca had done to earn Unsari's hatred, but he knew it really didn't take much, and that the boaraco went to great lengths to let other people know just how much he hated Macoca.

"Well, whatever the matter," Draha began. "I think Macoca's rise to boyiti was remarkable, and I'm sure his contribution to the meeting must have been equally remarkable."

"Remarkable?" Unsari jumped to his feet. "Remarkable? There has never been a remarkable thought in that tiny hutia head of his! You want to know what remarkable matter Macoca discussed for nearly the entirety of the meeting?" Unsari was waiting for him to reply but Draha played dumb. "Well, Drahoo, I'll tell you. He wasted our entire evening discussing public baths for Yapaca." He nodded in self-satisfaction and slumped back down on his stool.

Draha was confused and asked, "They don't have public baths on Yapaca?"

"Of course they don't have public baths on Yapaca! Those people bathe in the harbor all the time. But what Macoca waited until the end of his blathering, nonsensical waste of valuable sleeptime to say was that it was a health issue that could affect all of Itabacan!"

"How do you mean?" Draha honestly wanted to know.

"Because most of the workers on all of the islands live on Yapaca. If they don't have regular baths, then all of our food, all of our clothing, all of Itabacan society becomes contaminated with their filth."

He was right. Boaraco Unsari was absolutely right. *Why don't they already have public baths?* he wondered. There were at least six of them in Badhan, and Badhan had maybe one tenth the population of Yapaca. Draha was still confused why such an important matter irritated the boaraco, and so he asked, "But why should such an important matter irritate you so much?"

"Because it was the simplest argument to make," he explained. "Workers are dirty, those same workers harvest our food, then they weave our clothing, all after they've cleaned out the very public baths Macoca was trying to get them! That's all he had to say, but instead, Macoca talked and talked, and talked and talked, and my backside became numb, and my legs now feel like they've been boiled in crab water!"

Draha was surprised to see Boaraco Unsari so animated. The old man always loved to tell a story, but he had never gotten up and down so many times or been so red in the face. "Did the council agree with Boyiti Macoca? Are they getting public baths?" he asked.

"A hundred times more efficient than any in Itabacan, most likely."

There was a long moment of welcome quiet as the heated conversation settled around them. Draha thought it funny, the only reason Unsari was in such a poor mood was because he had been made to sit on a stone bench for a long time so other people could take a bath. No wonder the first thing he brought up when returning from the council meeting was Draha's odor! But then he had another thought – what matter did Boaraco Unsari take to the round?

So, he asked, "Boaraco Unsari, what matter did you take to the round?"

The boaraco leaned forward as if to tell another secret, raised one eyebrow, looked out the northeast window and said, "Look up there."

Draha shuffled over to the window, knelt down so that his gaze was in line with the boaraco's, and then he looked up. "Do you see that really bright star and the three that go up from it in almost a perfect line, almost like it might be a slightly bent reed?" Unsari pointed to the sky.

Draha nodded. They had learned about groups of stars called mul in Mayu Hall, and how an araco long ago had divided the sky into thirteen mul, one for each kuranan of the year, which was how the Itabayiti tracked the cycles of the moon.

"There are two more stars on either side of the first reed. They form another reed that appears to be lying across the first reed, do you see that?" Draha nodded again. He knew Boaraco Unsari was pointing to the Urgoca-mul, but he had already learned his lesson about interrupting the old man. "Now, we call that formation Urgoca," Unsari said, his eyes glistening with starlight.

Draha acted surprised. "Echo bird?" he asked.

"Don't *appear* to be foolish, Drahoo. Someone may just believe you," Unsari snapped, rolling his eyes. "You know perfectly well what I'm pointing at. Now, look, just to the right of Urgoca's belly button, what we call Sakimi. There, beside the belly button is another bright light. Do you see that, or are you going to pretend to be blind now too?"

"Yes," Draha said instantly, but he had to squint. "It's really faint." He thought he did see something.

"That star, Draha. That star does not move across the void like the others. That star is something else entirely," he said and then reclined back on his stool.

It was clearly an interesting discovery, and worth taking to the round and informing the Yaya, but all Draha could think about was that Boaraco Unsari had said his name right for the first time all evening.

CHAPTER FIVE

One Who Dwells in Darkness

There was a foreboding to the darkness, she had to remind herself. The sun went to sleep, and a guttural sensation activated a deeply rooted warning of potential threats on the other side of the light. She knew this. Those who chose to ignore this warning did so in great desperation. She felt it, right there, in the fog of disparate thoughts weighing on her like a mountain of rocks.

Dwellings were once in the trees high above the jungle floor. She knew this too. It was once thought that anything dangerous would alert those sleeping in the tree as the dangerous things climbed up to eat them – things with claws and sharp teeth. Eventually, dwellings moved to the ground and became enclosed spaces with a single doorway that was usually covered by strings of shells, or pieces of wood that clacked together noisily, warning of trespassers. And then – her thoughts swirled around in her mind. And then they grouped their dwellings into villages and placed early warning systems around them to further ward off threats. It was as if she was remembering the fuzzy false end of a frayed thread. She felt it, like the fires they once lit and tended to all night. They had effectively eliminated the darkness, armed with light, and slept until the sun woke up again.

Those who lived in the darkness, who woke with the moon and slept at the dawn, had a slightly different approach. *Yes*, she was remembering, a root warning activated by light, and there were only so many leaves to hide under, rocks to squeeze beneath, or holes in trees. This was familiar. Burrowing into the earth – *dizzying, swirling thoughts*. Burrowing into the earth was the preferred means of escape, but there were some who were not equipped with sharp claws. Some had to find those great holes in the earth that had taken millions of years to form and offered refuge from the light in deep, dark, far away corners.

In these spaces, cave crickets chirped discordantly in a cacophony of noise, but it was a necessary annoyance, because their silence warned any cave dweller of potential threats. Silence in light, noise in darkness. Bats roamed the night skies in search of flying bugs to consume and returned to their perches, only to be easily startled and would screech loudly at the first sound of danger – a danger that might snatch them out of the sky. The cave itself leaked constantly from gnarled points on the ceiling, dripping water into pools, which echoed off the rock walls. It was impossible for a threat to move through the puddles, or around the bat droppings, or over the loose rocks on the ground without triggering the silent alert.

Through a tight gap high up on the cave wall, she was able to read the activity beyond without leaving her nest. Her hearing was so acute, her eyesight so clear, and her sense of smell so refined that any potential threat was acknowledged and analyzed within a single breath. She couldn't help it. At least, she wanted to believe she was being compelled. It was some sort of involuntary response, of which she had little understanding. Every time she tried to figure it out, she would find herself growing tired and would fall asleep – *or crushed by the rock*.

She couldn't remember specific events, or days, or even years of her life, but understanding of the ancient past seemed so clear. She had feelings and senses which guided her with a general understanding of where she was, had been, and was about to go, but formulating a rational thought was exhausting. It was an odd existence, and there was this nagging feeling that she had at one time known something else. It was like a fog of disparate thoughts weighing on her like the crushing depths of the Great Sea.

There were times when the solitary warmth of the nest became uninviting, even suffocating, and constricted her with a force so great she actually believed being crushed to death might bring relief. She had once known relief – *a release of spirit*. Without the breath in her body, perhaps the exhausting thoughts would leave her as well, but then she might realize that relief would be just another exhaustion, which would then offer little, if any, actual satisfaction.

Were there other possibilities? Were there other options that might render her own thoughts irrelevant? If there were, she would wholly embrace them and be able to finally thank the Great Spirit for giving her life. But the mere thought of it all made her so drowsy – *swirling drowsiness –*

that she only wanted to snuggle into her warm coil, return to sleeptime, and commune with her ancestors in their trees. But she could no longer ignore her need to feed. It was compulsory. Reluctantly, she forced herself out of her nest and triggered the silence.

There was a family of thick-tailed scorpions around a boulder that could satiate her, but she hated scorpions. One time she thought she had snagged a helpless beetle only to discover it was a scorpion pincer, and the scorpion's stinger-strike response made the entire left side of her body numb for several moons – or had it been longer? Either way, she did her best to avoid the scorpions and continued over the wide trench, past the bat droppings covered in worms and maggots, and toward the mouth of the cave.

With the abundance of food in the jungle came an abundance of dangers. There were howlers, uca birds, gosu with their short but strong claws. She had even seen a fox once, but that was a long time ago. She remembered it felt like a long time ago. She almost lunged at a singing koki frog that darted in front of her, but she knew she had to be careful. Some of the frogs in the jungle had a powdery substance on their backs, and she accidentally got some on her tongue once. *I remember it made the grass turn into worms*, the dirt tickle her belly, and there were glowing eyes everywhere. She had decided that eating frogs was a bad idea.

She ventured on through the damp underbrush, the full moonlight piercing the canopy and casting strange shadows on the gray shrubs and short palms. There was a dance of moonshadows on the jungle floor, and she could smell an uca somewhere in the distance. She could hear a howler struggling to climb a tree not too far away, its matted fur riddled with insects smelling tasty, but she knew they were anything but. And then she caught the scent of a giant hutia digging nearby – burrowing into the earth.

Baby hutias were the most delicious critters in the jungle. They were tiny, soft, and very juicy, but giant hutias were dangerous and would defend themselves with their large teeth and strong hindlegs the size of tree trunks. If the hutia smelled her coming, it would likely run in a random direction for fear of leading a predator to her nest. What she needed was a threat that would cause the hutia to race back to protect her babies, and the first threat she thought of was the uca bird. With their perfect eyesight, silent wings, and sharp claws, uca could be unpredictably dangerous. Even if it took the bait, her plan might still fail.

Fortunately, the hutia had been between her and the uca, blocking its line of sight while she got the trap in place. Now she just needed the hutia to get out of the way to allow the uca to see the bait. She didn't have to wait long. Everything happened so fast; the hutia moved, the uca saw the bait and instantly swooped down with its mighty gray wings, startling the hutia which ran through a patch of gray-leafed shrubs. The uca silently flew just above the shrubs and short palms of the underbrush, appearing to grow bigger as it came closer. At the final moment, she flipped over a big piece of tree-bark and covered herself entirely – *hiding under leaves or holes in trees*. The uca halted its descent, flapping and hovering just overhead, before turning and flying off in the opposite direction. *This is my chance and I'll take it.*

Normal sized hutias were fairly quick little rodents, but giant hutias were big and slow and plowed through the underbrush, leaving a clear trail of destruction behind them. She easily followed the creature, but she made sure to keep an eye out behind her in case the uca was as clever as she was. She is – *I am.* Before long, she caught the scent of the hutia babies – they smelled tasty! Thankfully, giant hutias weren't very smart and were easily distracted. She had only to disguise her scent with a layer of mud and wait until the mother abandoned her nest, which didn't take long.

After lying still as a stick in the mud for a while, she watched the hutia family squeaking to one another. She remembered this too. She remembered the babies were hungry and needed their mother to venture out once again. After a brief hesitation, the giant hutia mother conceded and trotted away. She didn't hesitate and quickly silenced their hungry squeaks.

She remained there a moment, her belly full of baby hutias, allowing her body to adjust to the new weight. Like the heaviest thoughts, shadows confusing her mind, she saw a real shadow moving through the moonbeams. It wasn't the giant hutia, unless it had grown wings – no, it was the uca! She struggled to make her way farther into the underbrush, to hide under the leaves, or burrow in the earth, to hide herself from the uca, but it was too late. There was a burst of wind, as the uca landed on top of her, its warm claws tightening around her body – *death might bring relief.* And then they were flying, up, up, and up into the air. And that's when something very peculiar happened...

CHAPTER SIX

The Rise of MAWOI

The Temple of the Dawn faced the waking sun from the highest point on the island of Bahaca. The island was surrounded by jagged cliffs and resembled the trunk of a strongbark tree. Long before the Itabayiti arrived, Yuraca's mighty storms eroded the eastern face of the island, causing the eastern rim to collapse and create a steep slope that now rose sharply to the base of the temple. Intense rains carved away the western interior of the island, burrowing into the earth and forming a cave, which wormed its way through the sand, dirt, and rock until it emptied out to form the western shore. Because it was the only beach on the island, the western shore was also the only access point for the akin, their attendants, and the rare visitor.

The Mawoakin were not fond of visitors and forced them to walk up through the island if they wanted to reach the interior. There, they would find stables near the mouth of the cave and a shrine to Boynay, the Rain Spirit. A gravel path wound its way back and forth up the gradual slope from the stables eastward, until it came to a stop at the temple. Just to the north of the temple were the sleeping quarters and more stables, and beyond that a pair of meager gardens wrapped around part of the northern rim of Bahaca.

Before Mawoi could wake from his nightly slumber, the Mawoakin needed to perform the Rise of Mawoi ritual, which they had been performing every day since the first dawn on Itabacan. Most Itabayiti woke up naturally with the rising sun. It was an instinct from long before the Yayapti when the Itabayiti lived nomadically, or so Tabba had been told. She was the twin sister of Draha, born and raised by Elder Sengri and the Cult of Mayu. She was a star gazer, an intercessor for the ancestors, and she absolutely loved it – even if she was stationed in the middle of nowhere on the island of Bahaca. But like some of the workers on the other islands, the

Mawoakin needed to wake up before the dawn in order to prepare their morning ritual, and they relied on an araco stationed on the island to read the stars and do the waking.

Tabba only recently graduated from the Cult of Mayu and had been personally chosen by the Mawoakin to be their resident araco, though she didn't know why. Her brother was chosen to succeed Boaraco Unsari, and she didn't understand that decision either. Unsari hated her brother, like he hated most men, but Tabba never had a problem with the grumpy old boar. She thought it would have been nice to be the next and first female boaraco. It wasn't that she was ungrateful for the opportunity to serve the Mawoakin, but unless she got real interested in sun rituals really quick, she was going to be bored out of her gourd for a long time.

Being tall for her age and having a similar build to her brother, Tabba was often mistaken for him, which was why she started keeping her hair straight and long over her shoulders. But straight hair was a pain to maintain, especially in the middle of nowhere. Once she was assigned to Bahaca, far away from everyone she knew, Tabba put her thick black hair into a more manageable single loose braid that ran down the center of her back. She had taken out her braid for the third time and was in the middle of redoing it when she noticed a flicker of light slowly rising up out of the Great Sea. Tabba rubbed her tired eyes and looked again, but the flicker was gone. "What was that?" she asked herself, looking around at the barren landscape for an answer.

Bahaca had little foliage and was mostly lumpy patches of grass scattered around sandy soil in which hardly anything else would grow. There weren't many creatures on the island either, but it had once been home to several families of giant hawks known as muwan that were believed to be the guardians of the Great Light, or so Tabba had been told. They were revered by the Cult of Mawoi, especially one they called Uansu, but she hadn't been told why. The giant hawks first hunted the spiny rats on the island to extinction, and then they turned to the ekuki, or tiny mice. Unfortunately, as the wildlife population declined, so did the muwan. The last of them relocated to Amaca, and the island of Bahaca grew increasingly quiet.

The incessant wind started to pick up, blowing harder from the northeast and just strong enough to untangle Tabba's unfinished braid. She huffed and quickly finished braiding it, making the last few braids tighter than she normally would, and then she tossed her long braid back over her shoulder. Analyzing the diagram on her clay tablet once more, she didn't think there was enough light on the horizon to conclude that the flash she had seen was Chuka preceding the dawn. Then again, she also knew distant clouds sometimes obscured Mawoi's arrival. The araco had cataloged hundreds of thousands of ancestors in their precession across the void, but only a dozen or so were known to immediately precede Mawoi. One was known as Chuka, the Great Boar ancestor who pulled Mawoi's cart across the sky.

Tabba stood up, brushed off the seat of her dark-azure tunic, and squinted her eyes, scanning the horizon for Chuka. She had to be sure, otherwise she would be waking up the akin too early and their ritual might be ruined. Boaraco Unsari told her the last araco assigned to Bahaca needed to be replaced because he had fallen asleep and failed to wake up the akin. Tabba definitely didn't want to be replaced – at least, not until she could figure out why they had selected her to begin with.

After a moment, the flicker suddenly reappeared a little higher in the sky than before, but in roughly the same spot. Tabba looked at the other bright stars, double-checked her tablet, and then nodded her head. "That's got to be it," she determined and started walking toward the sleeping quarters.

Before Boaraco Unsari escorted Tabba to the island, she asked him what one thing she should know about the Mawoakin. Without hesitation, the boaraco said, *"Every single one of them, old and young alike, male and female, snore horribly."* She pushed the squeaky door open and walked into the deafening chorus of snoring. It was so loud it made her left eye twitch. A single reed-torch basin near the entrance provided the only dim light, and she squinted with her other eye and counted the beds on the right like she had been instructed to do.

Unlike every other leadership position in Itabacan, Boakin Tanoc slept in a regular bed in the same open-bay quarters with his fellow akin. As strange as Tabba thought that was, the fact that the boakin was a six-year-old boy was doubly strange. When she counted the seventh reed bed, she saw the child leader of the Mawoakin curled up in a ball beneath a pristine white sheet that seemed to glow a little in the faint torchlight.

Tabba shrugged. "Excuse me, Boakin Tanoc? It's time to get up," she whispered. The little boy squirmed, rolled over onto his side, and promptly went back to sleep. Tabba sighed, but before she could try again, one of the akin behind her sat up and rubbed his eyes.

"Already?" he yawned. "Fine." He then leaned over to the next akin and woke him, who then leaned over and woke the next one, and on it went like reeds in the wind around the room.

"Should I stay until he's up or what?" she asked the yawning akin.

"No, we'll get him. He doesn't have as many pre-ritual duties as the rest of us and can sleep a little while longer. Thank you."

As more akin were waking up, the snoring slowly dissipated. Her job done, Tabba nodded, turned, and quickly left the sleeping quarters. Being that it was her first time witnessing the ritual, they were going to allow her to observe as long as she didn't get in the way. So, she found herself a nice patch of grass to watch the whole thing unfold. She looked around Bahaca's barren landscape and thought it really was a shame there weren't any prancing critters on the island. She imagined seeing Elder Sengri's pet fox Ranar, bouncing around the patches of dune grass and digging in the sandy soil, his little nose getting filthy and him having to sneeze. The thought made her giggle.

When she was around the same age as Tanoc, Tabba recalled how she and Draha accidentally slept through morning meal and, instead of waking them up to admonish them, Sengri sent Ranar in to wake them with wet kisses. The little fox zipped around the room, bouncing off the bed, then the wall, then the floor, and then back on the bed in the opposite direction, yapping the whole time with his little red tongue dangling out of his mouth. It was the most adorable thing she had ever seen or was likely to ever see. Consequently, she and her brother may have accidentally slept in more than once.

Out of the corner of her eye, she saw the akin filing out of the sleeping quarters dressed in just their bright-white undergarments, glowing even more in the moonlight. Boakin Tanoc had told her earlier in the day that the first step in the ritual was to purify their bodies with oil. He had nodded along with his own words as if reciting the colors of a rainbow or counting his fingers and toes. She thought it would be too icky, but the little boy leader assured her that all of the excess oil got wiped off with a cloth and their garments were then made into fire sticks. She thought it was funny how he called torches fire sticks. The little boy seemed so happy to be a part of the ritual and only mentioned in passing that he was actually in charge. He said, *"We all wear fresh tunics, but I get a beautiful robe because I am Boakin!"*

There were six male and six female akin all glistening under the waning moon, their skin thoroughly oiled before being dressed in tunics even brighter than their undergarments. Tabba thought they all looked like finely dressed manati. And then the attendants came out carrying trays of paints and began meticulously covering every bit of their visible skin in colorful characters and geometric shapes. The boakin received special attention and was painted gold from head to toe, sparkling in the moonlight like a precious gem. As the torch bearers appeared, they signaled to the others that it was time to move the preparations into the temple itself.

Tabba had already been given a tour of the temple and thought it was the second most interesting building in all of Itabacan; the first being the Pyramid of Mayu. The Temple of the Dawn had two entrances, one north and one south, and there was a straight half-wall facing west. The eastern wall was curved and divided into four half-wall sections alternating between three open doorways, which sort of made it look like a mouthful of missing teeth. In the center of the temple was a pillar with three flat sides about half a reed wide and one rounded side. Various symbols were carved on the rounded side, but only a single image of a long-toothed creature adorned the backside. Tabba had never seen the creature before, and tried to get a better look at it, but she was asked to leave. The floor was divided by the pillar, with the eastern half dropping several steps down to the offering floor.

She watched the attendants remove the previous night's ashes from two copper-lined basins in the southwest and northwest corners, and then the torch bearers placed the new reed torches in the basins. Firelight instantly rippled across the ceiling, walls, and floor of the temple, reflecting off the white paint that coated every surface like seafoam. Magnificent, colorful murals on the walls came to life in the flickering light and depicted the Yayapti in vivid detail. The ceiling was adorned with bright-white stars in the same patterns she had seen in Mayu Hall back on Itabaca. They were mul, named after Boaraco Amul who first started cataloging them, and there was one for all thirteen kuranan of the year. But the mul on the ceiling of the Temple of the Dawn were arranged differently from what Tabba had seen before.

After the torch bearers left, the attendants poured the ashes in the center of the offering floor and spread them evenly into a large circle with their hands, which Tabba thought kind of made the offering floor resemble a big eye. Then the attendants left, making sure to leave no trace of their presence. And then in walked Boakin Tanoc. The little six-year-old looked twice as tall in his robe, wedge-heeled sandals, and an elaborate and massive headdress. It was hard to see in the dim firelight, but the headdress appeared to be made from long gray and brown feathers arranged in a tall column, which was wrapped and held in place with strips of yellow cloth. He walked with a professional confidence Tabba rarely saw in most adults, but she couldn't help but smile at the adorable little boy. Tanoc carried two paddles in his hands crossed at his chest, which looked to Tabba like miniature oars. He abruptly stopped in front of the backside of the pillar and gazed at the image of the long-toothed creature. The twelve akin lined up behind him in two rows of six facing west, each carrying their own miniature paddle and gourd drum.

Tabba watched as everyone involved stood in silence for a long time. She scanned the horizon for any hint of sunrise. It was dark, just like the rest of the night's sky. For a moment, a flutter of panic entered her mind – *did I read the stars wrong?* Tabba quickly triple-checked her tablet to make sure. Yeah, there were the eight ancestors that made up the Chuka-mul. The flutter dissipated a bit, but she still took a deep breath to ease her anxiety. At that moment, she caught a glimmer of light on the eastern horizon, and then the ritual began.

THUMP! The akin slapped their drums in unison with their paddles.

"We sleep in darkness, Maboti we fear!" Boakin Tanoc shouted in his little boy voice.

THUMP!

"Mawoi, asleep in the Durali, your light is never diminished!"

THUMP!

"Oh, Great One, Supreme Sovereign Ruler!"

THUMP!

"Although you sleep, you see all, oh Ancient One!"

THUMP!

"Who upholds the world, Lord of All, Creator, arise!"

THUMP!

Tabba was starting to wonder what the boakin was talking about. *Durali? Lord of All? Creator?* First, she had never heard the word *durali* before, but second, and more importantly, most of these titles were the same as those the Itabayiti bestowed upon Yucahu. Here the akin seemed to be worshiping Mawoi as if the sun was the Great Spirit. She anxiously searched the lumpy grasses she was sitting on with her hands for a stick or rock, or anything hard enough to... "Ah!" she whispered, finding a piece of a shell. She then flipped her clay tablet over and began taking notes by frantically scratching Itabayitian symbols on its backside.

"Owner of the Day, arise and defeat Maboti!"

THUMP! The first traces of light appeared on the eastern horizon, exciting Boakin Tanoc who slapped the sides of the pillar twice with his paddles, and the drums answered him in double.

WHACK-WHACK! THUMP-THUMP!

"We exalt you, Mawoi, One Who Bears the World!" His little voice shook with excitement.

WHACK-WHACK! THUMP-THUMP! Sunlight began pouring through the temple, and Tabba had to hold up her hand to shield her hazel eyes.

"Maboti is defeated! Mawoi rises and we are awoken!"

WHACK-WHACK-WHACK! THUMP-THUMP-THUMP!

And then Boakin Tanoc rushed down the steps directly into the center of the circle of ash, his hurried steps clopping as he went. Tabba had to stand and move closer to see what was going to happen next. The twelve akin turned around, got on their knees facing the rising sun, six on each side of the pillar, and began bowing repetitively in unison, sweat dripping from their bodies. Attendants appeared carrying basket after basket of fruits and vegetables, six in total, and lined up against the western half-wall. At this point, the boakin was thrashing about and tossing ash into the air. Sunlight pierced through the missing teeth in the eastern wall and made the ash glow like a storm cloud over the boy. Ash covered his entire body as he wailed like a baby bird, "*Eee! Eee! Eee!*" His elaborate headdress swung around like a broom, stirring the cloud into a mesmerizing swirl.

When the sun had risen above the horizon and the entire temple was filled with a glowing ashen cloud, two attendants helped the sweaty, ash-covered boy to his feet while the others dumped the baskets of food offerings all over the offering floor – gourds, yuca, pineapples, and beans mixed with the sweaty, oily, ashen soup. And then it was over. The akin filed out of the Temple of the Dawn and into the morning light like ants from their burrow.

Tabba was amazed beyond measure. She didn't know what she had expected. Maybe a song and dance, or the recitation of a poem to Mawoi, but not the spectacle she just witnessed. When she was much younger, she once had the opportunity to witness a Yucaakin ceremony, but that was nothing compared to this. She had a lot of questions for both Boakin Tanoc and Boaraco Unsari, but she decided she would wait until after the attendants had given the boakin his morning cleansing. That would give her some time to sleep before midmeal. Unfortunately, she wouldn't get to ask Boaraco Unsari anything until she returned to Itabaca in a few days. Tabba sighed and rubbed her tired eyes. She had been up all night and only wanted to go to bed.

She gathered her things and walked across the lumpy terrain to the sleeping quarters and her tiny room in the southwest corner. When on assignment to the akin, araco were expected to refrain from disturbing their daily routine as much as possible, and to sleep outside under the shade of a tree or any other spot that was far removed from the akin. But there was only one tree on Bahaca, and it grew right in the middle of the largest patch of grass on the island directly between the temple and the sleeping quarters. It would have been impossible to sleep, never mind not disturb their daily routine. So, she was genuinely relieved when Boakin Tanoc said they had prepared a room just for her. She was equally surprised by how quiet and peaceful the room was. There were no windows and only a single small door in the north wall, which seemed to easily swivel on squeaky hinges, but it did close tightly behind her. To her right was a low-lying bed made from driftwood and covered in dried dune grass. On the left, a driftwood table displayed a gourd of freshwater and a lit candle, bathing the room in a soft, warm, orange glow.

Tabba yawned, "This will do just fine." She set her things down on the table, picked up the gourd, and took a large swig. The cool water was refreshing and reminded her how hungry she was, but there would be time for food after she slept. She quickly drank her fill, set the gourd down, blew out the candle, laid on the bed, and closed her eyes. "Huh," she yawned. "It's actually pretty comfortable."

A moment later, she heard a squeaking sound and snapped awake. She was disoriented. The room was still as dark as a hole in the ground, but she oddly felt like she had been asleep for days. There was a strip of light at the bottom of the door, and she caught a whiff of... Tabba sniffed the air. "Baked beans?"

She swung her legs over the edge of the bed, shuffled across the tiny room, and then opened the door in one swift motion – *squeak!* Daylight momentarily blinded her, and she waited for her eye to slowly adjust. She saw the open window across from her room and the rows of empty beds to her right. She smelled the beans again, but the smell wasn't coming from out there. Tabba spun around on her heels and saw, in the center of her driftwood table, a baked yam overflowing with beans and topped with some sort of honey and pea puree. Tabba had been initially concerned when she learned the Mawoakin were vegetarians, but her midmeal was possibly the most delicious thing she had ever tasted in her life.

After she ate, Tabba found most of the akin were in the gardens, a few in prayer, and Boakin Tanoc was sitting on a stone bench next to that lonely tree. It was impossible to feel bad for the tree, because it had an amazing, unobstructed view overlooking the Great Sea. The wind constantly blew over the landscape of Bahaca and gently tousled the boy's hair. She ran her fingers over her long braid, making sure it was intact. Satisfied, she approached the bench. When she got closer, she noticed Tanoc was swinging his short legs like the child he was. In a way, he reminded Tabba of her brother when they were little.

"Taycoay, Boakin Tanoc," she said, yawning.

He turned. "Mawoi-coay, Araco Tabba," he said, and then patted the bench next to him. "Sit with me."

Mawoi-coay? Tabba sat and crossed her legs, noticing her feet didn't touch the ground either. She gave the moment a chance to be peaceful and the view to be undisturbed. She knew her questions might be too difficult for the boakin to answer, and there was the possibility he would not be pleased by her implications, so she was relieved when he spoke first.

"Did you enjoy the Rise of Mawoi this morning?" he asked, looking up with his boyish cheeks and big brown eyes.

"I did," she answered. "It was a beautiful ritual. I especially liked the sunlight through the ash cloud that looked like a great thunderstorm!"

"Yeah, Mawoi is the Source of All Things, his lightning, his wrath, and his wrath is just."

He was reciting again and Tabba noticed this time he was confusing Mawoi and Yuraca – or maybe he wasn't confused at all. She thought it best to start with a simpler question. "Yeah, the effect was pretty neat. Was that the only reason for the ash?"

Boakin Tanoc got excited about her question, swung his legs up onto the bench, and adjusted himself so that he was sitting on his heels facing her. "No!" he exclaimed and then leaned forward, gesturing with his arms and hands. "It's the burned body of Maboti and I am the incarnation of Mawoi rising from the ashes!"

"Oh, I see!" she said, smiling, trying to hide her shocked confusion.

"Yeah, I didn't understand what I saw in my vision until they told me what it meant, but now I know. I can feel it, sitting here, my warmth is his warmth because we are one and the same," he said. And then he tossed his legs back over the edge of the bench and faced out to sea.

Tabba was having a tough time wrapping her head around what the boakin was telling her. It was completely unheard of in Itabayiti society. Possession was a real thing, sure, the ararun were known to afflict people from time to time, but the Sun Spirit taking Itabayiti form every morning was something entirely different. She took a breath and decided she needed to make sure of what she was hearing. She needed to consult her tablet, but then she realized she had left it back on the table in her room. The moment this thought passed through her mind, Tabba remembered her midmeal had been placed on the table while she slept, and she didn't remember her tablet being there while she ate.

"Uh-huh," she finally said. Not knowing how to proceed, she pointed at the sun shining brightly over their heads and asked, "So, if you are Mawoi then who is that?"

"Also, me." He got a concerned look on his face and added, "Why don't you know these things?"

Tabba could tell he was getting upset, or maybe suspicious, so she tried a less direct approach. "Oh, well, of course! I was just seeing if you knew, you know? I guess Yucahu just blessed me with silliness."

"Yucahu?" he asked. His tone was nowhere near his initial boyish joy, or even that of a concerned child, but of cold and suspicious.

She swallowed hard. "Yes, Yucahu, the – uh – Great Spirit?"

Suddenly, Boakin Tanoc jumped to his feet and stood on the bench. "Yucahu is evil," he yelled at her. "Itabayiti are not Itabayiti anymore, but the Great Cleansing will come." Tears welled up in the boy's eyes. "Oh yes, the Itabayiti will witness a new dawn!" he shouted, his little boy face turning bright red. Tears streamed down his chubby cheeks.

Tabba stood and backed away from the raving child, not knowing what to do, but then she saw one of the akin suddenly rush over, pick Tanoc up like the six-year-old boy he was and carry the boakin back to the sleeping quarters.

She fell to her knees in the patchy grass, sobbing, completely disabled by her anxiety and fear, and then anger, and then a deep sympathy for this little boy washed over her. What were the Mawoakin telling this poor little boy? She knew she wasn't wrong in thinking this was all confusing and very troubling, but Boakin Tanoc had been so passionate and seemed to believe implicitly everything he was just screaming at her. She needed to go immediately to Itabaca and talk with Boaraco Unsari. There was no time to waste. Tabba started to get to her feet, but then she looked up and saw a half-dozen akin dressed in bright-yellow robes surrounding her.

Tambu could tell he was getting upset, or maybe suspicious, so she
struck a less direct approach. "Oh, well, of course I was just seeing if you
knew," she said slyly.

CHAPTER SEVEN
A Tangled Wad of Threads

Chief of Wares Abensu did not believe for an instant his son filled the palm oil jar with vinegar, because his son couldn't possibly know that vinegar would attract the wasps. He wasn't sure Anki even knew what vinegar was to begin with. Of course, Anki and his friends had pulled some pranks in the past, but they had always been silly and harmless. This prank was dangerous and seemed to specifically target Jokimbi. In Abensu's mind, there was a vast difference between pranks for pranks' sake and targeted attacks.

Unfortunately, when answering for themselves in the reception hall of the palace, the boys admitted they knew the wasp's nest was under the reed bath and that was all the Yaya needed to hear. It didn't matter that Anki swore on his mother's spirit he had nothing to do with the prank. Jokimbi feverishly pointed to the dozens of welts on his face, his big mud-brown eyes bugging out like a koki frog, and Anki and Biacoya started snickering right there in front of Yaya Amnu. Fortunately, everyone but Jokimbi and Unana Wani saw the humor in the prank as well, and the Yaya agreed that children should be allowed to be children and only suspended the boys from lessons for three days.

Afterward, they took the ferry back to Conaca and Tambu took Biacoya back to Pacca. Abensu put his son to work in the clay pits that very morning. Anki had always said being a waki digger looked like fun, but Abensu knew it could be back-breaking work. He felt it would be good for Anki, but he didn't want his son to overdo it and have an episode, so he placed Olari in charge and instructed him to keep an eye on his boy. By midmeal, Olari reported that Anki had been an excellent student and had earned a promotion to artisan.

"The youngest waki artisan in the history of Itabacan!" Elder Artisan Ikmo said, slapping the boy on his back.

Ikmo was the son of the former Chief of Wares Sabayi, who was appointed by Yaya Shakali during the beginning of his over-thirty-year rule and had been the chief for decades. By now, Ikmo was a severely wrinkled old man, thin and frail, and wore the loose clay-colored tunic of the waki that he somehow kept impeccably clean. Abensu wasn't sure how the old man did it with as much as they worked around wet clay and the glazes, not to mention endlessly tending to the roaring fires in the ovens. But Ikmo smartly wore an undyed, plain white apron, which Abensu noticed was perpetually filthy.

They walked down the shelly path from the chief's residence on top of the hill toward the clay ovens, the late midday sun bright and hot overhead. Abensu and Olari were in the front, while Anki and Ikmo followed along behind them.

"I'm not really a waki," Anki said, rolling his eyes, repeatedly kicking a single, oddly shaped shell down the path. "I'm only here because the Yaya didn't believe me and Biacoya hadn't done anything wrong and suspended us."

"You've grown up in the pits, son," Abensu said over his shoulder, making a point to ignore his son's complaints.

"By my count, you've been a waki for ten years now," Ikmo added.

There was a light breeze from the northeast, pushing them down the hill and cooling the sweat on the backs of their necks. It had turned out to be a near-perfect, late rainy, early dry season kind of day, and Abensu was encouraged to take full advantage of it. He had his son working with him, as well as two of the best artisans Itabacan had seen in the decade he had been the Chief of Wares. After they finished the ceremonial plates, they would enjoy a well-deserved break.

"You know," the elder artisan started to say, "you've been helping your baba as his dukyat, ever since your itaba..."

"Ahem," Abensu interrupted him and gave Ikmo a stern look.

"Ah – yes, what I mean to say is ever since you were a little boy." Ikmo mouthed an apology.

Abensu forbade his waki from speaking about Tiam in front of his sons, which then became an unspoken rule to not speak about her at all. He had done well not thinking about her for years, even though their sons reminded him of her every single day. He found detangling the saddest memory threads from the happier ones to be too difficult, and he eventually shoved the whole frustrating wad far back into the darkest corner of his mind. When he was alone, away from the judgmental eyes of his peers or the disappointed faces of his boys, Abensu allowed himself to get tangled up in his grief. Sometimes, it was the only way to fall asleep. The rest of the time, it was just easier to forget and focus on his duties as the Chief of Wares.

"What's a dukyat?" Anki suddenly asked, still kicking the same shell down the path.

"Go ahead, Ikmo," Abensu said with a little chuckle. "You brought it up."

"Gladly!" he exclaimed.

They rounded the bend of the shelly path, the sparse but noisy jungle on their right, the terrain dropping to the clay pits on their left, and arrived at the row of three enormous cibmani ovens used by the waki to fire the clay. Two more artisans were there and waiting for them.

Stopping at the bend, Ikmo explained to Anki, "Long, long ago, back when Itabacan was no older than you are now, the Yaya had a vizier – his second in command and immediate successor. They called this position the dukyat after the eldest daughter of Bitabay and the sister of the Biyaya."

"The title was abolished by...Yaya Osanek, I believe," Abensu added. "But it was replaced by the Order of the Yaali!"

"Hey!" Anki shouted. "I'm a yaali!"

"Yes," Ikmo said, a finger to his chin. "Yaya Osanek – I think you're right."

"My son, a yaali. I'm very proud of you." Abensu squeezed his son's shoulder and then turned to the artisans waiting for them at the ovens. "Now, it looks like this batch is about ready to come out of the ovens. Correct?" he asked the artisans, and they nodded enthusiastically. "Good. The last batch is still drying under Mawoi's great light, which means we" – he looked at Anki and Olari – "need to get started on a new jug of glaze."

"Yes, Chief," the artisans nodded in near unison, before turning back to the ovens.

"Chief Abensu, do you mind if I join the glazing party?" Ikmo asked.

"I don't see why not," the chief answered. "In fact, since your baba discovered the glaze recipe we've been using, it will be good for Anki to take his lesson from you."

"Wonderful!" The elder artisan beamed with pride. "Come, young Anki. We'll begin by gathering ash from below the ovens."

Ikmo guided the boy over to the last oven on the right, so as to not disturb the other artisans who were crowded around the first oven on the far left. Behind them were the cibmani cooling racks, partially filled with the previous batches of ceremonial plates, and on the top was a shelf where they stored unused candle-timers.

Abensu turned to Olari, his head artisan and personal assistant. He wasn't especially tall, but he did have broad, meaty shoulders tightly hugging a thick neck, which was attached to a rather large head. He had dark ebony skin from working in the sun, and the small sponge of hair on his head was sun-bleached light, almost sand colored. He had been one of Abensu's waki diggers for a few years and got along very well with the other workers, as well as the chief's family. Of course, Olari getting along with everyone was no surprise because his grandfather was Bolari, one of the Yaya's elder attendants, and his sister was the always delightful Lewa. It seemed being personable ran in their family. Knowing the pressure his waki were under to fulfill the Yaya's order in time for the festival, Abensu appointed Olari head artisan. It had been the right choice, and he was strongly considering making the promotion permanent.

"Chief Abensu?" Olari asked, giving him a confused look.

"Yes?"

"May I ask why you are staring at me like that?"

Abensu politely smiled. "It's nothing, Olari. Come, let's inspect this last batch."

He led the way off the shelly path to a packed-flat dirt section of a wide field where row after row of hand-molded clay plates had been lain out in the sun to dry. Beyond the plates to the west, dune grasses continued farther west, waving in the wind as they dipped slightly toward a rocky shoreline and disappeared into the shallows. The field stretched from the northern tip of the island all the way south to Conaca Harbor in the middle. Abensu felt the light breeze that had been following them on the path suddenly shift to a much stronger breeze from the north. Conveniently, it made some of the unbalanced plates wobble and clatter against the packed earth, sounding like woodchips clacking together and announcing their imperfections to the Chief of Wares.

Abensu watched Olari bend over to pick up one of the wobbling plates. "It's nice of Kayki to help us identify them," he said. "Or should we thank the Wind Spirit?"

"Hmm – I'm more inclined to blame my head artisan for allowing so many imperfections to begin with." Abensu smiled at Olari, whose ebony cheeks turned deep red.

Olari quickly stood up. "I apologize, Chief!" he said, clearly about to launch into a tirade of excuses, but Abensu held up his hand for him to stop.

"It's alright," the chief said, chuckling. "I'm only messing with you. We always expect to lose roughly ten percent to discoloration, cracking, and other common faults. Creating a balanced plate may be easier than a bowl or a jug, of course, but I would never demand perfection."

"Thank you, Chief," he said, and then after a pause, "I think."

"Besides," Abensu took the plate out of Olari's hands and tossed it over his shoulder, shattering the dried clay into a hundred tiny pieces on the packed dirt behind him. "These can be recycled. We'll just add a little freshwater – not saltwater – and then mix it back into the raw materials from the pit."

"Of course, Chief," Olari replied, nodding his big head.

They continued down the rows, picking up the clattering plates and tossing them into a pile – *crack!* Others had started to split and were discarded as well – *crack!* But by the time they returned to the ovens, Abensu was pleased to find they had only lost about five percent. He saw Anki sitting on the ground, a large jug between his legs, stirring the glaze inside with a long wooden stick. Ikmo was squatted next to him, expertly adding one handful of ash at a time from a small pile he held in his apron and Abensu saw there was still not a single smudge on the old man's tunic. He could only smile and shake his head, looking down at his own dusty clothes, even though he had hardly lifted a finger all day.

"Hey," Olari said, stepping up beside him. He pointed to Anki and asked, "What did you say earlier about him being a yaali? What is that?"

"When a Yaya has ruled for seven years," Abensu explained, "a list of boys, ages five to ten, is compiled as candidates to become his successor in the event of his untimely death. They're called yaali."

"Oh, I'd never heard of such a thing."

"That's because the yaali are always picked from the children of council members."

Olari nodded his head but appeared confused. "Why council members?"

"Because we're better than non-council members," Abensu joked, and then walked over to the elder artisan, leaving Olari's jaw open like a fish. "Ikmo, are we getting close?"

"Just about there," Ikmo answered without looking up, a fistful of ash suspended over the glaze jug. He shook his fist back and forth, allowing a drizzle of ash to fall into the jug and then he stopped. "There. I think that will do it. Now, stir until you don't see a single speck of dry ash," he instructed Anki, to which the boy sighed but nodded that he understood.

Abensu helped his waki artisans carefully arrange the hot ceremonial plates they had removed from the ovens around on the cooling racks. The plates were blackened by the soot and required additional polishing, but he could already tell the new glaze mixture had turned out beautifully. He looked up at Mawoi's position in the sky and then counted the candle-timers. The Day of Biyaya festival was in two days and they were surprisingly ahead of schedule. They might even be able to stop early for the day. Abensu glanced over at Anki, stirring the ash glaze and smiled at his son's bored expression.

"Did you already add the bone powder?" he asked Ikmo.

"About halfway through adding the ash, yes," he replied.

"Good – good. From what I could just see, it seems to be turning out great!" Abensu knelt down to get his son's attention. "You can stop stirring now," he told him.

"Finally!" Anki said, sullenly. He pushed the jug as far away as his arms could stretch.

"Here, I'll take that," Olari said, and moved the jug over to the rows of drying plates.

"Thank you, Olari," Abensu nodded, seeing a puzzled expression on his son's face. "What is it, Anki?"

"Elder Ikmo said the Mawoakin use ash in their rituals in the temple on Bahaca."

"He did?" Abensu gave the old artisan a dirty look; Ikmo mouthed another apology.

"Yeah," Anki continued. "He said the boakin bathes in it, which I thought was a little strange, but then I realized, in a way, we're basically bathing the clay in ash as well. Which made me wonder if there was something special about ashes that I'll learn when I'm older?"

The sincerity in his voice made Abensu chuckle. "Oh!" And then he mistakenly glared at Ikmo, who must have interpreted his glare as the signal to respond to Anki.

"Not just when you're older, but when you've witnessed your first bonefire," Ikmo began. "You see, ash is all that remains after the Great Spirit has been released."

"And from the wood in the fire?" Anki asked.

Ikmo nodded. "Yes, and our bodies. Actually, we put bonefire ash in the omaki the lowaki use to fertilize the soil on Hamaca and Coyaca. Your baba knows abo..."

"That's enough," Abensu interrupted. His traumatic childhood as a lowaki field worker remained a faded memory, of which he had no interest in sharing. He saw his son rubbing the ash glaze from his clearly sore arms. "I bet you wish you were back in the reed yard with your friends, huh?"

"No," Anki answered quickly. "Just tired, baba. Digging in the clay is hard work, you know. It may look like a lot of fun, but now I know why Yucahu put a little extra spirit in Olari's big shoulders." Abensu and Ikmo laughed, but Olari hadn't heard what Anki said.

"What about my shoulders?" he asked.

Anki shied away from Olari's question, but Abensu answered for him. "It seems the Great Spirit blessed you with big shoulders to make you a better waki."

Olari laughed, "Does that mean I'm being demoted back to the pits?"

"I must consider it," Abensu joked.

"That's not what I meant!" Anki protested, while the other two laughed. "Honest!"

"We know, son."

"We're ahead of schedule, wouldn't you say?" Olari asked, checking the glaze consistency before starting to apply it.

Abensu nodded again. "I was just thinking that, yes."

"And the sky appears clear – well, as far as we can see anyway." Seemingly satisfied with the glaze, Olari put down the boar-hair brush, and then hopped on the balls of his feet, trying to see over the great wall. Abensu saw that he was doing it intentionally to make Anki smile, and it was working. "What do you think, Anki? Maybe if you get on my big shoulders?"

"Are you making fun of me?" his boy asked.

"No! Of course not!"

Anki appeared perplexed for a moment, as if suspicious Olari was definitely making fun of him, but then he looked up at his father. "Can I?" he asked. Abensu nodded a third time and his boy leapt up from the ground and rushed over to Olari.

"Here – climb on up."

Abensu watched Olari kneel down so that Anki could step on his leg before swinging himself around and onto Olari's broad shoulders. He looked like a baby monkey climbing onto its mother's back. The two of them laughed and ran around, trying to find the best spot from which to jump and see farther over the wall. Abensu enjoyed watching them. He enjoyed having his son there learning the trade and being useful, but he mostly just missed his sons. He missed them being around and at the residence during the day. As much as it aggravated him, Abensu even missed hearing them fighting. As soon as they were both old enough to train in the reed yard, they were gone and Abensu often ate midmeal in the quiet residence by himself.

"Chief Abensu?" Ikmo called to him from over by the ovens.

"Yes?" He turned to see the elder artisan wiping the soot away from a plate with his apron, a sour expression on his aged face.

"Chief Abensu, the glaze is remarkable," he said, turning the plate around in his hands, his sour expression unchanged. "It has an excellent sheen. It came out even and smooth. But..."

"Yes? But what?" Abensu asked, a bit more impatience in his voice than he intended. He knew the old man often rambled to avoid confrontation.

"I hate to be the bearer of bad news, but there's something off about the Yaya's image on the plate."

"What do you mean?" Abensu quickly grabbed a plate that was cool enough to touch, and then he used his tunic to rub off the soot.

"If I was to guess, I'd say adding the bone powder to the glaze did it."

With the majority of the soot removed, Abensu was crushed to see what the elder artisan was talking about. Yaya Amnu's face in the center of the plate appeared tan, almost white, and there was a weird grainy look to it. He rubbed his thumb over the area, expecting it to feel like tree bark, but it felt as smooth as polished stone. It meant the clay hadn't finished drying before they applied the glaze and caused steam to develop. But Ikmo was right, it did have a beautiful continuous sheen. No matter which way he turned the plate, the new glaze mixture almost sparkled in the sunlight, making the rays of burnt-orange and yellow emanating outward from the center appear more vibrant. Unfortunately, the sparkling rays only accented the glaring mistake in the middle.

"Baga!" he exclaimed.

"We could – if I may suggest a remedy," the elder artisan said, looking at him. Abensu gestured for Ikmo to continue. "Well, we could simply paint this batch to match the others."

Abensu considered the option, along with the dozen others that were suddenly tumbling through his mind. They had already completed the bulk of the Yaya's order for the festival and these final batches were supposed to be Abensu's special contribution. They were a gift to the Yaya, the council, and their families. The rest of the plates were for everyone else and would be recycled like they usually were, but these batches were special and meant to be kept and displayed. He had no one to blame but himself for rushing the job. Abensu grabbed another plate, and then another, ignoring his burning fingers. He rubbed away the soot, revealing the faulty image, and then set each one aside, becoming more frustrated as the stack grew taller.

"I'm afraid they're all corrupted," Ikmo said.

"If we have to hand paint them, we'll ruin the finish." Abensu worked through their options aloud, continuing to disappoint himself – burning fingers, wiped soot, corrupted image, stacked, repeat. "It wouldn't take as long as if we redid the entire batch, but..."

"But it's a compromise." The elder artisan interrupted him. "Sometimes, the Great Spirit places an obstacle in our path. Whether we beat our heads against it or find a way around, he leaves that for us to decide."

Abensu smirked, "That sounds like something Tiam would have said." He looked over his shoulder at Olari and Anki. They had made their way farther down the sloping field toward the shore, likely hoping to jump off one of the large boulders. "Olari! Anki! Come back!" he shouted. Abensu hadn't made up his mind, but whatever they were going to do to remedy the situation, they needed to get started sooner rather than later.

"She was always kind to me," Ikmo added, stepping closer and staring up at Abensu with his old, wrinkled eyes.

The Chief of Wares stopped what he was doing, his hand hovering over the tall, teetering stack of corrupted plates, unsure how to respond. "I'm not sure this is..." He tried to express his discomfort, but the old man interrupted him again.

"A bouquet of wildflowers," Ikmo blurted out. "When my wife died and went on to be with our ancestors, Tiam gave me a bouquet of deep-red, orange, and yellow wildflowers." Ikmo looked down at the ceremonial plate in his hands, thumbing the unglazed base. "My apologies, Chief Abensu. I don't mean to cause you any pain."

"It's quite alright, Ikmo," he replied, and then realized Anki and Olari hadn't returned and quickly looked for them again. As he suspected, they had made it to the shore and were leaping from boulder to boulder and flapping their arms like seagulls. "AN-KI!" he hollered. The boy instantly turned to look at him. "HERE!" Abensu waved for them both to return to the ovens. He waited until he saw that they were on their way before turning his attention back to the old man. "Now, Ikmo," he started. "I'm not sure..."

"You may not remember," Ikmo continued, rudely ignoring Abensu's attempts to protest. "But after Midu's bonefire, I didn't return to the clay pits right away. I remained on Yapaca, shut up in our sad little bohi for a long while."

Of course, Abensu remembered. How could he forget? Ikmo's absence was the reason Abensu was bumped up to head artisan, even though he was only sixteen years old at the time. Midu's unfortunate passing was the catalyst that led to him being appointed Chief of Wares.

"Just after midmeal every day," the old man said, "I would gather my scraps to take to the docks and feed to the tiny fish that swam around in the shallows. It was something Midu loved to do because she loved fish – not so much eating them. She didn't like the taste of fish, or clams, or even crabs. I think it was the smell, but I'm getting off topic here. The point is every day I opened my door I found a kikuri lying there at my feet. I might not have noticed, had the dark-red petals not stuck out against the dusty white shells beneath them. Each day it was a different flower, until I had a beautiful bouquet in a bowl on my bedside table. I still fed the fish, which became a sad daily routine, but I grew more and more curious where the flowers were coming from." He paused, as Anki and Olari came running up behind Abensu.

"Baba," Anki said, out of breath. "You — need to see — the size of this giant sea turtle we found!"

"We'll tell him about it later, Anki," Olari told him. "By the look on Chief Abensu's face, I think something more important has happened. What's going on, Chief?"

"We have to redo these last two batches," he said, handing one of the faulty plates to his head artisan. Abensu saw Ikmo quietly wander off, likely to help the other waki artisans at the ovens. Trying to ignore what the old man had said, he let out a long sigh. "As you can see, moisture was trapped beneath the glaze, causing that bubbling and the discoloration of the Yaya's image."

"Yes, I see that," Olari said. "Sure it's not just because of the new mixture?"

"It could be, but then I'd expect the rays to be discolored also."

"Hmm..." Olari turned the plate this way and that, examining it from every angle.

"Is it my fault?" Anki asked. "I was stirring the glaze like you said."

"No, son." Abensu quickly dismissed his son's concern so he could address Olari again. "We can't recycle these, so we'll have to start again from the pits."

"But the festival's in two days," Olari politely objected.

"And in two days we'll have finished remaking these two batches. Go round up the waki — we'll need to start digging immediately. Based on a rough estimation, I'd say we'll need another five or so baskets of raw material, beyond what we already did today." Olari hesitated a moment, clearly wanting to object again, but Abensu didn't have time for any more discussion. "Great Spirit help me! I'm not saying redo everything, just this one batch. We'll let this one finish drying, adjust the glaze mixture, and that's it. Now, move!" he yelled. Olari handed back the plate and started running down the shelly path to the clay pits.

Abensu's nerves were on edge, he could feel it in his ears. First the plates were ruined, then Ikmo got him flustered thinking about Tiam, and then his head artisan wanted to argue with him instead of obeying his chief. Abensu released another heavy sigh, feeling a tightness in his chest, and looked down at his son. Anki had tears in his eyes but was trying to keep himself from crying. His lips were tightly pressed together and shifted off to the side, tucked into his left cheek and quivering along with his little chin. It was the exact same face the boy's mother used to make when she was upset. Seeing him flooded Abensu's mind with more memories and his heart with more ridiculous, fluttering, painful emotions.

"Come here, my son," he said, kneeling down and pulling Anki in for a hug.

"I'm sorry," Anki whimpered, sniffling and pressing his face into Abensu's shoulder. "I – didn't mean – to ruin – the plates..."

"You didn't ruin the plates, Anki. These things happen."

"But – I was – in charge – of the glaze..."

"No...listen, Olari was in charge of making sure the clay had fully dried before we applied the glaze, and I am in charge and responsible for all of you – like you may be one day." Abensu lifted his son's wet chin and smiled at him, doing his best to not cry as well. He chuckled, "You're just like your itaba."

Anki pushed himself away and wiped a slimy string of snot from his upper lip. "Itaba?" he asked, still sniffling.

Abensu nodded. "She used to make that same face when her flowers would wilt, and we would have to throw them into the scrap pile."

"Really?" Anki asked and his father nodded again.

"Really. Now, why don't you go help Olari and the waki," he said.

"Alright."

"And, when your brother returns from his lessons," he added, "we'll have evening meal together, and afterward, maybe go up to the roof and try to find itaba among the ancestors?"

Anki got excited when he heard this. "We haven't done that in forever!"

"I know," his father said. "Get going now and remember to mind your temper."

"Alright, baba," Anki replied, wiping the last tears from his cheeks and trotting down the shelly path.

Seeing his son do as he was told without fighting with him reminded Abensu just how much Anki had grown. There were times when he would look at his youngest boy and still see newborn Anki swaddled in the crook of his mother's arm, quietly gazing up at him as Tiam released her final breath. Anki didn't cry when he was born. His forest green eyes instantly locked onto his father, unfazed by the raging storm outside, and he remained focused on Abensu until his tiny eyelids became too heavy and he fell asleep. Abensu knew he was supposed to turn his son over to the araco, and he told himself he would the following morning, but he didn't. Lesini Nun said that his son's destiny would be filled with conflict and pain because of his father's actions that day, but Abensu didn't care.

The years went by and Anki's temperament started to wax and wane like the phases of the moon. It was subtle at first, a spontaneous slam of his fist or an irritated grunt, but it gradually intensified to screaming fits and him throwing just about anything within reach that his little arms could lift. Anki could be as gentle as the manati drifting along in the shallows, but then, in an instant, be as volatile as a long-tusked boar after being whipped one too many times. To everyone else, his erratic behavior added to the suspicion that Anki might be a yaduka, but there was something else more revealing for Abensu.

In those moments, just before Anki would get upset, Abensu started recognizing little traces of his deceased wife in the boy. Unfortunately, he watched the same realization dawn on Atu. Before he knew it, Atu was picking fights with his brother, teasing the yaduka and begging it to come out. It was clear to Abensu, Atu was only hard on his brother because he missed their mother, but Anki didn't know that. How was Abensu going to explain it to the boy without terrifying him? How could he explain to him that his father also missed their mother terribly and it was nice to see her reappear in Anki now and then? That sometimes he ignored Anki's pain and frustration, turned a deaf ear and a blind eye to his suffering, because there was a chance, for the briefest of moments, Abensu could be complete again.

You don't, he told himself. *Wad up that tangled mess of threads, toss it way back there, forget about it, and focus on your duties as the Chief of Wares.*

CHAPTER EIGHT

The SEGIN of NIAMCA

Demican thanked ferryman Oboco and stepped onto the smooth cibmani dock. He took care not to slip on the wet stone, but then an unexpected wave suddenly lifted the ferry, launching Demican forward. He slid on one foot with his arms outstretched and waving frantically for balance, quickly slamming his other foot down in an attempt to halt his momentum and avoid coasting off the dock and into the neighboring slip. Thankfully, Niamca's docks were wide enough to accommodate several large freshwater jugs side-by-side, as well as anyone who slipped on the wet surface and didn't want to go tumbling into the water.

"Easy there, young man!" Oboco hollered behind him. "A boy your size could really do some damage without even trying!"

"I'm alright!" he announced.

"And the nani lives to wreak havoc another day!" Oboco cheered. He then pushed the ferry away from the dock with his long oar. "The nani lives!"

Demican watched the ferry drift away, bumbling over the gentle waves north toward the island of Hatca. "The nani lives?" he scoffed. "That is one weird old man." Composing himself, Demican carefully walked up the dock toward the harbor yard, his worn-out sandals continuing to slip and slide around. As soon as he stepped off of the dock and onto the crunchy shells in the yard, he suddenly noticed how quiet and unnerving the harbor was.

The shortest of all the islands, Niamca was shaped like the open-mouthed face of a howler monkey with two freshwater springs as its eyes and one near the southern tip as its mouth. A spattering of trees sparsely covered a narrow shelf between the northern and southern halves of the island, but the jungle grew thick and inhospitable around the springs. They were named Anikna, Obnil, and Sakimi, after the three Yayas who ruled immediately after the Biyaya. Demican knew Anikna was the Biyaya's brother, the howler's right eye, and Obnil was his son, the left eye, but he wasn't sure who Sakimi was, except that it represented the mouth of the island. Uphill from Sakimi was the Temple of Niama, the Chief of Springs' residence, his attendant's quarters and their stables. There was a pumping station and a deck beside each spring where the segin water purifiers could observe and treat the freshwater. Cibmani channels took the water up to a central hub directly in the middle of the island, and from there the water flowed back down to the treatment facility next to the harbor.

Demican had always felt calling them water purifiers was a little bit of an exaggeration. Sure, the segin maintained the systems the Itabayiti relied upon to filter and purify their water for consumption, as well as when they dumped their refuse back into Itabacan Sound, but it wasn't like they were conducting purifying rituals like the akin. They weren't even relying on generations of craftsmanship like the waki and their ceramics, or how the coani seemed capable of interpreting the movements of the wind and the temperament of the Great Sea. They were just performing a necessary duty the same as sanitation workers, which Demican suddenly realized weren't called segin even though they really should be.

The story his father told him was that, hundreds of years ago, Yaya Segin, the eleventh Yaya, ordered his council to investigate a wave of illnesses which had swept through Itabacan. It was fairly well known that stagnant water could make a person sick and, even long before Yaya Segin, the Itabayiti boiled their water before using it. But it seemed there was something else going on and boiling water hadn't been enough. Demican's father said the cause of the illnesses had been forgotten over the generations, but the systems they developed to remedy the situation remained in place. In honor of Yaya Segin, the council established the Order of Water Purifiers and named them after the Yaya.

Since then, the segin had been responsible for inspecting the springs usually for animal carcasses and other contaminants that might clog the pumps, operating the pumps, and maintaining the treatment and storage facilities. Demican's brother, Yaeel, worked in the treatment facility where freshwater entered through a series of holes high on the eastern wall and cascaded down onto to a bed of reeds and coconut husk fibers, which were lain over a copper net. His brother told him that the husk fibers and reeds collected the larger bits, like leaves, sticks, feathers, and such, while the copper wire stimulated the water and was what truly purified it. When he asked how the copper worked, Yaeel told him that he didn't know and to stop asking so many questions.

Demican could see the treatment facility on the other side of the shelly yard, beyond the stables and next to the jug storage facility, but he still couldn't see any segin or attendants, or anyone, for that matter. As he approached the stables with his sandaled feet crunching on the shells, he heard the startled boar loudly snorting. He found two of them unattended, their reins still slung over the hitching post. "Where is everyone?" he asked the snorting boar.

From the stables, a cibmani street curved south around a large depression, past the spirit shrine of Yucahu, and merged with the rest of the street on the other side in front of the storage facility. Demican thought about hitching one of the boar up to the cart he saw leaning against the side of the stable, but then he thought about having to wrestle the beasts into position by himself, attach them to the cart, and how he would have to fight their desire to wander in any other direction but his. It was an annoying hassle and the reason why there were usually stablemen around to help. "Where are the stablemen?" he asked the beasts. Of course, the beasts didn't respond and Demican had to admit it was silly of him to think they might.

Frustrated and confused, he decided to walk instead, thinking he needed to stretch out his massive legs anyway. There had been virtually no wind that morning, stranding their training canuti at the docks where Bocoani Numilla decided they needed to do rowing drills while they waited. After the previous day's excitement of nearly getting smashed against the great wall, everyone enthusiastically welcomed the drills there in the safety of Itabaca Harbor – until the drills turned into playful competitions, which then descended into bickering feuds. Demican and Atu thought it was hilarious. But sitting on the ferry all the way to Itabaca, and on the training canuti the whole day, and then once again on the ferry the entire way back home made his legs ache worse than if he had just swum across the sound.

"Stop!" he heard someone suddenly shout.

Demican immediately stopped walking. The voice sounded like it had come from the docks behind him, but no one was there. He could just see the backside of Oboco's ferry up the coastline, but the old ferryman was definitely not screaming from that far away.

"Hey!"

"Ah!" Demican screamed. "Who's yelling at me?" Just as the question came out of his mouth, he heard the distant but distinct sound of sandals slapping on stone. He quickly turned around and there, emerging from the jungle and sprinting like his life depended on it, he saw one of the segin waving to him. The runner wore the dull orange tunic of the segin, and he even had his hair in fluffy braids the size of yuca roots like many of them did.

"Stop him!" the segin shouted.

"Stop who?" Demican shouted back.

"Ferry!"

"Oh..." He looked back at Oboco. Demican couldn't imagine the weird old ferryman would be able to hear him, but he shrugged his shoulders anyway and started jogging back the way he came. "Oboco!" he yelled.

After a dozen paces, Demican's sandals crunched on the shells in the yard once again as he passed the stables and the stinky, snorting boar. After another dozen paces, he arrived at the edge of the docks to the sound of waves slapping against the stone, the creaking of several transport canuti tied up and bobbing in their slips, and saltwater splashing and misting through the air. He hesitated before continuing out onto the slick stone dock itself, preferring not to tempt fate a second time.

He cupped his hands around his mouth and yelled from where he was, "OH-BO-CO!" He waited for a response, but there was nothing but the sound of sloshing water around him. "*OHHH-BOOO-COOO!*" he screamed as loudly as he could, feeling the strain in his throat and a lightness in his head. "Whoa!" He felt like he might have to lie down. Demican gave himself a moment to recover, before cupping his hands around his mouth once more, but then he noticed Oboco's ferry appeared to be turning around. "Yay!" he cheered.

Just then, he heard the segin's sandals on the shelly yard behind him. "Is he – turning – around?" the segin asked, taking heaving breaths.

"Yeah, why? What's going on?" Demican watched the man stop to catch his breath. The man seemed short for his age, though he was about

Demican's height, but with scrawny arms like Atu. He was definitely one of the water purifiers, but a more recent addition. Demican was thinking the man's name was Lombi, or maybe Lolabi? He wasn't entirely sure. His father made it a point to tell him the names of all the new recruits, but there were dozens of them, and he already had four older brothers, a lot of friends, and so many other things to remember. He just didn't care to also remember the names of every person that worked for his father. "So?" he asked. "What's going on, Lobi?"

The man glared back at him. "*Lolombi*," he said, coldly.

"Right," Demican smiled. "Llollombi," he repeated, rolling the L's.

"Urlam drowned," Lolombi said, dryly. "We need the ferry – to take his body back to Yapaca."

"Drowned?" Demican was shocked. A segin drowning would be like the ferryman being impaled by his own oar – possible, but highly unlikely.

"They should be bringing him down from the spring – any moment now." Lolombi took a deep breath and then waved to Oboco. Demican watched the ferryman expertly bring his canuti into the slip directly in front of them. "Tayokun," Lolombi said to Oboco, still waving. "You should probably go see if they need any help with the body."

Demican smirked, thinking why old Oboco would help carry a dead body, but then he realized Lolombi was talking to him. "Oh – me? You're talking to me?" his voice squeaked.

"Yes, you! Look at you! They could definitely use your help."

"Right." Demican hesitated. The thought of touching a dead body made him queasy.

"Now!" Lolombi shouted at him.

"Right – yes," he stammered. "Going." He turned and started back across the shelly yard for the fourth time that day – *crunch, crunch, crunch.*

Demican had been to a few bonefires in his young life. Ohbaba-Metihi and ohtaba-Naada, his mother's parents, had both passed on to be with the ancestors, and within a mawa of each other too. He remembered sitting beside ohbaba-Metihi watching the flames from ohtaba-Naada's bonefire stretch up like vines of light into the void, and he remembered what his ohbaba told him about those flames. He said, "*We ascend Yucahu's braid, as we are nothing more than strands of hair to him.*"

Demican always thought it was a weird thing to tell a four-year-old. He remembered distinctly not seeing the connection between his own hair and the Great Spirit, especially when hair burned, and burning hair smelled horrible. But then he thought it might have had something to do with ohtaba-Naada having been a lesini. He remembered seeing her collect strands of hair and wondered if his grandfather had been trying to tell him something. *Or maybe not*, Demican shrugged his shoulders. He truly had no idea what to make of it all, except that he was glad to be twelve now and to have a more mature appreciation for life and death.

The previous day's adventure out on the Bocoa reminded him the Itabayiti weren't all going to grow old and pass on in their sleep. Orlil, the Ageless Daughter of the Great Spirit, wove their belts of destiny into unique patterns and it was up to her when and where the pattern would end. Demican often wondered when he would ascend his own hairy vine of light. Would it be on the spine of a canuti, having been smashed against the great wall? Or might it be at the bottom of a freshwater spring? The question made him swallow hard. If he did as his father wanted and joined the segin when he turned fifteen, then he might share the same fate as Urlam. The giant boy quickly forced the thought from his mind and focused on where he was going.

Demican arrived at the quiet intersection where the sparse forest met the dense jungle surrounding Sakimi. The street he was on continued south around the spring, climbing slightly northeast to the top where the temple and their residence sat in a grassy field. If he cut back hard left and took the street north, he would eventually arrive at the central hub. The third option was to follow the dirt path branching slightly off to his left, which he knew ended at a pumping station. With a heavy sigh, Demican suddenly realized he forgot to ask Lombi where Urlam had drowned. Not knowing which way to go, he closed his eyes and listened.

He heard the rustling leaves in the trees and the branches clattering together. The wind had finally picked up at the tail end of their canuti lesson, but it was too late for Bocoani Numilla to take them out of the harbor, which he responded to in several angry grumbles Demican and the other shoats found funny. Fortunately, the Wind Spirit hadn't been bothered by the bocoani's insults and remained blowing gently ever since. Now, he couldn't hear anything farther south except for the constant wind.

Lombi must have come from one of the northern springs, he decided, but he had to admit it was an odd route to take. The street in front of the processing facility ran north and south. If Lolobi had come from one of the northern springs, Demican thought he would have run to the harbor from that direction instead.

Picking up his pace, he started jogging again, his legs starting to feel pretty good. When he was younger, his brothers continually pushed him to eat everything on his plate as fast as he could, before they dragged him to the processing facility to help them fill and move the heavy freshwater jugs. Demican had been moving those unbelievably heavy things around for years, all of his brothers had, which was probably why they were all so much bigger than most of his friends.

Demican suddenly stopped, thinking he heard voices. He saw the central hub ahead on his right. It was a cibmani stone structure, about the size of two bohi stacked one on top of the other, and the street ended in front of it at a rock wall. Cibmani channels branched outward from the hub, one up and over the rock wall, a second along the base of the wall and heading toward the northeast, and one going back the way he had come. And then he heard the voices again. They were coming from Anikna, the right eye of the howler, the spring ahead and to the right. Demican immediately started running, his sandals slapping against the stone street.

Why Lombi came this way from the spring, Demican could not understand. He thought about it and thought about it as he ran past the hub, following the channel right in the shadow of the rock wall on his left. It was much darker on the east side of the island. Though hanging a little low in the western sky, Mawoi was still shining brightly on the tops of the trees above him, but where Demican was it appeared as if the Great Light had already gone to sleep. He leapt on top of the channel when the path narrowed more, and the terrain started to climb ever so slightly. A few reeds away on his right, the shelf dropped a dozen reeds toward a white shelly beach that now appeared dark and ominous in the fading light. Not far ahead, the jungle rapidly approached, bringing with it the sounds of birds singing their farewell to the light, accented by the voices of several people talking.

Once he entered the jungle, the birds loudly announced their displeasure and fluttered away from their perches. Demican ignored them, focusing on crawling up the steep incline as fast as he could, his wide hands digging at the soil, still following the water channel on his left. It was pitch-black under the crowded canopy, but he knew if he just kept climbing, he would eventually pop out on the ledge above the spring. No sooner had the thought crossed his mind than Demican crashed out of the dense jungle and onto a high ledge far above the spring below. It was much higher than he remembered, and he was thankful the ledge was also wider than he remembered.

"Dem?" he heard his brother, Yaeel, shout up at him.

"Yup!" Demican replied. He thought he had thought this shortcut through, but as he looked around and saw how extremely difficult it was going to be to climb down to the spring, he realized he hadn't thought it through at all.

"What are you doing up there?" his brother asked.

"I – umm – took a shortcut." He could just barely see Yaeel's face awash in torchlight at the bottom of the sinkhole. Demican recognized his father, Chief of Springs Hadim, standing beside Yaeel, and the bushy hair of his other brother, Macu, just behind them. He could also see several other people in the dim light, all dressed in dull orange tunics, but he couldn't see their faces clearly enough to guess their names.

"Well," Yaeel said, "congratulations, I guess."

"What's going on, son?" his father asked.

"I was told you needed help with Urlam."

"Oh." His father sounded surprised. "Mina and Kataka took his body on a cart a little while ago. They're likely to have made it to the docks by now."

"Oh," Demican said, silently scolding himself. He knew he should have gone back and asked Lolbi which spring it was. Of course, how was he supposed to know the dumb segin would take the longest way possible to the docks from the Anikna spring?

"Dem?" Yaeel called up to him again.

"Yeah," he shouted down.

"Did you just get back from lessons?"

"Yeah."

"Who told you about Urlam?"

"Lombi."

"Lolombi?"

Demican smacked his forehead. "Yes, Llollombi. Why?" He saw Yaeel look at their father, and their father returned his brother's look. They talked among themselves for a moment, but Demican couldn't hear what they were saying, so he asked. "Hey! What are you saying?"

They didn't immediately reply, but then Yaeel looked up at him and asked, "Was there anyone else with him?"

"With Lolombi?"

"Yeah."

"No," he shouted. Demican was starting to feel very uncomfortable on the ledge. "Well – umm, if you don't need my help, I'm going back the way I came." He turned to leave, but before he could reenter the frighteningly dark jungle, Yaeel shouted up at him again.

"Hey, Dem!"

Demican carefully turned back around. "Yeah?"

"Where did you see Lolombi?" his brother asked.

"At the docks," his voice squeaked. His voice had been squeaking a lot lately.

"Is he still there?"

Demican thought a moment. "I'd assume so," he answered. He waited precisely one long breath for his brother to reply, and then Demican was done standing on the ledge.

He half-slid, half-ran down the steep decline and burst out of the thick jungle and onto the shelf. His foot felt weird and when he looked down, he saw he had lost one of his worn-out sandals along the way. "Baga," he groaned. "Whatever," he told himself. "Macu's got an extra pair I can steal."

Tired of running and now missing a sandal, he slowly started walking back toward the central hub. Insects buzzed around his head, biting at his sweaty neck and making him furiously swat at them. He gazed east over the great wall to the darkening horizon. There appeared to be a thin strip of clouds out there where the Great Sea merged with the void. If he were to guess, it looked like a big storm was coming and could arrive in a day or two. It would be good to get some rain, especially in time for the Day of Biyaya. Festivals were always so much more enjoyable after Boynay had cooled off the Grand Plaza and flooded the almec court. Demican had always wanted to be an almec player. He, Atu, and Hamsi would likely spend most of the Day of Biyaya down at the practice courts before the ceremonial match, picking up pointers for the next time they challenged Tunku, Kachi, and their little friend Amoc to a game. Sadly, he doubted Orlil had been kind enough to weave *becoming an almec player* into his belt of destiny.

By the time he passed the hub and reached the intersection once again, night had fallen on Itabacan. The sky was nearly entirely black, with only a splatter of stars here and there. Demican looked west and could see the attendants had lit the torch basins down at the harbor where he also noticed his brothers and father were standing on the back of a boar-drawn cart talking to someone. He couldn't see the person's face, but he also didn't care that much to know who it was anyway. He kicked himself for having not taken a cart earlier. He could have gotten to the spring quicker and not lost his sandal. Maybe he would even have met up with Lombi sooner and not wasted so much daylight running in the wrong direction. This thought led Demican to wonder why his brother had been so interested in Lolobi, which made him wonder if it might have something to do with Urlam's drowning.

CHAPTER NINE

A Voice with No Face

When Tabba woke up, her head wobbled about on her weak neck and felt as if it might split in half at any moment. Her eyelids were heavy and fought her every attempt to open them. She noticed her stupid arms and legs were equally unwilling to cooperate and could barely support even the slightest bit of weight. After an immense amount of effort, she propped herself up against something hard, cold, and damp. She forced her eyes open long enough to recognize the darkness surrounding her seemed familiar, but it was extremely annoying. She couldn't see a thing, not even her own thoughts. Her eyes opened or closed, it didn't matter, it was all black nothingness. There didn't seem to be a way to determine if it was morning or night, today or tomorrow, or even if an entire mawa had passed. She couldn't see where she was, and she had no memory of how she had got there.

"Just perfect," she grumbled, her light voice echoing faintly around her.

Tabba let out a long, deep sigh, unfortunately setting off an eruption of shivers that reverberated throughout her entire body. Her arms, legs, chest, and even her ears involuntarily shivered from the extreme cold she suddenly realized was actively draining her body of any warmth it had left. She blindly searched her immediate surrounds, her palms splashing in small pools of cold water that covered an uneven, bumpy, and rocky ground. As quickly and as delicately as she could, with one hand on the slick rock wall and the other on her knee, she forced herself to stand.

The air seemed to be slightly warmer up here and she wrapped her arms around her body to preserve some warmth. She instantly discovered her tunic was somehow both wet and stiff, as if the fabric itself had been soaked through and then covered in dried mud. Tabba suddenly realized she had been holding her breath and quickly let out a warm puff of air, only to inhale much colder air that sent another wave of shivers rippling down to her toes. She reflexively crossed one cold foot over the other and rubbed them together. She didn't want to do that again, but she had to breathe, even if it seemed dangerous to do so. It was a terrible game, seeing how long she could go without exhaling and losing the warmth within to the cold without.

Tabba quietly fumed. With one irritated, trembling finger, she reached out in front of her until she touched what felt like slimy clay, but clay that was as hard as a rock. Recoiling her arm back to her chest, she let out another puff of warm air and inhaled the cold. She then reached to either side and found more cold, wet, bumpy rock, and then she recoiled again. Her best guess – her only guess – was that the Mawoakin had thrown her into a hole in the ground, maybe somewhere in the cave entrance to the island. She could hear a droning wind somewhere above her head and reached up, stretching on to the tips of her cold toes, but didn't feel the shadow breeze. The droning reminded her of the humming in Mayu Hall when she was a little girl. The more she thought about it, the entire experience reminded her of her younger days, except for the splitting headache and the unbearable cold.

At around the age of four or five, she had her first true araco lesson. She remembered Elder Sengri leading her by the hand in the middle of the night to the inner chamber of Mayu Hall. There wasn't a single spark of light to be seen in the chamber. She recalled distinctly thinking it was brighter when she closed her eyes than when they were left open, and so she started blinking slowly over and over again. It was a sort of game to her, counting how many blinks it would take before the brightness faded. When it finally did, she discovered there was no distinction between her open eyes and her closed eyes. It was at this point she realized Sengri had let go of her hand.

At first, Tabba was only disappointed Sengri wasn't there to hear about her discovery, but then she called out to him. Her little girl voice called out to the darkness for her guardian, the only parental figure she had ever known, and it was met with cold, black silence. She remembered crying. Her crying turned into wailing, and then her wailing into trembling fear. At some point, she plopped down on the cool stone floor, pulled her little girl knees to her chest, and started rocking. She didn't dare run because she had been warned not to run. Elder Sengri didn't tell her why she shouldn't run, but her four or five-year-old imagination was enough to completely paralyze her. There could be an angry howler mother out there, or the Wicked Weaver, or the Dark Shadow himself.

When she was finally scared silent, Tabba suddenly heard a hum. She immediately called out to it, somewhere out there in the darkness, but the hum disappeared instead of replying. That was her second discovery; the humming only stayed if she didn't call out to it. Pretty soon, the first hum returned, but she remained quiet. When she did, a second hum sounded out of the darkness, but this one seemed like it was coming from a different direction. Her paralyzing fear soon gave way to her playful curiosity, and it became another game, where Tabba wanted to see how many hums were with her in the darkness. After counting eighteen separate, distinct humming voices, a single torch appeared not too far away, off to the right in her field of view.

Tabba recalled being initially irritated by the brightness of the single, small torch. It was as if she had become comfortable in the darkness and the torchlight was intrusive and disruptive. When a second flickering light appeared, she still didn't dare move to it and pulled her knees tighter with her little arms. This second torch was on the left in what she later recalled was the opposite corner of the inner chamber of Mayu Hall. One by one, eighteen torches were lit like eighteen twinkling ancestors in the void. When the last one sparkled to life, Tabba turned to find Elder Sengri was beside her once again, his hand silently reaching down for hers. Somehow, she knew she had passed the first test of the araco, and she was no longer scared.

From then on, her confidence grew stronger in knowing the araco were not afraid of the dark. They spent the majority of their lives embracing the absence of the Great Light. They were instructed to respect Maboti, but also to understand that what he wanted most was for them to fear the Dark Shadow. It was believed that fear weakened their grip on the Great Spirit, that part of them that longed to return to Yucahu, making fearful Itabayiti vulnerable to Maboti, ararun, and other wandering and invasive spirits. The araco bravely faced these dangers every night, because that was the sacrifice Yucahu demanded of those who might intercede with the ancestors. But from her experience, the Dark Shadow seemed more afraid of the moon and less interested in the Itabayiti than they were led to believe.

She laughed aloud, "Well, th-there's n-no...moonlight d-down...here!" She could hear her last word bounce off the walls and disappear into the droning wind overhead.

She assumed her captors wouldn't be hanging around in the pitch-black darkness with her, so she didn't feel the need to call out to them, or anyone for that matter. Bahaca was not an attractive destination like Amaca or Niamca were, and Tabba knew it was highly unlikely anyone would stumble upon her, wherever she was. The best thing she could do was to remain calm, listen, and wait for that first flicker of light to show her the way. She chuckled, wondering if Elder Sengri would consider her current predicament another lesson.

"Ba-ah-ga," she grumbled, her quiet voice trembling and her teeth clattering together. It was so cold, and she was so tired, but she didn't dare sit again. "An-nd...th-there the ss-similarities...end."

"Similarities?"

Tabba held her breath, *Was that me?*

"Similarities with what?"

Tabba didn't dare answer. Lesson number two had been very clear on this; be suspicious of a voice with no face. Their work was dangerous, often being alone night after night for years, and it wasn't uncommon for araco to attract curious ararun, or worse...

"Tayokun? Have you gone to sleep?"

The voice sounded like a woman, and it wasn't too far away, but could Tabba trust it? She had to admit, it was possible the voice could belong to one of her captors. Had she been wrong in thinking they wouldn't possibly be sitting there in the darkness with her?

"Hmm..."

Tabba was perplexed. The voice seemed so clear, like it might be coming from inside the hole with her, and it didn't appear to echo like her voice had. And that was when Tabba started to get scared for the first time in a long time.

CHAPTER TEN

The Beauty of YUKI'AT

Yaya Amnu shielded his face from the fierce and bitter wind tearing through the Council Rotunda. The sudden onslaught of stinging cold rain elicited yelps and grumbles from the council members seated below him, Boaraco Unsari clearly being the loudest among them. Amnu's adulu quickly sought shelter inside the curved cibmani walls, stepping out of the open doorways and making matters worse. He watched them shake the rainwater from their crimson tunics, creating little puddles beneath their sandaled feet. He could feel the shifting pressure in the rotunda crowd around his eyes and ears and forced a yawn to make his ears pop and alleviate some of the pressure. He looked out the open doorway toward the dark gray clouds, flashing like smoldering balls of cotton behind sheets of pouring rain, and he mouthed a thank you to Boynay for bringing the storm and an end to the meeting.

Amnu tapped the wahas on the floor between his feet. "Meeting adjourned!" he yelled over the howling wind. He then immediately stood and started for the south exit of the chamber, ignoring the protests of the council, his wahas clacking and mocking them with every other step.

He rarely used the south exit, preferring his private entrance that went outside and through the east hallway, but he didn't want to get wetter than he already was. The double doors before him led directly into the palace dining hall where he and his family would soon be having their evening meal, but Amnu knew he had time to relax in his bedchamber. He let Adulu Atriska use his long, thin body to prop open the heavy wooden doors. Atriska was one of Hadim's many mountainous sons, but Amnu suspected he had been last in line at mealtime. Amnu was impressed to see the adulu maintain a stoic posture, his fist clenched around the neck of his spear, and his chiseled chin held high.

"Thank you, Atriska," he nodded at the guard.

"My Yaya!" the adulu nervously shouted, clearly not accustomed to the Yaya speaking directly to him. Amnu smiled as he stepped through the open door.

The palace dining hall was shaped like the reception hall but offset west by a reed. It was seven reeds long by five reeds wide, with four separate entrances and exits, as well as a secret entrance beside a large fireplace set into the eastern wall. It was one of only two fireplaces in all of Itabacan, both of which were in the Yaya's Palace because the palace had to be on top of Mount Otaba and was the only structure that actually needed fireplaces. An enormous solid cedar dining table sat comfortably in the center, flanked on either side by equally long wooden benches and two tall chairs at the head and tail. The ceilings throughout the palace reached over five reeds above the polished cibmani floor, nearly twice as tall as the average bohi or chief's residence.

"My Yaya," Bolari quickly greeted him with a slight bow.

The strong wind crowded through the open door, past the Yaya, and ruffled Bolari's tan tunic. He was the oldest palace attendant, having served Yaya Shakali before Amnu, but had to remove himself when he lost his only daughter and son-in-law to one of Yuraca's great storms, forcing Bolari to raise his grandchildren on Yapaca. Unana had known them and convinced Amnu to invite Bolari back to the palace after Amnu became the Yaya. It was one of the best decisions he had ever made. Despite being a small man with delicate hands and an egg-shaped bald head that shimmered like a polished bowl in the torchlight, Bolari was devoted, efficient, and made an excellent fermented kosa drink.

"Ah – I see you are making preparations for evening meal," the Yaya said, and then glared back over his shoulder at Atriska who was trying to shut the large doors with his skinny arms against the fierce wind.

"Yes, my Yaya," the attendant said, lifting his head. "Roasted whitefish with grilled pineapple, honeyed yams, yatak bread..." The heavy doors finally closed behind them with a light thump, quieting Bolari and the wind at the same time.

"That's alright, Bolari," Amnu said, forcing another yawn before offering Bolari a generous smile. "I don't need to know everything they've prepared. I do enjoy being surprised now and then; you know?"

"Of course, my Yaya!" Bolari appeared to understand, bowed his head again, and then continued laying out the plates and cups on the table, brushing a bit of rain mist from his tunic.

Amnu noticed the fireplace to his left had not yet been lit, and the only light in the dining hall came from a single torch in a copper sconce on the wall. "Bolari, when you can, will you strike the fire? This storm has brought with it a bitter cold wind."

"Yes, my Yaya. Right away." Bolari bowed, quickly finished what he was doing, shuffled through the narrow attendants' door to the left of the rotunda entrance, and disappeared down the equally narrow hallway. The attendants' hallway ran the length of the north wall and led to a second narrow door in the northwest corner of the palace, as well as a third in the western outer wall, but Amnu never used either of those entrances.

Satisfied in knowing the dining hall would be warm and cozy by evening meal, Yaya Amnu turned and walked the few paces to the second set of heavy double doors that led into the reception hall. The pressure in his head was subsiding but the uneasiness in his stomach remained. Being that he didn't normally go this way, Amnu had to bang on the door with the wahas. After a moment, another adulu, one whose name escaped him, cautiously creaked the door open and peaked through the crack. When the guard saw who was on the other side, he quickly mumbled an apology, threw his shoulder into the heavy door, and stood like Atriska had, only with a little less enthusiasm and stature.

"Thank you," the Yaya said.

He continued toward his bedchamber on the opposite end of the palace, the dining hall door creaking closed behind him, and found the reception hall dark and quiet. Amnu could hear the muffled hum of the storm intensifying outside, and there was a whistle of wind he knew was coming through the gaps between the main doors and their old, worn-stone hinges. His sandals slapped against the floor as he walked, echoing off the cibmani floor, accented by the clacking of the wahas. He had been walking the length of the palace every day for over ten years. He knew every sound, every subtle imperfection in the floor, the cracks in the ceiling where the molds had been joined together when the walls were poured, and he was pretty sure his bedchamber was beginning to sag. It just had to be suspended over the southern face of the mountain, held up by two enormous pillars firmly bound to the rock outcropping below. There didn't appear to be any damage to the pillars, and there were no cracks around the seam between the chamber floor and the rest of the palace, but Amnu could feel the imbalance in his gut all the same.

As he thought about the uneasy feeling, his mind raced back to the uncomfortable council meeting that had ended so abruptly. A boy named Urlam had drowned. Amnu hated to hear about the deaths of his people, especially when they were so young and full of promise, and the meeting seemed to only get worse from there. Bocoani Numila, evidently trying to sympathize with Chief of Springs Hadim, admitted his training canuti full of shoats had nearly smashed against the great wall a few days earlier. Council members immediately demanded an explanation, which the bocoani hadn't expected because Amnu didn't think Numila intended to admit almost drowning their children in the first place. And then, as if that weren't enough ridicule, Numila claimed they had been attacked by a tiburana.

Of course, the council lost their collective minds. They leveled numerous accusations against the bocoani, challenging his leadership and his integrity. They naturally wanted Amnu to weigh in on the matter but all he could think about was his own stomach and lungs filling up with water, unable to speak or breathe. The thought pulled on a memory thread of him and Abensu sneaking out, borrowing a canuti, and taking a late-night sail beyond the Grand Gateways to the Bocoa.

He vaguely remembered it being a fishing canuti, but Amnu couldn't be sure. They were both accomplished shoats, but looking back, they were just young boys who had no business being so brash and reckless. He remembered Abensu was the voice of reason, arguing they should only go out far enough to circle back and return. There would be other vessels out there, other fishing canuti, and they definitely didn't want to get caught. And that was when...

The door to his bedchamber suddenly swung open, pouring torchlight down the hallway, reflecting off the polished floor and flashing into Amnu's eyes. With the interrupting light came a gust of that chilling wind, and he attempted to block both with his hands.

"There you are," he heard his wife, Unana, say. "Just wandering the palace again?" she asked, the wind howling past her and into his face.

Amnu scoffed, "You act as though you're surprised." She met him halfway across the shimmering pool of light wearing a sleaved robe made from alternating strips of dark and light-green fabric. A string of conch pearls adorned her neck, each a slightly different shape and shade of pink, which matched a pair of pearl earrings set into acorn caps wedged into her earlobes "Where are the adulu?" he asked her, a bit concerned there were no guards outside of their bedchamber doors like there were supposed to be. "And why haven't the attendants closed off the balcony?"

The south side of the Yaya's bedchamber was an open balcony overlooking all of Itabacan. Most storms approached from the northeast and were rarely an issue, but there were wooden shutters that could be latched into place to separate the balcony from the rest of the bedchamber when necessary. The storm now upon them seemed to have come from the southeast and was blowing directly through the open balcony, into the bedchamber and Amnu's face.

Unana threw her damp arms over his shoulders and kissed him on the lips. "When I saw the meeting had been adjourned and you didn't return, I sent the adulu to find you."

"That was unnecessary, my love," he said. But he had to acknowledge, sometimes, he did get lost in his thoughts and wandered longer than he may realize. "And the attendants?"

"They are preparing our evening meal," she answered, eyeing him. "Why so many questions?"

"Where's Kina? Is she in her room?"

Unana slowly nodded. "Has been ever since she came home from lessons. I believe the rain has dampened her mood," she said with a wry smile.

Amnu pulled himself away from his wife and walked the few paces down the hall to the right and stopped in front of his daughter's door. He knew she hadn't been on Numila's training canuti when it had almost crashed a few days earlier, but he needed to make sure she was safe all the same. He pressed his ear against the smooth wood to listen, but all he could hear was the rushing wind through their bedchamber. He gestured for Unana to close their door, which she did, and then he listened again. He could hear the muffled sound of the storm like before in the reception hall but there was nothing else.

"Is she sleeping?" he whispered, to which Unana shrugged her shoulders. Despite his desire to check on his daughter, if she was actually asleep, he didn't want to disturb her. Amnu sighed and walked back to his wife. "Come, we must put the shutters up ourselves."

"Are you feeling alright?" she asked him, taking his proffered hand.

"Fine – fine," he lied. His thoughts were still muddled by the council meeting.

Amnu pushed the heavy bedchamber doors open and was instantly blasted by the wind. It seemed to be getting stronger, but he could see traces of light on the horizon just behind the gray clouds that told him the storm couldn't last much longer. He was surprised to see the torch basins in the corners of the room hadn't been blown out by the wind and were still lit and flickering.

"We will start on the left and make our way across," he told her, as he led the way.

"If that's what would be best."

"That way we only have to affix two of them, and then we can lie down and rest before evening meal."

The Yaya's bedchamber was roughly four reeds wide by five reeds long, with the additional length taken up by the balcony on the far side. There were two pillars splitting the southern wall into three equal-sized openings, and on the other side were three wall-length steps leading down to the balcony. The pillars supported the ceiling and contained the necessary notches to hold the shutters in place. In the center of the eastern wall was the Yaya's large bed, while directly opposite the bed and set into the western wall was the other fireplace. In the northeast corner a private bath also contained a cibmani toilet, both of which fed into a stone channel running down and out onto the eastern face of the mountain. Their attendants regularly flushed the channel with seawater and hung freshly cut flowers on the walls. Just outside of the curtained doorway into the bathroom was a copper-lined torch basin, matching another basin in the northwest corner.

The southeast corner of the bedchamber pressed outward half-a-reed, forming a niche that was dark and obscured by a white curtain hanging from the ceiling. The niche in the southwest corner didn't have a curtain, but it was well lit and where Unana's many tunics and the Yaya's robes were stored – along with the three floor-to-ceiling shutters.

With the wind pushing at them, Yaya Amnu and Unana Wani slowly made their way toward the corner of the room. Stinging rain pelted their faces and hands, which they sacrificed to protect their eyes. Unana had to walk to the left of her husband to avoid his long flapping robe, while her long braids whipped around behind her, causing the shells braided into the ends to clack together. Amnu could see thick raindrops between the pillars pummeling the balcony as he reached the niche first. He leaned the wahas against the wall, slid his left hand around the corner, and easily pulled one of the shutters out. They were made of kapok tree wood, which wasn't especially heavy or strong, but was charred and covered in a thin layer of bitumen to protect each one against the weather.

As soon as the shutter was fully out of the niche, Amnu felt the full pressure of the wind slam the flat wooden shutter into his shoulder. Unana quickly stepped up beside him and braced it with both hands. They moved forward together, keeping it steady and turned slightly, redirecting the wind, and then maneuvered the shutter between the first pillar and the niche. Once it was turned back parallel with the wall, the wind pushed the shutter against the notches. Amnu then slid a wooden latch into place on both sides to keep it from being blown in the opposite direction.

"Whoo! One down, two to go," he said, smiling at Unana. She had a sliver of bitumen running up the center of her left palm and was picking at it with her manicured nails. "You might want to wait until we have the last two in place."

"I am aware," she replied without looking up.

"I know you are, I simply wanted to..." he started to say but Unana glared at him, making Amnu sigh. "Understood. Shall we continue?" He gestured toward the niche.

With the first shutter in place, the second and third shutters popped into their notches more easily. Once that was done, they both slumped down on the edge of the bed to rest. The wind continued to rattle the shutters and squeeze through the slits, keeping their bedchamber colder than Amnu preferred. He decided he would have Bolari strike the fireplace in the bedchamber during evening meal.

"Maroha be merciful!" Unana shouted. "What happened to starting on the left?" she laughed.

"We must be nimble like the reed and sharp like the chaak."

"Sounds like something your baba used to say."

Amnu chuckled, "No, that was Bocoani Gabeni."

"Ugh...it's times like these that I am reminded to be nicer to our attendants." She was looking at her hand again, having resumed picking at the now three strips of bitumen on her palm. "I'll need to wash this off before evening meal, and Kina will need a new tunic before lessons tomorrow."

"I'm sure the one she wore today will dry by tomorrow," Amnu said. "Besides, she already has – what – a dozen to choose from? For once, she can wear one of her other tunics."

Unana turned to look at him, resting her head on her clean palm. "You know that won't be good enough."

He knew what she meant. Kina could be temperamental when it came to her tunics. If the fabric didn't feel right on her skin or the color had faded, she didn't wear it. Amnu didn't look at his wife, preferring to continue staring at the ceiling and ignore the uneasiness in his stomach. "Well," he sighed. "It will have to be."

No sooner had the words left his mouth, Amnu could feel her eyes on him. His wife had her mother's cold, dagger-like stare, which could either stir the embers of rage within him or create a hole wide enough to vent the smoldering pressure. Amnu forced another yawn, popping his ears, and then turned to look into Unana's dark-azure eyes. She was his guiding star, the embodiment of Bitabay, and the love of his life. She had given him Kina, his precious obsidian gem and the second love of his life. The thought of losing either of them was almost too much to bear. It was worse than drowning, or being stung by a thousand wasps' nests, or being set ablaze alive on a bonefire. It was unimaginable. Amnu understood the responsibility of the Yaya; his responsibility was to do everything in his power to ensure their fates remained woven in their belts of destiny, guided by the will of the Great Spirit.

"Get out of your head and talk to me," she abruptly told him, taking his hand.

Amnu took a deep breath. He didn't want to involve Unana in the matters of the council, because he knew she often took matters too personally, and that was precisely what the council had done. On the other hand, if she figured out what was bothering him on her own, then he would really be in trouble. "A segin drowned in one of the springs on Niamca," he reluctantly admitted.

"Oh – that's terrible."

"He was young too. Just a boy, really."

"Does Hadim know how it happened? I can't remember the last time a segin drowned."

Amnu shifted his whole body on the bed so that he was lying on his side. "He speculates another segin was involved – young man named Lombi or Lolobi."

"When did this happen?" she asked.

"Two days ago."

A curious expression formed on Unana's face before she asked, "Why did Hadim wait so long to inform you?"

He sighed, "Because, he said there were other factors that needed his attention."

"What other factors?"

Amnu could see his wife was arriving at the same conclusions he had drawn during the meeting. "That is a good question," he said. The truth was, Amnu didn't have a chance to ask his Chief of Springs to explain himself because Bocoani Numila's comment had diverted the council's focus to him and the near drowning of their children. And then the storm hit, and the meeting was adjourned.

"You didn't ask," she said, reading his mind and figuring things out on her own. "Something else came up."

He looked at her and took a deep breath. "Numila – and don't ask me why – thought it was a good idea in that moment to admit his shoats were nearly killed returning through the Gate of Mawoi a few days ago."

"What?! A few days ago?" Unana was getting agitated. She quickly sat up and glared at him. "You are the Yaya. How are you not being informed of these things?"

Amnu sat up as well. "My love, Kina wasn't..."

"I don't care if our daughter was there or not!" she exploded, taking it personally. "You need to reconvene the meeting and get to the bottom of this." She stood and started marching around their bed toward the bathroom, her long braids swaying and the shells clacking.

"I *need* to do nothing," he quickly responded. Seeing her clearly so upset, Amnu didn't think it wise to mention the tiburana.

"Well, then, you ought to," Unana amended her statement.

"Do you think this lack of communication and clear show of disrespect doesn't trouble me?" he asked, rhetorically. Amnu struggled with his long, damp robe as he stood. "I have been fighting this council for years. The oldest members want nothing to do with progressive ideas or innovations, themselves having been appointed by Shakali who always appeared to me like a frightened giant hutia bumbling through the jungle and leaving overturned soil and broken bushes in his wake. While, on the other side of the round, in the howling kugo seats, progress and innovation are all the younger members want to discuss. It seems impossible to find common ground on the simplest of matters, and I don't want to end up like Shakali and rely on unilateral decrees that cut the council out of my rule entirely."

"Would that be such a bad thing?" Unana asked from the bathroom where Amnu assumed she was rinsing off her hands. It was hard to hear what she was doing in there over the rattling shutters and droning wind.

"If I want them to implement any of my decrees without also having to order the adulu to stick spears in their backs, then yes, that would be a bad thing," he said, starting to pace behind the wall of shutters, thinking about the former Yaya.

Shakali had halted trade with the Gusiti because the bocoani at the time was attacked and his men were injured. Of course, no one was killed or even seriously hurt, and the coani had put their spears through plenty of the Golden People in response. But Shakali used the incident to justify isolating Itabacan anyway, cutting them off from the only somewhat civilized people the Itabayiti had come into contact with in nearly a thousand years. Some of the current council members thought Amnu was crazy to send Bocoani Gabeni to reestablish contact, but they ate their words when the resumed trade was widely popular, despite the fact that Amnu had acted without the council's consent. He stopped pacing and huffed – *you're getting off topic*. He blew out his frustration in a puff of air and stretched his back.

"The point I want to make, my love," he continued, "is that I want to be remembered, not just for reestablishing trade with the Gusiti, or even building new baths on Yapaca, but for being inclusive. For bringing the Itabayiti together and expanding our understanding of this..." He gestured toward the view of Itabacan beyond the open balcony, but then he immediately recognized it just looked like he was pointing to the rattling shutters. "Well – we can't see it now, but Yuki'at."

Much like the Yayapti, the Yuki'at explained how all things came into being and was taught to each Itabayiti child by their parents in the form of bedtime stories. There was the story of the twins Yucahu and Yuraca attempting to repair a crack in Ora, resulting in the formation of the Earth Spirit, Kayki. There was the story of Sikulka the Frost Spirit coming down every day from Kayki's mountainous shoulders to melt in the warmth of the sun, which eventually created their homeland, the Land of Many Rivers. But Amnu's favorite story, the one which immediately came to mind, was when Ma'an the Great Sky cried three tears to form Osani the Great River, Boynay the Rain Spirit, and Maru the Dark Mist. When tamed by the Great Spirit and brought together, the three sisters formed Niama the Water Spirit. Listening to the stirring of Boynay beat against the shutters, spraying mist over the top and through the slits, Amnu felt like a boy again – curled up against his mother in the candlelight listening to her tell of the Yuki'at.

He heard Unana step out of the bathroom and turned to see her drying her hands with a tan towel. She casually inspected her palm to ensure it was no longer sticky from the bitumen, all while raising one eye to Amnu. "What do you hope to understand that Yucahu hasn't already revealed?" she asked him.

Amnu thought a moment. He and his wife had heated discussions about this before, and he knew her stance and that it was unwavering. "You and your sisters may think you've figured it all out," he said, "and perhaps you have." He nodded his head as if giving her position serious consideration.

He knew Unana had joined one of the many cults in Itabacan, but he wasn't exactly sure which. The cults encouraged strangers to embrace as brothers and sisters through the sharing of ideas, goods, and kindness, usually in association with one of the many spirits. It was nothing out of the ordinary. There were wonderfully unique groups throughout the islands all searching for alternative explanations for things that their Itabayiti traditions couldn't. Some were as benign as the Cult of Kuruan who wore black cloaks and squatted in the rain, flapping around like the giant black birds and squawking at anyone who happened to walk by them. And then others were as troublesome as the Cult of Utuchu, or as dangerous as the Cult of Kano had once been.

"I prefer to listen to my fellow Itabayiti," Amnu continued. "I've seen them struggling to find reason and meaning, as I often do."

She offered him a polite smile, tossing the towel on the floor and stepping closer to him. "What meaning? Orlil weaves our..."

"Yes. Yes," he snapped, unintentionally. "The Great Spirit determines what threads to use, and his Ageless Daughter weaves them into our belts of destiny." He tugged on his own golden, boarhide belt for emphasis. "And who's to say if any of that is true?"

"It's all we have..." she tried to say, but Amnu cut her off.

"Look what happened to Yaya Obac. His wife died while in labor, and Obac lost her and the child. The Biyaya Spirit couldn't prepare him for that! He didn't know how to rule after he lost them, and then he was poisoned a few short years later..."

"That was never confirmed," Unana corrected him, taking another cautious step closer.

"And if I'm destined to lose you? To lose Kina? Great Spirit, my heart bleeds for the parents of that boy! If anything ever happened to you or Kina, Yaya or not, I would have nothing. I would be nothing!"

She quickly closed the gap between them and pulled him in close to her chest, rubbing his weary back with her clean hands. "You have learned to hear and speak, but your thoughts remain empty," Unana whispered.

"You don't need to quote the yaali creed to me," he scoffed, to which she just compassionately squeezed him.

"You have seen both light and dark, but your eyes have never opened."

"Unana, please..." Amnu tried to lift his head from her shoulder, but she forced it back down.

"You have lived for many years, but living is unknown to you," she continued despite his protestations. Amnu sighed heavily, and his wonderful wife squeezed him tighter. "We are not meant to know the reason for Yuki'at, but to marvel at its beauty and tremble before its power. You are the Yaya, the embodiment of the Biyaya Spirit, and we Itabayiti are meant to follow you."

"And if I am destined to..."

"You aren't," she said quickly, with another tight squeeze. "But even if *we* were, you are destined to be our Yaya. You needn't worry about our destinies, Kina's or mine, but that of Itabacan. She is your responsibility. She is your destiny."

Unana relaxed her hold on Amnu, and he slowly pulled himself away so that he could look into his wife's beautiful eyes. "I am the Yaya. The Biyaya spirit flows through me. I believe this, but I feel there must be a greater truth beyond belief," he said.

Suddenly, there was a soft rapping on the bedchamber doors. It was just barely loud enough to be heard over the storm outside and Amnu knew who it was. He swiftly kissed his wife and strolled across the room to the door. The air pressure made the door stick, but once he got it moving, it swung open and slammed against the wall – *THUMP!*

"I'm hungry," his daughter said, holding her hand up to the torchlight instantly pouring out of the bedchamber. Yaya Amnu silently scooped her up into his arms and Kina reflexively wrapped her arms around his neck, her legs around his waist, and laid her head on his shoulder. "Are we going to have evening meal soon?" she asked.

Amnu didn't immediately respond, allowing himself a quiet moment to hold his daughter. Just as he was about to answer her, he saw Bolari walking toward them, clearly on his way from the dining hall.

"Are we ready?" Yaya Amnu asked the old attendant.

"Yes, my Yaya," Bolari said, stopping where he was and bowing.

And then Amnu noticed the two adulu standing on either side of their door with their spears in hand. "Oh – there you are!" The adulu didn't say anything but silently and slowly bowed their heads toward their Yaya. It was dark in the hallway with the only light coming from his bedchamber and the open doors of the dining hall far on the other side of the palace.

"Shall we go?" he heard Unana say behind him.

"Yes!" Kina shouted enthusiastically, making her father laugh.

"Of course!" Amnu set Kina down, taking her hand and holding his other hand out for Unana to join them. "Bolari."

"Yes, my Yaya."

Unana took his hand and the three of them started making their way toward the dining hall. "Bolari, would you please get someone to light the torches in the hall."

"Yes, my Yaya."

"And the fireplace in the bedchamber," Unana added.

"Yes, the fireplace as well," Amnu echoed her.

"Of course, my Yaya, Unana Wani," Bolari answered, his head still bowed. "Would there be anything else, my Yaya?"

"Not at the moment, Bolari. Thank you."

"Yes, my Yaya," the old attended said and scurried off ahead of them.

"Nawuni said all twins are given the same name," Kina told them. "Is that true? Because Yucahu and Yuraca don't have the same name."

Amnu smiled, thinking how ironic it was for his daughter to be asking such a seemingly random question after he had just been thinking about the Yuki'at. "Well," he started, pausing when their sandaled feet slapped against the floor of the reception hall like a dozen oars slapping the waves. "Your itaba and I were just discussing the Yuki'at, and actually you are correct on both points."

"Baba?" Kina asked, looking up at him with her big turquoise eyes sparkling more and more the closer they got to the bright firelight of the dining hall.

"Yes, twins are always given the same name, except in rare instances where they end up not actually looking identical," he explained, but she still looked confused.

They entered the warm dining hall and saw the cedar table in the center covered with ceramic trays of steaming whitefish, grilled pineapple, glazed yatak bread, all kinds of nuts and berries, jars of golden honey, baked yams, large jugs of oycu for Amnu and Unana, and a smaller jug filled with coconut milk for Kina. It was more food than they could eat in a lifetime, but the Yaya always made it a point to allow his attendants to take a plate before he and his family began eating. The damp wood in the fireplace crackled and popped, flooding the room with heat and orange light. Amnu hadn't realized how cold he was until he was standing behind his chair at the head of the table and felt the heat from the fire against his back. He nodded at the adulu who was closing the south doors, leaving them to dine peacefully as a family.

"This looks marvelous," Unana said. Amnu saw her turn to say as much to Bolari, but the old man had already scurried off through the narrow attendants' door.

"Ooh – num-num fruit!" Kina exclaimed, climbing onto the bench to Amnu's left. Unana circled around behind him and took her seat on the bench that ran along the right side of the table. "I love num-num fruit!" their daughter continued, stuffing her mouth with juicy, red, bite-sized chunks.

"Take it easy, Kina," Unana told her.

"No – let her enjoy herself," Amnu said, finally sitting down as well. "How were lessons today?" he asked as he took a sip of his oycu. It was a fermented drink made from the plant of the same name, and it was delicious.

"Fine...until it started raining."

"You said earlier that Jokimbi left early," Unana prompted her.

"Yeah," Kina said, smacking her lips together. "It was alright because Lewa took over, but then the rain came, and it didn't matter anyway."

"Did he say why he had to leave?" Unana asked, but Kina's mouth was full, and she couldn't answer. Fortunately, Amnu was able to answer for her.

"I would assume Elder Sengri summoned him up to the plaza," he said, "because I gave him permission to help with the Tara'apti rehearsal."

"The play for the festival? Unana asked.

"Yes. Being the son of Yaya Shakali, Jokimbi has just as much experience with the Tara'apti as Sengri. After the – uh – incident, I felt bad and offered for him to take part."

"It's so exciting!" Kina said, gulping down a bite of whitefish. "The Day of Biyaya is tomorrow!"

Amnu smiled, feeling much better than before now that he had his girls there with him and enjoying an excellent meal. Suddenly, the attendants' door swung open, slapped against the wall, and Bolari barged into the dining hall.

"My Yaya," he said, out of breath.

"Bolari! What is it?" he asked, and the old attendant whispered in his ear.

Yaya Amnu felt he had always been a reasonable ruler. He wanted the Itabayiti to feel like they could approach him at any point during the day with any matter, so long as the preferred and official methods had failed. There were council members and assigned representatives for nearly all walks of life in Itabacan, and council members had a schedule for approaching the Yaya that would not interfere with his personal family life. But even with all those safeguards Amnu had put in place himself, there was Bolari interrupting his evening meal with his family.

Amnu looked at his beautiful wife and daughter sitting beside him at the table in the dining hall, their evening meal steaming and smelling delicious in front of them. The expression on Unana's face told him an argument was coming, but like she had said, he was the Yaya, and the Yaya had a responsibility to Itabacan that overshadowed any familial obligations. He let out a deep sigh.

"You say Bogula is with them?" the Yaya asked.

"Yes, my Yaya," Bolari said, still bowing.

"With whom?" Unana interrupted.

"Abensu," he answered her, but then he sighed at seeing Bolari bowing again. "There's no need for all of that," Amnu told him. "Tell them I will be with them in a moment."

"Yes, my Yaya," Bolari said. He seemed unsure of what to do, but then he quickly bowed again and left the dining hall through the floor-to-ceiling double doors in the center of the south wall.

The large ornate fireplace behind the Yaya crackled and popped some more, casting warm light upon his wife's and daughter's cheeks while the table in front of them remained in a cool shadow.

"This is evening meal, Amnu," Unana said, her tone firm, but Amnu could tell she was trying to be sincere. "You're not seriously going to leave now?" She had gotten used to having him there for evening meals, no matter how many times he told her the Yaya needed to be accessible day and night.

"My guiding star, you were right, this is my destiny. Besides, I feel the Biyaya Spirit telling me something is different this time." Amnu finally stood and kissed the top of her head.

"That does not mean you have to listen," she said and took a bite of her roasted fish.

"Is Anki out there, baba?" Kina asked, her eyes brightening with excitement.

"I *must* listen, my love," he replied to his wife, but then looked at Kina. "I believe he is, but you need to finish your evening meal with your itaba." Kina frowned and stabbed at her fish with her finger. "I'll be back shortly," he said, and then left through a concealed door beside the fireplace along the eastern wall.

Anki didn't like it, but he had to admit he actually enjoyed his first day of suspension working in the clay pits, making the ash glaze for the ceremonial plates, and hanging out with Olari. He had joked around with Lewa's brother on occasion over the years, especially once Atu had gone off to the reed yard and left Anki on Conaca alone with their father, but now he was starting to wish Olari had been his older brother instead. Realizing how mean that sounded in his head, he thought maybe what he meant was that he wished Olari had always been older brother to both of them. Then maybe Olari could have picked on Atu the way Atu picked on him, and then maybe his brother wouldn't have been such a pain in the butt.

Unfortunately, once Anki's father realized they needed to remake the last batches of plates, being anywhere near him quickly became dangerous. If he wasn't yelling at the waki to dig faster, he was yelling at the artisans to be more careful, but also work faster. Olari frantically organized the waki, and they had made respectable progress before running into an enormous boulder that needed to be cleared. His father ordered them to work through the night under Kuraka's pale light, digging out twice as much clay as necessary to complete the order. By morning, the waki diggers were exhausted but their chief was satisfied and allowed them to stumble down to the harbor, where they loaded a transport canuti bound for Yapaca.

Anki hadn't been awake when Olari and the other waki diggers left, his father either let him sleep late or simply forgot to wake him. When he finally made his way down to the clay ovens, there was Chief of Wares Abensu screaming at the artisans for ruining another dozen plates. Anki learned they had been doing much smaller test batches from the hundreds of dried clay plates that were not ruined the day before, and that was why his father made the diggers work through the night. Unless he wanted to get yelled at along with the artisans, there was nothing for Anki to do on his second day of suspension and he ended up wandering around Conaca, playing with the howler monkeys, and planning something marvelous for the next day.

"If you get into trouble and the adulu bring you home at the end of a spear," his father warned him, "I will tell them you ran away. Understood?"

"But baba, the adulu are palace guards," Anki explained, as if his father didn't already know. "What would they be doing on Niamca?"

"It doesn't matter *who* brings you back! Do you understand?"

Anki nodded that he understood, though he only sort of understood. "Yes, baba," he said.

Because Anki had only been in the way the day before and his father was really busy, he asked if he could go to the springs on Niamca his last day of suspension. His father wasn't initially going to let him go, but enough annoying begging would have convinced his father to let him do just about anything. Eventually, his father agreed to look the other way, but he hadn't said anything about stopping on Pacca to get Biacoya and neither did Anki.

He wore his yaali tunic because he thought, if he was already going to draw attention when taking a midmorning ferry alone, he should look his best. It was a white tunic with gold stitching along the seams, a gold-colored boarhide belt, and the symbol of the Yaya embroidered in the center. The symbol of the Yaya was the outline of a canuti overlaid with the head of a spear, and then a circle representing Ora in the center. Anki thought it just looked like an uca bird had stepped on his chest. The council had gifted him and the other yaali each a ceremonial garment over a year ago, but it had just been lying around, and Anki wasn't going to let such a fine-looking tunic go to waste.

"Taycoay, Haro," he said as he walked down the dock to the ferry.

"Taycoay, Anki. Where's your baba?" Haro asked, his cheek twitching.

"Oh – he's up at the ovens," he replied, looking down at his feet. "He has the big ceremonial order to fill by tomorrow." Anki stood next to the ferry slowly swaying, trying his best to not stare at Haro's twitching cheek.

"Ah, yes, the Day of Biyaya." He leaned toward Anki. "Don't you think it's weird that we celebrate the Biyaya on the day of his death?"

"I don't know," Anki shrugged. He had never thought about it like that before, but as curious as the ferryman's question was, Anki didn't want to stand around on the dock any longer than he had to. "Can I get a ride to Pacca?" he blurted out.

"Oh, this isn't a social visit?" Haro looked sad, which made his twitch turn into a full-blown spasm. "I should have known. Look at you, all dressed up! I'm sorry. Of course, young man." Haro adjusted a few things on the ferry and invited Anki to get on.

"Thank you," Anki said and climbed onto the reed boat.

Haro maneuvered the ferry away from the docks and headed into the sound, turning south toward Pacca. Anki thought it was nice of Haro to not expect something of trade for the ferry ride. Ferrymen had a specific schedule running morning workers to and from work and, in the evening, taking them to and from home. Unless someone was on official business, a ride any other time often came with a haggle. Anki looked down at his yaali tunic and smiled.

There was a brisk breeze on the water that caught Haro off guard, nearly tossing him into the sound. His string of shells pulled on the tiller and suddenly shifted the canuti southwest. Anki watched him struggle to right their course and was glad he would likely never have to be a ferryman. He was the son of a council member and chosen to possibly become the next Yaya. Some Itabayiti, he thought, were simply not born to work, but to rule. Anki found comfort in the thought as they approached the island of Pacca.

Pacca sat low in the water between Conaca and Bahaca and featured the thickest jungle of all the islands. Anki's father told him it was because storms only knocked over the trees and shrubs instead of ripping them out of the ground, which was what often happened on the taller islands. It made it easier for Kayki to return the fallen foliage to her soil, enriching and allowing it to grow more trees and bushes and grasses. Anki told Biacoya what his father had said, and he just laughed. He said his father told him it was because the Temple of Maroha was on Pacca and protected them from Yuraca's strongest winds. Whichever the case, Anki always marveled at just how many trees there were. The island was shaped like a skinny shark's tooth, with the northern tip surrounded by boulders poking out of the shallows like the ridges of the tooth. The only accessible beach, where the Itabayiti built the few docks that would fit, was on the southwestern corner.

Palms and mangroves grew all the way into the water along the shore like giant crab legs, and there were more manati around Pacca than all of the other islands combined.

Haro swung the canuti into the slip and flung the mooring line around a pillar. "Alright, young man, off you go!" he said.

Anki nodded and then leapt off onto the dock. He got a few steps and then turned to the ferryman, "Thank you, Haro."

Haro smiled, his cheek giving an extra twitch, and said, "You're welcome. Taycoay!" And then the ferryman shoved off the dock and drifted back into the sound.

Biacoya didn't know Anki would be showing up and expecting to go on a little adventure, and Anki wasn't sure if Biacoya's father would be home, which could complicate things. Biacoya's father was Tambu, the Chief of Vines. He was a burly man of average height, but he had thick, rough, dark skin which seemed to be more like the scales of a lizard than the flesh of a man. He had gone bald at some point long before Biacoya was born and Anki swore Tambu must polish his shiny scalp with coconut oil, because it reflected the sun like an obsidian mirror. Tambu was extremely strict and often violent, and he once broke his son's nose because Biacoya accidentally let one of their boar get loose. His father later apologized and said he didn't mean to strike Biacoya so hard, but the real damage was done. Now, Biacoya was scared to death of his own father and found any excuse to avoid going home after lessons.

Thankfully, there was no one in sight as Anki walked up the dock toward the cibmani stone street. On the other side of the street was the spirit shrine of Yucahu, which was exactly where it was located on every island except for Itabaca where a giant shrine to Bitabay took its place. Every island also had a temple dedicated to one of the spirits. The Temple of Kayki was on Conaca, and the Temple of Maroha was on Pacca.

Anki could see the roof of the temple through the palm trees, nearly two hundred reeds up the only hill, and in between was the vine yard where jara workers processed various trees to make rope, baskets, and lumber. The jara were named after the Itabayiti word for vine because they originally used the plentiful vines on the island to make rope, but that all changed when they discovered that rope made by weaving thin strips of palm tree wood was much stronger. The backside of the vine yard buildings faced the docks and Anki didn't see any workers, but he could hear them over there talking, sawing, and generally making quite a bit of noise.

He decided to go ahead and stroll east up the street toward the chief's residence on the hill, and if someone asked, he would just point to his official tunic and say it was none of their business. Anki was a little disappointed when no one bothered him as he strolled right past the vine yard and up the street into the jungle. After a while, the street curved north and Anki could see the temple ahead on his left. The Temple of Maroha was quiet as Anki approached it, likely meaning they were in prayer. He knew their rituals were typically done at first light, unless the Wind Spirit became angry and demanded that they deviate, but he couldn't be certain what any of the akin did during the day. Anki took a deep breath and continued strolling on past the stables on his right, then the attendants' quarters, and up the three steps to Biacoya's front door. He knocked.

There was a brief moment of silence and then he heard someone shuffling to the door. Anki took another, deeper breath – *please don't be Tambu, please don't be Tambu...*

The door opened and there was Biacoya eating a bowl of dried peach palm fruit. "I thought you might show up," he said, and then he turned and walked away, leaving the door open.

"You thought nothing." Anki poked his head in and looked around for Tambu. "Is your baba home?"

"He's down at the vine yard. Come in, ya dope!"

"Good," Anki said, stepping in and shutting the door. "First, give me some of that fruit. And second, grab your yaali tunic, because we're going on an adventure."

Biacoya held the bowl out for Anki, and Anki noticed his friend's right cheek was bruised and swollen. "What?" Biacoya said with a mouthful of dried fruit.

"Your baba is something else, isn't he?"

"Imagine what he might have done if he honestly believed we put that vinegar in the jar."

"Baga! Well, save your other cheek for when we get back." Anki chewed on the dried fruit and looked around Biacoya's home.

They had been best friends for as long as he could remember, but this was the first time he had ever been in the Chief of Vines residence. Of course, they were all the same. There was a main entrance that led to a hallway, and the hallway went right upstairs to the roof and left around a corner into a dining area. A fire basin sat in one corner beside several narrow wooden tables running along the same wall, while the opposite wall had two curtained doorways leading into two separate bedchambers. Anki noticed Biacoya's walls were completely barren, unlike the walls at his residence, which were entirely covered in flowers in varying states of decay.

"Depends on where we're going," his friend finally replied.

"You still have your training canuti beached on the east shore?"

"*Ikadun?* Of course, why? You want to head over to my hut? Oh, I found some starfish I wanted to show you!" Biacoya got really excited, set down his bowl of dried fruit, and ran into his bedchamber.

"Starfish? That sounds awesome, and I'm definitely interested, but I had something even better in mind!" Anki picked up the bowl of fruit and continued stuffing them in his mouth.

Biacoya hollered from his bedchamber, "Hey, why am I getting my yaali tunic?"

"Just put it on! We'll need it for this little adventure to work. And don't forget your sandals again!" Anki knew his friend was notorious for going barefoot.

"Look, frog breath, just tell me what we're doing," he said, emerging from his bedchamber in his yaali tunic and carrying a dead starfish the size of his head in one hand and his sandals in the other.

"Nice! Where'd you find it?"

"Promise you won't tell anyone? And I do mean *anyone!*"

Anki nodded. Biacoya gave him a side-eye and then whispered, "The Deeps."

"What?!" Anki shouted. The Deeps was what Anki and his friends called the area near the great wall where the shallows disappeared into a deep, dark, black nothingness.

"Shh!" Biacoya shushed him. "Let's sneak out my window in case baba's coming for midmeal. I'll explain on the way."

They went into Biacoya's bedchamber, pulled the shutters open, and climbed out one at a time. It was about the same distance from the docks to the residence as it was from Biacoya's window to the east shore, but they had to shove their way through the dense jungle to get there. Once Anki felt they were far enough away that no one might hear, he asked Biacoya to explain where he got the starfish.

"I found a hole in the great wall and went through it," he said matter-of-factly, ducking under a series of low tree limbs.

"How? Where? Details, Biacoya. I need details!" Anki followed Biacoya, ducking limbs and kicking through the underbrush. Jungle critters scurried away from the boys as they went.

"I was sailing over to my hut yesterday and decided I'll just keep going and sail along the wall a ways. There's that inlet grate at the base of the north wall, ya know, and sometimes I can find neat stuff there." He pushed through a clump of vines, each the size of the boys' arms, and then they emerged onto the east shore beach. "But when I got there the grate was busted, leaving a big hole. The current didn't seem that strong, so I went out."

They pushed Biacoya's training canuti off the beach into the shallows and climbed on.

"You went out? Like, out into the Great Sea!" Anki was impressed. He knew Biacoya was already an excellent sailor for his age, but tackling the wild waves of the Bocoa was another feat altogether.

"Wait," Biacoya stopped. "Where *are* we going?"

"Oh – Bahaca!" Anki puffed up his chest and held his head high. "Originally, I wanted to go to Niamca, but I also wanted to wear my yaali tunic. It felt like a waste to wear it to the springs, where we've been a hundred times, and I'd just take it off anyway. So, now, we are on official yaali business and have been sent to introduce ourselves to the Mawoakin."

"That may be the most incredible idea you've ever had!" Biacoya exclaimed, excitedly unfurling the sail. "And Abensu-baba said it was alright?"

"More or less. He gave me permission to go to Niamca, but what's the difference?"

Biacoya giggled while he tied off the kona-line, and then handed the chok-line to Anki. "Here, when I tell you to tie it off, loop this part of the rope through the oar-port here, and then run this part of the rope through that loop. Got it?"

Anki nodded. They had sailed several times before to the tiny island just off the east shore of Pacca where Biacoya's secret hut was and where he kept his stash of starfish, broken chaak blades, snake skins, and other collectables. Anki was fairly confident they could handle sailing to Bahaca. The wind had been reasonably strong all morning since it nearly blew Haro off the ferry and quickly caught the sail, thrusting the little canuti forward.

"Hey, look at that, we're making way in no time! Alright, tie off the kona-line, Anki!" Biacoya shouted over the wind.

Anki did as he was told. It was a bit more difficult than he expected what with the wind pushing on the sail and the sail pulling on the rope. Of course, he didn't know what he expected. Biacoya had always done this part already, but he had watched his friend ready the canuti to make way plenty of times. Finally, with the sail taught, Anki looked back at Biacoya and asked, "Well? The Deeps?"

Biacoya pulled the tiller toward himself, bringing them around the southeastern corner of Pacca. "Alright, on the other side of the wall, the Great Sea was kind of peaceful. I didn't get tossed around at all. The wind was a little stronger, but even that was manageable. And then I saw there were mooring posts along the waterline of the wall near the grate. I guess they were put there so someone could tie off and work on the grate, ya know, since the water is too deep to anchor. And that's when I got the idea to see if I could dive to the bottom."

"You went to the bottom of the wall? I don't think anyone has been to the bottom of the wall in a hundred years!" Biacoya never ceased to amaze Anki.

"Yeah! Well, it took a few tries, and the current was strong and tried to drag me away from the coral. Turns out, there's a lot of coral on the walls below the waterline. Every time I tried to dive, the current pulled at me, so I had to tie a rope around my waist to keep from getting pulled out to sea."

"What was at the bottom? What did you see?" Anki was getting impatient.

"It was really dark down there. I could hardly see my hand in front of my face. But I found a bunch of starfish *and* I can say that I have walked on the bottom of the Great Sea!"

Anki whistled and cheered, "My hero, Biacoya the Sea Walker!"

Biacoya bowed. "Thank you. Thank you."

They talked and joked some more, but it wasn't long before they needed to adjust the sail as they rounded the northwest cliffs of Bahaca. Compared to their islands, Bahaca was a monstrous beast. Cliffs wrapped around the entire island like bark on a tree and towered over their heads, making them have to crane their necks to see the northern rim. Biacoya aimed the canuti for the only beach instead of the docks. A moment later, they squished up onto the wet sand and the boys hopped off, pulling the canuti farther up the beach in order to avoid the tide taking her.

"I still think we should have pulled into a slip to look more official," Anki said as they made their way across the beach toward the wide-open mouth of the cave entrance to Bahaca.

"I can sail, Anki, but I can't pull into a slip yet," Biacoya admitted. "And there's only one Ikadun!"

Bahaca's cave entrance had been widened at some point in the past thousand years and was squared off on the sides where there were two copper-lined stone basins with blazing sponge torches in them. In the center of the curved roof hovering five or so reeds over the wet sand was a wedge-shaped stone and the carving of a perfect circle with a dot in the middle. Anki recognized it as the symbol of Mawoi, which he thought was fitting for the stump-like island.

As they walked in, he noticed they were actually walking on a cibmani stone street that had been poured into a carved path in the floor of the cave. He had not been expecting a street in the middle of a cave. A dozen paces in, the cave split with one tunnel going to the right and down, while another went up and to the left. Another symbol of Mawoi was carved into the rock wall of the tunnel on the left in the direction of the street, which was a good sign.

"I wonder what's down there," Biacoya said.

Anki pointed to a symbol carved into the rock wall of the other tunnel of one vertical line separated by three horizontal lines. "Means danger, right?" he asked and Biacoya nodded. "I guess we'll be going that way when we leave, huh? Got your sandals?"

"Yup," Biacoya replied and quickly slipped them on.

The incline of the cave up ahead was a bit steeper, and they could see flickering light after a bend in the ceiling, which they walked a little more briskly toward. Anki reminded himself they were supposed to be there and to remain calm and confident at all times. After the bend, they found a fresh reed torch in a copper-lined stone basin casting light in all directions, and up ahead was another flicker of light beyond the next bend – they ran toward this one. Their wet sandals slapped on the street and echoed off the rock walls of the cave. It sounded to Anki like when the Itabayiti held a festival in the rain, and everyone was dancing in the plaza. He was thinking about the dancing when he noticed Biacoya had suddenly stopped running. He turned around to find Biacoya's eyes were wide, and his face was a bit paler than usual.

"Taycoay, Yaali. Please, come with me," someone said behind him.

"Ahh!" Anki jumped as he spun around.

There, in a long yellow robe standing a few reeds away and holding a blazing torch was a girl. Her eyes were almost as black as obsidian and the firelight danced across them like moonlight on the sea. Her voice was also unlike any Anki had ever heard before. It was almost as if she were singing instead of talking, each word drifting into the next like notes from a jatbay. As unsettling as the girl's eyes were, Anki was intrigued by her hair. He had never seen anyone with hair like that, girl or boy. It was straight, short, and flat against her scalp, and was parted in the middle with each side tucked securely behind her ears.

"Will you *please* come with me?" she asked again.

Biacoya nudged Anki with his elbow and Anki cleared his throat, "Ahem, we *are*, um – yaali here to meet the Mawoakin."

"Yes, we know," the girl said. "We've been expecting you. Please, come with me." She turned and started walking up the slope toward the interior of the island, hiking her robe up with one hand and carrying the torch in the other.

"Of course," Anki said, nudging Biacoya to follow. Biacoya nudged Anki back, and then the two slapped at each other a moment before regaining their composure.

The girl in yellow led them out of the cave and into the light. The boys could see a spirit shrine to Boynay at the start of a shelly path that wound up a very steep slope. Anki thought it was a little odd and wondered where the shrine to Yucahu might be. The slope looked as steep as the steps of the Pyramid of Mayu, and at the top he could barely make out a couple of buildings that were painted white against a graying sky. Immediately to his right were the stables and the girl in yellow was calling them over with a big smile as she climbed onto a boar-drawn cart. Anki noticed the wooden handle of the torch she had been carrying was resting in another one of the copper-lined basins just outside of the cave.

"Well?" he asked Biacoya.

Biacoya raised his eyebrows and feigned a smile. "This is your plan. Lead the way, Yaali Anki."

Anki puffed out his chest again, held his head high, and said, "Follow me, Yaali Biacoya." And he marched over to the cart and climbed on.

After a moment, Biacoya hesitantly did the same, and they stood in the cart behind the smiling girl in yellow. She snapped the reins and the boar started forward – slowly at first, but then the boar found their stride.

Winding back and forth up the steep slope, taking in the scenery, the boys were wondering the same thing: who was this girl and how did she know they were coming? *She's very pretty*, Anki thought. The girl had long legs like Sheka, and a touch of freckles on her clay-colored cheeks like Numila. She had eyes as black as the darkest, moonless night, which Anki had only ever seen in uca birds. Her dimpled chin looked like it could have been molded out of clay. As fascinated as he was by her, it really was weird, if not kind of awesome, how their plan was actually working. Neither of the boys knew any children that had been to the Temple of the Dawn. And other than old Ikmo, Anki was fairly certain most adults had never been either. What the Mawoakin did to awaken Mawoi every morning was one of the many assumptions in life, like that the field workers were planting, or the fishermen were fishing. No one truly paid much attention until something went wrong.

They crested the southeastern edge of a crescent shaped plateau that wrapped around the eastern rim of the island. The wind on the plateau ripped at their clothes, forcing Anki to turn away. Getting a little queasy with his eyes closed, he opened them and looked back down the slope. He saw the darkness of the cave at the bottom and the only way he could describe it was like the mouth of some sort of ancient monster devouring the earth.

The cart came to an abrupt stop behind a large building about twice the size of Anki's residence on Conaca. He noticed the western wall was only half-finished and was more like a giant window. He could see clearly into what he suddenly realized was a temple. Up ahead to the north he saw

127

the two white buildings from before, which he now assumed were the attendants' quarters.

"You may get off now," the girl in yellow said, waiting for Anki and Biacoya to get off the cart so that she could. Realizing this, they hurriedly jumped off. "Thank you," she said. "Now, which one of you is the eldest?" Biacoya half-raised his hand, giving Anki a confused look. "Very well. You will be speaking with Boakin Tanoc, and you," she pointed to Anki. "You will only listen. Is that clear?" The boys nodded pensively. "Good," she said with a smile and turned to leave.

Anki stopped her with a raised hand. "Um – excuse me, but what is your name?"

"My name is Soci," she said, placing her right hand on her chest. "Now, come with me to..."

Anki interrupted her. "Nice to meet you Soci, my name is..."

But before he could introduce himself, Soci put her soft finger to Anki's mouth. "No-no, we do not need your names. The boakin insists. Now, follow me."

Biacoya shrugged his shoulders and followed Soci around the northwest corner of the temple, while Anki lingered a moment looking in the window of the temple. He saw carvings and paintings on the walls and ceiling, and a towering pillar in the center with more carvings all around it. He leaned his head in the window to get a closer look and was amazed by the vast number of colorful murals all over the inside. There were images of men and women fighting what looked like giant howler monkeys dressed in green loincloths. A black snake with dark-azure eyes, bigger than any snake he had ever seen, instantly reminded him of the carving of Kanu next to the grand staircase, which then made him wonder if the murals were meant to depict the Yayapti. He was about to climb through the window to get a better look when Biacoya suddenly grabbed his arm and yanked him away.

"Come on, they're waiting," he said, frantically.

"They?"

On the other side of the temple, the boys walked toward a bench where a little boy was sitting next to a tree. He appeared to be about six years old and was dressed in a similar yellow robe, except his robe had elaborate red-stitched patterns running down the sleeves and around the cuffs. Anki noticed the boy's hair was similarly flat against his little head and

128

cut short to where it didn't quite touch his eyebrows. And then the wind through the tree leaves caught his attention. The tree was similar to the mangroves he knew well, but the teardrop leaves were shiny and light green on one side and dark green on the other. There was what looked like green fruit dangling from its thin branches, which looked like thousands of long ugly fingers poking into the air.

The little boy squinted against the wind and smiled as they approached. "Yaali! Mawoi-coay," he said and bowed slightly. Anki bowed, knocking Biacoya's elbow in the process, and then Biacoya also bowed. "I'm Boakin Tanoc and I am happy to meet you!" He was addressing Biacoya. Biacoya started to say something but appeared to think better of it and nodded instead. Boakin Tanoc patted the seat next to him and said, "Come, sit with me."

Biacoya looked at Anki, but Anki was looking at Soci who was staring at Biacoya expectantly. Biacoya smiled at the girl in yellow and sat down next to the little boy.

It was weird, Anki thought his friend looked nervous, even though he knew Biacoya was the bravest and most confident of all their friends. He swam to the bottom of the Bocoa, the current pulling at him, running out of breath, all just so he could get a starfish. It was strange to see Biacoya uncomfortable on dry land, so Anki looked up at the dark clouds starting to block out the sun. He sniffed at the wind – *smells like a storm coming.*

"We had a meal planned, but you're early." The boakin was looking at Biacoya, waiting for him to say something. Anki was surprised by how well spoken the little boy was.

Biacoya answered slowly and paused often, "Yes, there – uh – had been an issue with the – umm – ceremonial plates." Astonishingly, Anki's friend wasn't telling a lie.

"The Day of Biyaya is tomorrow," the boakin said, more of a statement than a question.

"Yes," Biacoya looked at Anki. "So, the Chief of Wares needs us later." This also wasn't a complete lie because Anki's father would probably have them help load the Yaya's order onto the transport canuti when it was finished. He watched Biacoya wipe his sweaty palms against his tunic, and then he pointed to the sky, adding, "There's a storm coming."

Boakin Tanoc nodded, "There is. Mawoi needs to cleanse us all." Anki was pretty sure the boakin had misspoken. It wasn't Mawoi who brought the storms, which was Yuraca, but he was told not to speak and so he didn't. "Will you leave soon?" the boakin asked, a hint of sadness in his little voice.

Biacoya looked at Anki who was nodding his head urgently. "Yes, I'm afraid so," he finally answered.

"Then we will talk of other things." The little boy looked up at Soci who nodded and gestured to another akin in a yellow robe, who neither Anki nor Biacoya had seen join their meeting.

He was a full-grown man with a big curly beard and a prominent brow over dark-brown eyes, which Anki thought made him look like an uca bird – fitting, considering they were wearing yaali tunics with that big uca footprint on the chest. The big man leaned over the boakin's little shoulder and handed him a small wooden box. As he did, a dark cloud growled over their heads.

"Thanks, Goacolo," the boakin said and turned to Biacoya. "Take this to Boadulu Urtulu but be careful with it." The little boy looked up at Soci. "It's a gift," he said and then handed the box to Biacoya with a tiny smile. There was a roll of thunder and the boakin laughed, "Mawoi is pleased."

Anki was watching Boakin Tanoc and Soci closely. The boakin was giddy and bouncing on the bench like the little boy he clearly was, and Soci had the same unwavering smile on her face, but it still felt like something wasn't right. It was hard to believe Tanoc was so young, when he seemed to form better sentences than most of Anki's friends. Besides that, he and Biacoya came up with a spur-of-the-moment plan out of boredom. Had he not seen his yaali tunic folded up and sitting there at the foot of his bed, he wouldn't have thought to put it on. And if he hadn't put on the fine tunic, he wouldn't have felt like playing the role for Haro. And if he hadn't allowed his imagination to run wild, he and Biacoya wouldn't be there, exposed on the eastern rim of Bahaca with the boakin about to send them on a clandestine errand to deliver a box to the chief of the palace guards.

"Do you understand?" the little boy asked of Biacoya.

Anki didn't hear what the boakin had said, but Biacoya was playing the part well. *We are yaali and on official business*, he could almost hear his friend telling himself.

Biacoya smiled. "Of course, Boakin Tanoc. We will deliver this to the boadulu as soon as we return."

"NO!" Soci shouted, but then she quickly composed herself. "Sorry, my Boakin. No, it must be delivered tomorrow before the ceremony."

"Of course, yes, that's what I meant," Biacoya corrected himself. He then stood nervously and then bowed. "We must go now."

Boakin Tanoc stood as well and made a small hand gesture to Soci that was too quick for Anki to make out what it was, but Soci instantly bowed and darted off toward the attendants' quarters. There was a loud crackle of thunder as the bearded man called Goacolo grabbed Anki and Biacoya by their arms. His hands were warm and strong, and it made Anki want to scream, but he bit his lower lip.

"Mawoi will not be happy if you are dishonest," the boakin said. He felt the fabric of Biacoya's yaali tunic between his thumb and pointer finger, paying close attention to the stitching with a troubling expression forming on his little boy face. A few drops of rain fell on his hand, and he suddenly put his hands behind his back, smiled with a mouthful of little teeth, and said, "Mawoi-coay, Yaali."

Goacolo yanked the boys by their arms back the way they had come from behind the temple, and then pushed them toward the boar-drawn cart. "Go," he said and walked away toward the attendants' quarters without looking back.

The boys couldn't move fast enough. Anki grabbed the reins while Biacoya hopped onto the cart behind him, the small wooden box in his hand. They sped down the slope, skidding around the corners of the gravel path as it wrapped back on itself, the cart at times even pushing the poor boar who were huffing and squealing loudly the entire time. It seemed to have taken a very long time to ascend the slope, but they made it back to the stables and the mouth of the cave in what felt like a single breath.

Biacoya hopped off and grabbed the half-burned torch from the basin as Anki rode the cart directly into the stables. Suddenly, a sheet of rain dropped from the sky in thick, heavy streams like the waterfall on Amaca, and the boys ran into the cave. Rainwater was already starting to trickle down the stone path and Biacoya led the way holding the dying torch. They didn't speak at first and reached the next basin in silence where they swapped the dying torch for the slightly-less-dying torch in the basin, the flickering light shimmering off a widening stream beneath their feet.

Anki looked back up the path behind them, making sure they weren't being followed. "What in the name of Kayki was all that about?" he asked, allowing his internal confusion to finally erupt from his mouth.

"I don't know, and I don't want to know. All I want to do is get *off* this island!" Biacoya almost shouted, peering ahead in the dim, flickering light.

"What are you going to do with that?" he pointed to the box Biacoya was carrying.

Biacoya examined it for a moment, as if he had forgotten he had the box, and then tucked it into his belt. "I don't know that either."

The reed torch finally died as they reached the split in the cave, but even with the storm the midday light filtered through the opening of the cave, and they noticed the trickle of rainwater had become a rushing river that was now curving to the left and down the other tunnel.

"Want to at least check it out before we go?" Anki asked.

"Sure do, but I really just want to sail Ikadun far away from this island."

"Why'd you name it that anyway?"

"Because she'll be the death of me," Biacoya answered, matter-of-factly.

"Oh." Anki feared there was a good chance that name could come back to bite them. And that's when they both heard a noise coming from the tunnel on the left. "What was that?"

"Shh," Biacoya shushed him, listening intently.

"Help," a soft voice seemed to cry out in the darkness.

Biacoya started cautiously walking down the tunnel while Anki raced to the mouth of the cave. "Where are you going?" Biacoya asked over his shoulder.

"We need light!"

Anki ran out into the rain to the basin on his left, but it was already filled with rainwater, a soggy sponge floating on the surface. He looked to the other basin and was relieved to see a hint of light. He dashed through

132

the deluge and found the basin was better protected from the rain and only half-filled, the sponge just barely sticking above the surface of the water. He reached in and grabbed it, dashed back under the cover of the cave, and used his tunic to soak up some of the moisture. He then cracked the tip of the wooden torch handle against the rock floor, gently squeezed the bottom of the burning sponge into the crack, and, after a moment, the flame came back to life.

Biacoya was already a dozen paces into the dark tunnel when Anki came running up behind him, torchlight bouncing off the rock and the rushing river, growing stronger and louder with each step. They waded through a section of the cave that had already flooded up to their hips before emerging onto a drier bank a reed wide. Black smoke trailed upward behind them, while the cave continued downward with a slightly smaller stream trickling between their feet.

"Help...m-me!" They heard the weak voice again, barely audible over the cacophony of water behind them as they came to another split in the cave.

Anki shoved the torch into both openings. "Well?" he asked.

Biacoya closed his eyes and listened. Anki thought he looked silly, but after a moment his friend confidently pointed down the tunnel with the widening stream. "This way," he said, his sandaled feet sloshing through the water.

"I beg-g...you, p-please, h-help?" The voice was strained but getting louder.

After a few more paces, they watched Anki's torchlight bounce along the cave floor until it suddenly vanished down a hole, along with the flooding rainwater.

"Hey! Who...ev-ver you are, help...m-me!"

The boys both leaned over the edge of the hole, Anki's torch first flickering off the damp rock walls, but then off the dirty face of a terrified girl about five reeds down. She was standing in water up to her armpits, her long black braid of hair over her shoulder, wearing what looked to Anki like the dark-azure tunics of the araco.

"Ch-children?!" she whimpered, her teeth chattering. "Just...p-perfect!"

"Hey, who are you and what are you doing in this hole? You could drown, you know?" There wasn't a trace of irony in Biacoya's voice.

"Oh, I d-don't know, I j-just...th-thought I'd give it a t-try," she said sarcastically. "What do you th-think?" Her voice was weak and cracked from exhaustion, and they could clearly tell she was both extremely cold and extremely bitter.

"We can do that, I think." Anki looked around for something to use to pull the girl out.

"Rope!" Biacoya shouted. "I have rope on my canuti! Be right back." Then he ran off into the darkness, his frantic steps splashing and echoing throughout the cave.

"Who are you?" Anki asked.

"T-Ta-ba-ba," she said, the water up to her shoulders and still pouring in.

"Taycoay, Tutababa, I'm Anki," he said with a wave.

"*Tay...c-coay?*" she coughed. "If you're f-friend doesn't...g-get back s-soon, I'm p-probably going to...d-drown. I hope m-my s-spirit...p-p-possess-ess you!" She spit out a mouthful of water and continued to shiver.

Anki backed up a step. He felt himself getting upset, but he took a deep, humid breath and told himself this wasn't about him. He wasn't in trouble, Tutababa was, and she needed him to be calm. "Fine, I'm sorry," he said.

Tutababa rolled her eyes, "Ch-children."

Anki thought Tutababa didn't look much older than he was. "How old are you?" he asked.

"F-F-Fourteen...I think." She sighed and rolled her eyes. "I'm n-not...s-sure."

"Why not?" Anki asked immediately.

"Ugh! Be-Because my b-brother and I...w-were handed-d over to the C-C-Cult of M-Mayu when we were b-born, and they d-don't...k-keep ba-baby records."

"I knew it!" Anki almost danced. "You're an araco. I always wanted to be an araco."

"T-Trade you...p-p-places," Tutababa joked. They both laughed nervously while the rainwater kept coming and the hole continued to fill.

"Hey," Anki had a thought. "Why don't we just let the hole fill up and then you can just walk out with me and Biacoya?"

"Because it's already flooded back there," Biacoya said, appearing seemingly out of nowhere and soaking wet. "Here." He handed Anki one end of a bundle of equally wet rope. "If we stay here much longer, we won't be able to swim out."

"*Swim?*" Anki didn't like the sound of that.

Biacoya tied the rope around Anki before looping it around himself, and then he tossed the rest of it down the hole to where it dangled about a half-a-reed above Tutababa's head. She quickly ducked her head under the water, crouched at the bottom of the hole, and then sprang upward like Okid out of Maboti's boiling pot. She reached out with her right arm for the rope and caught it, and the rope instantly tugged on the boys who slid forward a bit before finding their footing.

"Whoa," Biacoya groaned from the sudden weight. "First try!"

"Whoo-hoo!" Anki exclaimed.

"Backup, Anki," Biacoya directed.

The boys slowly walked backward through the rushing water, making sure to alternate their steps. Bit by bit, Tutababa was hauled up and out of the hole. She lay there on the edge catching her breath for a moment while the boys plopped down on their butts panting as well. There was a crunching sound as Biacoya sat.

"What was that?" Anki asked, just before the torch went out.

CHAPTER TWELVE
The Spark of Twin Fires

The waves in the sound had become increasingly choppy, tossing the training canuti from side to side and almost rolling them several times. There were a few scattered graying clouds in the sky, but Atu knew Bocoani Numila was listening to Niama. If the waters of the sound were this rough, it meant the Great Sea would be much worse. They could all see a storm was rapidly approaching, it was obvious, and the bocoani finally ordered the shoats to turn the canuti around and head back to the docks.

"Aww," some of them moaned, though Atu couldn't understand why.

"Knock it off, shoats. I don't need your baba or your itaba coming down on me when one of you drowns," Numila said, holding on to the headrib. A moment later, Hamsi pulled on the tiller and brought them round swiftly.

Atu held onto the kona-line, leaning against the midrib, and looked over at Joba. They had been eyeing each other for two days straight, but Atu hadn't figured out what any of it meant. She was promised to Draha, and challenging arranged marriages was completely unheard of. *Well, not completely unheard of,* he thought. Everyone knew Yaya Amnu had stolen Unana Wani away from Boyiti Macoca when they were his age, but it was still very rare. Joba caught Atu staring at her, and she shied away, pulling on the chok-line and tying it off.

"Well done, Joba and Atu. Maybe you're capable of learning after all!" Numila said. "Hamsi, I know you're not great at pulling into the slip but please, try not to break *another* pylon."

"Yes, Bocoani," Hamsi yelped, nervously.

"I have faith in you, Hamsi," Demican squeaked.

His voice had suddenly started getting deeper the past couple of days, but it sometimes seemed unable to make up its mind. Atu noticed Kachi and Tunku snickering at his friend, eliciting a threatening look from Demican, but Atu didn't want to get involved. He had come too far with Joba to ruin it by behaving like a silly boy, even if he was staring across the sound with a silly smile on his face.

"Furl the sail," Numila ordered. The boys stopped snickering and went to work while Hamsi gently guided the reed boat. They slowly coasted toward the docks. "Keep her steady," Numila said, his eye on one of the pylons. "Steady, Hamsi – ease her in." There was a slight scraping sound as the canuti skidded snuggly into the slip, and then Demican tossed the mooring line over the stone mooring post. "Alright, get off my canuti," Numila ordered.

The bocoani leapt past Atu over the kona side and onto the dock. He then turned and walked away, looking up irritatingly at the thickening gray clouds overhead.

Atu watched the other boys hop off as well, but he waited for Joba, thinking maybe he could offer to help her. He wasn't sure what he would do, only that he wanted to do something. The tension he felt between them had been growing, but Draha had been standing at the dock every day they returned from lessons. He looked at the dock now and, so far, Draha was nowhere in sight.

"What are you waiting for, milky?" Kachi said, sticking his tongue out at Atu.

Tunku laughed, but Atu just smiled back and shook his head. He did not want to make a fool of himself in front of Joba. He glanced at her and saw the concern in her eyes.

"Baby brother isn't around to stand up for you is he, cotton-ball? Are you just going to stand there and wait for him?" Tunku started pretending to cry and then Kachi joined in, but there was a sudden crackle of thunder that startled all of them.

Just then, a few drops of rain sent Kachi and Tunku running toward the harbor. Demican and Hamsi both knew Atu had a thing for Joba, because most of the boys had a thing for Joba. They each gave Atu a nod of encouragement and then chased after Kachi and Tunku, hollering insults at the jerks.

"Well," Joba said, sliding across the spine toward him. "What *are* you waiting for?"

She held out her hand delicately for him to take and he did, a feeling of supreme elation washing over him, and then he helped her step off the canuti and onto the dock. As they did, the rain started to come down in sheets. Laughing, they raced for cover beneath the palms that lined the other side of the street. More thunder erupted in the sky and flashes of lightning reflected off of every wet surface. The palm fronds dipped from the weight of the sudden pooling rainwater and dumped it right on top of their heads.

"Aww, man!" Atu exclaimed, stepping out from under the palm and into the downpour.

Joba was right there beside him. She looked over to the dark lighthouse not too far away. "Come on," she said and dashed through the sheets of rain.

Atu gave chase and they laughed and played tag, their sandaled feet leaving crisscrossing prints in the soggy sand all along the way. Their game of tag quickly developed into a one-on-one game of Okid, but the game was usually played with seven people, making it less of a game and more of a dance. When played right, a circle was drawn on the ground to represent Maboti's pot and one player was picked to start as the frog ancestor. He crouched in the middle of the pot while the other six spaced themselves evenly around the pot. Okid's goal was to leap out of the pot while the other six ran in a circle and could use one hand to stop him. If Okid caught one of the six, then Okid yelled "Maboti!" and they switched places. As it was just the two of them, Joba and Atu were just switching places between themselves, gradually spinning their way toward the lighthouse.

There was a near simultaneous flash of bright light and a crack of thunder, which made them both shriek. They immediately rushed through the open doorway and into the ground-level chamber of the lighthouse, the rain outside echoing throughout the stone structure and sounding like an endless yawn. Joba abruptly turned to Atu and smiled.

"Did you know," she started excitedly, "originally, the Itabayiti relied on two huge bonefires here to light up the rocks and protect the canuti? They only built the lighthouses so the fires could see over the wall." Atu stared at her blankly. He hoped she could see how in awe he was of her, but he was pretty sure he just looked like a wet rat with a broken jaw. "I think this level was originally used to house the agur before they were relocated to Chacuca."

"Really?" Atu asked, definitely impressed. The things she was saying seemed familiar, as if he had once known more about the lighthouses but had forgotten about it for one reason or another. And then he remembered having a similar conversation with his father not too long ago.

"Yeah. The lighthouses actually extend above the walls another two reeds where the giant cibmani basins and their polished copper mirrors can direct the light downward."

Atu knew Joba was knowledgeable and that she was an excellent sailor, but this was another level of intelligence he had not expected, and he liked it. "I wonder if somebody already lit the basins," he said, just to have something to add to the conversation, which made him sound like Hamsi.

"They better have, or we're going to lose some canuti today!" Joba shook the rain off her body like a wild boar and hollered up to the next level, "Hey, anybody up there?!" Only the wind and torrential rain replied.

Atu looked up the circular staircase to the second level where there was another smaller chamber and doorways leading right and left onto the top of the wall. He felt great, though a little intimidated by Joba. Besides her immense lighthouse knowledge, there was something about her that made him feel exceptionally feisty and sure of himself. Without any further hesitation, he started up the stone steps, his soaking wet sandals squishing beneath his feet. "Taycoay?" he hollered. Joba followed behind him, kicking excess water from each long leg as she took the steps two at a time.

The howling wind grew louder and louder the closer they got to the second level. Atu could feel a near deafening pressure in his head, and there was a pulling sensation all over his body as if a monstrous beast was sucking them up into its mouth. The wind tore through the small chamber from the northwest doorway, swirled in the center like a funnel cloud, and then rushed out the doorway to the southeast. Bits of debris and sand spun around and scratched at their faces and any exposed skin.

"Sweet Bitabay!" Atu exclaimed, shielding his face and eyes with his arms. He saw Joba do the same, joining him in the chamber. He quickly grabbed her hand, "Let's keep going!"

He took them up the second staircase, which was much narrower than the first, to the third and final chamber. Although they were higher and more exposed to the storm, the angle of the walls kept most of the wind and rain out of what was known as the fire chamber. It was much smaller than the other two, with a quarter of the wall open to the harbor below and the fire basin and mirror in the center, which they instantly noticed was definitely not lit.

"Ha!" Atu shook his head. "Someone's going to get reassigned."

"Not if we help," Joba said.

Atu rolled his eyes, or at least he thought he had. He looked at her, a pleading expression on her pretty face, and then he shrugged his shoulders. "How do you suppose we do that?"

Joba walked around the dimly lit chamber looking at the floor near the basin. Then she turned to the walls, looking everywhere until she appeared to find what she was looking for. "Ah-ha!" she exclaimed, pointing to a niche in the center of the curved wall. "A sparker!"

"Wonderful! And where's the wood?" Atu was definitely not going to go hack down a tree in this storm. Then again, he thought, for Joba? He might do just about anything for her.

"Uh – right below the sparker," Joba replied.

There, directly below the sparker, was a neatly arranged pile of very large and very dry logs. She strained picking one up and waddled over to the basin. Atu sighed. He didn't want to move the logs, they looked heavy, and he wasn't a fan of starting fires ever since Anki accidentally set Atu's bed ablaze playing with a sparker. But that something about Joba pulled him toward her until he found himself grabbing the end of one of the smaller logs and dragging it across the floor. It surprisingly didn't take them long to get all of the logs into the basin, and then Joba snatched the sparker out of the niche in the wall.

"You do it," she said, offering the sparker to Atu.

"Me?" Atu raised his hands. "No, no, this is your idea."

"I really don't know what I'm doing, but fine," she said.

Joba examined the sparker a moment, turning the device around a few times, opening and closing the sticks, and then she slapped them together – *SNAP!* A few sparks popped up into the air making her giggle.

"This is so neat!" she exclaimed, and then moved over to the basin and leaned over the logs. "Alright, stand at my side and block the wind."

Atu tried to roll his eyes, but they seemed to be locked in a perpetual, silly, mesmerized stare. All he could do was smile and stand beside her as she opened and closed the sparker numerous times in a row – *SNAP-SNAP-SNAP-SNAP-SNAP!* Sparks flew everywhere, falling all over the dry logs, onto the stone basin, and even landing on Atu's arm, which stung. A moment later, the fire roared to life, forcing Joba and Atu to back up around the side near the staircase to get away from the blazing heat.

"Whoa!" he exclaimed, rubbing his singed arm. The sudden flash of firelight momentarily unlocked his mesmerized eyes.

"You alright?" Joba asked.

"Yeah," he lied.

She looked over the edge of the chamber, through the pouring rain, to the rocks below, and then turned to the mirror. "Hmm, the light isn't hitting them," she said, before grabbing the bottom of the mirror. Joba instantly pulled her hand away, shouting, "Ow! It's hot!"

"Well, there is a big fire right next to it," Atu smirked, still rubbing his arm.

She took off her sandal and used it to pull on the bottom of the mirror, which started tilting. "Let me know when the light hits the rocks."

Atu looked over the edge, waited until the beam of light struck the rocks, and then he said, "We're good!"

Joba skipped over to look, trying to put her wet sandal back on at the same time. "You know what we should do?" she asked, and then looked toward the dark lighthouse at the other end of the harbor.

"What?" he asked, pensively, feeling his dumb eyes starting to lock on hers again.

"Light the other fire." She tapped Atu on his forehead. "You're it." And then she ran down the stairs to the second chamber below. Atu blinked several times, his broken rat jaw dangling open, and then he gave chase.

The wind on the second level was strong enough to push them through the southeast doorway and onto the narrow catwalk that stretched over the Steps of Ajan. Rain washed over them in waves as lightning crackled through the dark clouds in the sky and flashed off the wet stone beneath their feet. If it wasn't for the wind trying to blow them over the edge, they would have made it to the other lighthouse in no time, but they had to move slowly, bent over, and with one hand on each of the knee-high walls on either side of the catwalk.

Joba reached the other side first and immediately charged up the staircase to the fire chamber, but Atu wasn't too far behind her. They went through the now familiar motions and Joba offered the sparker to Atu again, but he insisted she be the one to finish what they started. She snapped the sparker several times, sparks flew, and the fire roared to life. They were professionals.

"Look at us," she said. "The Yaya should give us this job. We're great at it!"

Atu laughed. "If you say so. I just enjoy watching you get excited about lighting fires!"

Joba smiled and pushed him. "Only because it helps keep people from dying on the rocks!" She turned the sparker around in her hand. "But this thing is awesome!"

"So..." he started to ask about Draha but stopped himself.

"So, what?"

"Nothing," he spun away.

"What's nothing? What were you going to say?" She put the sparker back in its niche.

"I feel weird." Atu squirmed.

Joba giggled. "Well, it's been a bit of a weird day." She grabbed his hand and pulled him down to sit beside her on the top stair, and then she frowned, the wind and rain howling around them. "It's about me being promised to Draha, isn't it?"

Atu rubbed the back of his head and shrugged, "Maybe?" His stomach was tickling him like crazy, and he could feel his heart beating harder than a plaza-full of gourd drums. They had been having fun and running around lighting fires, which only intensified his feelings for this girl. She was sitting right there next to him, alone, in a lighthouse, in the middle of a storm.

"My itaba used to bring me to see these lighthouses," she said, thankfully interrupting his spiraling thoughts. "She thought it was important to visit all of Itabacan's great structures and learn about our history from all perspectives." Joba looked at him and smiled meekly, rainwater still clinging to her chin. "Baba has never been interested in anything that doesn't directly involve Amaca. He takes his position seriously, I guess. Itaba lets him. She gave up trying to get him interested in anything else long before I was born. At least, that's what she says."

Atu was pretty familiar with Joba's father, Mugan Galo. During the peak of the rainy season, he and Anki traveled over to Amaca and floated down the Osani River, snaking back and forth through the densely forested interior of the island and passing the Mugan's three huts along the way. Every now and then, Galo would yell at them to get out of the river, but if they remained in the river, it was pretty easy to avoid him. A towering plateau called Osanum dominated a third of Amaca where a waterfall ten times taller than the Pyramid of Mayu cascaded down the cliff face and crashed into the ground far below. After creating an unbearably cold lake, the waterfall fed into the mighty river. Some said there was a lake of healing waters at the top of the plateau feeding the waterfall, which was why the lesini prayed at the Temple of Osani at the foot of the plateau.

"Is the river really filled with healing waters?" he suddenly asked her.

"I don't know," she answered with a sigh. "That's what baba says, but he also swears he saw a woman appear out of a herd of brocket, scaring them away just before he could spear one." Joba giggled and then wiped her face on the collar of her tunic.

Atu really liked hearing her giggle, but he especially liked making her giggle. "Your baba would've speared me and Anki, if he ever caught us messing with his huts," Atu admitted.

Joba smiled at him, "Really?"

"Promise, you won't tell?" he asked. Joba quickly turned toward him and pressed two fingers from her right hand to her lips. He understood the gesture, she was saying her lips were sealed, but Atu had never seen anyone do it that way before. "Fine, I guess."

"That's how my baba says he promises," she explained and then giggled again. "I think it's a Mugan thing."

"Sure – a *Mugan* thing," he teased her, and Joba elbowed him playfully as a series of lightning flashes illuminated the inside wall of the stairwell in front of them, causing their shadows to dance and overlap each other. A moment later, deep rolling thunder grumbled through the lighthouse, and then the rain seemed to grow quieter. Not wanting to waste anymore of the storm, Atu abandoned his story about messing with the Mugan and leapt headfirst into what he really wanted to know. "Joba?" he said, quietly.

"Atu," she mocked him with a goofy grin.

"Why Draha?" he asked, and Joba's smiling face instantly saddened. It was the fastest change of expressions Atu had ever seen on anybody, and then, as troubling as her now sad face was, Joba turned away from him.

"He wasn't my choice," she answered, coldly.

"I'm sorry, I just..." Atu tried to apologize, but she cut him off.

"Stop, please," she told him, putting her hand on his. "Let me explain." She looked into his eyes with the fire behind them reflecting in hers, mesmerizing him until he nodded. "I did not choose Draha, my itaba did. We were visiting Mayu Hall after the Canutaloc last year, and Elder Sengri introduced us." She looked out the open wall of the lighthouse to the still-grey clouds hovering over Itabacan. "I was just there with my itaba to learn about Mayu Hall, not to have the rest of my life decided for me."

The Canutaloc festival came during the dry season and celebrated the gift of the canuti to the Itabayiti by Kanu, the Great Serpent. Atu remembered seeing Joba at the festival covered in dust, her long black hair down and swaying while she danced with everyone else in the Grand Plaza. He recalled Demican nudging him and encouraging him to go dance with her, but he had refused. He gave some stupid excuse like if Orlil destined them to be together, then Joba would come to him.

"Anyway," she continued. "Draha led us around the hall, explaining all of the different mul painted on the ceiling, the relevance of the thirteen pillars, and other things like that. I guess at some point, itaba and Elder Sengri lingered farther back from us and, well, they...made it all happen." Joba threw her hands up and shrugged her shoulders. "The next thing I knew, my itaba began sewing my marriage belt."

Atu didn't know what to say, except that he hated himself for not having listened to Demican and danced with Joba during the festival. "It would be a shame to allow one frayed thread to unravel the whole thing," he said quietly, mostly to himself.

"What was that?" she asked, looking at him again with her mesmerizing eyes. "I couldn't hear you over this ridiculous wind."

"Nothing. It's – just, nothing," Atu replied. It was his turn to look away, not because he didn't want to stare into her fiery eyes, but because he didn't want her to see the pain in his.

"I like you, Atu," she said behind him. "But I'm not supposed to. I was glad you waited for me at the dock because I wanted to be able to at least spend some time, any time with you before I'm married to Draha. After that, you and I might never see each other again." He heard her start to cry and quickly spun around to put his hand on her shoulder.

He wanted to console her, to hold her, to make her happy, but he was also so angry. He was angry at himself, angry at Suga-itaba, and Elder Sengri, and at the Ageless Daughter for weaving the whole terrible mess for them. Atu wanted to storm right out of the lighthouse, march up to the Pyramid of Mayu, and tell Draha to his face that he was taking Joba away from him and that there was nothing he could do about it. Forget destinies, marriage belts, promises broken or kept. How could Atu forget his own feelings? How could they forget the love clearly sparking between them, like the flames of the two fires they just lit? Unfortunately, there were so many thoughts and emotions running wild through his mind that Atu didn't say or do anything.

"I understand if you're upset," she said and then stood to leave, while he remained seated. He couldn't decide what to do. "I better go," she said and started down the steps.

"Wait." Atu grabbed Joba's hand and stood. With her down one step, they were actually the same height, which was convenient because Atu had decided he was going to kiss her.

The lighthouse fire was raging behind him, wind howled around them, and a low rumble of thunder accented their heated encounter. But as Atu closed his eyes and leaned in with his lips puckered, Joba suddenly let go of his hand and ran down the stairs as fast as she could. Atu's momentum carried him forward and down a step, causing him to almost fall over in the process.

"Aww, man!" he exclaimed, alone, to himself and the lighthouse.

CHAPTER THIRTEEN

A Shudder of Visions

Biacoya couldn't breathe, or he didn't want to breathe. He coughed again and the pain in his throat and chest was excruciating. It was a sensation like nothing he had ever experienced before. He imagined thousands of crazy ants racing back and forth from his mouth to his stomach, biting and tickling with their tiny legs, all while wasps built a nest in his throat that kept getting bigger and bigger. He tried to crawl to the stream, thinking maybe a drink of rainwater, even the salty seawater of the Bocoa might soothe the agony, but his arms were like the thick vines on Pacca and crumpled under the weight of his body.

"Biacoya?" he heard Anki call out to him, but he couldn't discern direction. His thoughts were cloudy, his sight useless in the black nothingness, and his hearing was being bombarded by a high-pitched buzzing.

"Tabba?" Anki called out again, maybe a little closer, or so he thought.

He tried to get Anki's attention and moaned, "Hhnn..." The pain from his effort was too much. He writhed in agony until there was a strange sort of peace...

A fuzzy rope in his hands stretched upward through a gap in the canopy of the jungle, straight up to Kuraka. The Moon Spirit's face glowed with anticipation, and Biacoya could hear the sound of gourd drums thumping through the trees in all directions. He felt palm fronds embrace him, folding around his cold body, and the breath of the Great Spirit rippled through his limbs, out the tips of his fingers, and then back into his nose and mouth. His grip on the fuzzy rope was strong and he climbed effortlessly through the gap and broke through the canopy.

All at once, Biacoya's mouth was filled with seawater. He was choking and coughing. The gurgling pain shocked open his eyes to a hazy darkness that was bumpy and passing just a reed's width away from his face. He could feel his warm breath rebound off the cold rock and back into his eyes.

"Hhnn..." he tried to moan, a test to see if he was awake or still asleep. There was a loud splash nearby and he heard Anki's voice.

"Don't worry, buddy, we've got you..." But then there was a burning and piercing sensation, like ember needles stabbing all over his body, and the high-pitched buzzing returned...

Biacoya laughed, the cool breeze in the stillness of the night tickling his skin. The thumping from the gourd drums was distant now, below him, and he heard a spattering of voices like a chorus of birds in perfect harmony. The singing was neither near nor far, but within him and about him at the same time. Their tonal vibrations coursed through every muscle of his body, and he rode on their wave through the void toward the smoldering embers of Mayu.

A salty mist suddenly struck his cheek and splashed into his eyes. Biacoya blinked, seeing stinging flashes of a swirling light-gray sky, and then he turned his head. He saw Anki caked in mud, a trickle of blood running down the side of his face from the top of his head to his chin, and then he only saw the stormy clouds again. His field of view rose and fell, and he quickly realized he was lying on Ikadun in the tumultuous shallows. "My...hhnn..." He wanted to help, but there was a buzzing wasps' nest lodged in his throat, swelling like a puffer fish.

"...you tie it off when I say, understand?" he heard Anki shouting.

"I do, I think," came a muffled reply.

Biacoya blinked again through the agony, looking over the midrib of the canuti toward the docks of Bahaca where he thought he saw another reed boat. He coughed, his lungs on fire, half expecting flames to shoot from his mouth, but he tried to focus his eyes on the other canuti. It was a ferry, and he was able to make out three people stepping onto the dock, one taller in a crimson tunic carrying a palm frond over two children in white. He thought he recognized the short, spiky hair of one of the children, but then a large wave obscured his view.

"It's going to be alright, buddy. We're getting you off the island!" he heard Anki say. And then his canuti was moving, his view of the docks drifted away, and then Biacoya closed his eyes to his pain...

Streams of ash cascaded through the fingers of his right hand, forming three pyramids beside a field of swaying reeds. Beneath his left hand was the head of Chuka, the boar ancestor, ashy breath billowing out of his heaving nostrils and blowing across the reeds. Biacoya raised and lowered each hand, weighing them against each other, before hearing a low rumble from across the Great Sea. There, in the distance, was a ring of smoke traveling above the waves and heading toward him. He continued weighing the ash, keeping a watchful eye on the traveler. A sudden shudder within the ring startled him, and then an object appeared, like the tip of a spear, which caught the reflection of Kuraka and seared into Biacoya's eyes. He heard screaming. There were hundreds, if not thousands of screaming voices rising in pitch until they combined into that single, familiar, droning buzz.

Biacoya opened his eyes and the buzzing instantly receded to the back of his head where it festered. He was in his bed, several blankets weighing down his body with only his neck and head above them. His mouth was dry, and he had to blink from the sweat dripping down over his brow and into his eyes. He couldn't move. Every muscle tingled, limp and useless, and he had to take short puffs of breath to avoid a torturous burning in his throat. To his left, seated in a chair, he saw his baba sleeping with his head tucked into his arms crossed over his chest. At his feet, through the doorway into the dining area, he saw Anki talking with that girl from the hole, both of their faces illuminated by firelight, her long black braid running down her back. He wanted to say something, maybe thank them for getting him off that island, but he knew he couldn't. He was unbelievably exhausted, and thought if he closed his eyes for just a moment...

CHAPTER FOURTEEN

The Fruit of KINCHAM

Tabba and Anki sat quietly at the dining table in the Chief of Vines' residence, relieved to finally be safe on the island of Pacca and out of the storm. A gentle fire provided a bit of warmth and light from the basin in the corner, casting a somber yellow-orange flickering glow over the walls, the table, and their faces. The storm outside had started to die down, but there continued to be intermittent bursts of heavy rain and the distant rumble of thunder. Tambu was in the other room with Biacoya, and Anki was pretty sure they were both asleep, which was a good thing.

He had seen Biacoya's father angry before, and he had seen him furious, and both times ended in Biacoya getting smacked across the face. But when they arrived at the docks with Biacoya unconscious, hardly breathing, and clinging to the last threads of life, there was no anger in Tambu's eyes. The terrifying man didn't even yell at them, which was surprising. He just scooped his big boy up into his strong arms and effortlessly carried Biacoya up the street to their residence in the pouring rain. Tambu then gently placed his son in his bed, immediately sat down next to him, and hadn't moved since.

Anki watched Tabba unbraiding her damp hair. She had explained that her name wasn't actually *Tutababa*, and that she was just shivering so much it came out wrong. Afterward, he felt embarrassed and chose not to talk anymore. One of Tambu's attendants brought them each a towel, but he hadn't used his yet. Tabba, on the other hand, had already wiped off her face, arms and legs, and was busy squeezing the water out of her hair. Anki sat beside her, spinning a piece of broken wood the size of his palm on the table with his finger.

"What is that anyway?" she asked.

"A piece of a box the boakin gave Biacoya – *a gift for the boadulu*, he told us. Biacoya had it under his belt in the cave. It must have been crushed when he sat down." Anki turned the piece some more, noticing tiny sparkles of a green powder in the cracks.

"For Boadulu Urtulu?" Tabba asked. "I wonder what reason the Mawoakin would have to send a gift to the chief of the palace guards." She reached over and snatched the piece of wood from him.

"Hey!" he complained.

"I just want to look at it," she said, bringing it close to her face and squinting. Anki watched her, a little hurt, but then he saw her expression change. He guessed she had noticed the green powder too. And then she ran a finger across one of the cracks. Suddenly, the front door of the residence burst open, startling them and waking up Tambu.

"Great Maroha's wind!" Tambu hollered in his deep, gritty voice, immediately jumping to his feet with his fists raised and ready.

"Anki?" Abensu shouted, charging into the dining area and leaving a trail of rainwater along the way.

"Here, baba." Anki stood and took a step toward his father who instantly swept him up into his arms and squeezed him tightly.

"Oh, it's *AH-BEN-SU*. Omaki boy!" Tambu moaned, before plopping back down on the chair beside his son's bed. Anki heard the chair screech in protest.

"What's that supposed to mean?" Tabba whispered, setting down the piece of wood.

"It's nothing," his father replied with a dismissive wave.

"They don't like each other," Anki clarified, as his father set him down.

Abensu glared at them both. "It is *nothing*, Anki, and – whoever you are." He stepped into Biacoya's bedchamber. "How's your boy, Tambu?"

Tambu gestured with his upturned palm to his unconscious son. "Here, then there, hot to the touch, but then cold and clammy," he said. "But he's alive, I guess, thanks to your boy." Tambu offered Abensu a clearly forced smile, which Anki realized was the first time he had ever seen the man smile.

"A lesini was on the ferry with me," Abensu said, "but you know how quickly they move. She should be here shortly." He came back into the dining area and grabbed Anki's hand. "Let's go, Anki."

"Baba, you have to hear what happened," he protested, squirming.

"Later. Right now, I have to get back to finish the plates, and you are coming with me."

Anki ripped his hand from his father's grip. "NO! You must hear it now!" Tears welled up in his eyes, his emotions having been suppressed for much too long.

"Anki, we don't have time for this..."

"Anki said you've been best friends with the Yaya since you were yaali yourselves," Tabba said, standing. Tambu scoffed from the other room, making Anki's father sigh.

"That was a long time ago, and irrelevant at the moment." He grabbed Anki's hand again, but Anki yanked it away, causing his father to huff in irritation.

"My name is Tabba," she said, placing a hand on her chest. "I'm araco for the Mawoakin."

Abensu looked at Tabba, appearing to notice the color of her tunic for the first time. "So you are," he said, but didn't introduce himself to her.

"The Mawoakin tried to kill me," she said, but then suddenly lost her balance and plopped back down in her chair. Anki watched her rub her fingers on her tunic aggressively.

Growing a little concerned, he asked her, "What's the matter?"

"I-I don't know," she stammered. "My fingers feel like they're on fire!"

"Did you say the Mawoakin tried to kill you?" Anki's father seemed to be processing what Tabba had just said, but very slowly.

"Yes," she snapped, and then quickly stood up but fell over into Anki's arms. "I need some water."

Anki helped her back into her chair. "I'll get you some," he said.

"Why would the Mawoakin want to kill their araco?" his father asked.

There was a ceramic pitcher and cups on a small table in the corner opposite the fire basin. Anki poured two cups and brought them back to the table, handing one to Tabba. She took a sip of the water, tilted her head back, and closed her eyes.

"Do you feel better?" he asked.

"Give it a moment."

"How did they try to kill you?" his father asked, still processing.

"They threw her in a really deep hole at the bottom of the cave," Anki answered.

"And how do you know that?"

"Because that's where we found her – Biacoya and me. She would have drowned if we hadn't pulled her out with Biacoya's rope." Anki took a sip of his own water, making sure Tabba drank some more with him, but then she shoved her fingers into the cup. "What are you doing?"

"My fingers are burning!"

"Wait – you're dizzy, and your fingers are burning?" his father asked, as if he had just woken up. Tabba nodded, her eyes still closed and her fingers in the cup of water. "Anki, tell me everything that happened, and include every little detail."

"Um..." he gulped, seeing Tambu join the three of them.

"What's going on?" Tambu asked, leaning in Biacoya's doorway.

"Just a moment, Tambu. Anki's going to tell us." His father looked at him sternly, "Go on, son. What happened?"

Anki collapsed into his chair, but before a single word came out of his mouth, he was startled silent when he saw a woman standing at the end of the table. She was dimly lit by the fire basin on the opposite side of the room, but he could see she was small, maybe even as short as Biacoya was. She had extremely long hair that was bunched together into thick, fuzzy clumps like the segin, but hers nearly touched the floor. Her tunic was either very dirty or dark-brown, and she wore a jungle-green sleeveless robe over the top that was open and dragging on the ground behind her. She didn't appear to be old enough to need a walking stick, but she leaned on a gnarled staff, her bright-azure eyes flashing in the firelight.

"Tayokun, Bogula," Tambu greeted her.

"Tayokun, Tambu," the creepy woman quickly replied. "Abensu, I saw you earlier and I see your son here now – Anki, is it?"

"Bogula," his father said, nodding at the woman.

She made Anki feel uncomfortable, and he tried to hide behind Tabba.

"No need to be shy, boy," the creepy woman said with what might have been an attempt at a smile. Then she addressed Tabba, "And you are Tabba, daughter of the Cult of Mayu and sister to Draha. However, I do not see the boy I came for."

"He's in here, Bogula," Tambu showed her.

The way Bogula seemed to float across the room mesmerized Anki. He noticed there was a hollowed-out acorn in each of her earlobes, which were stretched wide like the mouths of whooping howlers. As she passed, he could have sworn she whispered something to him, and he almost asked her to repeat what she said, but then he realized her mouth hadn't moved. Anki's father joined Tambu and Bogula in Biacoya's bedchamber, while he pulled Tabba out of her chair and over to the fire basin in the corner.

"What?" she groaned, stumbling along with him. "You're lucky I feel a little better."

"Who is that?" he whispered loudly. "She's not going to hurt my friend, is she? He's already been through enough."

"Relax," she told him. "Bogula's a lesini."

"None of the lesini I ever saw looked like her."

Tabba appeared to consider this for a moment before saying, "Well, not all lesini are exactly alike. They do their own thing, wander around and develop their own style. Unfortunately, they also don't tend to live very long. I think it has something to do with exhausting their healing spirit, but I don't know."

"What do you mean?" he asked quietly.

"The Great Spirit imparts only so much of himself in us. The lesini are said to be born with an excess of spirit, which bubbles over and cannot be contained. They feel obligated to share it with others, but I think they have a hard time knowing when to shut it off."

"What? Do you mean like..." Anki looked around the room. "Like a pitcher of water?"

Tabba thought about it then said, "Yeah, kind of like that." They could hear Bogula softly singing in the other room and stopped talking to listen. "Hey, I recognize that tune," she said, grinning, and then her grin turned into a grimace. "Anki, you're bleeding."

"I am?" He instantly reached up to feel around on his face.

She went back to the table, grabbed his towel, and brought it back to him. "Hold still," she said, grabbing his chin.

As Tabba cleaned Anki's wound, he heard Bogula stop singing, and then he watched the three of them emerge from Biacoya's bedchamber.

"Anki, I think it's time to tell us what happened," his father said.

"Spare no details," Tambu added, glaring at him, causing Anki to hesitate.

But Tabba encouraged him, "It's alright, go on."

After a few deep breaths, Anki told the entire story about their trip to Bahaca, only excluding the part about the starfish because he didn't want his friend getting into even more trouble. He described what the akin were wearing, what he saw inside of the temple, the strange tree, Soci's strange black eyes, and then Tabba added details about what the Mawoakin planted in their gardens. But when Anki came to the wooden box, his father suddenly interrupted him.

"What box? Where is this box?" he asked.

"The box broke in the cave...and Biacoya must have inhaled that powder!" Anki said, pointing to the broken piece of wood on the table, the realization suddenly dawning on him.

"Powder?" His father went to pick it up.

Anki shouted, "Baba, no!"

"It's alright, son. I see what you're talking about." He gripped it by the edges.

"Are there more trees like the one you describe on the island?" Bogula asked, and then drifted to a chair, her flowing robe and fuzzy hair billowing outward as she sat with a heavy sigh.

"There's only one tree on Bahaca," Tabba answered for him.

"And I bet it's the kincham," Abensu said.

"Kincham?" Tambu asked.

Abensu turned to Bogula. "Do you think?"

"There's only one way to find out," the lesini replied.

His father showed Bogula the piece of wood and said something to her, motioning toward Anki, and then he called him over to see the lesini. Anki suddenly noticed, ever since leaving the cave, there was a high-pitched ringing in his ears. He tried to stretch his jaw as he walked.

Bogula sat for a moment in thought, looking at him strangely, and then she asked for Tabba's towel. Tabba handed it to her, but Bogula immediately handed it back. "No, no – too wet. Is his bloody one drier?" Tabba nodded. "Good, give me that one."

Anki watched her take the towel, tear a strip off, wrap it around the piece of wood, and then shove it into a pocket somewhere in her robe.

Where the frail-looking old woman got the strength to casually tear a towel in half, he did not know. She then turned her attention to Anki's wound.

"You saved your friend's life. You know that don't you?" she said, pulling a wooden vial from somewhere else inside her robe.

"I guess," Anki answered shyly.

Bogula unstopped the vial, poured a drop of purplish sap on her finger, and then rubbed it into the little gash on his head. He instantly squirmed. "Hold still," she said softly.

"It hurts," he whined.

"All things hurt in their own measure, boy. We must listen to the hurt and allow it to teach us what the spirits intend. Now, did you inhale any of the powder?"

"No, I don't think so."

She made him open his mouth and looked at his tongue and teeth, running her finger around inside his cheek. Anki pleaded with watering eyes for his father to help him, but his father shook his head and motioned for Anki to remain calm. Then Bogula tousled his hair and smiled from ear to ear, exposing her yellowing teeth and red gums.

"You're a good boy, Anki, son of Tiam," she said as she stood. "I will go with you now to see the Yaya," Bogula told Anki's father. "Tabba should come too."

"Wait, you knew my itaba?" Anki asked, pulling on Bogula's robe.

"There's no time for that," Abensu dismissed him. "You don't think this can wait?" he asked the lesini.

Bogula seemed to consider responding to Anki but stopped herself and started toward the door. "Tambu's boy is lucky to be alive. If what I've been told is true, then whatever their motivation, whoever the intended target was to be, the Mawoakin were going to kill someone with that poison." She paused to look back at everyone. "When one deadly snake is killed, her hungry babies will strike out from their nest." Everyone stared at her blankly until she rolled her eyes. "The Mawoakin will try again."

"Oh, of course," Abensu said, nodding his head.

"I need to stay here with my boy," Tambu told them.

"That is best," Bogula said.

"Wait," Anki shouted. "Will you be back to cure Biacoya?"

Bogula shook her head. "It is kincham and the only antidote comes from the tizaka tree, which no longer grows on these islands. I must go see the Yaya."

"But what about my friend? Will he be alright?" Anki started to cry.

"He will live," she told him. "But he will never be the same again."

CHAPTER FIFTEEN

Creature Games

Alight drizzle persisted over the Buku Market, keeping all the hanging rolls of fabric damp and the stained boarhides glistening in the early-evening gloom. Varying colors of dye trickled down the shop stall walls and snaked through the mud into the center of the market where two men were struggling to remain standing in the deepening muck. Their upper bodies were dripping with sweat and rainwater, while their legs were coated in a rainbow of mud. Sheka arrived late to the dispute match taking place and watched from beneath a woven reed awning with several other onlookers.

There were few things the Itabayiti loved more than a balanced and fair wrestling match. It was common for matches to spontaneously erupt between friends to settle bets, or for boys to impress the girls, or for girls to impress the boys, but wrestling was also encouraged communally as a way to settle disputes between strangers. Unfortunately, dispute matches were rarely balanced or fair, which was what Sheka liked most about them.

The sudden and heavy downpour had brought her lessons in the reed yard to an abrupt halt. She thought about returning to Yapaca but didn't want to sit on the ferry all that way in the storm, if the ferries were running at all, so she decided to attempt to be friends with the other girls again. They sought shelter in one of the rib drying huts, while the boys and Jokimbi braved the wind and rain and headed for Badhan. After what felt like a lifetime listening to Kina, Nawuni, and Matata gossip about boys, Sheka kicked herself for having not gone on the ferry back to Yapaca. When she darted out into the pouring rain, she paused to look back at the other girls and see if they might say something, but they didn't. It was as if they hadn't noticed her presence to begin with and couldn't be bothered to notice her absence. Sheka suspected she knew why.

She grew up in Badhan, the daughter of Jokimbi and Matia, but she didn't want her friends to know her father was their instructor because she also wasn't sure it was true. She didn't lie, she told them she was the granddaughter of Yaya Shakali, which would explain why she was allowed to train with the children of council members, but she always tiptoed around who her parents were. Then Kina Wani showed up and just had to say something.

Being the daughter of the current Yaya, Kina claimed to personally know all of Shakali's children and swore there was no way Sheka was his granddaughter. Sheka was so mad that day, during midmeal she went into the jungle, caught a snake, and then dropped it on Kina's head from atop the binding hut. No one knew she had done it, of course, and Jokimbi blamed Luculati instead, which was absolutely perfect! But Sheka had to admit, if Kina was being honest about Shakali's children, then she might not be the daughter of Jokimbi and Matia after all.

The whole way up the steps through the inner wall, down the street past the Temple of Yucahu, and back to the grand staircase on her way to Badhan, Sheka fretted about her parents. The strangest thing was that Sheka's earliest memory was of a festival where everyone slapped bundles of reeds on the ground, stirring up a cloud of dust that glowed orange in the afternoon sun. She stood between her parents, holding their hands, when an extremely tall woman approached them wearing a dark-red robe over an even darker red tunic. She remembered the woman smelled sweet, like honey and num-num fruit. Her parents freely let the woman take Sheka away, through the orange cloud, and into the jungle where they played all day, pretending to be all sorts of different creatures.

Her parents never spoke about the woman and a full year passed. Not long after Sheka turned five, the Canutaloc Festival occurred, and it was what she remembered attending before with the reed beating and the orange dust cloud. Again, the tall woman in red showed up and her parents allowed her to take Sheka into the jungle to play. She didn't remember what she called the woman the first time, so she recalled asking her the second time.

"What's your name?" she remembered asking while they pretended to be armadillos and burrowed in the dirt.

"Ibaka, of course!" The woman had called herself an armadillo.

"No," Sheka pressed her. "My name's Sheka and yours is?"

Sheka remembered the woman becoming very serious and bringing her dirt-covered face close to hers until they were nose to nose. The woman's beautiful azure eyes were bright and shimmered like the Great Sea on a sunny day. "You may call me itaba," she told Sheka with a hand to her chest. "But you cannot tell anyone this little secret. Promise?"

"But I already have an itaba." Sheka remembered feeling confused but also, somehow, excited and anxious all at the same time.

"Ditaba, then," the woman said. "But promise, not a word!" The woman had raised her voice and gripped Sheka by her shoulders, but Sheka didn't remember being scared. The memory was like a heavy blanket, warm and comforting, even though it pinned her down and she was unable to move out from under it. She promised to keep the secret and continue meeting with her ditaba, her second mother, every year during the Canutaloc Festival.

Year after year, the creature game, as Sheka started to call it, became increasingly involved. When she was six, a fierce wind tore through the jungle, stirring up leaves and whipping Sheka's long hair around her face, but they continued pretending to be birds with their arms outstretched like wings. She remembered imagining her ditaba was an echo bird with bright red, green, and azure feathers, gliding between the vines as Sheka watched through her tangles of hair. When she was seven, they climbed trees and whooped and barked like monkeys. Ditaba wanted Sheka to pay close attention to how useful it must be to have a tail, but especially how strange it would feel. When she was eight, her second mother said they should pretend to be people, focusing on all the unusual ways arms and legs and fingers and toes could move. But then, after Sheka turned nine, she stood with her parents and the slapping reeds and the orange dust cloud, but her second mother never came to retrieve her.

SPLAT!

Sheka nearly tripped over the smaller wrestler's head, as the bigger one slammed him into the mud right in front of her. Her attention now fully reclaimed by the dispute match, she watched the two men tire themselves out, splattering multi-colored mud on the sandalled feet of the excited onlookers. She wondered how the clearly mismatched dispute had started. One of the two was tall and thick and looked to Sheka like a giant manati with hairy legs. He was twice the size of the second man, who was frail and sickly in appearance and reminded her of a hairless gosu. The Itabayiti actually called the weasel-like creatures kugosu, but her ditaba told her to call them gosu.

Standing next to Sheka was a man wearing the whitest tunic she had ever seen. It was spotless, even with the rain and the splattering mud from the wrestlers. On the man's right was a boy she recognized, Kachi, who was a few years older than her, short for his age, as thin as she was, and constantly moving. As she slipped around behind the man in white to talk to Kachi, she noticed Kachi was subtly bouncing on the balls of his feet.

"Hey!" she whispered loudly, poking Kachi in his boney back.

"Ow! What..." He spun around and then rolled his eyes when he saw it was Sheka. "Oh, it's only you. What did you do that for?"

"How did this start?" she asked excitedly, ignoring his question.

"You shouldn't sneak up on people, Sheka. It's rude," he said, turning back to watch the wrestling match.

"I'm *so* sorry!" she said sarcastically. "I didn't know I was *sneaking*. Tell me what's happening here?"

Kachi sighed. "Why should a little girl care?"

"Hey! I'm the same size as you – ya spiny little rat!"

"Spiny rat!?" Kachi spun around again.

"Shh!" the man in white demanded. "Quiet down, son. And stop bouncing! Stand still!"

"Sorry, baba," Kachi said, shrinking a bit as he turned around once more.

SPLAT!

The giant manati slammed the frail gosu into the muck, sending fist-sized chunks of wet, colorful mud flying everywhere and on everyone. Kachi and his father were both hit hard with the splatter, ruining his father's pristine white tunic. Sheka looked down at her rain-soaked but otherwise clean tunic and started laughing.

"Coki!" Kachi's father shouted.

"Yeah?" The giant manati looked up with a satisfied grin on his chubby face. "Oh – Kasim, what happened to your beautiful tunic!"

"You know what happened to my beautiful tunic, you maniac!"

"Hmm...I am deeply sorry, Kasim," the man called Coki said with what Sheka thought was the perfect amount of sarcasm. "Would you like me to get you a new one? If only we were... Hey! Look, we *are* standing in the Buku Market!"

"Let's just go, baba," Kachi said, picking clumps of mud off his legs.

"Coki..." Kasim started to say something but stopped himself. "Come on, Kachi!" he huffed and shuffled off into the drizzling rain. Kachi shuffled off behind his father.

Sheka couldn't stop laughing and watched in awe as the massive man called Coki helped the other, scrawny wrestler get to his feet.

"You're alright," Coki said, brushing the larger chunks of mud off the man with a rough and aggressive hand. "At least now you know not to call me names!" he said with a wink.

"I guess, Boyiti," the man whimpered, rubbing a sore arm.

"I said it before and I'll say it again, I am no longer the boyiti! Macoca won the election six years ago. Where have you been?" The scrawny man didn't reply, he just slinked away. "Sheesh!"

Most of the other people in the market were returning to their business of the day, but a few stepped forward to pat Coki on the pack or offer him a courteous bow. Sheka had heard the name Coki before, but she didn't know he was the former boyiti of Yapaca. Now she absolutely had to find out why he was in a dispute match during a rainstorm in the middle of the Buku Market.

She slid through the mud and into the drizzle as Coki held up one of his sandals and was clearly searching through the muck for the other. "So, you are Coki, *former* boyiti of Yapaca, and I am Sheka – a new resident of Yapaca and currently your biggest fan!"

Coki chuckled, still looking for his sandal. "Nice to meet you, Sheka, resident of Yapaca. How did that happen?"

"How did what happen?"

"You said you're a new resident of Yapaca, but here you are wandering around Badhan. So, how did that happen?"

Sheka thought Coki's reasoning was surprisingly sound. Now she was even sadder that he was the former boyiti. "Well," she began, "my parents had a long argument, and my itaba and I went to live with ohtaba-Elaya. She lives on Yapaca in Ciba Village."

"Ciba – *dusty bodies*," Coki said, still searching for his sandal. "Fitting."

"Uh – what?"

"Ah-ha!" he shouted, holding his other sandal high into the air. "I found you!" Coki quickly stepped out of the mud pit, brushed the colorful chunks from his legs and feet, and then squished his foot into the mud-soaked sandal.

"So..." Sheka looked up at him confusedly.

Coki sighed. "That's why the workers on Risca are called ciba, because they get extremely dusty making cibmani."

"Oh, that is fitting."

"Yes. Now, I guess you're probably ten or eleven?" he asked, and she nodded. "If you live on Yapaca, you should be at the reed yard right now having lessons with Coani Chaladu. What are you doing in the Buku Market?"

"Yes. No!" she quickly corrected herself. "My baba is Jokimbi, so I was given special permission to continue my lessons here on Itabaca."

"Alright, but that still doesn't explain why you're not at lessons," Coki said, stretching his back and twisting from side to side. His back cracked several times, and Sheka giggled at the way he sighed after each one.

"That's simple," she said quickly. "It's raining."

Coki looked up and squinted against the raindrops landing on his face. "Right," he mumbled, and then finished stretching. "Do you mind if we get out of the rain?" he asked, and she agreed. He motioned for them to move over into the alley beneath a stone archway. It was quieter in the alley and Sheka noticed she must have been ignoring the howling wind the entire time in the market. "That's better, right?" Coki asked and Sheka nodded. "So, I get the feeling this conversation is just getting started."

"A couple questions," she said. Coki chuckled, but then smiled and nodded. "One, were you just playing around with that other guy? Because I bet you could have won whenever you wanted, couldn't you? And second..."

"That would be three questions then?" he asked with another chuckle.

"Uh – no, yes...what?" Sheka's mind seemed to twirl in on itself. "No, see, the first question was about you being able to win whenever you wanted, and the second..."

"Yes, but then you asked that question twice."

"Well...I guess it was more of a clarifying continuation of the first question."

Coki smiled and shook his head. "I concede, then. What is your second question?"

"Oh, what was...wait, you didn't answer the first question!" Sheka said and put her fists on her hips.

"Of course I did."

"No, I asked the question, and then you said there were three and that I asked the same question twice." Sheka was amazed she was talking so much. She never talked this much. Maybe it was because she hadn't been able to talk to anyone all day, she wondered.

Coki shrugged his large shoulders, and sighed, "Look, little girl..." He paused, seeing the genuine interest and childlike curiosity in Sheka's eyes. "Yes. I was just playing around with Dimgal – *that scrawny guy* – and could have beaten him at any moment, but he is also my friend. So, who's to say? Now, please, ask your next question so that we might get on with our lives."

"I knew it!" she shouted. "So, um – you're obviously much bigger than he is. What caused the dispute in the first place?"

"Oh! You want to know why we were wrestling?" he asked, and Sheka nodded vigorously. "It was silly, really. He bumped into me, or I bumped into him, and words were exchanged. I was going to walk away, but then he..."

Coki stopped mid-thought and stared over Sheka's head toward the main street at the end of the alley. Sheka turned to see what he was staring at. There, walking up the street toward the Grand Plaza in a soaking wet clump, was Anki, his father, that weird lesini named Bogula, and a girl araco in a filthy azure tunic Sheka didn't recognize. They were the strangest looking group of people Sheka had ever seen.

"Manati," Coki said behind her.

"What?" she asked, spinning back around to face him.

"Dimgal, he called me a manati and I pushed him into the mud."

"Oh!" Sheka said with a nervous snicker. "That makes sense."

CHAPTER SIXTEEN

Trusting the Children

The reception hall was dark when Abensu, Bogula, Tabba, and Anki arrived, and an attendant had to hurriedly retrieve a reed torch and light the copper sconces along the north and south walls. It was nearly sixteen paces from the palace doors to the dais, which Anki had counted when he was there a few days earlier. The dais continued a further two reeds to the eastern wall behind three stone thrones, and there was a window a half-a-reed tall running the length of the east wall near the ceiling. Anki couldn't see out of the high window and thought it didn't seem to be very useful. He would have to ask his father about it later.

He was exhausted and leaned on his father to support his flimsy legs. His plans for a day full of adventure had come true, but it was just not the kind of adventure he had hoped for. He looked down at his filthy yaali tunic. Mud still clung to the front in streaks, having turned the pristine white fabric to a reddish-tan, and there was dried blood on his shoulder. Undisturbed bits of golden stitching here and there were the only evidence of what his tunic had once symbolized.

He watched Bogula tapping her foot impatiently, changing hands on her staff with increased irritation. Looking up, Anki could see the strain in his father's eyes, and he could feel the dried clay that perpetually covered his father's calloused hands. Anki's tired eyes wandered over to Tabba with her tunic just as destroyed as his, even more so, and wondered if she was hungry after being in that hole for so long. He hadn't seen her eat a thing at the Chief of Vine's residence. Of course, neither had he. And now they were both at the Yaya's Palace, and he was pretty confident they weren't going to get anything to eat here either. Suddenly, Anki heard a noise up on the dais and there was the Yaya sitting on his high-back stone throne. Anki hadn't even seen him enter the hall and wondered how he got up there.

"Alright, Abensu, Bogula," the Yaya nodded at each of them, seeming to intentionally overlook Anki and Tabba. "What drags me from my evening meal with my family?" Anki's father started to speak, but the Yaya cut him off. "And, please, don't ramble. Get to the point."

Anki heard his father swallow hard, but then he forced a smile. "Tayokun, my Yaya," Abensu began. "Knowing how ridiculous what we are about to say may seem, I must first remind you of our history, of our childhood, of all the years..."

"Yes, yes, Abensu. We were friends once, now get to the point."

"Then you should know that I have never in all these years abused that friendship, even though we were *best* of friends once — no matter how troubling a matter may have been." The Yaya rolled his eyes and almost said something, but then he admitted a smile and motioned for Anki's father to proceed. "This is Tabba. She is the araco to the Mawoakin." He pointed to Tabba and then raised Anki's hand. "And you know my boy, Anki. Both of them had a disturbing experience on Bahaca, which must be heard to be believed."

"Fine," the Yaya said. "Tabba, is it? Go ahead, speak."

Anki was surprised to see Tabba so nervous. They had only spent part of one day together, but he could already tell she was a determined and outspoken girl. He watched her shift her feet around as if trying to get something out of her sandal.

"Um — I was only assigned to the Mawoakin for a couple of days when I asked to observe the Rise of Mawoi ritual," she began. "I had never seen it before. Actually, I'm pretty sure most people haven't, because it's very shocking and anyone who has seen it would immediately report what..."

"And when was this?" the Yaya interrupted, rolling his eyes.

"Um — two, maybe three days ago."

"So, why didn't you report this *shocking* ritual immediately?"

"Well," Tabba looked down at her wretched appearance. "I will tell you."

Tabba's story was powerful and filled with big, beautiful words, some of which Anki didn't know. When she described the Rise of Mawoi ritual, he felt like he could hear the gourd drums and see the sunlight piercing through the ashen cloud right there in front of them. He had been to the temple and, even though he was not an araco and was not learned in their ways, there seemed to be more carvings on the walls related to the other spirits than just to Mawoi. In fact, Anki suddenly realized he hadn't seen the sun symbol of Mawoi on or in the temple at all. When Tabba's story came to where Anki and Biacoya showed up with their rope, the Yaya stopped her, appearing to be reasonably disturbed by what he was hearing.

"Thank you, Tabba," the Yaya said before turning to Anki. He rubbed his forehead and called over one of his attendants who were standing on either side of the dais. He whispered something quickly behind a cupped hand, and then the attendant bowed and rushed out a secret door to the right of the Yaya Anki hadn't seen before. Yaya Amnu then feigned a smile and asked, "Anki, your baba says you have something to add to this story."

Anki hid behind his father, gripping his calloused hand tightly. "It's alright, son. Tell the Yaya what you told me," his father encouraged him, pulling him forward. His father then gripped Anki's shoulders in his large, rough hands.

"Wait," the Yaya abruptly said, before Anki could speak. "Are you wearing a yaali tunic?" he asked, as if noticing it for the first time.

Anki was ashamed and angry at himself for ruining such a fine tunic. He was so embarrassed, he started to get upset. He nodded and said through his sniffles, "I'm sorry. I didn't know it was going to get ruined, honestly. I only wanted to wear it once because it's been folded up in a basket for over a year, but then I saw it at the end of my bed, and I got suspended from lessons and couldn't help baba in the pits, and I didn't know how to help with the ash glaze, and then Biacoya was dying and..." Anki started to cry.

"It's alright, Anki," the Yaya said, his tone quickly becoming gentler and more fatherly. He stepped down from the dais and knelt in front of him. Abensu, Bogula, and Tabba instantly took a step back and bowed their heads. Amnu looked up at Abensu and said, "Anki, do you want to come up and see my throne?" Anki's father nodded, and then the Yaya took Anki's hand and led him up the steps of the dais.

The Yaya's throne was the biggest of the three and stood tall in the middle. It had the names of every ruler since the dawn of Itabacan carved into it. On its right was a slightly smaller throne, which Anki knew was reserved for the mother of the Itabayiti, and on its left was an even smaller one for Kina. Anki tried to read the names on the Yaya's throne, but the Itabayiti tongue had developed quite a bit since the throne was created, and he could only guess the biggest name on the headrest was YAYA. As he went down the list, he finally came to the wedged characters he recognized in the seven last and most recent names on the list. He read: ENGAR, OBOLO, MOBO, OBAC, ANACACU, SHAKALI, and AMNU.

"Sit," the Yaya said, inviting Anki to sit on his throne.

"Really?"

"Of course. Who knows, maybe one day this throne will be yours," the Yaya joked. "You are a yaali after all."

Anki giggled and climbed on the cold stone seat. "Don't be silly."

"Anki, watch your tone with the Yaya," his father warned him.

"Yes, baba."

"It's alright, Abensu," Yaya Amnu said, and then he sat next to Anki in the mother's throne. "Now, Anki, it was only a few days ago that you were standing in this room because of another incident." Anki shrunk down in the stone chair as far as he could. He glanced at the Yaya and saw him lean over and whisper in his ear, "I believed you, by the way. But my Kina was hurt, so I couldn't simply let you and your friend go without any form of punishment."

"Really?" Anki whispered back.

"Really." This revelation made Anki feel a thousand times lighter, and he instantly sat up tall on the throne and smiled brightly at his father.

"Now," Yaya Amnu continued, "can you tell me what happened on Bahaca?"

"Yes, Yayamnu," Anki mumbled, mushing the title with the name.

"I need you to be as clear and detailed as you can, alright?"

"Yes, Yayamnu."

Anki leaned back in the throne, running his palms on the smooth stone armrests, and started telling the Yaya everything that happened. Again, he hesitated when he arrived at The Deeps and Biacoya's starfish, but then the Yaya gave Anki a stern look and he had to come clean. He told himself he would apologize to Biacoya later. His story moved on to the girl in yellow named Soci, and how the Mawoakin seemed to be expecting the yaali. He told of the ride up the slope to the Temple of the Dawn and how the cave looked like a monster swallowing the earth. He made sure to point out details Tabba had missed when describing the temple, which elicited a bit of light-hearted laughter from everyone. But he confirmed what she said about the tree, and how the boakin talked about Mawoi as if the Great Light was also the Storm Spirit, and the Wind Spirit, and the Rain Spirit combined. When he started talking about the box, Bogula approached the throne and laid the piece of wood wrapped in the strip of towel at the Yaya's feet.

"What's this?" he asked, picking it up.

"Anki will tell you, my Yaya," Bogula said, returning to where she had been standing.

"Alright. Continue, Anki," he said.

Anki explained the boakin called the box a gift for the boadulu. Then acted out how they raced down the slope in the boar-drawn cart, and how he drove the cart right into the stables. He said Biacoya tucked the box under his belt before entering the cave, and that he must have accidentally crushed it and inhaled the powder after they pulled Tabba out of the hole. Anki pointed to the towel and said there was a piece of the box in it, at which point, the Yaya opened the towel and saw the broken piece of wood.

Then Anki got choked up while describing how he and Tabba carried Biacoya's lifeless body together as they swam through the flooded sections of the cave. He described in great detail how Biacoya kept going in and out of consciousness, trying to speak but couldn't, and how they had almost lost him when he slipped off the canuti and into the angry waters of the sound. He told them how he had to teach Tabba how to sail the canuti in the storm, even though he had only just really learned earlier that morning. His harrowing tale seemed to tug at the Yaya's heart strings because Anki heard him disguise a sniffle as a cough.

At that moment, Kina Wani suddenly burst through the secret door the Yaya's attendant had gone through and tackled Anki on the throne, hugging him with all of her might. Her disappointed looking mother slowly followed behind her, but Unana Wani stopped near the mother's throne and hovered there over the Yaya.

"Thank you!" Kina said, her soft cheek pressed up against his.

"Have you been there this whole time?" Yaya Amnu asked his daughter and wife.

"Well, if you're not going to come back to evening meal, then we had to come to you," Unana Wani replied, and then she waved at Anki's father. "Tayokun, Abensu."

"Tayokun, Unana Wani," he replied, bowing slightly to her. "It's been a long time."

"Too long," Unana said. "Alright, that's enough, Kina."

Kina loosened her tight grip and backed away a step, leaving Anki with bright-red cheeks and that giggly feeling tickling his stomach again. He couldn't help but smile and instantly turned away, feeling horribly embarrassed.

"After you didn't return, Kina and I followed you and have been eavesdropping through a crack in the door," Unana added, seemingly to fill the silence in the reception hall.

Anki finally turned back to find Kina smiling at him, her turquoise eyes watering and her soft cheeks appearing to be just as red as his likely were. And then Anki's eyes wandered a bit farther to the right where he saw the Yaya was grinning at the both of them, a strange little sparkle in his eye. He quickly looked away, only to realize his father, Tabba, and that creep lesini were also smiling at them. Everyone but Unana Wani had the same silly grin on their faces, and that was when he noticed he and Kina were still holding hands, and he snatched his hand away.

"Yaya, may I?" Bogula asked to approach the Yaya where he was sitting on the mother's throne, and the Yaya nodded.

"Is Biacoya going to be alright?" Kina asked abruptly, as if she had been holding it in.

"That is yet to be seen," Bogula answered her. "It is kincham, my Yaya. We need to send someone to Bayamaca to bring back the fruit of the tizaka tree immediately."

"Kincham?" The Yaya was confused. "We eradicated that tree a hundred years ago."

"There is one on Bahaca as we speak. If what these children say is true, if there was an intent to use that poison to harm the boadulu or even you, then we must have tizaka. Its fruit is the only antidote." And then she repeated what she had said earlier on Pacca, "When one deadly snake is killed, her hungry babies will strike out from their nest."

"To scatter in the reeds, where more nests they'll build," Amnu finished the saying.

It was then that an attendant entered through the front doors of the palace, followed by Boadulu Urtulu and six of his palace guards. Urtulu was a massive man with massive shoulders, biceps as big as Anki's head, and bulging veins snaking down to fists of chiseled stone. But he walked with a strange, uncomfortable looking gait, which Anki thought might be because of some old wrestling injury. Urtulu had been a fan-favorite for years before the council appointed him boadulu, and Anki always wondered why he gave it up just to be a palace guard.

Abensu, Bogula, and Tabba made way for the guards by pressing themselves against the north wall, and Anki and Kina quickly jumped down off the throne. Kina then ran to her mother and Anki to his father, as the Yaya took his rightful seat once more.

"You sent for me, my Yaya?" Boadulu Urtulu said, snapping his heels together and bowing.

"Come, Urtulu," the Yaya said, waving for the chief of the palace guards to come closer.

"Yes, my Yaya."

Anki watched the giant boadulu march the few extra paces to the dais, one hand on his long obsidian spear, the other swaying dramatically from front to back, and then he stopped, snapped his heels together again, and bowed. Because of its brittle nature, Anki knew only the most skilled warriors could wield the deadly obsidian blades without breaking them. They were the sharpest of all Itabayiti blades, but his brother told him they could only be found on the island of Risca.

"Boadulu Urtulu, if I ask you to hand your spear and sling to your men, will you do it?" Yaya Amnu asked.

Boadulu Urtulu didn't hesitate and immediately handed his obsidian spear and boarhide sling to one of his men. Urtulu then snapped his heels again and, with his chin high in the air, he shouted, "Adulu!"

"Adulu!" his men echoed.

"Boadulu Urtulu, I had initially asked you here for one reason, but now I find that there may be another reason altogether." The Yaya stood and addressed the other adulu standing behind Urtulu. "As you are palace guards whose sole purpose is to protect the Yaya and his family, I regretfully ask that you raise your spears on this man." He pointed to Urtulu.

There was a brief hesitation, the adulu looking at one another, unsure if they should follow the Yaya's order, but then their spears slowly angled down one by one and pointed at their chief. The polished coral points individually reflected the torchlight onto the ceiling and walls, creating a brief dance of light that captured everyone's attention.

"Urtulu, you have been my boadulu for quite a while now, and I have not once been disappointed in your conduct. It grieves me to be in this position, but I have been presented with compelling testimony regarding a possible secret plot against Itabacan, and I need to know right now, before those gathered here, whether or not you knew about it. Do you understand?"

The boadulu remained standing firm and resolute, but his shifting eyes seemed to reveal a conflict happening in his thoughts. "Yes, my Yaya," he finally answered.

"Good, good." The Yaya looked relieved. "You have always been a loyal member of the palace guards, but there are two ways you can answer my next question, and I do hope you choose the right and proper path." Yaya Amnu paused to allow his words to sink in. "What do you know about the Mawoakin seeking the assistance of yaali in order to deliver this box to you?" The Yaya lifted the broken piece of wood from the towel for Urtulu to see. "Well – what is left of the box, anyway," he corrected himself.

Breaking from his stoic professionalism, Boadulu Urtulu looked menacingly at Anki and the other people lined up against the wall. His frightening eyes lingered longer on Anki, but Anki didn't look away like he might have on any other day, which surprised even him.

"I assume by your facial expression you have an answer for me?" the Yaya asked.

"I do," Urtulu replied and then bowed his head. There was a tense moment of silence, as everyone held their breaths in anticipation. "You, my Yaya," he said slowly, ominously. "You are in far greater danger than you could possibly imagine." There were several audible gasps in the hall as Boadulu Urtulu fell to his knees and raised his hands together, offering to be bound. "My fate has been woven, and I embrace the will of Mawoi. May his

Great Cleansing purify the Biyaya Spirit," he said, and then the boadulu started to laugh.

Yaya Amnu immediately ordered the adulu to bind their chief's wrists, which they reluctantly did. Anki was in shock the boadulu didn't struggle at all. And then the Yaya turned to the rest of them witnessing this extraordinary moment.

"Thank you for your service to Itabacan and your Yaya," he said, nodding to Abensu, Bogula, Tabba, and then Anki. "But it is time for you to leave. You will keep silent about what you have seen and heard here," the Yaya commanded, and everyone agreed. "Abensu, I am postponing the Day of Biyaya, but I will send for you shortly. Please, escort Tabba back to Mayu Hall."

"Yes, Yaya," Abensu bowed and started leading Anki and Tabba out of the palace.

"Bogula, I don't know if you have strong sea legs but..."

"No one else will be able to recognize the tizaka tree, my Yaya," Bogula interrupted him. "I will go and be happy about it." She smiled with her yellow teeth and added, "I also travel light and am ready to go as soon as you give the order."

"Thank you, Bogula," the Yaya said.

Outside, a full and bright moon shined down upon the palace grounds, creating an artificial day with a bit of a chill in the air. There was a distant crackle of thunder and Anki saw a mass of storm clouds receding to the west. He was beyond tired and stumbled through the shelly yard on his long legs, which were acting like soaking wet reeds at the moment. His father helped him onto the boar-drawn cart, Tabba climbed on behind them, and then his father took the reins.

"I can take you to Mayu Hall, or it might be safer for you to come to Conaca with us." He snapped the reins and the boar lazily started forward.

"Actually, can you take me into Badhan?" she asked.

"Any particular location in Badhan?"

"Do you know the Caru Market?"

Abensu steered the boar around a tight turn before answering. "It's been a while, but I think I know the place. Any particular reason why the Caru Market, if you don't mind me asking?"

"No, it's just where I grew up." Tabba warmed her hands with her breath and rubbed them on her arms.

"You weren't given over to the cult when you were born?" he asked. Anki noticed a bit of surprise in his father's voice.

"I was – we were, but twin araco are kind of rare and Elder Sengri wanted to raise us with him. He lives in Badhan now."

Abensu pulled the reins hard to the left, as they skidded around the last turn down the mountain, arriving at the backside of the Pyramid of Mayu. "Sengri is still around, is he?"

"Yeah, we always poked fun of his wrinkly face, but he joked his wrinkles were from the wisdom of the ancestors weighing down on him like a basket of chacu lard." Tabba laughed and Anki's father gave a hearty chuckle, which was the most Anki had heard him laugh in some time.

As they passed the pyramid, Anki thought he saw someone he recognized and tapped his father's shoulder. "Baba, is that Atu over there?" It looked as if Atu was hiding behind a bush.

"I believe you are correct, son." His father pulled back on the reins, bringing the boar to a halt and hollered, "Atu!" Anki's brother was startled and turned around, but Atu appeared even more startled to see them all bunched together in the cart. "What are you doing here, son?" Anki's father never appreciated having to shout.

"Um – I was just hanging out after lessons." Atu was lying. Anki knew his brother, and he knew when he was lying. He watched Atu jog over to the cart. "What are you doing here? Tayokun, Tabba."

"Tayokun, Atu," she replied with her arms crossed.

Anki saw his father swallow his irritation with Atu before he said, "Get on the cart, Atu. We're going home."

"But there's already too many of you on the cart," he protested.

"There's room and this is not a debate." Abensu's tone was stern and Atu wisely conceded.

With another body weighing down the cart, the poor boar squealed – their own form of protest – but begrudgingly started scraping their way forward. The village of Badhan wasn't much farther down the street and popped up on their right as they came down the slope. Its many candle-lit windows sparkled like the stars in the sky, which seemed to almost be choreographed to the hustle and bustle noise from within. Half of the shop stalls in the Caru Market were still open and there was a jatbay band playing their stringed gourd instruments in the center while men and women danced around them.

"Sengri's bohi is just there, after the stall selling plucked heron," Tabba pointed.

Anki saw half-a-dozen of the birds dangling from the roof beams by their feet, all of their feathers plucked out except around their heads. There was a jovial man behind the hanging heron, trying to draw business by hollering about the quality of his birds, "Fresh caught today! Gutted and drained! Ready to trade!"

"You can let me off here," Tabba said. She jumped down off the cart, but then she turned back, grabbed Anki, and hugged him, squeezing him even harder than Kina had. "Thank you, again, Anki. You may never know how grateful I am to you and Biacoya," she said, just as a graying old fox ran up to her and started licking her hand. "Ranar!" she shouted with joy. "I'm glad to see you too!"

Anki had never seen a fox before. His father told them foxes used to run wild all over the island of Amaca, but the agur had hunted them for their pelts to near extinction. To this day, there were thought to only be a few left, even though agur chiefs still wore fox pelts.

"Tayokun, Abensu – boys." Tabba waved, picked up Ranar, and walked toward the alley next to the heron vendor.

"Tayokun," they said, and then Abensu snapped the reins, and the boar sprang to life – no doubt, thankful the cart was now a little lighter.

As soon as they pulled back out onto the main street, Anki told his brother everything about his adventures during the day and made sure to not leave out a single detail. They made their way down to the docks and climbed onto the ferry, Anki still talking but his story getting broken up by his frequent yawning. Atu feigned a smile at his story, trying to listen politely, but Anki could tell he wasn't really paying attention to him. A cool breeze washed over the ferry which coasted effortlessly upon the still waters of the sound. Anki cuddled up to his father for warmth, his eyes closed but still mumbling about the cave and Biacoya and going to the palace to meet the Yaya.

He popped one eye open and watched Atu look out over the water to the Grand Gateways and the Great Sea beyond. He knew Atu was becoming a man and that he had a big crush on a girl named Joba. Anki was pretty sure she was already promised to someone, he wasn't sure who, but he did know Atu complained about the other boy a lot. Actually, now that he thought about it, his brother complained about everything. He complained about his friends for making fun of him, the bocoani who Atu said always talked down to him, and Atu even complained to Anki about all the attention Anki got all the time. It was then that Anki realized blathering on about his adventures, and then Kina, and then the Yaya probably didn't make his brother feel any better.

He watched Atu spit into the water, hugging his cold thin legs to his chest and resting his chin on his boney knees, and hoped Orlil had woven something amazing for his brother. As mean and frustrating as Atu could be, he was Anki's one and only brother. They laughed more than they fought, and Anki hated it when they fought. He decided right there on the ferry, from that day forward, Anki was going to do his best to suppress the yaduka and not get so angry with his brother all the time. He yawned a long, big yawn and closed his eyes. What an amazing, tragic, enlightening, painful, and tiring kind of day, he thought. And then the memory thread of Kina's soft cheek pressed against his popped into Anki's mind, and then a giant smile crept across his face, just before he fell asleep.

CHAPTER -SEVENTEEN

And Rises with the Moon

Deep in the cool, damp, dark recesses of the cave on the cliffs, Ennu opened her Itabayiti eyes to the blackness. There was a sharp pain in her back and her left leg was unresponsive. She ran her palms over her bare skin and began inspecting her body. A wave of relief washed over her as she marveled at her smooth skin, long thin fingers, and chubby little toes. She felt her thick, matted hair and did her best to tease through it with a bit of saliva and her fingernails. Her lips were chapped, and her mouth tasted gross, but she wasn't sure why. She checked her ears, feeling all over them and snapping her fingers near the opening to make sure they still worked. Her snaps echoed around her, telling Ennu she was in the cave. Pleased to know everything seemed to be in the right place, she closed her eyes to complete the transformation.

Breathing in and out and paying close attention to the sensation in her chest, Ennu caught the expected dank smell of wet rock, but also the surprising odor of rotting bird eggs. It was both alarming and exciting at the same time. She recognized the odor as belonging to the many thick-tailed scorpions which lived in the deepest sections of the cave. In her Itabayiti form, the scorpions would pose a deadly threat to her recovery, but the fact that she was able to retain such a precise sense of smell after her transformation was phenomenal. She sniffed the air again, now focusing on the scorpion scent and found it was strongest to her right, and a bit closer than she initially thought. She dragged her right foot back so that her heel pressed against her bottom, took a deep breath, and then braced herself against the rock wall as she stood. Her wobbly right leg worked well enough to support her, but her left leg dangled at her side like a fleshy vine. She needed water and could hear a plunking sound coming from around the corner to the left.

Ennu had been through enough transformations to know her recovery would take time, food, and, above all, water. Other than being able to recall those three elements, her memory was a bit foggy. Transformations were always disorientating, but this one was exceptionally so. There was a feeling like she needed to be doing something else, but she wasn't sure what. She had an itch on her forearm and scratched at it passively as she struggled along the rock wall toward the not-too-distant dripping. Her heart beat rhythmically at what she felt was a normal rate, and she could hear the scuttering of various critters somewhere in the darkness. She sniffed the air again like a hutia detecting a predator. *Ah-ha*, she thought, licking the inside of her mouth again – *baby hutia*. Her arm was still itchy, and she scratched at it again before reaching out blindly toward the dripping sound next to her.

The cool water was exactly what her disgusting mouth, exhausted body, and clouded mind needed. She awkwardly angled her head directly beneath the drip, allowing the water to splash all over her face, and then she drank her fill. The water was refreshingly cool but gritty, grinding between her teeth and coating her tounge. In her mind, she ran backward through the most recent events starting with her itchy arm, attempting to piece together a thread which she could gently pull until more of her memory came down the line.

Before the darkness of the cave, she was crawling through the jungle, which might explain her itchy arm. She was crawling because her legs wouldn't work after she had fallen into a patch of large-leaf bushes, which was where the uca had dropped her. Images of recent events were starting to appear on the thread. Her back hurt from the fall, which also explained why her left leg was currently useless. She painfully shifted her body, leaned against the rock wall, and slid down until she was sitting on her bottom. The water dripped on top of her matted hair, which smelled awful, but then the smell sparked a memory-flash of gray and white feathers, a pain in her side, and a similar musty smell. After a moment, the thread snagged, and her memory went dark again.

Ennu was almost certain she had transformed back from being a snake, but it remained unclear how long or why she had been a snake in the first place. What do snakes do? she wondered. *They slither around on the ground licking the air, snapping at ankles, and hissing when you won't let them eat you!* Her response to her own question made her snicker in the darkness. And why do they do that? *Because they're angry the Great Spirit forgot to give them arms or legs...* She held her tongue, her thoughts revolving around a new or, perhaps, the absence of a memory thread. She had never transformed into a snake before, and that was why she had done it. She pressed her aching back against the cool rock, feeling a bit more confident in herself.

Where do snakes live? *Holes in the ground, trees, and caves.* Another flash brought the threads more quickly now; the Womb of the Earth, *Libanu, Karun'kalu...* The dense fog obscuring her memories was lifting. Memory threads continued to form, stretching out from the recesses of her mind. Each strand effortlessly wrapped around the next as they wove themselves into a colorful cloak Ennu imagined being draped over her shoulders.

Karun. Karun Village was where she first discovered her ability to take the form of other creatures, which she called her kalu – her threat guardian, her blessing from Karun. Of course, the village no longer existed. It had outgrown itself long ago, all the villages had, and eventually merged with the others to form Badhan. The Itabayiti had turned her home into the Caru Market, which was infuriating. She spit on the ground, the stale, earthen taste of baby hutia still lingering in her mouth. The passage of time had not diluted her anger one bit, and over the years she learned to redirect her animosity for the Itabayiti to more productive activities, like perfecting her kalu and growing her family. She made secrecy a priority and went to great lengths to avoid detection for centuries.

She knew there were stories about her, of course, tales told to keep children in bed at night. Each new generation needed guidance and control without requiring the Yaya to institute additional time-consuming training. To this end, the Itabayiti manipulated ancient stories passed down through the generations to be more educational, filling them with little lessons in morality and cleanliness. However, no matter how much they changed their stories, hints to their original intent remained. There were even a few stories which were said to be based on ancient truths the Itabayiti had long since forgotten. The truth of Ennu's kalu was one of these stories, she was sure of it, and she had devoted a substantial portion of her long life to repairing that frayed thread.

Suddenly, the faint sound of someone talking startled her eyes wide open. She could hear the dripping water, the distant hum of wind, and then, there in the faint distance, was the voice of a little girl. It was a voice that sounded oddly familiar.

"Hkkk..." She tried to speak but only a horrifying hacking came out. In response, she heard the pattering of sandaled feet on wet rock. "Hkkk..." She tried again but the second time was almost more terrifying than the first. She stood on her one good leg and hobbled after the sound, sniffing the air. There were the scorpions, but also – *sniff, sniff* – smoke, fresh flowers, and both male and female body odor. There were two of them.

Ennu passed the scorpions, rounded a corner, and then stubbed her toe on a rock which skidded forward into a chasm of some sort; the rock ricocheted off the chasm walls as it went down and faded away. She could still hear the pattering of sandaled feet to her left and followed them, tiptoeing around the chasm and squeezing through a narrow crack in the rock wall. Suddenly, she stumbled into an open area illuminated by a smoldering little fire. Ennu chuckled as the light reminded her of her nakedness, but she was pleasantly surprised to see that she was standing firmly on both legs. Willing herself forward, she charged into the darkness she now knew would take her to the mouth of the cave.

"Whoa! Thanks!" one of them said.

Ennu could see the silhouettes of a boy and a girl against the moonlight straight ahead, but she was having trouble breathing. There was a process to the libanu for a reason, and chasing children was not part of that process. She was pushing herself too hard and had to slow down. With an exhausted wheeze, Ennu plopped down on her backside and tried to control her labored breathing.

"Ahhh!" the children screamed and ran off around the corner into the jungle.

Ennu chuckled again. She looked out into the night with her Itabayiti eyes and saw the ancestors dotting the dark sky. Fresh air poured over her face and her breathing eased. She could smell the rich and complex scents coming from the jungle, the salty seawater at the base of the cliff, and then her own pungent aroma hovering wherever she went. She needed to retrieve her clothes, get off Itabaca, and return to Osanum where she would summon the others, her daughters, the Numkalu.

Unsurprisingly, her clothes were right where she had left them and, with a few grunts, Ennu slid a maroon tunic over her matted and greasy hair. Instantly, the fabric felt uncomfortably stiff and foreign. It was as if her skin was rejecting the covering and she shivered and gritted her teeth, forcing herself to not immediately rip the fabric from her body. Next, she wrapped her brock-hide belt tightly around her waist and fastened it, but the constricting sensation was nauseating, and she quickly loosened it until the sensation passed. Lastly, Ennu draped a crimson robe over her irritated shoulders and growled at her clothing.

The lively jungle quieted as she strolled confidently down the well-worn path through the underbrush. She popped out onto the full-moonlit street and arched her back, cracking it in several places. It didn't take long for her to reach the Pyramid of Mayu and the Grand Plaza, which were both dark and silent. She meandered around Mayu Hall and down the slope toward Badhan without encountering another person and did her best to make her wild hair presentable as she went. In the moonlight, she was able to see and brush off most of the dirt and grime from her limbs and face, but her hair was uncooperative. As she slipped into the alley before entering the Caru Market, Ennu snagged a dark-red, almost black wildflower from the ground and stuck it in her hair.

Jatbay players strummed beautifully in the southeast corner of the market, their vibrant music filling the air while couples danced in their bare feet and drank from gourd cups filled to the brim with oycu. They weren't paying any attention to her, allowing Ennu to easily slip between the dancers and the empty stalls along the north side of the market. She stopped at a non-descript wooden door set into the cibmani wall like a knot on a tree. After a quick glance to ensure no one saw her, she knocked softly.

PART TWO
The Orders of the YAYA

CHAPTER EIGHTEEN

A Quest for TIZAKA

Bocoani Numila was summoned before dawn and taken to the Yaya's private chambers where he noticed neither Unana Wani nor Kina Wani were in sight. He met with the Yaya alone who instructed him to organize an expedition to the island of Bayamaca immediately without any explanation as to why, except that he would have a passenger named Bogula. Numila knew the name, but he had never met the eccentric lesini until that morning, when she was standing on the dock waiting for him as Mawoi appeared over the eastern wall.

She was a short woman with long ratted hair that smelled awful and glistened in the sunlight like bubbling bitumen. Numila saw her fingernails were long and chipped, and there was dirt or something like mold underneath them. But Bogula waved and Numila smiled as he approached.

"Taycoay, Bocoani Numila," the strange woman said.

"Taycoay, Bogula. I have been instructed to take you to Bayamaca, correct?" Numila had his hands on his hips, flexing his rippling muscles, and squinting at the sun.

"Correct, young man. Did the Yaya tell you why?" Bogula grinned with yellowing teeth.

Numila looked at her with unconcerned eyes. "No, he did not, and that is just fine with me. However, you should know that sailing to Bayamaca is not going to be easy."

"Oh, and why is that?" she asked, leaning on her gnarled staff.

"Because the storm yesterday stirred up the Bocoa, and dangerous creatures come up from the deeps to feed after a storm."

Bogula seemed to ponder this for a moment and then looked at the fishing canuti in the slip next to them. "Do we need a bigger canuti?" she asked with a little chuckle.

Before Bocoani Numila could respond, his crew arrived. They were five of the best sailors Itabacan had to offer, and one of them happened to be his wife, Koyay, the only female coani in the Yaya's fleet. She normally supervised the harbor when Numila went out to sea, but he knew he needed her for this mission.

His crew greeted one another in the customary way and then began climbing onto the canuti and got right to work, ignoring the strange woman standing next to him. There was Madiri, a quick-witted man with unnaturally long tan arms, a neatly trimmed but graying beard, and a ga'an the size of a coconut on top of his head. Madiri came in handy when furling the sail and would man the kona-line. Ruruga had pale skin, but no one would know because every last bit of him was covered in tattoos. He had a reddish-brown ga'an on top of his head and would man the chok-line with no sense of humor at all. Dimgal was a slippery-sort-of man, short and quick on his hands, feet, bottom, or whatever the moment called for, and had big, fluffy, wild hair and a dozen shell necklaces. Dimgal was easily distracted and Numila had to keep him busy as their scrounger. And then there was Gisal who was as tall as he was wide with a delicate tiny black ga'an knot perfectly centered on his head. The canuti dipped nearly a whole hand in the water when Gisal climbed on, but he could row them out into the sound by himself and was proficient in every position; Numila gladly sacrificed their speed in favor of Gisal's skill.

Koyay patted Numila on the cheek as she walked by. She was petite with rich ebony skin and exceptional legs and was the fiercest navigator in all of Itabacan. Unlike the other coani, Koyay had several smaller ga'an knots arranged in a five-pointed star pattern on top of her head – one for every year she had been a coani. The island of Bayamaca was surrounded by thick coral reefs, and they would need Koyay to get them there without ripping their canuti to shreds.

Together, Numila and Koyay had a young boy named Kaseo who stayed with Koyay's mother, father, and baby brother, Mulak, on the island of Hatca. Their son spent most days learning everything there was to know about crabs, but when he was old enough, he would be right there with his parents.

"Alright, everyone, this is Bogula," Numila said, helping her onto the canuti.

"We know," Koyay said.

Numila looked up to see everyone nodding in agreement. "Well, why didn't you say so!"

"Taycoay, Bogula," Koyay said as she checked the tiller and rudder. The others followed with the customary greeting as well.

"Taycoay, everyone." Bogula smiled and got comfortable, sitting on the spine right in front of the mast.

"Bogula is on an important mission for the Yaya, which we are helping to facilitate by taking her to Bayamaca." Numila strutted to the head of the canuti.

"Which is why I'm here," Koyay joked, eliciting a bit of laughter from the men. They all knew how important Koyay was to the mission, but Numila was aware they also knew it was rare for both the bocoani and the harbor chief to be away from Itabacan at the same time.

"Who's running the harbor while we're gone?" Dimgal asked, as if reading Numila's mind.

"Kaseo," Madiri joked, and the other men laughed.

"Ha-ha, not funny," Numila mocked him. "The Yaya has postponed the Day of Biyaya and ordered the harbor closed. I'm sure you have all noticed the agur hanging around."

This news surprised everyone. Closing the harbor was rare, and postponing the Day of Biyaya was unheard of. Numila couldn't remember a time when Itabacan was without both a bocoani and a harbor chief, or the harbors closed, and contemplated what it might mean while he watched his crew go to work.

Gisal had pulled up the anchor and was readying the oars when he asked, "Were you going to tell us why?"

"He doesn't know!" Madiri laughed, but no one laughed with him.

"Honestly, I don't know," Numila responded, noting the wiggling ribbon at the top of the mast. "All I know is we need to make way. We have the wind and with the harbor closed, we have the best coani at the tiller." He smiled at his wife and asked her, "Ready, Coani Koyay?"

"As I'll ever be," Koyay replied.

"Good, take us out boys!" Numila shouted.

"Ahem!" Koyay gave her husband a look and the men snickered like little girls.

"My apologies. Take us out *shoats!*"

Everyone cheered and squealed like baby boar. Numila didn't need to go through his usual instructions he gave the shoats, because these were the best sailors Itabacan had to offer. All Numila needed to do was keep them focused and bring them back alive. He glanced over at Bogula sitting in front of the mast and added her to his list of responsibilities. Surprisingly, she seemed to be watching all of the activity on the reed boat with a passing fascination, as if being on this epic journey, a journey the vast majority of the Itabayiti would never get the opportunity to take, was no different from any other boring trip across the sound.

Of course, Numila knew all too well the amount of skill and cunning he and his crew – any crew, for that matter – needed just to survive the first part of their journey, the half-day sail to Sanaca. He looked over the headrib as they passed under the Gate of Kuraka. The waters of the Great Sea were murky due to the churned-up seagrasses and sediment floating on top and just below the surface. Koyay expertly angled them into the Trough of Tranquility where the calm waters of Itabacan Sound collided with the raging sea. The wind always shifted at this point, and Numila watched Madiri and Ruruga to make sure they harnessed the Great Wind with the same amount of excellence his wife was displaying on the tiller. All at once, the sails popped, their canuti jerked a notch to chok, climbed out of the trough, and then they crested the wave and were met with the roar of the Bocoa once again. The canuti slapped back down hard, sending a shower of salty seawater over the entire crew.

"Woo-hoo!" Dimgal hollered, and the rest of the crew cheered along with him.

"As expected," Numila said, smiling proudly.

Up and down the canuti rode on the rolling waves like a pelican soaring into the sky, the cano on either side their wings, and then they dove back down toward the water. Numila loved it. He honestly loved sailing more than anything and so did his crew. And then he noticed Bogula was filling a water gourd with vomit, the contents of her stomach spilling over the lip of the container and dripping onto the spine. He shook his head, chuckling. *The old lesini doesn't seem to be so bored now*, he thought.

"Dimgal!" he shouted for his scrounger.

"Bocoani!" Dimgal bowed to Numila, prostrating himself on the wet spine of the canuti.

"Knock it off, will you?" He had to laugh. "Help our guest and get her to the midrib. We can't risk any of you getting sick because Bogula forgot her sea legs back on Amaca."

"Bogula, do you need me to empty your gourd for you?" the scrounger asked, saltwater dripping off his soaking wet face.

The old lesini looked up and shook her head, but then she looked past Dimgal to the extreme rising and falling of the horizon and quickly tucked her head back into the gourd.

"Guess she's not finished with it yet," Madiri joked. He was calmly manning the kona-line a reed away, his entire body drenched from the waves constantly splashing across the canuti.

Dimgal chuckled and said, "Come on, Bogula. We have to get you to the midrib, else your nasty puke is going to make everybody sick."

"He's not joking, lesini," Madiri added. "I've seen an entire transport full of vomiting ciba workers, all because one of them ate a bad pagsha." He chuckled to himself.

"Dim, NOW – please!" Numila shouted at him.

"Yes, Bocoani!" Dimgal helped Bogula crawl to the kona-side midrib, doing his best to keep her puke gourd level. The canuti rose and fell again with a mighty splash, dousing the crew in a salty mist. The scrounger twisted his body like a wet weasel trying to confuse a snake. Numila thought he looked ridiculous, but Dimgal didn't spill a drop from the gourd.

"You understand," Ruruga said from the chok-line in his dry, dead-pan manner, wiping seawater from his tattooed face and long beard. "Lesini prepare remedies for sick and hurting bodies, and she will likely do so for herself. Bogula will let us know if she needs our help."

"Right," Dimgal replied, raising his eyebrows to Numila, but Numila knew the scrounger's sarcasm was lost on Ruruga. "I'll be back in a bit," Dimgal told the lesini. "Don't you go anywhere!" He then carefully dumped the contents of the gourd into the sea and returned to the mast where their spears and freshwater gourds were stored.

After she had expelled every last bit from her stomach, Bogula slumped against the midrib, her long vine-like clumps of hair snaking across the spine. "Feeling any better, Lesini Bogula?" the bocoani asked, watching Dimgal return and hand her a gourd of freshwater.

She didn't immediately respond to him but looked up at Midiri instead. "Young man," she said. "It's pa-*ga*-sh-*la* – toe-pinchers, they call them, not...whatever you said."

"What did I say?" Midiri asked the rest of the crew.

"Hmm...foot shake?" Koyay said, making everyone laugh.

Once they had traveled farther out to sea, the waves seemed to settle and their canuti cut through the water at an incredible rate. Bogula eventually made her way back to where she had been sitting in front of the mast while Dimgal sat behind the mast. The string of gourds clacked together against the wooden shafts of the spears above the scrounger's head, adding to the noise of the sea and the persistent creaking of the reed boat. Numila glanced to make sure Ruruga and Madiri had tied off their lines before he reclined in the neck and watched everyone else relax.

They all enjoyed the voyage in their own ways. Bogula had fallen asleep at some point, her head hanging down and swaying left to right with the rhythmic movement of the vessel. Ruruga had a ball of string, which he used to create dozens and dozens of intricate knots. For as long as Numila had known him, Ruruga had loved to invent new knots for the coani to use, and some of his knots had actually replaced the ancient knots the Itabayiti had been using since before the Yayapti. Madiri and Dimgal found a handful of beetles in the baskets of provisions and were playing with the skittering bugs like little children might. Gisal, the monstrous mountain-of-a-man, snored almost as loud as the crashing waves of the Great Sea, and was fast asleep with his head on the coiled anchor rope, his fingers interlocked and resting on his belly, and his outstretched legs crossed at the ankle. Numila had never seen anyone look more comfortable.

Before long, only Bocoani Numila and Koyay were still awake, the rocking vessel having put everyone else to sleep. He tilted his head to the side to see around the mast and Bogula's swaying head to his beautiful wife back at the tail, still standing with one arm slung over the tiller. Every now and then he would catch her eye and Koyay would make a silly face at him. They made a game of it, seeing who could make the silliest face without cracking a smile. She was winning, of course, but that was only because Numila had gotten used to losing the same game with their son, Kaseo. After a while, they both lost interest in the silly-face game, and Numila looked up to see Mawoi high in the western sky, having just past midday. He thought it strange they hadn't spotted Sanaca yet and was contemplating closing his eyes. It was going to be a long voyage, and there was never any guarantee when they would be able to rest. He opened one eye to ensure all was well before trying to get some sleep and noticed Koyay pointing.

Numila quickly stood and turned to see what she was pointing at. "Sanaca, straight ahead!" he shouted enthusiastically through a yawn.

Everyone started waking up and looked, as the canuti dipped into the shadow of a large wave and then cut hard to kona through its crest, dousing the crew in seawater. When they emerged, there was a sliver of land on the horizon. Sanaca was one of the many islands Bocoani Tiktali had discovered a century before when Yaya Anacacu had sent him to find the end of the Bocoa. From Sanaca, if they sailed both day and night, Numila knew they could reach Bayamaca in roughly half-a-mawa.

"Tiburana!" Koyay suddenly screamed, and then she pulled the tiller to her stomach as hard as she could, causing the entire crew to lose their footing and nearly fall off the canuti as it swung hard to kona.

Numila braced himself against the chok-side headrib and saw an enormous fin a dozen reeds out, about twice as far away as the cano. Fishermen told stories of an unusually large shark that was known to eat other sharks and would even attack their canuti from time to time, but Numila had only recently seen one up close. He felt like he might be able to reach out and touch it. Of his small but experienced crew, only Ruruga claimed to have encountered a tiburana before. He even had the outline of one tattooed in the center of his back running up his spine. As the enormous fin dipped below the water, Numila looked at Ruruga on the chok-line and silently asked him with his eyes to confirm, and Ruruga slowly nodded in reply.

"Keep calm, everyone!" Bocoani Numila immediately addressed the rising tension. "We're not far from shore. Do you have eyes on the beast?" he called to Koyay on the tiller.

"Not anymore," she said, scanning the turbulent waves around the tail of the canuti.

"There!" Madiri shouted and pointed to a dark spot moving below the surface.

It was hard to see through the murky water. Numila had warned Bogula that very morning about the massive creatures that came up from the deeps to feed after a storm. Most of them paid no attention to canuti and appeared to be gentle like the manati. The biggest of them didn't even have fins but massive flippers and wide flat tails. They gulped up mouthfuls of seawater and anything unfortunate enough to be floating in it. Numila lost sight of the dark shadow. "Koyay, get us back on course. Gisal, ready the spears just in case!"

"Yes, Bocoani!" Koyay and Gisal replied in turn.

Their course was corrected with the head of the canuti pointing directly at Sanaca, and Gisal untied the barbed spears from behind the mast. He first handed one to Numila, then Dimgal, and then he laid one next to both Madiri and Ruruga who each stepped on their spears to keep them in place.

"Do we see the beast anywhere?" Numila asked his crew, but the only response was a bump on the belly of the canuti.

"It's beneath us!" Dimgal shouted.

Everyone looked, and to their astonishment they could see flippers reaching all the way to the cano on either side. Numila guessed the gigantic shark was easily twice the size of their reed boat.

"What's it doing?" Bogula asked, her voice squeaking with fear.

They crested another wave and the crew briefly lost sight of the beast, but as they leveled out again, its shadow reappeared directly below them. Thankfully, the wind hadn't died down at all and the canuti was tearing through the water faster than ever.

"It seems to be perfectly content to just cruise along with us," Numila said, but had his barbed spear ready to throw just in case.

WHAM!

Everyone jumped, startled by the tiburana bumping the belly of the canuti again, but it didn't hit them hard enough to knock them off course. The Bocoa had started to calm a bit and the rolling waves settled into a medium chop. Before long, Sanaca grew until Numila could clearly make out palm trees on shore and the light-green shallows straight ahead.

"Hey, it's gone!" Koyay exclaimed.

They had all been biting their nails, focusing on maintaining speed and direction, and assumed their shark-shadow was still with them. Bocoani Numila searched the waters with wide eyes. "Any sign of it anywhere?"

No one said anything, but after a moment Ruruga replied, "I think it's gone, Bocoani."

Numila let out a relieved sigh, "Fine, I'll put it to a vote. Do we continue on, or do we anchor in the shallows of Sanaca for the night? I only ask because we won't see land again for two days if we continue on." Numila looked at his crew, waiting patiently for their votes.

To his surprise, it was Bogula who stood up and addressed the crew, wiping a dribble of vomit from her chin. "What just happened scared the Osani out of me!" she began. "I could see it in all of your eyes as well, but my mission – our mission cannot be postponed like a festival, or even for a *tiburana*, or whatever that thing was! We must reach Bayamaca as fast as we can."

"What *is* our mission?" Dimgal asked as he collected the barbed spears from everyone.

Numila's crew looked to him first, but then they all looked at Bogula together. The old lesini just smiled and answered, "If we continue on, then I will tell you."

After a moment of reflection, they all agreed to continue on and Koyay pointed the head of the canuti south toward the island of Oubayoca.

The amazing tale Bogula told captivated Numila's crew for a long time, thankfully taking their minds off of the tiburana. The old lesini became lost in the intricate details she seemed to have heard so many times she forgot about her lack of sea legs. She walked about the spine of the canuti with her staff like a seasoned coani, acting out bits of the story, and she even got emotional and started to weep when she pretended to cradle the boy, Biacoya, in her arms. Bogula called her story *Part One of the Quest for Tizaka*, and was asked to repeat the epic tale again the next morning. And then Gisal asked to hear it again that next evening, and the lesini obliged him. But when Gisal asked that she tell the Quest for Tizaka a fourth time, just when they spotted Oubayoca on the horizon, Bocoani Numila had heard enough.

"Stow it, Gisal," he said, and then turned to Bogula. "Thank you for entertaining my crew, but I think we've heard enough of that story for now."

"It was getting a bit stale," she admitted and returned to her seat in front of the mast, using her staff to ease herself down.

Numila felt bad for snapping on Gisal. He had to remind himself, although he had brought together the best possible crew, they were all coani and chiefs in their own right. Except for Koyay and Dimgal, everyone else on the canuti was also older than Numila. There was only one thing he could think of that might bring them all together, and so he started to sing.

Between the sky and earth, we ride our canuti far from home.

Reed to rutter, Bocoa Cutter, a sail from cotton sewn...

Koyay giggled, but then joined her husband and sang along:

"Come back," they cry with tearful eyes from docks made of stone...

And then the rest of the crew chimed in on the next line:

Yucahu bless their sorrowness but keep us free to roam!

They sang verse after verse as the waves splashed against the ribs of the canuti, their voices slowly lifting the island of Oubayoca out of the sea like a crab from beneath the sand.

Oubayoca was known as the Island of Blood, because its beaches were often blanketed with dead fish and their blood soaked into the sand, creating a muddy-red ring around the whole island. Some said the fish chose to die there because the island was cursed by Niama, while others claimed the fish had been rejected by a sea monster that left them to rot in the sun. No one was absolutely sure why the fish washed up on shore, but with the dead fish came a wall of flies and other insects. Sand crabs came by the thousands to feed on the carcasses, and the smell of it all would hobble the strongest Itabayiti. But once those hazards were overcome, the interior of the island was very peaceful and provided most of the comforts and provisions of home.

With the canuti anchored in the shallows and the sun low in the sky, they waded to shore and started hacking their way through the buzzing barricade, stepping over the dead fish, crabs, and bugs.

Madiri heaved, "It's so thick, I could roll it up like a sail." He chuckled to himself, grabbing handfuls of flies as if they were huge grains of sand.

Numila glanced to his left at Madiri, but then Gisal stepped between them and batted at the insects with an oar like he was playing a game of almec. Dead flies soared through the air in every direction, hitting their crewmates, but the others didn't seem to notice one or two flies from the rest of the wall of bugs. Numila then looked to his right and saw Bogula collecting some of the flies in a wooden vial. She stoppered it before putting the vial inside her robe. Dimgal was watching her as well and laughed, but then he got a mouthful of flies and broke through to the other side gagging and spitting them out.

"Why do I always let you talk me into trips like this?" Ruruga asked as he plucked buzzing insects out of his beard.

"Because I order you to," Numila answered.

"Oh," Ruruga said, without a hint of irony.

"You boys done playing with the bugs?" Koyay hollered at them. "We have to set up camp and get some food in our bodies before I pass out!" She was waiting up the hill from the beach, tapping her foot. Numilla thought she looked lovely.

The evening sun had almost disappeared over the horizon, creating a mesmerizing display of reds, oranges, yellows, and greens, which they all watched with heavy eyes. Bocoani Numila could feel the tug of sleep upon him as Dimgal roasted whitefish on a spit over their modest campfire. Unlike some of his companions, Numila had always been skeptical of the idea Yucahu spoke to them during sleeptime. He had the same vision every night and stopped trying to understand it a long time ago. It was said, what the Great Spirit revealed in sleep could only be realized if the vision was recalled in its entirety upon waking. His vision was too weird and convoluted to be remembered entirely, no matter how many times it had repeated. But as Numila watched the whitefish sizzle and smoke, rotating and making a *tsss* sound as it dripped into the flames, he thought he recognized something about the moment. It was as if he had seen these roasting fish and experienced this exact campfire before.

"You alright, my loving jellyfish?" Koyay asked, clearly seeing the strange look in Numila's eyes.

"Ye-Yeah," he stammered. "I'm just hungry and tired, that's all." He blinked several times and rubbed his face. "And don't call me that in front of the men," he whispered.

"Almost done," Dimgal said.

"Finally!" Gisal licked his lips.

They ate their fill of whitefish and talked a bit about their expedition until the campfire died. Numila explained there would be no more stopping until they reached Bayamaca in three days, and he encouraged everyone to ask Yucahu to allow his Great Spirit within to sleep restfully through the night. The next part of the journey would be excruciatingly monotonous. As far as Bocoani Numila knew, only he and Koyay had ever been as far away from Itabacan as Bayamaca, and he worried the crew might not handle the stress as well as they had so far. But, as much as he worried about the men, Numila was more concerned about old Lesini Bogula. There was definitely something strange about her, and he got the uneasy feeling she wasn't being entirely honest with them. He heard her story about the quest for tizaka enough to suspect Bogula might be skipping over an unknown, pivotal plot-hole, and Numila knew there was nothing more dangerous on a long voyage than a great big hole in their canuti.

CHAPTER NINETEEN

The Tusks of CHUKA

Yaya Amnu's orders were clear; Boagur Gudugu was to send a small force to secure the harbors of all the islands, while taking the majority of his men to arrest the Mawoakin and their attendants. He sent six agur to each of the other ten islands, leaving a contingency of twelve men on Coyaca, while he personally escorted an army of sixty agur warriors to Bahaca. They arrived on shore under the cover of darkness, squishing up onto the beach well before dawn on three transport canuti. Their assigned coani were ordered to not waste time docking or anchoring because speed was the aim. A few agur would be left behind to protect the coani who were instructed to be ready to make way at a moment's notice. The agur were burly enough to push the canuti off the beach after their task was completed.

Gudugu stood firmly on the beach with his arms crossed over his boulder-like chest. He had dark honey skin and stretch marks over his broad shoulders that looked like jagged streaks of lightning. He wore a boarhide tunic the agur called a chaccus that was so tight it could have been painted on his body. Two support straps came up over his shoulders and crossed at his chest, before attaching to a polished boarhide belt around his waist. An orange and brown fox pelt hung from his left shoulder strap, while his agur braid draped over his right shoulder. A leather sheath holding an obsidian saber hung from his right hip, and the saber had a highly polished bone handle that glistened in the fading starlight. A gourd full of oycu dangled from his left hip, but it only glistened if Gudugu spilled any of the precious liquid inside, which didn't happen very often. His lean legs were toned after years of supporting his substantial torso, making him appear like an extremely muscular, though nearly hairless boar.

Gudugu was easily a hand taller than the majority of his men, and he wore a boar jawbone headdress wrapped with tanned leather straps in varying shades, signifying him as the chief of the agur. His men were all relatively tall and strong boys, but the boagur was simply that much larger. His wife, Gigal, was taller than most of his men, and they knew their son, Luculati, would likely be as well. She was also smarter than most of the agur, and she was happy to remind him every day with her extensive knowledge of Itabacan's history. Of course, the one fact she had neglected to tell him over their decade-long marriage was how she knew so much. Gudugu's newly appointed second in both command and height was Duagur Addo, the oldest son of Chief of Springs Hadim, and the only other person in the boagur's life whose intelligence rivaled Gigal's. He eyed the young man, thinking if any of his men were going to challenge him for leadership, it would be Addo.

He watched as his small army of agur quietly arranged themselves into three equal kanbati, or formations, and then Boagur Gudugu lifted his headdress high into the air, signaling rather than telling them to follow him.

Though they trained to march in unison, once they reached the mouth of the cave entrance to the island, Gudugu immediately noticed how loud their sixty-one pairs of sandals were on the stone ground. He quickly raised his headdress again, causing his men to stop, and made a show of removing his sandals and setting them aside. Getting the idea, the rest of the agur followed their boagur's lead and removed their sandals as well. He nodded to Duagur Addo who understood and swiftly scanned the feet of their men. When Addo was satisfied that everyone's sandals had been removed, he nodded back to the boagur and their march into the cave continued.

The low thumping of their bare feet echoed off the rock walls and seemed to resonate through the cave like a constant rolling thunder. Gudugu had noticed two dark torch basins at the entrance of the cave, and he knew there would be at least two more basins before they reached the interior of the island. Without their comforting glow, the cave rapidly grew darker than the darkest Hekura. Not even the sun-bleached and polished bone handle of his saber reflected even the faintest trace of light. The only reassurance they were headed in the right direction was that they were still moving uphill and hadn't run into any walls or fallen into that hole the Yaya had described.

Initially, Gudugu intended to bring his entire one hundred-and-twelve-man army and leave securing the harbors to the Yaya's adulu, but then the Yaya explained there were supposedly only a few dozen akin and attendants at most on Bahaca, and that they were all vegetarians. Gudugu had never heard of a vegetarian and thought he was suggesting the Mawoakin were possessed by the Earth Spirit. When Yaya Amnu did explain what it meant, Gudugu was immensely disappointed.

Just up ahead, he caught a glimpse of light – a long but thin sliver of slightly less blackness that curved upward like a jagged smile in the rock. As they marched toward it, their thunderous footfalls radiating around them, the jagged smile started to widen like a slow yawn. Gudugu hadn't seen the two torch basins he remembered being in the cave, but it had been over ten years since he had been there, and he assumed things had changed.

He tilted his headdress down, looking up over his eyebrows and checking to see if the jawbone was reflecting enough light to signal and it was. The wide-open mouth of the cave approached and just before his bare toes dipped into the smile of faint light, the boagur raised his headdress and stopped. The men directly behind him stopped as well, but the rest of them got the signal by bumping into the man in front of him. Grumbles reverberated from kanbati to kanbati, but Gudugu silenced them.

"*Stug!*" he whispered as loudly as he dared.

"Stug," he heard Duagur Addo echo him, or he assumed Addo had repeated the order.

THUMP-thump...thump... The agur stomped in intervals as they responded to the echoing order to come to attention.

Boagur Gudugu held his breath and cringed at the amount of noise coming from his army. They might as well put down their spears, build a fire, and have a cave festival. After a moment, the echoing slowly died away and he listened for the alarm he was sure the Mawoakin would sound, but there was nothing. He let out a deep sigh and shook his head, allowing himself to breathe freely once again.

From what he could see, the terrain outside of the cave was exactly as he remembered it. There weren't any trees to hide under, and the scattered prickly shrubs and patches of dune grass were insufficient as cover, except for maybe a few spiny rats. They were going to be exposed all the way up the slope and the entire time they were on the island. To the right, Gudugu saw that the stables appeared to be empty, but it was hard to tell in the dim light of night. The only reasonable plan of attack, as far as he could tell, would be to run as fast as they could, as quietly as they could, and hope they made it to the top before getting noticed.

He turned back to his men, squinting to find Addo in the bleak darkness of the cave. Once he found him, Gudugu motioned for his duagur to come to the front.

"Hmm," Addo mumbled as he approached.

Gudugu gestured for him to come closer and then whispered in Addo's ear, "We run. No talking. Spears at the ready. If anyone falls out, you scoop them up and follow in a second wave. Understood?"

"Hmm," Addo nodded, and then went back to relay the order. "Run. Silent. Spears ready. Run. Silent. Spears ready," he continued whispering down through each kanbati.

Boagur Gudugu was glad he had promoted Addo. The young man was big, he was intelligent, and he was just young enough to take orders and not question them. As the thought crossed his mind, Gudugu suddenly remembered he had brought Giri along. Giri was like most of his men, thirsty for combat and eager to test his finely honed skills, but he was also young, scrawny, and not the quickest bee in the hive. Gudugu had made Giri a duagur in training and placed him in charge of the yakanbati, the third formation, to give him some leadership experience without putting Giri in any imminent danger. He scanned the dark faces of his men but couldn't pick him out of the crowd. *I'll find him when we reach the top*, he told himself.

Once again, he raised his jawbone headdress into the air, turned back to the mouth of the cave, and scanned the surrounding terrain one last time for any sign of alarm. As satisfied as he could be, Gudugu's arm came down and he was running.

The sudden rush of energy burned through Boagur Gudugu's bird legs. His bare feet punched the cibmani path like a waki digger's fists, but the stone street wasn't nearly as forgiving as clay, and then it turned into a gravel path and stabbed the bottoms of his feet. He and his men wound back and forth up the slope like a snake being startled out of its nest. Their dark-red tunics rippled like scales, and their coral spears flashed in the starlight, mirroring the ancestors passing overhead. His breathing was heavy but controlled, as was that of his men. He wasn't surprised, necessarily. The agur trained every morning on the sandy beaches next to Chacuca Harbor, wrestled in the muddy boar pits, and ended their morning routine running up the steep shelly path to the plateau overlooking Itabacan Sound. For them, this was like a leisurely evening stroll, except for being barefoot and stomping on small, pokey rocks.

Since leaving the comforting darkness of the cave, other than their pounding feet, the rustle of their clothing, and their heavy breathing, the agur didn't make a sound. As soon as Boagur Gudugu reached the summit, he realized it wouldn't have mattered if they had been screaming the entire way.

A warm eastern wind roared across the nearly flat, crescent-shaped plateau before him, drowning out everything else and nearly knocking the jawbone headdress off of his head. He could hardly hear himself breathing and wouldn't have known there were sixty men running up the slope behind him if he hadn't been the one leading them there in the first place. Directly up the path northeast he could clearly see the Temple of the Dawn and two more buildings just beyond it, while the remainder of the landscape north and northwest looked barren and was made up of nothing but more pathetic looking shrubs and scattered patches of dune grass. From the look of it, and much to Gudugu's disappointment, there didn't appear to be any alarm or Mawoakin in sight. But then a flicker of light caught his eye from behind the temple.

"What – is it – Boagur?" he heard a small voice ask.

Gudugu turned to see Giri standing beside him, trying to catch his breath and making his entire scrawny body heave. "Giri! Where's Addo?" he asked, just as the duagur arrived at the top of the slope. "Ah! Good, you made it."

"By the tusks of Chuka!" Addo shouted. "This wind is ridiculous!"

"It is, and Maroha might just have saved our butts," the boagur suggested. He watched the last few stragglers join the rear formation, and then he turned to look for the flicker he had seen before. "Do you see that?" He pointed toward the temple.

Duagur Addo followed the boagur's finger and squinted his eyes against the blasting wind. "Is that...a fire?" he asked.

"I'm going to say, yes. I'll take the first kanbati around the right side of the temple, between it and the eastern cliff. Unless we're overwhelmed, and I can't imagine how that might happen, we'll meet you at the third building over there." Gudugu pointed again. "You take the okanbati right through that door into what I assume is the akin quarters. I don't expect you to get much resistance from them, so do your best to not harm anyone. The Yaya wants them all brought back alive for questioning."

"Hmm," Addo nodded but then looked puzzled. "What about the temple itself?"

Gudugu smiled. "Glad you asked. Giri!" he called, forgetting the little agur was standing right next to them. "Oh – there you are," he said, seeing Giri had finally caught his breath. "You will lead the yakanbati – that would be the third formation down there." The boagur pointed at the gaggle of nineteen men down the slope behind everyone else. "Lead them through the temple, clearing every corner and any niches there might be. If you find anyone, do not harm them but bring them right back here. Do you understand?"

Giri nodded but asked, "Which one is the temple?"

"The first building there – the big one," Gudugu pointed it out for him.

"Got it."

"It looks like there might be a door on the north side of the temple. But if not, just climb through that big open window there. You and your men need to return to this spot in order to stop any Mawoakin from escaping who happen to get past us."

"Got it."

"Do you?" Gudugu asked, and Giri nodded enthusiastically. He looked at Addo who was nodding as well. "Good. May Chuka guide us," he said.

"Over the horizon!" Addo and Giri replied.

"Over the horizon!" the rest of the men echoed, their voices rippling down the slope and fading into the ferocious wind.

The boagur waited until the men were in position with their respective formations before he raised his headdress high into the air, having to hold it tightly against the strong wind. A single loose leather strap suddenly wiggled free and waved about wildly as if it were attached to the

200

top of a sail. Gudugu watched it for a moment, noticing how it seemed to be dancing with Maroha, and then a smile stretched across his face and his arm swiftly came down.

Boagur Gudugu and his kanbati of twenty agur moved quickly up the path a few hundred paces before branching off to the right. From there, they wove between prickly shrubs and the patches of dune grass. He noticed the ground beneath his feet was dry and cracked, and there were several strange looking green bugs hopping around. To his left, he saw Duagur Addo and the okanbati continuing down the gravel path, and Giri and the yakanbati were right on their heels. To his right, just a dozen paces away, was the eastern cliff's edge and the Great Sea stretching as far as he could see. As he neared the south wall of the temple, Gudugu pulled his obsidian saber from its sheath with his left hand and held it high, slowing himself to a stop before pressing his back against the wall.

He peeked around the corner, allowing his men time to form up along the wall beside him. Having forgotten how the temple was shaped, all he could see was more wall. Cursing under his breath, he scooted forward until he could see around the curved wall, squinting against the wind. A few dozen paces away, there appeared to be three copper-lined torch basins arranged in a row with blazing fires in them. Behind the basins on the eastern rim were what looked like one or two white sheets attached to stakes jammed upright in the ground. Whatever it was, he couldn't wait any longer to figure it out, as he suddenly realized Giri and the yakanbati had started clearing the temple.

He swiftly raised and lowered his obsidian saber, and then charged around the corner. Boagur Gudugu didn't make it two full strides before running face-first into the shoulder of a large man who seemed to have leapt through the wall of the temple at that exact same moment. Both men tumbled to the ground while the kanbati were suddenly forced to either jump out of the way or trip over them, grunting and yelping like children playing Okid. In all the jumble of arms and legs, Gudugu wasn't sure if he was playing the part of Okid, one of the six, or Maboti.

Gudugu got to his feet as quickly as he could, readying himself in a wrestling position with his right hand open and free to grab, his left hand maintaining a tight grip on his bloody saber. The boagur had to look twice at the obsidian blade, momentarily confused by the bright-red liquid coating the shimmering black rock beneath.

"Baga!" he exclaimed, rapidly checking all over his chest, legs, and arms for any accidental wounds. To his great relief, other than a tear around the collar of his tunic, everything seemed to be in its rightful place. Obsidian blades were the sharpest of all Itabayiti blades, but they were also surprisingly fragile. Gudugu was amazed it wasn't broken.

He continued to inspect his handful of men, who had tripped and were struggling to get to their feet in the lumpy terrain and deafening wind. And then Gudugu's eyes drifted up to the large, tree-like man standing before him. He wore a long yellow robe that hung loosely over a tan tunic, making the enormous man beneath it appear small, but Gudugu could see he was anything but. He had a black curly beard, bigger than the boagur's entire head, and the man's prominent brow sat low over a pair of dark, nearly invisible eyes. And then the tree-like man abruptly slumped to his knees, and Gudugu noticed a thin line of red on the man's yellow robe just behind his right elbow.

"*NOOOOO!*" came the ear-piercing scream of a woman from inside the temple. "*Goacolo!*" And then her voice became muffled as if by a hand.

Gudugu watched as the tree-like man rocked forward and backward a couple times before falling face-first into the dune grass like a great cedar crashing to the forest floor. He had never stabbed anyone before, let alone killed them, and remained fixated on the yellow robe covering the lifeless body, flapping in the wind like a sail. There was a great deal of shouting coming from the direction of the next building, which broke Gudugu's mesmerized gaze.

"May Chuka guide us!" he shouted to his men, who were standing around and equally mesmerized by what had just happened.

"Over the horizon," they responded casually, as if waking up from a deep sleep.

Boagur Gudugu stepped over the fallen tree and led the way to the torch basins. The flames whipped around wildly, sending blasts of heat and smoke in seemingly random directions. Gudugu guessed the sheets had been erected in order to prevent the flames from being blown out, but then he looked more closely at them. They weren't sheets at all but white tunics that had been cut open and spread out. Gold stitching ran along the sides and the symbol of the Yaya was embroidered in gold thread on one side. And that was when Gudugu noticed the slashes in the fabric, and each slash was surrounded by a red stain. Behind him was a wooden bench beneath a small tree. And then he heard more shouting over the persistent wind.

He and his twenty agur ran north past the torch basins, keeping to the cliff-side of the akin quarters. The wind pushed them west toward the cibmani wall of the building, and Gudugu had to switch his saber to his right hand in order to brace himself against the wall with his left. When they emerged around the northeast corner, he briefly saw Duagur Addo chase several yellow-robed figures into the next building, which Gudugu immediately recognized were stables.

"This way!" he yelled and led his men to the left between the buildings, intending to cut off anyone trying to escape out of the open stalls, and switching his saber hands again.

"Boagur Gudugu!" one of his men hollered behind him, but he ignored the man, rounding the southwest corner of the stables.

A half-a-dozen boar burst out of the open stalls right in front of him and ran west across the plateau, squealing into the night. They were followed by several startled birds that had evidently been taking a nap in the stables.

"Boagur Gudugu!" he heard the same small voice again, but this time he realized it was Giri and turned to see what the scrawny young man wanted.

"What?" he snapped. "Can't you see I'm a little busy at the moment!"

Giri shrank back slightly but continued walking timidly up to the boagur. "Excuse me, Boagur, but the woman wants to talk to you," he said, as the rest of Gudugu's men ran past them.

"Woman? What woman?"

"Umm..."

"Well? Did she give you a name, or should we just call her woman?"

"I think she said her name was Soci? She said she needs to talk with you."

"Soci?" he asked and Giri nodded. "Don't know her." He turned to continue the assault with his men, but then saw they had already joined up with Duagur Addo's men, and it looked like they were surrounding nearly a dozen akin on the northern rim with their yellow-robed backs against the cliff's edge. "Baga," he huffed, wiped the blood from his saber on his chaccus, and then slid it back into its sheath. "Alright, take me to her."

As Giri led him back toward the Temple of the Dawn, Gudugu admired the efficiency of their raid. It seemed to be over just as quickly as it had started. Addo's men were dragging the last of the attendants in their tan tunics out into the open and binding their hands with palm rope, while he only counted two men and one woman dressed in yellow robes. He felt good, though a little unnerved by accidentally killing that big guy, but good otherwise. It felt like morning and Gudugu looked east, expecting to see the sun starting to rise, but it wasn't. He did see Chuka emerge on the horizon and the sparkling boar ancestor made him wonder, if they were arresting all of the akin and their attendants leaving no one on Bahaca to conduct the Rise of Mawoi ritual, would the Great Light awaken? *Of course it would*, he told himself. *What kind of silly thought is that?*

"Mawoi-coay," the woman sneered. "*You* are the boagur?"

Gudugu saw the woman's hands were bound at her waist. She wasn't wearing a belt of any kind, her filthy white tunic was torn at the shoulder, and her yellow robe had fallen off her back and hung from her elbows. He then looked into her astonishingly black eyes, glaring at him as if wishing him dead. He had never seen anyone with eyes so dark. They give off the illusion she didn't have eyes but holes in her head, and he was looking straight through to the void in the sky behind her. Her short hair was parted in the middle, slicked to the sides of her perfectly round head, tucked behind her perfectly symmetrical ears, but then smushed up in the back like the head feathers of an excited cuckoo. She was, quite possibly, the prettiest woman Gudugu had ever seen, which he immediately decided was a detail he would not be sharing with his wife and son later.

"I asked a question," she snarled, suddenly not seeming so pretty.

"Yes," Gudugu answered, crossing his arms over his boulder-like chest. He saw that she was about to launch into a big speech and stopped her with a wave of his hand. "Before you go yelling at me or any of my agur, you should know that we can't help you – not me or any of us. We serve the Yaya, and what he has planned for all of you is his business. Now," he paused to adjust the torn collar of his tunic. "Speak, and keep it brief."

"We are the Mawoakin, the Bringers of Light, who awaken the dawn and..."

"Yeah, yeah, I know. Briefer." Gudugu didn't care to hear any ramblings from any of them. He snatched the gourd of oycu from his hip, popped off the palm seed stopper, and took a long swig.

"If we do not conduct the Rise of Mawoi ritual, the Great Light will not awaken, and there will be endless night!"

"Is that so?" he mocked her. Though he knew most of the akin rituals were merely symbolic, there was a tiny flicker of doubt in the back of the boagur's mind.

"It is," she said sharply. "You are desecrating...sacred ground!"

Boagur Gudugu spit out a mouthful of oycu, "Bahaca?!" He pointed to the barren landscape around them. "You must be joking!" This made her mad and she lunged at him, requiring him to block her attack and spill his oycu. "Chuka's tusks!" he shouted.

"You have spilled blood before the One Who Bears the World!" she was screaming, struggling to get at Gudugu's saber. "You will suffer – you will all suffer when his Great Cleansing is upon us!"

He shoved her off him and to the ground. "You spilled my oycu!" Gudugu shouted. "Baga! Take her with the others down to the transports."

"NO!" she pleaded, now struggling against the two agur lifting her off the ground. "Boakin Tanoc! He needs me!"

"Ah – yes, the boakin." Gudugu looked around at the few yellow robes that had already been detained, wiping spilled oycu from his boarhide tunic. "Where is the boakin?" he asked.

"Tanoc," Soci added, glaring at him with her obsidian eyes.

"Don't care," the boagur dismissed her. "Addo!" he hollered across the plateau. The wind had died a bit, and he was beginning to hear the rest of his men talking near the northern rim. "ADDO!" This second yell got the duagur's attention, and Gudugu waved at him. Seeing Addo jogging over, the boagur turned back to Soci. "Who was the man I killed?"

"Goacolo."

Boagur Gudugu stopped mid-sip. Goacolo was the name of the former boakin. The Mawoakin raised their leader from birth and replaced him after he turned fifteen, which was similar to how all Itabayiti typically transitioned from childhood to adulthood. Why they always followed a child, he never understood, but the realization he had stabbed the former boakin added an immense weight to Gudugu's guilt. "I am sorry," he said, offering her the gourd of oycu, but she just stared at him in response. He shrugged, put the stopper back in the top of the gourd, and reattached it to his belt. "For what it matters, I didn't do it intentionally. Yaya Amnu requested that we bring all of you back to the palace alive."

"Boagur!" Duagur Addo called to him as he approached.

"There are no accidents," Soci growled, sounding quite a bit like an angry fox. Gudugu scanned the area just in case there actually was a fox nearby.

"Boagur?" Addo asked, a little out of breath.

"Is Boakin Tanoc over there with the rest of the Mawoakin?"

"Yeah, and it doesn't look good for the boy," he said with a heavy sigh.

"What do you mean?"

"You should come see for yourself."

Boagur Gudugu looked at Soci, her black eyes only conveying her intense hatred, and then he motioned for the duagur to lead the way. "Giri, bring her with us," he ordered and Giri complied.

They made their way across the plateau, choosing to weave between the patches of dune grass and prickly shrubs like the boagur had done before. The wind had settled substantially and was now very refreshing. Gudugu looked east into the breeze at the still-dark horizon, and that tiny flicker of doubt at the back of his mind started to grow.

"When we flushed them out of the stables," Addo was saying, "they immediately retreated over here to their garden."

Gudugu noticed him limping and using his spear as a staff. "What happened to your leg?"

"Ehh — I twisted my ankle jumping over a broken cart. It'll be fine. I'm more worried about keeping these crazy akin from leaping to their deaths."

The boagur looked past Addo at the eight people in yellow robes, one of whom had their hands on the shoulders of a little boy in white. All nine of them were no more than a single step away from the cliff's edge. "What's stopping them now?" he asked.

Addo chuckled, "Well, it's kind of strange. They keep asking for Uansu."

"Uansu?"

"Yeah, they claim Uansu will save them."

Gudugu looked back at Soci, seeing a devious smile on her pretty face. Uansu was the Great Hawk, the ancestor of the few the muwan that still nested around Osanum. The Itabayiti had hunted them to near extinction hundreds of years ago, because they were big enough and fierce enough to snatch a baby right out of a mother's arms. Every dozen or so years, their population rebounded and decimated the brocket herds on Amaca, becoming a huge pain in Mugan Galo's side. The muwan would then inevitably get tired of feeding on smaller creatures, expand to the other islands, and become a pain in everyone's side. He agreed with Addo, it was definitely strange for the Mawoakin to be praying to the Great Hawk.

"*Uansu! Uansu! Uansu!*" the akin were chanting as Gudugu and the others arrived.

"No great hawk is coming to save you!" the boagur shouted at them.

"*Maboti! Maboti! Maboti!*" they started yelling and spitting at him.

Gudugu laughed and crossed his arms. "They're crazy!"

"I told you," Addo said, leaning on his spear.

"Do it! Go on. Jump!" Gudugu continued to chuckle at the absurdity of it all.

"They will," Soci warned. "They will jump, and they will take the boy with them."

Boagur Gudugu's jovial expression sank into a dark grimace. One accidental death, especially a man Goacolo's size, wouldn't upset the Yaya much, and even nearly a dozen others killing themselves would only be slightly disappointing, but Gudugu was pretty sure losing the little boy would be a huge problem. "How do we stop them?" he asked her.

"You let me go."

"Ha!" He laughed nervously, but then a glimmer of light suddenly appeared on the eastern horizon. Gudugu pointed to the clear sign of the soon to be rising sun. "Still think Mawoi needs to hear your little ritual?" he asked her.

And then he saw, out of the corner of his eye, Boakin Tanoc drop to his knees and prostrate himself toward the dawn. While they were all marveling at the Great Light, Boagur Gudugu seized the opportunity. He grabbed Addo's spear out from under him, causing the duagur to stumble, and threw it into the chest of the akin that had been holding on to the boy.

The immense force of the thrown spear drove the unfortunate man straight off the cliff, while Gudugu followed his own momentum forward and grabbed the boakin's arm. Several of the agur who saw what was happening quickly moved toward the akin with their spears, but instead of accepting defeat, all seven remaining Mawoakin leapt off the cliff in their yellow flowing robes.

"*UANSU!*" they shouted, their voices trailing all the way down until they were lost to the crashing waves on the rocks far below.

"NO!" Soci screamed, trying to pull away from Giri's surprisingly tight grip. Just as she got free, she was instantly surrounded by agur spears.

Gudugu dragged the boy back away from the cliff's edge, fighting his flailing arms and legs. It was like trying to hold onto a live whitefish flopping around the spine of a fishing canuti. Tanoc bit him several times before Gudugu was able to restrain the child.

"Take her to the transports," he ordered. "And Addo, help me with this one!"

Duagur Addo helped the boagur wrestle the boy into submission, binding both his wrists and his ankles, and then Addo tossed Tanoc over his shoulder as if he were a basket of yams.

"Thank you!" Gudugu said. "Now, can we get off this stupid island!"

"Why'd you have to take my spear?" Addo asked, limping around a prickly shrub.

"Oh – sorry. Hey, you!" he shouted at one of the men. "Give Duagur Addo your spear." The startled agur immediately handed Addo his spear. "There. Feel better?" Gudugu asked him.

Addo took it, thanking the young man. "Better, yes, but..."

The boagur rolled his eyes, "But what?"

"That was my favorite spear."

Gudugu couldn't help but laugh all the way back to the transport canuti.

CHAPTER TWENTY

A LESINI Knows Many Things

By the end of their fifth day on the Great Sea, the Quest for Tizaka crew hardly spoke to one another. Numila's sailing song fell out of favor, becoming annoyingly repetitive and the cause of numerous arguments, especially from Ruruga who insisted they replace Yucahu with Kuraka throughout the verses. Not even Gisal wanted to hear Bogula's continuing story about their quest anymore, rendering the old lesini nearly silent throughout the day. Conversation on the canuti was replaced by the flapping of the sail in the wind, the creaking of the reed bindings, and the rhythmic swooshing as they surged through the water. Their provisions were dwindling, but that was to be expected. Numila had already told them that replenishing their provisions for the return trip was second on their very short list of things to do before leaving Bayamaca, right behind Lesini Bogula finding the tizaka tree.

Bogula had been sleeping less and less as the days dragged on and woke up just before dawn. Her back was as stiff and as gnarled as her staff, and the motion sickness seemed to return every time she tried to sleep on her side. After tossing and turning with the rocking vessel she thought it would do her some good to stand up and stretch her legs. With the aid of her staff, she got to her feet, hiking up her robe to avoid stepping on it, and then collected her long fuzzy braids and tossed them over her shoulder. She gratefully let the persistent wind do most of the work, blowing her braids back and pulling her upright to where she could admire the sky. It appeared as an eternal darkness off their kona-side to the west, but gradually lightened to white-azure eastward behind scattered clumps of black clouds, ending in a thin vein of orange light that split the horizon. Rippling black waves surrounded them on all sides, reminding Bogula how desperately alone the seven of them were, and put a slight smile on her aging face.

It was good to have her sea legs back, she thought, confidently stomping forward with her staff clopping against the bound reeds of the spine. It had been so long, Bogula was growing concerned she might spend the entire voyage bent over the midrib vomiting. She looked around in the faint light, finding Numila and Koyay curled up together in the neck of the canuti. They truly were an irritatingly disgusting couple, always flaunting their infatuation with one another. But Bogula had to admit she thoroughly enjoyed Koyay's feistiness, seeing a bit of herself in the girl, and thought she was much too good for Numila. *The youngest bocoani ever*, she scoffed, recalling what Numila had said when they first met. Of course, the other young men with them were also disgusting, all men were, but at least the coani spent their lives out in the open air and were constantly being bathed by the Great Sea. *Things could be a lot worse*, she told herself.

She continued around the mast, squinting to see the spine ahead of her and sweeping her staff back and forth. She was not in the slightest bit interested in tripping over the mountainous Gisal. She could handle running into the scrawny Dimgal, or one of the others, but Gisal was a beast, the largest coani Bogula had ever seen, which was saying something. She recalled back before any of these young men were born, back when her father would take her out on the Bocoa. There were large Itabayiti then too, some taller and wider than Gisal, but they were wrestlers, or ciba workers breaking volcanic rock, or waki diggers, and they were never permitted to be coani. There was a place for men of his size, and it was definitely not on a reed boat.

Seeing Madiri was the only one awake manning the tiller, Bogula cautiously made her way to the tail. He was a bit older than the rest of them. His graying beard reached all the way up to his cheek bones, where the wrinkles around his eyes seemed to drip down and merge with his beard. Madiri seemed like a nice enough man, though Bogula found his attempts to turn anything into a joke to be tiresome. She wasn't going to speak at first, not wanting to deal with it, but then she decided, since it was just the two of them, and he had been up for most of the night, she might as well say something.

"Nice breeze," she said, her staff scraping on the spine as she walked. Madiri smiled at her, a twinkle of tears in his eyes, no doubt thanks to the nice breeze.

"*Maroha harnessed, as she blows upon us, to Niama we turn to tame,*" he sang, rubbing his eyes with the tips of his fingers. After a moment with just the sound of her staff scraping on the spine, he asked, "Can't sleep?"

"It's been a long time since I've had to sleep on a canuti," Bogula answered honestly. "May Osani, the Great Healer, keep me from ever getting sick again."

Madiri chuckled, "That can ruin a perfectly good trip. How long has it been?"

"Oh – I'm doing well. Haven't had an issue since morning meal yesterday."

"Good. That's good, but I was asking, how long it's been since you've had to sleep on the spine of a canuti."

"Oh..." Bogula wasn't entirely sure how to respond. "Just a few years," she lied. If she had been honest, Madiri might think she was crazy, or worse, believe her. She quickly changed the subject. "Feeling tired yet?"

"NO – no, I could do this for days," he said, tapping the handle of the tiller affectionately.

Bogula caught him hiding a yawn in the crook of his elbow. "Are you sure about that?"

"As sure as I am, if we don't get enough provisions on Bayamaca, Gisal will eat us." He chuckled.

Bogula wanted to laugh as well, but she reminded herself men like Gisal not only needed more room but provisions as well, which was another reason they didn't belong on canuti. "You laugh, because you know there is truth to what you say," she said, adjusting her long, fluffy braids in the wind.

"Of course!" Madiri laughed again. "Imagine we arrive at Bayamaca only to discover its volcano has erupted and the entire island is consumed by fire. No tizaka. No provisions. It's a terrifying thought," he said with a crooked smile.

"We are most vulnerable to the Dark Shadow when we are afraid," she told him. "You strike me as the type who disguises his fear with humor."

Madiri scoffed, "I'd much rather be a fraud who makes others laugh, than one who might get the rest of her crewmates killed."

Bogula fell silent, glaring up into Madiri's mud-brown eyes. *What was that supposed to mean?* she asked herself. She decided she didn't want to talk anymore and thought it might have been a bad idea to start the conversation in the first place. She huffed and looked away, staring across the sea to the darkness of the western sky. Men were truly awful creatures. The only man pure-of-heart Bogula had ever known was her father.

Her thoughts tumbled down one memory thread after another, images of her father flashing before her eyes in a hazy collage of emotions. She hadn't thought about him or their ill-fated voyage to Bayamaca in a very long time, and Madiri's words made her worry history might repeat itself. Bogula took a deep breath and told herself to listen to her own advice. There was nothing to fret about. And then it dawned on her, *but there might be something I can learn from these memories*. What if Madiri was right? Of course, there was no way he could have known how right he was, but Bogula's mind started to wander.

She remembered they were gone for several kuranan at a time, returning only to report what they found to the Yaya, re-seal their canuti with fresh bitumen, gather provisions, and then they would leave again. On one occasion, she recalled having to repair a torn sail, and Bogula's cousin, Yahuba, joined the crew. As a shoat, he only knew the basics of sailing. Even as a little girl, Bogula knew more than Yahuba, especially how dangerous it was to have someone so unskilled on such a long voyage. But Yahuba was also Yaya Anacacu's nephew, and the Yaya insisted they take him along to find the end of the Bocoa.

The Yayapti mentioned that the Biyaya traveled west forty days and nights to reach Itabacan, and they expected the southern edge of the Great Sea to be no farther than that, but Yuraca had other plans. The Storm Spirit sent his most brutal storms, one right after the next, pounding their çanuti until they crashed on the reefs of a densely forested island with a ferocious looking volcano poking up out of the center like a jar stuck in the sand. Her father would later name the island Bayamaca, but at the time, Bogula remembered calling it Hurassa's Palace after the Fire Spirit.

The reeds that grew on Bayamaca were thinner and shorter than what the Itabayiti cultivated in Itabacan, but they were strong enough to construct a new canuti. Unfortunately, after the first night stranded, Yahuba gave into his fears and ran scared into the interior of the island. Bogula remembered searching for her idiotic cousin for two days, but they eventually had to call off the search. The canuti was ready, and they needed to figure out where they were and how to make it back to Itabacan. They had no other choice, they had to abandon him on Bayamaca as they set off to wander the Great Sea, discovering new islands, new plants and creatures, and even another civilization they called the Gusiti. After nearly six kuranan, they finally found their way back to Itabacan with amazing stories to tell.

Bogula remembered a festival was held in her father's honor, complete with a game of almec and a night of feasting and dancing. It wasn't until the following morning that her father informed the Yaya his nephew had been lost. Yaya Anacacu demanded her father return at once to Bayamaca and bring back his nephew, but her father refused. She couldn't remember why her father refused, but she suspected it had something to do with her mother. Whatever his reasoning, the Yaya stripped her father of his titles and banished him to Coan Village on Yapaca where he lived out the last of his days without honor or attendants. Bogula later found out the Yaya sent several expeditions with dozens of good men for his nephew, but the boy was never found and many Itabayiti lost their lives. Bogula's father went on to be with the ancestors a few short years later, and her mother took the Vow of Osani immediately after her father's bonefire.

Forcing herself away from the knotted memory threads relating to her father, Bogula once again tried to focus specifically on the terrain of Bayamaca and where the tizaka tree might be. With the volcano directly in the middle of the island, she thought they could walk in a line all the way around the volcano and would be certain to stumble upon the tree at some point. If only she could remember precisely where the tree had been, then they could save precious daylight, and she could return to Itabacan sooner.

"You're awfully quiet," she heard Madiri suddenly say behind her.

"It's peaceful," she replied without turning around. *Focus, focus...*

"I'm told it typically is this far out to sea," he said, and then added, "But I don't have to tell you that, do I?"

Bogula's eyes popped open as she slowly turned to look at him. She smiled politely but was caught off guard by the serious expression on Madiri's face. He didn't appear to be joking any longer. "I-I'm not sure what you mean," she stammered.

Madiri smirked, "You may have the rest of the crew fooled, but I'm old enough to remember the stories my ohbaba told me about the infamous

Bocoani Tiktali and the discovery of Bayamaca." He paused to adjust his hand on the tiller, clearly taking the opportunity to read the expression on her face. "After you told us about our mission, I started to wonder how we were going to figure out which, of all the trees on the whole island of Bayamaca, was the right tree. The mission is so very important, after all, and we wouldn't dare come all this way for the fruit of a specific tree without one of us knowing exactly what that tree or its fruit looks like."

Bogula thought about what he was saying and ignored his implications before she explained, "We, lesini, know many things most Itabayiti do not."

"Of course!" Madiri said, sarcastically. "I mean, you probably work with kincham and tizaka constantly. And I'm sure you would be able to spot it in the jungle while still standing on the canuti anchored in the shallows."

"Young man, I don't appreciate your tone," she snapped, feeling a little nervous. "Kincham and tizaka used to grow in Itabacan, and descriptions about the trees and their fruit have been passed down from generation to generation, much the same as whatever stories your ohbaba may have told you." This comment made Madiri smile. Bogula thought it was an ugly smile, like that which a mischievous child might use when trying to manipulate a parent.

"And my ohbaba told me Tiktali had a daughter who sailed with him on all of his voyages, but specifically on the voyage that discovered Bayamaca."

"And I'm sure it was an exciting story, but I don't see..."

"His daughter's name was *Abogu*," Madiri cut her off.

Bogula stared at Madiri, trying to hide the shock on her face as they swayed side to side with the rocking of the canuti. No one outside of the Sisterhood of Lesini had said her real name in at least forty years, and she had convinced herself no one ever would again. "How do you know this *Abogu* is me?" she inquired, undoubtedly failing to hide her vulnerability.

"As I said, I'm old enough..."

"I heard that part," she sternly cut him off. "What I want to know is how you came to this conclusion about me?" She pointed to herself with her staff.

"Oh," Madiri shrugged. "I've been thinking about it for days. Yaya Amnu sends us to retrieve a fruit that none of us would be able to identify, that is on an island only two of us have ever been to, and the only reason we have to believe we might find it there is because Tiktali claimed he saw it there over a hundred years ago?"

"You realize that you..." she tried to tell him how insane he was sounding, but Madiri interrupted her.

"But then the Yaya happens to provide us with a lesini named Bogula who can somehow identify it, even though the trees that once produced the fruit were eradicated from Itabacan and no one has seen it in – oddly – over a hundred years. And then I remembered my ohbaba's story about Tiktali and his daughter, Abogu. And I thought, huh, that's weird, the lesini with us is named Bogula, which sounds awful similar to Abogu to me."

Bogula laughed, nervously. "You must be joking! Do I look like I'm over a hundred years old?" she asked him, holding her arms out for him to inspect her. "This is ridiculous. You, young man, are ridiculous!"

"Well," he shrugged again. "I guess I don't *know* for certain."

Bogula flicked her chipped fingernails in Madiri's face. The old lesini was anxious. She felt cornered, like a spiny rat under a market stall. Thankfully, she heard a few of the others beginning to stir and decided to change the subject. "Well, I can't help you with that. Now, are we still on course for Bayamaca?"

"It's there," a groggy Numila answered her, surprising both Bogula and Madiri.

Just then, the rising sun shot across the Great Sea and smacked into their sail, before continuing on to illuminate the upper rim of Bayamaca's volcano in the distance directly ahead of them.

"Thank you, Mawoi. You woke up just in time," Madiri said, squinting over his shoulder.

Bogula started walking up the spine, rattled by her confrontation with Madiri and hoping to take her seat in front of the mast. She watched Numila poke Koyay on her shoulder.

"Hey, you're on," he said, but Koyay just mumbled and rolled onto her back. Numila laughed, "Ko-Ko, it's time to wake up. We need you on the till...." He started to poke her again, but Koyay snatched his finger and bent it backward, making Numila squeal for her to stop.

"Poke me again and I'll break it, my loving jellyfish," she said and sat up, reaffirming Bogula's liking for the girl.

"You two have the weirdest relationship," Dimgal joked through a yawn. He then started gathering their gourds and hoisting them up the mast.

"Alright, everyone," Bocoani Numila began, rubbing his finger with a smile on his face and stretching his back. "We have arrived at the moment of truth. I need everyone on alert. These reefs are treacherous, and we will not survive to complete the Yaya's mission unless we give Koyay our undivided attention." He looked at his crew and locked eyes with each of them, including Bogula, before nodding to Koyay. "Well, my love, you're the bocoani now."

Bogula didn't recall sailing to Bayamaca the first time because Yuraca had done the hard part for them. This time she decided she would sit near the tiller and watch Koyay order these disgusting men around. She turned back to the tail, intentionally bumping into Madiri along the way, but he didn't say anything. She nodded at the new, temporary bocoani, and then sat beside Koyay against the chok-side tailrib. From there, Bogula could easily see the men pull their ropes, port their oars, slide from rib to rib on the wet spine, and all at the command of a woman – no matter how young or petite she was.

Koyay stood with her fierce eyes fixed on Numila who was squatting on his knees at the neck, half of his body dangling over the headrib and signaling the path to Koyay with his hand in the air. The tiller was tucked up under her right arm and both of her hands were wrapped tightly around the well-worn handle. Bogula watched her make subtle adjustments with her hips, causing the reed boat to dance through the coral reefs like a bumblebee going from flower to flower.

By midmorning they were safely in the shallows just offshore with Bayamaca's smoking volcano towering over their heads. Koyay gave the order for Gisal to drop anchor and for Dimgal to scrounge their gear into one of the cano, which he then detached from the arms of the canuti and started rowing to shore. Bogula cursed under her breath as she slipped over the midrib and into the cool water, wondering why they didn't allow her to get into one of the cano. Instead, she had to use her staff to push off the sea floor until it was shallow enough for her to find her footing.

She knew how impressive it was for them to have made it to Bayamaca at all, and she was fairly confident they would find the tizaka tree in the single day Numila had allotted for them to search. But now she had to keep one eye on Madiri, and Bogula thought it might do her some good to be slightly less talkative moving forward.

CHAPTER TWENTY-ONE
The Hunt On YAPACA

Boagur Gudugu bent over the edge of the stone dock and dipped one of his meaty hands into the gentle waters of the shallows. He wiped the warm salty water over each hand, rubbing vigorously between his calloused fingers and around his chewed-on nails, let them drip-dry a moment, and then reached for the hand towel Giri was holding out for him. Yapaca's harbor was eerily quiet with only the sloshing of the water against the docks and dozens of empty creaking reed boats nearby to fill the silence. Even the dreaded army of seagulls typically squawking overhead were gone, no doubt realizing, for the second day in a row, no fisherman had gone out or would be bringing back any fish for the annoying ravenous beasts to squawk about. Gudugu handed Giri the damp towel, retrieved his gourd of oycu, and took a monstrous swig.

"Ahh!" he said after a hard swallow. He stoppered the gourd and reattached it to his hip. "Duagur Lakum!"

He strutted up the dock toward the harbor yard, Giri following behind him, wringing out the towel. Ahead of them in the middle of the yard, a group of agur reed huts had been erected the day before. There were three huts in total, one per two agur warriors who would be staying on the island indefinitely. Each hut had reed-tall walls and a pitched roof that added an additional half-a-reed in height. Duagur Lakum and his five men were ordered to close Yapaca's harbor, erect their huts, clear the streets, and place the Yapati on a strict curfew until further notice from the Yaya.

The island of Yapaca was shaped like a squat yam that had been smashed flat. Its more bulbous end faced south, while the rounded-off tip pointed north and featured the only hill on the island. The short but broad hill was nearly a third the size of the entire island of Niamca and spread out over its gentle crest were the Temple of Ma'an, the residence of the boyiti, and his stables. The eastern slope dipped gradually to the shore, while the

218

northern slope featured a noxious quagmire that stretched down to a rocky beach and smelled worse than the boar pits. To the west, a wide field of grassy dunes followed the curvy coast south and ended in an uninhabitable brackish swamp they called The Niknob, which took up the entire southwest corner of the island and swallowed every attempt to build there. The southeast corner was also difficult to build on because the terrain was uneven, rocky, and nearly devoid of soil. Midway up the east coast, Yapaca Harbor rivaled that of Itabaca's, complete with a lighthouse and a massive fish processing facility. There were no mountains, terraces, or dense forests dotting Yapaca's landscape. The flat and arid central plain was suitable for only one purpose and that was to accommodate Itabacan's ever-growing population.

Gudugu's sandals crunched on the shelly yard where he stopped with his arms crossed over his boulder-like chest, admiring the work Lakum had done. His oblong shadow stretched out before him in the midmorning sun, making Gudugu smile. It was almost midmeal and there wasn't a single Yapati in sight.

"You know what, Giri?" he said rhetorically.

"What?" Giri just had to ask, making Gudugu sigh.

"I was ready to nominate you and Addo to receive the Order of Kareb for your bravery on Bahaca, but Lakum and his five men against the boyiti and all of the Yapati might have changed my mind."

There was a moment of silence, and then Giri asked, "What's the Order of Kareb?"

"Seriously?" he asked, and the scrawny little agur shrugged his shoulders. Gudugu took a deep breath. "The Order of Kareb is one of the oldest Itabayiti titles," he explained. "It's said, the Biyaya had a favorite guard named Kareb who sacrificed himself to protect the Biyaya from the Amunti. Because of his heroic act, the Biyaya decided to honor Kareb by awarding his friend's name to those who displayed the same level of courage."

"Like you did yesterday?"

"Well – while I may have led the most successful raid in the history of the agur, perhaps even more successful than when Yaya Anacacu's agur crushed the Cult of Kanu on Amaca," Gudugu admitted, as humbly as he could. "It isn't proper for the boagur to nominate himself."

"Maybe I can nominate you," Giri suggested.

The boagur grabbed his gourd of oycu and took another swig. "No, it doesn't quite work like that."

Another peaceful moment of silence passed while Gudugu drank, waiting for Lakum to appear, and then Giri added, "I don't think the Cult of Kanu was crushed."

"You don't, do you?"

"I mean," Giri shrank a bit. "That was nearly a hundred years ago, and I saw a Kanuakin swallow a snake in Badhan just a few years ago."

Gudugu nodded, finishing off the last drops of oycu from the gourd dangling over his open mouth. "You're probably thinking of the Mabotakin. The akin for the Cult of Kanu wouldn't swallow snakes." He started chuckling. "That would be like the Hurassakin eating fire." He shook his head.

"Oh," Giri replied quietly. "How do you know so much about all this, Boagur?"

"Because," he said, putting his empty gourd away and re-crossing his arms, "your boagur is also the boakin of the Chukakin. I'm actually surprised you don't know that."

"I guess I never thought about it before." Giri looked down and kicked a few loose shells around. "How does that work?" he asked.

"What – me being both boagur and boakin?" Gudugu asked and Giri nodded. "Well, during the battle with the Cult of Kanu I mentioned before, the Yaya lost multiple boagur and the boakin took over command of the assault. In fact, the battle resulted in such a massive loss of life that the council actually turned on Anacacu, which was why he's now remembered for building those apartments over there and other civic improvements, instead of eliminating the Cult of Kanu." The boagur pointed to a row of two story cibmani buildings up the street in the direction of the north side of the island. "By the time they were able to crush the cult, all of the Chukakin had been trained as agur, and the council made the change permanent. Every single one of us since then has also been trained in the priestly ways of the Chukakin. That's why you are likely to hear us referred to as warrior-priests, or *agurakin*."

"Boagur?" they suddenly heard Lakum say from inside the hut on the right, just before the duagur poked his head out of the open doorway and looked at them. "Oh..." Lakum mumbled, and then his head disappeared back inside the hut.

"Don't worry about us, Lakum," Gudugu called out to him. "Giri and I are happy to wait."

"We are?" Giri asked, confusedly.

"Shh..." he elbowed Giri's tiny shoulder, causing the little agur to stumble to the side.

Lakum was the elder duagur and afforded certain privileges, but Gudugu would not tolerate being made to wait much longer. There was a blur of motion across the harbor yard and around the stables, and he wondered if the Yapati might be getting ready to exit their bohi for midmeal. He hoped they would. He was still under orders to detain the Cult of Mawoi and suspected there was a substantial population of them there on Yapaca. It would make his job a lot easier to not have to kick down everyone's door on the island.

"Taycoay, Boagur Gudugu!" Lakum shouted, finally emerging from his hut with a big goofy grin on his long face.

Duagur Lakum was what Gudugu liked to think of as the average agur. He was of average height and build, and he was just smart enough to follow orders without questioning them. He had a respectable agur braid draped over his right shoulder, and cocoa skin that was sun-bleached in spots like oil on the surface of muddy water. The only thing about Lakum that truly annoyed the boagur was his ridiculously goofy, yellow smile that was perpetually planted directly in the middle his shaggy black beard, which was also very patchy and kind of reminded Gudugu of spiny rat fur.

"Lakum," the boagur said over his crossed arms.

"Yes, Boagur? I'm sorry, I wasn't expecting you until after midmeal," Lakum explained, grinning like he was trying to attract insects with his teeth.

"Don't worry about it, Lakum," Gudugu said dismissively, and then took a step toward the hut the duagur had exited. "I see you were successful in clearing the streets last night."

"Umm..." Lakum bounced along beside the boagur, smiling. "Yes, it was nothing. Well..." Lakum paused to watch him poke his head into the hut.

"Go on, I'm listening." Gudugu saw another agur, one whose name he couldn't remember, sitting next to a young woman who he was sure wasn't one of the agur. "Taycoay," he greeted the woman.

"Taycoay," she replied politely, but he saw a hint of nervousness in her light-brown eyes.

The boagur reached in past the woman and grabbed one of the agur coral spears leaning against the reed wall of the hut. "Lakum, do you need your spear?"

"OH! Yes, Boagur. Thank you!"

Gudugu handed him the spear while stepping back away from the hut and dusting off his shoulder. "You know, Addo had a favorite spear?" he said rhetorically, wiping off his hands.

"No, well, I..."

"He lost it, Lakum. Do you know how Addo lost his favorite spear?" Gudugu watched Lakum search the sky and then the shelly yard for an answer, but the duagur could only continue grinning and shrug his shoulders. "I threw it off a cliff."

"You – you threw his spear off a cliff?"

Gudugu nodded. "Well – to be precise – it had one of the Mawoakin attached to it, and when he went off the cliff, the spear had no choice but to follow." He watched Lakum shuffle his feet nervously, leaning on the spear one way and then another, grinning all the while. Gudugu wondered what was making the duagur so nervous. Having a woman in his hut wasn't something the boagur was going to make a big fuss about. After all, Lakum was the elder duagur and afforded certain privileges.

He quickly moved past Lakum to the middle hut and poked his head inside. There were two more agur – a young man named Nagi, and another new recruit whose name Gudugu couldn't immediately remember. They both went rigid, clearly startled by the boagur's sudden presence. He saw they were playing a stick game called omabu-disha. It was a simple game in which a small object like a rock or, in this case, a shell represented the dry tumbling omabu shrub, and the players tossed three-sided sticks to determine how many spaces they could move the shrub closer to their opponent. The game was originally played using reeds, but the Itabayiti eventually started making the game pieces out of wood that could be carved and reused many times, at least that's what Gigal had told him.

"Hmm," he grunted and stepped away from the middle hut, moving to the last one.

He heard the two men call after him, "Taycoay, Boagur Gudugu!"

"Boagur!" Lakum shouted. "You asked about last night? Yes, we — we set up and..."

The duagur was talking and bouncing around beside him again but Gudugu wasn't listening. Something strange was going on, or maybe something had happened, but whatever it was, he was going to find out... As soon as he poked his head in the last hut on the left, Gudugu saw three more young women huddled together against the reed wall opposite the entrance. Their wrists and ankles were bound with rope, and each had what appeared to be a palm seed jammed into their mouths and held in place with a strip of cloth. They didn't look to have been physically harmed, but he couldn't imagine the three of them being dangerous enough to warrant being treated like this.

"I can explain," Lakum said behind him.

Boagur Gudugu instantly spun around and slapped the spear out of the duagur's hand, snatched him up by his collar with both fists, lifted him off his feet with ease, and then tossed him into the hut. Lakum landed hard on the reed mat flooring, loudly crunching the shells beneath it. "Release them immediately!" Gudugu ordered him.

"Yes — but I can expl..."

"NOW!" he screamed, pointing and glaring at Lakum with all the hatred and disgust boiling up from his oycu-filled gut. "You — Nagi and the other one — get in here and assist your duagur!"

Gudugu stepped out of the hut and stormed past the two agur scrambling across the shelly yard, Nagi helping the other one move aside to keep from running into the boagur. When he arrived back at the first hut, Gudugu reached in without looking, grabbed the fourth agur by his foot and yanked him out, dragging him into the yard on his back.

"Giri!" he yelled, but instantly saw the little agur was standing just a reed away watching him in shock. "Oh, there you are. I need you to go back to Coyaca and have Duagur Addo bring me a kanbati of twenty men immediately."

"Yes, Boagur," Giri said, nodding.

"And Giri, don't let that big guy intimidate you. You want to be a duagur? You have to grow some tusks!"

"Yes, Boagur!" Giri shouted and then ran off toward their waiting canuti.

Boagur Gudugu returned his attention to the matter at hand and saw the young woman he had greeted before sneaking out of the hut. "Don't worry," he assured her, "we don't really have tusks."

"Can...I go?" she asked timidly, hugging the outer wall of the hut.

"Yes, with my apologies." He watched her nervously fix one of her two braids as if unsure whether or not the boagur was being serious.

"Thank you," she peeped, but before she could run off, the boagur stopped her.

"Just a moment, if you don't mind," he said, and she paused to listen. "Tell me, did any of these men harm you?" he asked, fearing how the woman might answer. He watched her slowly shake her head, no. Gudugu sighed. "Were you afraid they might?" he asked, and she nodded. "I am sorry for that. Do you know – and this will be my last question – do you know if any of the other women were harmed?"

"This will go a lot smoother, if you'd stop squirming!" Lakum was yelling loud enough at one of the young women for all of Yapaca to hear.

"Lakum!" Gudugu hollered over his shoulder. "Be gentler, or I swear, by the tusks of Chuka, I will skin you alive!" He turned back to the startled woman, instantly recognizing how horrifying all of this must seem to her. "I promise you; I will not skin him or anyone alive. We, agur, sometimes..." Gudugu found himself stumbling over his attempt to explain the confusing and, understandably, disturbing behavior the woman was witnessing, and then he suddenly realized, looking into her young, startled, scared, nearly-on-the-verge-of-tears eyes, she just wanted him to shut up and let her leave. "I'm sorry," he apologized again. "Taycoay."

She didn't respond but sprinted away like a fawn escaping from a hunter. Gudugu felt horrible for the woman, for all of them, and he vowed to do something about Duagur Lakum. The grinning man said he could explain, and Gudugu was going to make him do just that, or the duagur was going to spend the rest of the year cleaning the boar pits with his tongue. Maybe that would finally wipe that ridiculous smile from his face.

"You – what's your name?" Gudugu pointed at the agur he had dragged out of the hut by his ankle, still lying on his back and staring up into the clear sky like a dazed maniku.

The young man scrambled to his feet. "Tolan, Boagur!" he answered with a stomp of his foot – *crunch!*

Gudugu chuckled, "You're smarter than you look, Tolan." He crossed his arms and leaned forward until their noses were almost touching. "Or am I wrong?"

"Yes, Boagur!" the young agur quickly shouted, nervously. "I mean...no..."

"Good," Gudugu laughed. He retrieved his empty gourd and handed it to him. "Fetch me some more oycu."

Tolan hesitantly took the offered gourd. "W-Where am I...supposed to..."

"Get it!"

"Yes, Boagur!" Tolan shouted, stomped his foot again, and then ran off. At first, he went back toward the docks, but then Tolan spun around on his heel and headed west toward the village of Coan instead.

"Lakum!" Gudugu called for the duagur. He was beginning to think, maybe, it was possible Lakum hadn't done much of anything wrong. It was only the appearance of wrongdoing that had riled up the boagur. He looked down at the shelly ground and dug the toe of his sandal between a few loose shells, and then he noticed the dust and dirt on his hands. "Baga. Lak...oh!" he started to shout but saw the duagur was right behind him. "Have you released the women?" he asked.

"Yes, Boagur," Lakum answered, always smiling.

Looking past Lakum and the huts, several hundred paces west, Gudugu could see people starting to venture out into the streets. Unfortunately, he was going to need every last agur to weed through the Yapati and determine who was a member of the Cult of Mawoi, which unfortunately meant he still needed Duagur Lakum.

He looked into Lakum's desperate eyes. "Why did you detain those women?"

"Boagur Gudugu, those women..."

Gudugu silenced him with a wave of his annoyingly filthy hand. "Don't you dare give me some story you've just made up. I have other sources," he warned, gesturing with his eyes to the duagur's men standing behind him. "And I know how to make them squeal like little baby shoats. Now, explain yourself."

Lakum swallowed hard, his smile fading for the first time in a long time. "We went street to street, clearing like you ordered us, but there was some...resistance. A man named Bayom argued with us about closing the harbor, making a lot of noise and shoving past us. He was carrying a basket of thread, tripped on his own, and the thread went everywhere." He paused to laugh, his yellow smile reappearing momentarily. "Anyway, he got mad and demanded we help him. Well, I said no, because there were only six of us, and I didn't want us to appear weak."

"You kicked his basket," Nagi added.

"I did not!" Lakum shouted, turning to face his accuser.

"You did, and the man's thread went blowing in the wind and down the street!"

Lakum tried to confront Nagi, but Gudugu grabbed Lakum's shoulder with one meaty hand. "No. We won't be at each other's throats – at least, not right now. You two can wrestle over this later. Right now, I need you to finish telling me what happened and why you detained those women."

"They got in the way!" Lakum shouted.

"Of you harassing the thread vendor?" Gudugu asked, half joking.

"Yeah! Like I said, there were only six of us and there are a lot of Yapati! The women shoved past us to help the guy, so...well, I detained them."

Gudugu shook his head. "You detained them for helping a thread vendor pick up his dropped thread?"

"You bet I did!" Lakum answered. "Boagur, had we not stood up for ourselves, what might've happened? First, Bayom disrespects us, and then those women? No, we had to do something!"

The boagur continued shaking his head, keeping one eye on the growing crowd of people spreading through the streets beyond the harbor yard. "Go on. Tell me what happened next and be quick about it. We'll need to be on guard here pretty soon."

Lakum looked back over his shoulder at what the boagur was seeing. "Baga," he sighed. "While we were binding their wrists, Bayom got really mad and tried stop us. What could we do but respond?"

"You could have walked away?"

"He tried to strangle me!" the duagur screamed.

"Take it easy!" Gudugu warned him like he might his own son, and then he turned to Nagi. "Is this true?" he asked and Nagi nodded. Gudugu was going to make himself sick from all the head shaking he was doing, which reminded him that Tolan hadn't returned with his oycu.

"I know we were only supposed to secure the harbor and clear the streets," Lakum continued. "But I felt we should take the opportunity to let them know who was now in charge of Yapaca."

"You did, did you? And who is now in charge of Yapaca?" Gudugu crossed his arms and stared Lakum down.

"Umm..." he squirmed. "Uh – you, Boagur? You're in charge of Yapaca?"

Gudugu laughed, "No! Yaya Amnu is in charge! We are instruments – the extended arm of the Yaya, his great spear, the tusks of the chacu that pull his woigir!"

"Woigir?"

"His warrior's cart," Gudugu explained. "It has bigger wheels, shielded sides, and there are slots to hold up to a dozen spears." He suddenly realized Lakum already knew about the woigir and was intentionally distracting him. Gudugu fumed, "You know what I..." He grabbed Lakum's collar with one fist but held his other menacingly at his side. "What did you do to the thread vendor?"

"We beat him!" Lakum admitted, shouting and bracing himself for a beating of his own with his eyes closed and face turned, but the beating didn't come.

Gudugu's attention quickly shifted to the people gathering at the edge of the shelly yard. "We'll continue this discussion later," he said and shoved Lakum away. "Grab your spears."

Boagur Gudugu's wife told him there were originally five villages spread out over the center of the island and connected to the harbor by long, branching shelly paths. Each village was eventually named after the common occupation of its inhabitants, which were Jara, Segin, Waki, Coan, and Ciba. Yaya Gahun had relocated hundreds of people to Yapaca nearly five hundred years earlier, which he recalled only because Gigal had been talking about it the night before. It was known as the Shiyiti, the Movement of the People. Gahun built rows of cibmani streets between the villages and lined them with huts. Nearly forty years later, Yaya Shango converted the huts into small cibmani houses called bohi. dug smooth cibmani ditches along the streets, and vastly improved the sanitation and overall health of the people. Yaya Anacacu began adding second floors to some of the bohi, something Gudugu didn't need his wife to tell him, which created apartments to accommodate more Yapati as their numbers continued to grow. All of this meant, the horde Boagur Gudugu and his agur were facing was more than a little intimidating.

Scanning the crowd, Gudugu hoped he might recognize a reasonable face, someone he could talk sense into and could persuade his neighbors that what happened the night before would not happen again. A warm, salty breeze blew at their backs as if Maroha was pushing them to confront the crowd.

"Remember," he told his men, "we are not here to harm anyone. Our orders are to secure the harbor and prevent anyone from leaving the island." He stomped his foot, crunching the shells beneath his sandaled foot, "Stug!"

CRUNCH!

"Agur!" his men replied, their spears held firm and upright in their right hands, their feet a shoulder-width apart, and their left hands resting on the lower parts of their backs.

A man dressed in a brown tunic the color of chan seeds stepped forward and shouted, "I just need to get back to Hatca! You stranded me here last night, and I have traps to tend to!"

"Yaya Amnu has ordered all harbors closed," the boagur replied in his best fatherly voice.

"Until when?" The man took a tentative step forward and seemed to be on the verge of becoming frantic. "Do you know who I am? I'm Dualuk Allun. I have twelve men and a hundred-and-seven traps that *should* have been cleared last night, but I was here!"

"I understand, but the Yaya's orders are firm." Gudugu knew the name Allun, but he had never met the crab trapper before. The aluk mainly kept to themselves on the island of Hatca, and it was usually Boaluk Palu

228

who delivered their nightly catches to both Yapaca and Itabaca anyway, which made Gudugu suspicious why Allun was there at all. "That said, I would like to speak with you privately, Dualuk Allun," he said, and the man in brown seemed to consider it.

"Now?" Lakum whispered.

"We have orders to weed out the Cult of Mawoi," Gudugu whispered back, without taking his eyes off of Allun. "The six of us..." he paused, and then snapped to look at Lakum. "Duagur Lakum, you came here with five men. Tolan is running an errand for me, leaving you with four. Why do I only count three?"

Out of the corner of his eye, Gudugu saw Allun take another tentative step forward. "I – I don't know about a private conversation," the dualuk said.

"Sagota's parents live in Ciba." Lakum nodded toward the northwest. "He was supposed to be back for morning meal."

"You can't keep us here forever!" a woman suddenly shouted, eliciting a grumble of agreement from the crowd.

Tensions were building. Boagur Gudugu crossed his arms, glanced up into the sky, and quietly observed that although the seagulls had stayed away, the squawking had clearly returned.

"I have to see a lesini," a different and much older woman said with a toothless mouth.

"Yeah!" several people shouted in agreement.

Dualuk Allun took another step forward.

"Not one more step, Allun," Gudugu warned, his mouth starting to feel parched and his tongue heavy.

"Or what?" the toothless woman sneered.

Allun took another, more confident step, but stopped and nervously looked at them.

Gudugu shook his head and sighed, slumping his boulder-like shoulders. "Giri, seize Dualuk Allun," he reluctantly ordered him.

Giri audibly gulped. "Uh – now?"

"Yes! Now! Go!" He pushed the scrawny agur forward, his spear dragging through the shelly yard as he stumbled.

"What errand did you send Tolan on?" Lakum asked, quietly.

Boagur Gudugu wasn't listening to Lakum. His mind was distracted and calculating their chances of peacefully containing the ever-growing crowd. He was beginning to understand why Yaya Amnu had ordered them to act so swiftly. In Itabacan's near one-thousand-year history there had been two recorded uprisings of the Cult of Kanu — once during Yaya Ajan's rule, and once more recently with Yaya Anacacu and his assault on Amaca. Both uprisings had resulted in countless deaths and the disruption to Itabayiti life had reverberated throughout their society, from the beggars in the alleyways of Badhan, up to the Yaya in his mountaintop palace. As the boagur quietly watched Giri stumble toward Dualuk Allun, his spear tipped back over his shoulder and his hand extended in a show of kindness, Gudugu admitted to himself, *I could really go for a swig of oycu, right about now.*

CHAPTER TWENTY-TWO

NIAMA Nibbles but HURASSA Bites

he island of Bayamaca was nearly twice as long as it was wide, a near perfect oval of green vegetation surrounded by crystal-clear teal water beneath a cloudless light-azure sky. Out of the center of the jungle, a crude red-rock tower roughly the size of the island of Bahaca emerged like an enormous jar filled with steaming bone broth. The very active volcano was massive and rumbled constantly, letting off a thin plume of gray smoke that billowed upward toward Ma'an. From the base of the volcano, a dense jungle extended outward in all directions, parts of which stretched into the shallow teal waters like the fingers of a giant green hand. If it weren't for the protection of the immense and colorful coral reef, the raging Bocoa may have consumed the island long ago. As it was protected, Bayamaca was a haven for all manner of birds that crowded the sky and were often mistaken for the smoke from the volcano.

At the suggestion of Bogula, the Quest for Tizaka crew split up to search the island. The old lesini gave them a detailed description of the tizaka tree but explained it was almost identical to the kincham tree, which she warned them not to touch. They anchored in the shallows and swam the short distance to the north shore, creating a commotion among the swarms of birds that had been peacefully feeding on sand crabs but were now circling overhead and squawking at them loudly.

"Gisal, you'll come with me," Bocoani Numila was saying. "We'll head straight into the jungle from here until we reach the volcano, and then start making our way around."

Gisal nodded along. He didn't care one way or the other who he was paired with, or in what direction they were going. All he cared about was finding the dumb fruit tree thing so he could go after the whitefish they had seen swimming around the reef. They were going to eat good tonight!

"Bogula, you'll go with Madiri, since..."

"I'd prefer to be partnered with Ruga, if you don't mind, Bocoani," Bogula interrupted him. Gisal knew the bocoani didn't like being interrupted, and Ruruga didn't like it when people said his name wrong.

Numila sighed, "Whatever. It does not matter to me. You two will search that way, circling around to the south side where we'll meet you in the middle," he said, pointing at the northwest shore, and then he turned to Madiri. "You'll go with Koyay and search the northeast side and meet us around back of the volcano." Madiri nodded, glaring at Bogula. There was something going on between them, Gisal just knew it. Of course, they didn't seem to be trying to hide it either. "Dimgal," Bocoani Numila continued.

"Yeah, yeah, I know," Dimgal moaned, handing out the barbed spears to everyone. "Scrounge the gear, Dimgal. Stay here and keep an eye on the canuti, Dimgal. Climb a tree and fight those bees because I'm pregnant and craving fresh honey, Dimgal…"

"Hey, that was one time and I apologized afterward," Koyay said, defending herself while the rest of crew started laughing. "How was I supposed to know one little sting made him swell-up like a puffer fish?"

"Crazy ants do it to him too," Gisal added, snickering and making his chubby cheeks jiggle.

"Enough," Numila ordered them to stop, trying to conceal his own little smile. He refused a spear, unsheathing his polished coral saber. "Before we know it, we'll be swapping stories, laughing our butts off, and quickly run out of daylight. Now, you have your orders, you have the description of the tree and its fruit, so let's get to it."

"Let's get to it, what?" Koyay asked, her big eyes as green as the jungle.

"Let's get to it, shoats!" Numila hollered, and they all squealed. The birds overhead answered them in a chorus of angry squawks.

Gisal watched everyone go their separate ways before following Bocoani Numila up the beach toward the wall of green ahead of them. He didn't know what he expected as they lumbered into the jungle, but he wasn't overly impressed. "This is it?" he asked, trying to use his spear to slash away at the underbrush.

"What did you expect?" Numila was making short work of the thick-leafed bushes and hanging vines with his saber, but he seemed to be having just as much trouble as Gisal navigating around the densely packed trees.

"It reminds me of Amaca," Gisal said. There were easily a dozen palm trees within an arm's reach of him. He wasn't able to swing the dumb spear at all. He reached out with his massive hands and simply ripped the bushes out of the ground instead, using the spear as a staff.

"Yeah, I guess," the bocoani said between slashes. "This jungle is definitely much thicker, though – more like Pacca."

With all the hanging vines, Gisal could see why it reminded Numila of Pacca too. He just expected something more. This was the infamous Bayamaca, after all. It was supposed to wow him. "It's hard to see which tree is which," he said, squinting up into the dark canopy overhead.

"Bogula said it has white bark and black sap oozing out of it."

"Sounds awful!" he shouted, seeing Numila had worked farther ahead of him. Gisal ripped another patch of bushes out of the ground between two short and fat palm trees. He was about to toss the bush aside when he noticed bright-red berries on it. "What is this?" he yelled.

Numila looked back, squinting at him in the dim light. There was a spattering of sunlight through the canopy, and Gisal was trying to swing the bush into one of the hazy beams for the bocoani to see. "Beats me," Numila finally answered. "It kind of looks like strongbark, but I've never seen strongbark grow so short."

"It's everywhere!" Gisal gave one of the red berries a sniff. It actually didn't smell too bad. Leaning his spear against the palm tree, he plucked one of the berries and nibbled it a little bit. Just then, the volcano sputtered loudly overhead, startling him. "Hey, is that thing going to come down on us?" he asked, taking another nibble of the berry. The berry tasted awful, and he instantly recognized it was definitely not strongbark. It was too hard, chewy, and not nearly sweet enough to be strongbark, but the berry didn't seem to make him sick, and he was starving.

"If it does, it does – no sense worrying about it."

"Has it always been so noisy?"

"Yeah." Numila had gotten even farther away, focused on hacking away the underbrush, and had stopped looking back at Gisal.

"Did it when you and Koyay were here before?" Gisal could barely see him. "Huh?"

"Yes!"

"Man, I'm either starving or these berries aren't as bad I thought," he said to himself.

"It's best we just ignore it, find this tree, and get back on the Bocoa as soon as possible."

"Sounds good to me," Gisal said, eating some more of the red berries. "Hey, I'm going to take some of these bushes down to Dimgal!" he shouted at Numila, but he wasn't sure if the bocoani had heard him. "ALRIGHT?!"

"Yes, Gisal! I hear you," Numila snapped. "Go. We need provisions anyway."

Gisal yanked some more of the bushes out of the ground, tossed a couple berries into his mouth, tucked the bushes under his arm, grabbed his spear, and started making his way back to the beach. Every now and then he looked up at one of the trees, but they all seemed to be either palm trees or kapok trees, tangled up with thick, hairy vines, and surrounded by the same green bushes with the red berries. He broke out of the jungle and trudged through the deep sand.

"Anything?" Dimgal hollered at him from down near the water.

"Nothing yet," he said as he arrived. He tossed the bundle of bushes down at Dimgal's feet. "Except this stuff."

"What is it?" the scrounger asked, poking at one of the berries.

"Not sure," he answered, tossing another berry into his mouth. "Maybe some kind of strongbark?"

"Strongbark leaves aren't this shiny." Dimgal paused, noticing Gisal chewing. "Should you be eating it, if you don't know what it is?"

Gisal just shrugged. "Anyway. Spread them out, will you? So, they dry out under Mawoi's great light." He closed his eyes and smiled up at the sun.

"Sure," Dimgal said.

"Great. Well, gotta head back. Don't want to leave Bocoani Numila alone in there. He might get lost." Gisal laughed, ignoring the fact Dimgal wasn't. He turned around and started trudging back toward the jungle.

Gisal was starting to feel great and charged into the jungle, the leaves slapping at his knees. He started grabbing more of the bushes, ripping them out of the ground, and created a pile, which he then scooped up and threw over his massive shoulder. "...*reed to rutter, Bocoa Cutter*..." he sang, as random parts of Numila's sailing song popped into his head.

He returned to the beach and dropped pile after pile next to Dimgal, who was still busy spreading out the green stems and leaves of the first pile. "Why do you want to take this back with us?" Dimgal asked.

"We'll ask Bogula later, but I think it could be helpful. I ate some of the berries, which don't taste very good, but after you get used to your mouth going numb, you start to feel pretty good," Gisal said as he quickly popped a handful of the berries into his mouth.

"And you're *still* eating them?" Dimgal protested.

"Of course." Gisal smiled and took off at a jog back into the jungle, tossing a few more berries into his mouth.

A little over a hundred paces east of Numila and Gisal, the dense jungle started to thin out and the terrain became more rocky and uneven. Madiri and Koyay had wanted to search using the parallel fishing technique where they walked in the same direction for a bit, and then rotated and arched outward to search a new area by walking back the opposite direction. Unfortunately, the terrain wasn't cooperating. They were still making good progress, but having to climb up and over the rocky terraces slowed them way down. Madiri could see Koyay a stone's throw ahead of him, cautiously crossing over a narrow stream that appeared to split the northeast and far eastern sections of the island. There was a gap in the jungle from the stream, like a rip in a sail letting sunlight spill through. Even though they had slowed, he remained confident they would be able to search the entire island by evening meal. He was hungry and hoped they might find anything to eat besides more fish.

"Hey, Madiri, get over here. I think I found something," Koyay shouted back at him.

Madiri glanced here and there at the palm trees, kapok trees, and others he had never seen before, but which disappointingly didn't have white bark or black sap. He was extremely surprised by the lack of wildlife on the island. There were the birds, of course, but he had yet to see so much as a mouse, and Madiri refused to let himself hope for a boar or brocket. He came to the trickling stream and glanced right toward the volcano, and then left and down toward the shore. The water appeared to be clean enough – clean enough for their crusty crew, at least. He stepped over it with his long legs and saw Koyay just a few paces away.

"I hope it's that stupid tree or a hutia nest – I'm so hungry I could eat a whole litter!"

Koyay didn't respond, but Madiri instantly saw why when he stepped up next to her. She was staring at a pyramid of flat stones waist high, topped off with a skull. There were several rings of ash surrounding the pyramid's base, which was set on an area of cleared soil.

Koyay knelt down and ran a finger through the layers of ash. "This looks recent. Maybe within the last few days."

Madiri's eyes widened to the size of oysters, and he slowly started scanning the surrounding jungle. "You think someone is living on this island?" he asked.

"That or visits more regularly than we do." Koyay stood and looked around as well. "We better meet up with Numila and the others and search the south side of the island together."

She stood and immediately started walking southwest toward the volcano. Madiri lingered a moment longer, analyzing the stones. They looked polished like they might have come from the stream he and Koyay had just crossed, but the stones looked too shiny to have been polished by just water. And then he thought they actually reminded him of the ceramic plates the waki artisans made.

"You coming?" Koyay hollered at him.

"Yeah!" Madiri stood with the help of his spear and followed after her, his mind beginning to spin.

If the stones weren't stones at all but some kind of ceramics, then someone knowledgeable about waki techniques must have been on Bayamaca in the past. He didn't think it likely there was anyone else on the island with them now. At least, he hadn't seen any evidence so far, and Madiri had been looking for howler tracks, hutia tracks, or any tracks or traces of anything besides their own sandal prints in the dirt. He stepped over the stream again, following Koyay's tracks through the underbrush. And then he thought, there were conveniently three people with him that had been to Bayamaca before, and one of them was Bogula. He looked up from his feet and saw that Koyay was scratching a hashmark into a tree with the barbed tip of her spear, at which point he noticed a few other trees also had hashmarks carved into them.

"Clever girl," he said to himself.

"What's that?"

Well, he thought he had said it to himself. "The hashmarks," he answered her.

"Yeah, leading back to the skull," she explained.

"Speaking of," Madiri began, but paused to step up on to the knee-high rock terrace where Koyay was standing. "There's something you should know about Bogula."

"Yeah? What's that?" she asked, scratching another marker into a tree, but then she suddenly looked up. "Woo-hoo!" she shouted and started dancing.

"What?" Madiri asked.

Koyay tapped the tree with her spear, still dancing, "Tizaka!"

Madiri stepped closer to examine the tree – white bark, green leaves, hanging fruit all, and he didn't see any black sap. Just then, Numila and Gisal approached from the direction of the volcano.

"What's all this about?" Numila asked.

"Bam!" Koyay tapped the tree again with her spear and danced around it a second time.

Bocoani Numila put his hands on his hips and flexed his sweaty muscles, examining the tree as well. "Alright then. We'll need to bring Bogula over here to verify. Gisal?"

"Yep?" Gisal answered quickly, and then he tossed some red berries into his mouth.

"Stop eating that! You have no idea what it is," Numila said, shaking his head.

"I know what it *does* – it makes me feel spectacular!"

"Kayki provides!" Madiri prayed, bowing his head toward the ground. He then held out his hand to Gisal, "Give me some!"

"No!" Numila shouted, slapping his hand. "Gisal, run over and bring the others here."

"Yep." Gisal didn't hesitate and instantly took off to the west.

"And stop eating those berries!" Numila shouted after him, but Gisal didn't respond.

"Where did he get those berries?" Koyay asked.

"The northern base is covered in the stuff. Gisal's been taking bundles down to Dimgal."

"Interesting. Also," Koyay gestured for Numila to follow her. "Madiri, stay here with the tree for a moment. Numila, I want to show you something."

"If I eat it and die before you get back, don't say I didn't warn you!" Madiri yelled after them, only half-joking, and then he kicked the tree. "Dumb tree."

On the opposite side of the island, Ruruga pushed through the palm fronds with his spear and stepped out of the jungle and onto the hot western beach. Bogula was right behind him. Across the shallows to the west was what looked like a massive boulder balancing on a tiny island, but when she looked more closely, Bogula guessed it must have once been a part of Bayamaca that had been eaten away by the Great Sea. She stepped out next to Ruruga with her gnarled staff in hand and shook out her robe, enjoying the slight bit of cooling air flowing up through her tunic. They had covered the entire northwestern section of the island and hadn't seen anything that resembled tizaka or kincham. Of course, she hadn't expected to find it on this side of the island either.

"Think it will be up there?" Ruruga pointed to some trees at the top of the boulder.

Bogula couldn't tell if he was serious or not. After spending so much time with him, she decided it was less frustrating to just assume Ruruga was always serious. "No, I do not," she replied and turned to go back into the jungle. "Come, young man. There's a lot of jungle to search and we'll soon be running out of light."

The volcano grumbled again, and they could see smoke drifting into the clouds above. "Think we'll see any lava?" Ruruga asked, ducking under the palms behind her.

Bogula sighed, "I don't know."

"I remember the Bleeding of Orisa."

"Mm-hmm." She directed them toward the western base of the volcano.

"I was very young, but my baba took me to Risca after the initial eruption to see how the lava burned the forest, and how it died when it met the shore."

"Uh-huh."

"There was an explosion of steam, and we prayed to Hurassa that night."

"The Fire Spirit? Why not Niama?" Bogula asked, clearing a path with her staff.

"It was a mighty display of Hurassa's power and my itaba says, *Niama nibbles, but Hurassa bites*," he said with an adorably tiny chuckle.

Bogula stopped and turned to Ruruga. It was the first time she had heard him laugh the entire voyage. She looked up into his smiling, tattooed face, and had to chuckle as well. "I believe your itaba and I will get along quite well," she said.

"Maybe, she died when I was born," Ruruga said, matter-of-factly, and then continued slashing through the jungle, leaving Bogula to digest what he had said. Suddenly, Gisal burst through a wide sheet of vines with the energy of a brocket buck.

"There you are!" he shouted. "I've been up and down, back and forth, all over this side of the island, and I was about to go over to the other side when I heard you talking. Right, you have to follow me. They found the tree. Are you ready, alright, let's go!" And then he took off again.

Bogula and Ruruga shared a look of amused confusion, but then they had to follow Gisal quickly before they lost sight of him.

Numila scratched his head, looking at the skull atop the pyramid. They hadn't done a thorough search of the island when he came to Bayamaca the first time, but he told himself they would surely have noticed an Itabayiti or Gusiti presence if there had been one.

"What do you think? Should we search the rest of the island together or get what we came for and leave as soon as possible?" Koyay asked him. "I'm leaning toward getting off Bayamaca as soon as we can, but you're the bocoani."

"Hmm," Numila grunted. He was kneeling down and prodding the pyramid with a stick. "Do you remember that story about Yaya Anacacu sending doomed expeditions in search of a brother, or son, or someone?"

"Vaguely. I think you told me about that when we were shoats together," Koyay said. "You don't think this has anything to do with that, do you? That was – what, fifty years ago?"

"I think it was more like a hundred years ago, actually." Numila stood and tossed the stick into the bushes. "If that's the tree we're looking for, let's finish our mission and let Yaya Amnu decide about this."

"Wooo!" Gisal jumped out of the bushes and scared Numila and Koyay.

"Baga!" Koyay said, breathing heavily. "You scared the Kuraka out of us!"

Numila held his wife. "What is wrong with you, Gisal?!"

"My apologies - logies," he said, repeating himself, but appearing confused by it. "But Bogula and Ruruga – Bogula, Ruruga – are at the tree. She – tree, she – says it is definitely tizaka. Ka – ka..."

Numila and Koyay gave each other a concerned look and then Numila put a hand on Gisal's shoulder. "Why don't you go help Dimgal, and take it easy, alright?"

"Yep," he replied and darted off toward the north beach.

They joined the others around the tizaka tree and waited as Bogula collected the various samples she required. She handed Madiri a bundle of fruits, flowers, and bark, and then gathered more, which she handed to Numila and Koyay. Once they all had their arms full of samples, they headed back to the beach together.

As Mawoi settled in the western sky and Bayamaca's volcano continued to cough, Bocoani Numila and his crew relaxed around a large campfire with bellies full of roasted whitefish. Madiri licked his lips and feigned satisfaction while Ruruga was on his third helping and chewing loudly. Gisal had gotten back to the beach earlier, drank two gourds of water, promptly passed out, and was sleeping soundly on a bed of wet sand from his profuse sweating. Dimgal settled in next to Gisal and was keeping an eye on his friend. Numila and Koyay cuddled and admired the stars popping into view overhead. Every now and then they glanced over at Bogula who was already grinding tizaka seeds and bark together while chewing the flowers and spitting the juice into the coconut-husk bowl. She would make enough to fill one of the many vials, of which she seemed to have an endless supply, and then would start the process over again.

"So," Madiri began, smacking his lips together. "Are we going to talk about that little skull shrine or what?"

"Not tonight," Numila yawned. "We all need to get some rest. Bogula, will Gisal be able to sail in the morning?"

"Kayki enchanted oka with the vitality of youth, but there will be a price to pay," she warned them.

"So, that's what you call it?" he asked and Bogula nodded. "Huh – well, what price will he have to pay?"

Bogula shrugged. "Don't worry, Gisal will be fine. He just needs time to recover."

She hadn't answered his question, but Numila didn't care. He was too tired and desperately needed to get some sleep. Once Numila and his crew quieted down, the jungle of Bayamaca came to life around them with the familiar and welcomed sounds of home, and then sleep came quickly for everyone.

CHAPTER TWENTY-THREE

The Information Game

Atu cursed under his breath as the smelly warrior patted him down. The agur were stationed at the docks of each island in their fiery-red tunics and carrying their shiny coral spears, searching everyone and everything that came or went from their ramshackle huts, especially teenage boys. The unfortunate agur running his filthy hands over him wore a sweat-stained tunic that looked a bit too big for him and had scratch marks on the back, which made it look like he had been dragged over a field of shells. *Strange*, Atu thought, but then he shrugged and held his breath, trying to avoid inhaling the man's body odor.

"You're clear," the warrior said with one final slap on his shoulder, and then he motioned for him to move along. Atu didn't respond and quietly started up the cibmani street shaking his head.

News of what was happening on Itabaca and Yapaca didn't travel between the islands, and by the time the Yaya opened the harbor and people were attempting to return to their normal routines, fantastic stories started to spread, and people couldn't tell fact from fiction. Atu overheard some of the waki diggers talking about attacks in Coan Village and Segin Village, but Olari would get really quiet when Atu and Anki came around. He would only say that he had never seen anything like it. Of course, Anki wouldn't shut up about his experience on Bahaca, which made Atu all the more frustrated because he couldn't care less about the Mawoakin. He eventually distracted his brother with the sparker he had taken from the lighthouse just to get away from him and get a moment of peace. So, when Demican sent a message with Haro that morning asking Atu to meet him on Niamca, he jumped at the chance to get off of Conaca for a while and maybe gather a little information along the way.

Niamca was a weird island, and he wondered how the two islands that produced the freshest water could be so completely different. Amaca was a paradise compared to Niamca. There was a lush and vast forest covering all of Amaca, two large lakes, a long rushing river, and an enormous, towering plateau, which was said to hold a third massive lake that was supposedly the size of the entire island of Niamca. There was even a waterfall pouring out of the side of the plateau, feeding the mighty river. And what did Niamca have? Three weird little sinkholes with springs at the bottom of them. The areas around the sinkholes were also the only places on the island with trees, while the rest of it was almost as baren as Yapaca.

Atu ducked off the main street and into the dense foliage on the left, half jogging, half sliding down the steep depression toward the south spring. Why they called it Sakimi, Atu had no idea, but he also didn't care to know. Whatever the reason, he thought it must have had something to do with the insane amount of prickly bushes that grew around it. None of the other teenagers complained about getting a few scrapes when taking the shortcut through the jungle instead of the long way around on the path, and neither did Atu, at least not out loud. He broke out of the underbrush between two palms right in front of the pumping station entrance. A few birds squawked disapprovingly at him from their perch on top of the station before flying up and away in disgust. As he watched them, Atu thought he heard the segin talking softly through the wooden door of the station.

"Atu, that you?" Demican called to him from the other side of the building. He stood there a moment, expecting the segin to come out and chase him and Demican away, but the door remained closed. *Guess they don't care we're down here*, he thought.

"Atu?"

"Yeah!" he shouted back, brushing burrs and other pokey plant seeds from his legs. "Man, what is with the agur? I got patted down before I got on the ferry from Conaca, and then again just now when I got here." His complaining continued as he walked around the building.

Demican was sitting on the wooden deck that hugged one side of the spring, his legs dangling over the side and in the water up to his calves. "Beats me," the giant boy said.

Atu plopped down beside him, "How's the water?" He slipped his sandals off and then tested the water with the tips of his toes.

"Fine," Demican said with a little nod, but he was staring off in thought.

"You alright, Dem?" The water was satisfactory and Atu submerged his feet, noticing Demican's masts-for-legs went a whole hand farther into the water than his. He looked at his friend who was unusually quiet and reserved. "Dem, what's going on?"

"Yaeel's dead."

"W-What?"

Yaeel was Demican's brother and a segin who worked at the treatment facility down by the docks. Atu couldn't believe he was dead, and he didn't know what to say. It wasn't that he didn't care, necessarily, but Atu had never met Yaeel and knew next to nothing else about him. He also wasn't very fond of seeing others get all emotional over people dying and their spirits returning to Mayu. If he was being honest, he probably wouldn't have come had he known beforehand. But he did think it weird Demican asked him to meet at the south spring instead of at the treatment facility where Atu assumed whatever happened had happened.

"He drowned," Demican continued.

"Really?" It immediately occurred to Atu how hard it would be to drown in the treatment facility.

"Right here," Dem clarified, as if anticipating Atu's next question.

"What?!" Atu jerked his feet out of the water.

"Or in one of the northern springs," he quickly added. "They didn't tell me which, and I doubt they will. I guess it has something to do with not wanting to worry people — what with all that is going on right now."

Atu glared down into the spring water. It went from pale-green and clear to dark, black-green and murky farther down. If there were a hundred bodies down there, no one would ever know. He had never heard of anyone drowning in the springs, and would never have guessed a segin, a person supposedly an expert on water, to be the first. "Did they say how it happened?"

"No." Demican kicked his legs, sending little ripples across the pool. "You know, now that I've mentioned it, I don't think I want to talk about it anymore," he said, and Atu gratefully agreed. "Thanks for coming all the same."

Atu blankly nodded, his thoughts lingering on all those potential bodies at the bottom of the spring. After a moment, he decided to change the subject. "So, what do you think is really going on around here? When baba came back from his council meetings I asked him, but he told me not to worry about it. Can you believe that? *Not worry about it?*" Atu chuckled. "So, I asked Haro, but he knew even less than I did. Anki attended one of those meetings before they closed the harbors, and he tried to say he already told me about it, but I called his bluff. I pinned him in the clay pits until he told me what it was about. He said the boadulu admitted to being a part of some conspiracy to murder the Yaya. Can you believe it?" He paused to gauge Demican's reaction, but his friend remained dazed. "Anyway, he said it had something to do with a little boy – an akin on Bahaca, or something. That's all I got."

After a moment, Demican seemed to snap out of whatever trance he was in and looked at him. "Yeah, I heard about the same from my baba. I learned a little more from my brothers, but we mostly talked about Yaeel," he said.

"Oh, and what is that?" Atu tried not to sound too eager.

"What? From my brothers?" he asked and Atu nodded "Um – well, you know Atriska?"

Atu thought for a moment, "Yeah, I think so."

"He's an adulu."

"Right, the skinny one!"

Demican smiled for the first time, "Look who's talking!" They both laughed, and Atu was glad to see his friend smiling again. Atriska was Dem's only brother who grew taller but not larger. "Anyway," he continued. "My brothers came last night for evening meal and to bear witness to Yaeel's bonefire, which was the strangest experience I've ever had." He drifted off again but immediately shook his head, avoiding wherever his sad thoughts might lead. When he turned back to Atu, he had what looked like a bead of tears threatening to pour over his eyelids. Dem took a deep breath. "Atriska said he overheard the Yaya and Unana Wani talking about their daughter, Kina."

"I knew it!" Atu shouted, getting to his feet before Demican could say anything else.

"They're going to promise her to your brother."

"I said, I knew it half-a-mawa ago!" He started pacing, his thin pale arms crossed at his chest. "That lucky maniku! And now you're gonna to tell me they're naming him the next Yaya!" He stopped to look at his friend, but

Demican didn't respond. He just continued sitting there quietly, slowly shaking his head with his pursed lips curled up in a mischievous grin. Atu threw up his hands. "What?" he asked but Dem didn't answer. "Speak – Oh, great Demican!" He jokingly bowed to his friend.

Dem chuckled, "If Anki is promised to Kina Wani, then he can't be named Yaya."

"What?"

"That rule has been in place since Yaya Asoc forbid the eating of yellowfish."

"Wait, how do you know that?" Atu asked as he plopped back down on the deck.

"My *other* brother," he said with a squeaky little chuckle.

Suddenly, a loud crashing sound came from the other side of the pumping station and startled the boys. Atu tiptoed to the end of the wall and peeked around the corner.

"What is it?" Demican whispered.

"Oh, nothing," he whispered back, but then he started snickering. "It's only Hamsi. He must have slipped and tumbled down the slope!" Demican started laughing as well and came up behind him. "Shh!" Atu put his finger to his mouth. "He's coming."

Hamsi didn't stand a chance. The instant he rounded the corner, Atu grabbed his arm, spun him into Demican, and the giant picked Hamsi up and threw him into the spring with a mighty *SPLASH!* The boys fell to the deck holding their stomachs and laughing.

Hamsi instantly resurfaced, spit out a stream of water, and shouted, "What was that for? Honestly! You guys couldn't at least warn me?"

But before the boys could respond, there was another crashing sound just like the first. Atu rushed and peeked around the corner again. It was Lewa and some guy he thought looked familiar, but he wasn't sure why. "It's Lewa and some guy I don't recognize."

"Lewa? What's she doing here?" Demican asked, sneaking up behind Atu like before. "What do we do?"

Atu looked at him and smiled. Having seen Atu's crooked smile plenty of times, Demican quickly got into position. Lewa also didn't stand a chance. The instant the girl rounded the corner, Atu spun her and Demican tossed her – *SPLASH!* It happened so fast, the guy she was with just stood staring in shock as the boys fell to the deck laughing again.

Lewa surfaced and coughed out a mouthful of water. Searching the spring and the surrounding jungle for an explanation, she first saw Hamsi bobbing in the water nearby and waving at her, but then her startled light-brown eyes locked on Atu and Demican. "What are you jerks doing here?" she asked, swimming to the edge of the spring.

"Probably the same as you," Demican answered.

She rolled her eyes and then glared at her friend. "You're just going to stand there?" she asked, to which her friend only shrugged in response.

"Who's this?" Atu gestured to the guy with his thumb.

"I'm..." he started to say but Lewa cut him off.

"Nobody!" She climbed out of the water looking like a drowned rat. "Atu, why are you such a pest?"

"Sorry, Lewa," Demican apologized through his squeaky chuckling.

Lewa threw her arms out, displaying her drenched tan tunic. "I know this wasn't your idea, Dem!"

"Can I say something?" the guy asked with his finger in the air, but Lewa glared at him. "That seems fair," he said and sat quietly on the deck.

Atu stared at the guy. He was tall and muscular, but not like the hulking muscles men got from cutting down trees or working in the clay pits on Conaca. They were smoothed out, as if he had been born muscular but then stretched out as he grew. He was also cleanly shaven, which was only typical of children, entertainers, the ciba who worked on the volcanic island of Risca, and... *SPLASH!* Atu's thoughts were suddenly interrupted by a wave of cool spring water.

"Hey!" he shouted, peeking over at Hamsi through the water dripping into his eyes.

"I got you back!" Hamsi laughed, swimming to the end of the dock where Lewa was wringing out her two long braids. "Hey, Lewa. What's happening on Yapaca?"

"Yeah!" Atu and Demican said in harmony. Atu was actually thankful for the splash to his face, but he raised a threatening fist at Hamsi anyway.

"I don't...well..." Lewa stammered, seemingly not in the mood to talk, but then it looked to Atu like something suddenly dawned on her, and her eyes grew as big as acorns. "Well," she began again, sitting on the deck next to her friend. "How about I tell you something I know, and then you tell me something you know?"

"Ah, so you want to play a game," Atu said. He looked at his friends who were nodding in agreement, but then he added, "You go first!"

Lewa rolled her eyes. "Fine!" She looked up and squinted at the midday sun high overhead, wiping the cool spring water from her smooth ebony skin.

Atu watched Hamsi stare at her with a big, dumb smile on his chubby face, as if he had never seen a drowned rat before. Of course, Atu also saw what Hamsi saw, that Lewa was a remarkably pretty girl, but he had promised his friend he wouldn't show any interest in her and he didn't intend to. Besides, she was way too good for Hamsi and, judging by the look of her so-called friend, maybe too good for Atu as well.

"The agur showed up four days ago," Lewa started. "It was probably the same time everywhere, I guess. At first, they just set up their huts and blocked off the docks. They wouldn't even allow the ferrymen to head out. It was weird." She stopped when a look came over her face that reminded Atu of when Demican had drifted off into his own sad thoughts, but then Lewa quickly recovered and smiled at everyone. "I overheard one of the agur explaining to Oboco the harbor was closed," she said with a soft little laugh, the kind girls typically hide behind their hands. "The old man nearly started crying, jumping up and down and waving his arms like a chubby heron — it was pretty funny to watch, actually. But now that I think about it, maybe he knew something we don't." She stopped talking again and crossed her arms.

"Hey," Atu protested. "We already knew the harbors were closed."

"And that Haro looks like a chubby heron," Dem added, causing a round of laughter.

"Stop, Dem!" Atu punched his friend's thick shoulder but immediately had to shake off the pain it caused his own hand. "She owes us something we *don't* already know!" Atu complained, nursing his sore wrist.

"Ugh!" Lewa groaned. "They cleared the streets and established a curfew..."

"What's that?" Hamsi asked, but then he must have sensed Atu's irritated glare because the interrupter quickly dipped his big mouth below the surface of the water. Hamsi knew what a curfew was, Atu was sure of it, he just liked to always be included in conversations.

"Like when your baba makes you go home before Mawoi goes to sleep," Dem answered, but he looked at Lewa for confirmation.

She shrugged and nodded, "Sort of like that, yes. The agur were enforcing the curfew, but I didn't know that. I was picking flowers in Coan garden and heard shouting. People were running." Lewa took a deep breath. "It was awful. I've never seen anything like it." She looked at her friend and then at everyone with sorrowful eyes.

Atu was getting impatient. "What was happening?" he asked, hardly able to contain himself. He swiveled his legs around and rested his elbows on his boney knees.

"The agur were beating a man in the street, right there in front of us! His children – well, I assume they were his children – were crying and trying to help him, but one of the agur held them back with his spear." Lewa bit her lip, her thoughts drifting off again.

Atu looked at Hamsi and then at Demican, seeing both of his friends hanging on her every word like a couple of seagulls bouncing at the feet of the fish vendors. He thought they looked pathetic. And then Atu noticed Lewa's friend was picking his nose with his long, delicate finger, and a giggle snuck out of Atu's dumb mouth. Immediately, they all turned to glare at him like he was the one that had been beating that guy in Lewa's story. "What?" he shrugged.

Lewa shook her head and declared, "That's enough. It's your turn."

"He was picking his nose!" Atu exclaimed, pointing.

"It needed to be picked," her friend said.

Lewa scrunched her face at him. "Eww."

"What's so gross about picking my nose?"

"Yeah, I do it all the time!" Hamsi added, joyfully, shoving his own chubby finger up his own chubby nose.

"Yuck! Boys are disgusting!"

"Why? Do girls not pick their noses?" Demican asked, completely serious.

"Of course we do!" Lewa scoffed. "We're only more discrete about it. You boys seem to think all of Itabacan wants to take part in your nose picking, and belching, and farting, and every little gross bodily function.

Ugh!" She tossed her still-damp braids over her shoulder. "I knew we shouldn't have stayed. Now I'm all wet *and* grossed out!"

"Did you want to leave?" her friend asked.

"No! Wait," Atu protested. "Dem, didn't you have something to add?"

There was a moment of silence as they all looked at the giant boy who was looking back at each of them with wide eyes. "Umm...well, my brother..."

"Besides the Yaeel thing," Atu interrupted him. "You don't need to talk about that, if you don't want to." Demican's head spun around, and he glared at Atu so quickly, Atu thought his friend's head might spin right off his broad shoulders.

"What Yaeel thing?" Hamsi asked.

Once again, everyone fell silent and waited on Demican for an answer, which Atu hoped would be as short as it was before. He really wasn't interested in learning more about Dem's drowned brother, but if it satisfied their turn in the information game, then he was willing to stomach it.

Demican let out a long, deep sigh, and then he looked across the shimmering waters of the spring and into the dark jungle beyond. "There has to be a reason for it," he said. "Something woven into his destiny, a purpose greater than this brief life Yucahu so quickly reclaimed."

"Oh!" Lewa gasped, picking up on Dem's subtle revelation.

"Baba and I were up at the residence. I was helping him fix a bench Yaeel and Macu had broken a few nights before. That was the same night Hamsi and I left you with Joba at the training docks, Atu." He stopped to smile at them, while Atu shrank away from Lewa's judgmental gaze. "They had argued over whose responsibility it was to stable the chacu before the storm and got to wrestling over it. Baba just cheered them on." Demican started to cry, but he forced a bit of laughter through the tears, which slowly made their way down his cheeks. "Ya lifted Macu up like this." He demonstrated with both fists raised up and over the edge of the decking. "And then, WHAM! Brought him back down hard, using Macu's back to snap the bench in two. I, of course, cheered, and I saw baba smiling..." he whimpered. "Baba smiled at him and said, well done. Baba rarely

250

compliments us, you know? And Macu was red-hot, angrier than a clawless hutia! But he's a lot like me – we know when we've been bested."

"That's only because no one else in their right mind would challenge you!" Atu joked, momentarily lightening the mood. He thought Demican's story would have been much more moving, if his maturing voice hadn't been squeaking and creaking like the trees around them.

"My brother..." Dem started again but stopped to clear his throat.

"Take your time," Lewa told him.

"Yeah!" Hamsi shouted, just needing to say something.

Atu decided he wasn't interested in talking about Yaeel anymore. They weren't learning anything new about what was really going on around Itabacan, and so he interjected, "What greater purpose could Niama have for drowning your brother?"

"Atura!" Lewa scolded him, and with his full name too.

He hated it when people used his full name, especially stupid girls who had no business being there at the spring with them in the first place. She was just another frustrating, meddling, irritating, wasp-of-a-girl, who needed to be swatted more than anything.

"Aww, is Atu going to pout now?" Hamsi joked, splashing at him again, but the water fell short.

Atu quickly put his foot in the water and kicked back. "No! I'm not pouting, ya curly-haired manati!" His cheeks were turning pink, he knew it, he could feel the embarrassment flooding his face. And that was when it dawned on him, "Hey! Dem, isn't your other brother one of the agur?"

"I think he was about to tell us," Lewa said with a smirk.

"Oh? You think?" Atu snapped, mocking her. He pulled his knees up to his chest and hugged them with his pale arms.

"What I was going to say," Demican said, hesitantly, "was that, yes, Yaeel drowned, but he wasn't the first. Urlam, another segin, was found in the Anikna spring..."

"Another one?" Atu cut him off. "You didn't tell me that!"

"I was going to, but then..." he gestured to Hamsi, Lewa, and the oddly familiar stranger still sitting there quietly like a caught maniku playing dead.

"Two segin drowned, and within a mawa of each other." Lewa looked at her friend, her little wasp eyes searching his eyes for answers.

"That's not all of it," Dem continued. "Lesini Turan examined him, and she said she suspected Urlam had been poisoned!"

"Poisoned?" Lewa asked and Demican nodded.

"Baba was furious! Said the lesini was being reckless and had no right making such *outlandish accusations.*" Dem paused, seeing Hamsi looking at him with a confused expression on his face. "Baba's words, not mine," he added.

Hamsi nodded, but his half-open mouth and arched brow gave away his persistent confusion. "So...your other, other brother," he started to say, still working it out in his mind. "He's an agur, right?"

"Nope!" Atu interrupted. "Thanks, Dem." He pat his friend on the back and then gestured to Lewa. "Alright, it's your turn. I want to hear more of your story."

"Well, before I respond to you!" She stuck her tongue out at Atu, which wasn't as bad as she probably intended it to be, and then Lewa placed a gentle hand on Demican's shoulder. "I'm sorry about your brother, Dem," she said. Demican quietly nodded but he seemed to be avoiding eye contact with her. "Truly." She moved her head along with his, until he looked up and she caught his wandering eyes, and then she smiled at him with a glint of tears in her own light-brown eyes.

Demican let out a large, labored sigh. "Thank you," he said.

"Now, where was I?" Lewa asked.

"The man in the street," Atu answered quickly, not wanting to waste any more daylight.

She nodded, arranging the pieces of her story in her mind. "Right. The agur were everywhere. They banged on doors before kicking them in and dragged my neighbors into the street by their hair. Can you imagine?" she asked but didn't give anyone a chance to respond. "The protectors of Itabacan, our warriors, beating their fellow Itabayiti!" Lewa shrugged and shook her head. "I honestly don't know. Like, my neighbors were crab trappers. The people I first saw being taken to the docks were lowaki."

"What happened the next day?" Hamsi asked, still swimming around in the pool.

"The next day was more of the same, and things seemed to settle down the day after that. It's what happened yesterday that truly made no sense!" she said and waited.

"Well?" Demican leaned toward Lewa with his giant head.

"Well, nothing. It's your turn! Why were all the council members detained on Itabaca for so long?" she asked and crossed her arms. "I heard they were going to arrest Boyiti Macoca."

"That's dumb," Atu said quickly.

Lewa tossed her hands up, "Oh? Then tell us!"

"I don't know, because my baba told me *not to worry about it*," Atu said as if he were mimicking a crying infant, making Demican and Hamsi laugh, but neither Lewa nor her friend thought he was funny.

"And you?" she pointed to Demican.

"Me?" Demican pretended to be confused.

"Yes, you! Ma'an, give me strength!" she shouted into the sky.

Atu hadn't seen Demican's cheeks get so red in a long time. "You alright, Dem?" he asked with a wry smile.

Demican let out a nervous chuckle. "Yeah, of course. Um – you asked me something, Lewa?"

Lewa threw up her hands. "Children! Yes, I asked you what your baba's council meetings were about!"

"Oh, uh – the boadulu conspired to murder someone, and the akin on Bahaca were involved," he finally squeaked out.

"Hey! That's what I told you!" Atu elbowed him in the arm.

"So, you lied!" Lewa pointed at Atu, accusingly.

"No, I told you what my baba said, word for word." He gestured to Demican with his thumb. "What he said was what I managed to get out of my brother."

Lewa's eyes widened. "You're brother? Anki?"

"Yeah."

"How would your brother know that?" the quiet guy asked, who still looked so familiar.

Atu looked at him and rolled his eyes. "Because he..." Atu stopped himself and then smiled and pointed to Lewa. "Nope, it's your turn."

"Ugh!" she grunted.

Hamsi climbed out of the spring and flopped down on the deck next to Lewa. "They were your rules," he said, clearly feeling like he hadn't spoken enough.

"Fine! Yesterday, most of the people that had been taken the first day were brought back, and the agur forced them at spearpoint to scratch the symbols off of their doorways."

"What symbols?" Hamsi asked.

"Like, the symbol of Mawoi..." Lewa's voice trailed off, as if something suddenly made sense to her. "That's it!" she shouted.

"What?" her friend asked.

"You said that Anki said the boadulu and the Mawoakin attempted to murder someone." Everyone looked at her with confused eyes. "The Mawoakin on Bahaca? The Temple of the Dawn?"

"Yeah, so?" Atu looked at her blankly, trying to get her to explain more, but then he thought of something and stood up. "So, you're saying it wasn't just the akin conspiring with the boadulu, it was Mawoi as well?"

"Yes, no!" Lewa shouted. "The *Cult* of Mawoi."

"Ah – makes sense," the not-so-quiet-anymore guy nodded.

"Ugh, I can't take it! Who are you and why do you look so familiar?" Atu demanded of Lewa's friend.

Her friend looked at Lewa, she rolled her eyes and nodded back, and then he said, "My name is Piddso, and I..."

Hamsi stood up with big round eyes. "The almec player?!"

"No way!" Demican was on his feet now too.

Atu couldn't believe it. Everyone played almec, and every island was represented by its own team during the Canutaloc Festival, but there were only a handful of really good players. Piddso was one of the really good ones. His father told him, many generations before, a cult developed around the game, and they believed the game ball represented Yucahu and the hoops were the cracks in Ora that Yucahu repaired with his Great Spirit. During the Canutaloc, the top two teams of the year were pitted against each other, one representing Kanu and one representing Chuka. Piddso had been the chief of team Chuka and scored the winning point during the last festival.

"I'm afraid so," Piddso said with a big smile full of pearl-white teeth. The boys were oozing with questions for him, and they formed a semi-circle around him on the deck, which Atu suspected was probably why Lewa didn't want them to know who her friend was.

She suddenly stood, clapped her hands together loudly, and said, "Hold it! Can we please save your slobbering over my friend until after we've finished our discussion?"

"Aww – come on, Lewa!" Demican pleaded.

"Yeah, or Dem will throw you in the spring again!" Atu threatened.

Demican put his large hand on Atu's tiny shoulder and smiled at her. "He doesn't speak for all of us."

"Well," Piddso interjected. "I have news from Badhan I can share."

Lewa snapped to look at her friend. "What?! You've been holding out this whole time?"

"No one asked me," he shrugged.

"Men!" Lewa plopped down on the deck and stewed. "What I think of boys of all ages!"

Everyone grew quiet, waiting patiently for Piddso to begin; so quiet they could hear the pump operators working on the other side of the station wall. Piddso leaned forward and started talking in a whisper.

"I was practicing with the team in the Badhan courts when we saw three or four agur carts come down the street. We didn't think much of it until I saw the second one had Boadulu Urtulu standing on the back with his hands bound. So, we followed them to the docks. We tried to stay out of sight, but when we saw there was a huge crowd already gathered down there, we just blended in with them. The agur loaded the boadulu onto a fishing canuti and took him out beyond the Grand Gateway, which could mean only one thing..."

"A walk with Niama," Hamsi whispered with big round eyes.

"That's what we guessed. We saw the agur return later that day *without* Urtulu."

Atu's father told him a walk with Niama was the most merciful punishment for the most egregious crimes. The convicted were taken out beyond the Grand Gateways to the Bocoa and left to swim for their deliverance. If they made it back, then they would be forgiven, but most people sank beneath the waves and were never seen again.

"And yesterday," Piddso continued, "when we were practicing, we saw another column of agur carts, but this time it was a little boy and a girl dressed in yellow robes with their hands bound behind their backs."

"The boakin and that girl Anki mentioned!" Atu almost shouted, but then he quieted again as he tried to remember the girl's name.

"What girl?" Lewa asked, clearly annoyed to still not have all the information.

"Oh – just someone who nearly got Tabba killed," he answered, matter-of-factly.

"What?!" she screamed at him. "Tabba? When did she get involved in all of this?"

Atu rolled his eyes, "Ugh...girls. What I think of girls..." he mocked her, eliciting a few chuckles from Piddso. Lewa quickly turned her irritation on him, but luckily for Piddso, there was suddenly a soft rumble of thunder from the east, causing them all to look up into the sky.

Lewa stood to leave. "Come on, Piddso, it's that time of day. We better head back to Badhan before the ferries stop running."

"Yeah," Atu stood as well and stretched his back. "I better get back before Anki burns down the residence."

Demican threw a hand out to help Piddso get to his feet, which Piddso gladly took. "Can I come by some time and practice with the team?" he asked.

"Any time," Piddso said.

"I wonder if my baba is back from his mission," Hamsi wondered aloud, pondering the graying midday sky.

The others instantly stopped what they were doing to grill Hamsi with their piercing and questioning eyes, but Atu was the first to ask, "What are you talking about? What mission?"

CHAPTER TWENTY-FOUR
Prices to be Paid

The Quest for Tizaka crew slept peacefully through the night, and Koyay was glad to let them. Everyone had worked hard and deserved a rest. She, on the other hand, had been startled awake by a garbled voice. At first, she thought it might have just been the volcano grumbling at them, but no one else seemed to have heard it, not even Numila, who was sleeping beside her. She sat up, listening intently to the gentle waves breaking on shore a dozen reeds away, and the equally gentle breeze rustling the jungle foliage behind her. Despite the looming threat of the active volcano constantly sputtering and coughing both day and night, Bayamaca was extraordinarily peaceful. Koyay laid back down and closed her eyes, but she immediately heard the voice again.

"Ora churns..."

"Wha..." she started to respond but thought better of it. Koyay didn't want to wake the others up, especially her husband.

She decided to move away from the rest of the crew to investigate the voice a bit more. She carefully stood, stepped between the smoldering coals of the dying fire and Bogula, and headed toward the shore. Judging by the position of Chuka on the eastern horizon, Mawoi would be rising soon, and she was awake anyway. Just when her toes touched damp sand, Koyay stopped and sat quietly on the beach. She listened to the waves, allowing their rhythmic whooshing to clear her thoughts, and closed her eyes once again.

"Now," she whispered, "what's all this about Ora?" Waves came to shore, wind rustled the trees, distant birds squawked, but there was no voice. "Come on...say something!"

Koyay waited and listened a little longer as the first rays of the Great Light appeared on the eastern horizon. Bright-yellow beams zipped across the calm waters of the Bocoa and pierced the lid of her right eye. It instantly popped open, and she glared at the sun. Koyay sighed, squinted, and stared north toward Itabacan, out there somewhere in the Durali. It was known as the Land Asleep, where Maboti reigns and Mawoi rests before being awoken for the dawn. But the Durali was perpetually beyond the horizon, and the Cult of Mawoi knew the only way they could ever help the Lord of All and put a stop to the endless struggle with the Dark Shadow was to find a way into the Land Asleep and defeat Maboti once and for all. Unfortunately, that could only happen if Itabacan was cleansed of its non-believers.

There was commotion behind her as the rest of the crew were roused by the dawn. She slowly got to her feet, brushed the sand from her backside, and walked back up the beach, slightly disappointed the voice didn't return.

Koyay saw Ruruga was just about to wake up Numila and called to him at a loud whisper, "Ruruga, I'll get him. You and Dimgal should go ahead and load the cano with the provisions." Ruruga didn't say anything in reply, he just turned and started waking Dimgal, who snapped awake instantly.

"Already?" Dimgal yawned, stretching his scrawny arms and arching his back.

Koyay knelt down beside Numila, stuck her finger in her mouth, and then slowly slid her finger into her husband's ear.

"I'm not kidding," Dimgal said, watching her and rubbing one eye with his knuckle. "You two are weird."

"Come, we have to load the provisions," Ruruga told him.

The scrawny scrounger nodded and jumped up, landing flat on his feet and dipped into a squat where he rocked side to side, rolling his head around in circles and loosening his joints. Koyay saw him out of the corner of her eye, but she was more focused on trying to wake up Numila in the grossest way possible.

"Whoa!" Numila suddenly shouted, scrambling away from her and slapping at his ear. Sand flew everywhere, on Bogula, the fire, Gisal, and Koyay, who laughed and laughed.

"Why are you so loud!" Bogula huffed, rolling away from them and covering her ears.

"Taycoay," she greeted her very alert husband.

Numila smiled, shaking his head. "Only the Great Spirit knows how much I love you," he said, and then started digging the sand out of his ear. "Well," he started, pausing to yawn, "I guess we should be on our way."

"Expeditiously," she said, smiling. "Ruruga and Dimgal are already loading the provisions, and Bogula is clearly awake. So, we just have the other two..." Koyay turned to see Madiri kick sand over the smoldering embers behind her. "Fine. Just the one left to wake up."

"Gisal!" Madiri yelled at him to wake up, but the big guy didn't flinch. "Hey..." he tapped Gisal's leg with his foot. "Ya overgrown manati, it's time to wake up and greet Mawoi!" When he still didn't respond, Madiri looked to Bogula.

"I told you; he needs time to recover," she said, checking on the vials in her robe.

"What's that?" Numila stood up and stretched. "What's going on?"

"Look," Madiri said, and then he kicked Gisal hard in his leg.

"Hey, don't..." Numila started to scold Madiri but noticed Gisal didn't respond. "Bogula, what's wrong with Gisal?"

"Ugh!" Bogula huffed, slapping at the sand. "Why aren't any of you listening to me? The man consumed a copious amount of oka berries. There are prices to be paid for disrespecting Kayki like that!"

"Prices?" Koyay interjected, slightly alarmed.

"How long will he be asleep?" Numila asked.

"Until he isn't," she answered matter-of-factly.

"What?" Numila almost screamed.

"No amount of yelling at me is going to help, young man!" Bogula lectured Numila. "You'll just have to wait it out here or drag him onto the canuti somehow."

"Dimgal, Ruruga!" Madiri yelled out to them, who were already transferring some oka bushes and other provisions onto the canuti. "Come back with the cano!"

"We're going to need both of them," Koyay added.

Madiri chuckled, "Both cano!"

With a great amount of effort, they dragged Gisal's massive body onto the two cano and towed him out to the canuti. It took all six of them to haul the giant up onto the reed boat, which dipped on the kona-side and dumped a hefty portion of their provisions into the clear waters of the shallows. When they finally managed to sprawl the unconscious Gisal out evenly on the spine, Numila turned on everyone.

"Which one of you is diving down there to retrieve that?" he fumed.

"We're exhausted," Dimgal answered him.

"Fine, you'll be the first to sacrifice your portions." He glared at the rest of them.

Koyay rolled her eyes, "Jellyfish, we'll be fine."

"I said not to call me that..."

She put her soft hand against his sandy cheek and stared into his bark-like eyes. "I'm sorry. Bocoani Numila, we will be fine," she told him, but he quickly snatched her hand away from his face.

"Listen up, shoats!" Numila stomped across the spine. "Getting here in one piece was impressive, but getting back without something going wrong would be astonishing. It is my duty to ensure you all get back alive, understood?"

"Yes, Bocoani," they answered in near unison. Koyay loved it when her husband took charge like this.

"Dimgal, re-attach the cano. Madiri and Ruruga, grab the oars. Bogula, take care of Gisal. And Koyay, do that thing with your hips and take us home!"

"*Squee!*" the shoats squealed and enthusiastically went to work.

For some reason, as Koyay checked the tiller, the word *prices* kept repeating in her head. She bit her lip and went through her routine, passively watching Numila march up to the neck with his fists on his hips and his muscles glistening with seawater in the morning light. She wondered, when she did finally tell him about her joining the Cult of Mawoi, if he would see the light and join her, or if he would have to be cleansed with the rest of them. *Prices, prices, prices...* Koyay sighed.

Before long, the Quest for Tizaka crew was making way through the hazardous coral reef. Koyay gracefully swiveled her hips, nudging and pulling the tiller right and left as they snaked through and out of Bayamaca's clutches. Mawoi continued to rise brightly in the eastern sky, but there was a strip of gray clouds far off to the northeast which was concerning. Koyay didn't want to think about the clouds, and it seemed that no one else did either. Conversation between the crew trickled off entirely, like the breaking waves on the reefs, enabling Koyay to relax and focus on the wiggling ribbon at the top of the mast. The calm open sea stretched out ahead of them and they had a strong southerly keeping their sails taut and the head of the canuti cutting through the Bocoa, forming a perfect trough in their wake.

By the time the sun arrived directly overhead to beat down on them, the topic of the peculiar skull cropped up again. Between the rhythmic whooshing of the waves and the constant but pleasant salty mist hitting her in the face, Koyay could hardly hear what Madiri was so upset about. He seemed to have lost his sense of humor and prodded Bogula incessantly. The old lesini became increasingly aggravated and started threatening Madiri with her gnarled staff.

"You don't scare me!" she heard Madiri mocking Bogula.

"That's because you're dumber than a rock!" the old lesini snapped back at him.

Numila was up near the neck of the canuti and seemed to be trying to ease the two down with a calming voice, but then they teamed up and turned on their bocoani. Koyay couldn't believe it. They were both yelling at him up in front of the mast, and her husband had to raise his hands to ward them off. Koyay was getting riled up, but there was nothing she could do because she had to stay on the tiller. As she helplessly watched, Dimgal and Ruruga joined in on the arguing, but their efforts weren't coordinated and, before they knew it, the entire crew was yelling at one another.

Suddenly, Gisal snapped awake like a stunned giant hutia. He was dripping with sweat and looked around with a warped and confused expression on his face. Koyay could just barely hear Madiri laughing at Bogula over the waves, but the sound that came out of Gisal's mouth was ear-piercing and everyone stopped arguing to stare at the screaming giant.

In that moment and without warning, the tiburana bit into the midrib of the canuti on the chok-side, taking a boulder-sized chunk of reeds and half of Ruruga's left arm with it back down below. At first, Ruruga didn't scream. He was in shock along with everyone else by the surprise attack. Dimgal was the first to respond, frantically ripping a piece of cloth from the bottom of his tunic and rushing over to Ruruga to try and stop the bleeding. As the scrounger applied pressure, the terror came out of Ruruga's mouth.

"*Ahhhhh...*" he screamed in horror.

"Spears!" Bocoani Numila shouted, and then he noticed Gisal was having trouble standing. "Madiri, get Gisal to his feet and on the chok-line!" He ran to the backside of the mast and retrieved their spears. "Koyay!"

"On it!" Koyay yelled back and quickly pulled the tiller into her stomach.

The canuti immediately leaned to chok and turned in the direction of the beast. Dimgal barely had time to shove Ruruga toward the tail before he fell into the hole where the chok-side midrib used to be. Numila instinctively grabbed Madiri's arm, keeping him and Gisal from following their scrounger into the dark-green water. Koyay pushed the tiller away, the canuti straightened out, and soon the tiburana's shadow appeared a dozen reeds ahead on the kona-side.

"Dimgal! We'll come back for you!" Numila hollered to him.

"After we kill the beast!" Koyay added.

"Gisal, Madiri, hold the lines! Ruruga?" Numila was moving quickly across the spine.

"Yeah..." he replied with the voice of a man in pure agony.

Numila saw that Bogula was kneeling beside Ruruga and tightening the belt from her tunic around the upper part of his arm, which immediately stopped the bleeding. Blood was everywhere. Ruruga clenched his teeth in aguish, obviously in no condition to fight, but Koyay knew that Numila knew they needed every spear at the ready.

"Bocoani, there's no...what do I..." Gisal was trying to catch the chok-line that was loose and being whipped around by the wind since there was nothing left of the midrib.

"Get that line and anchor it with your body, Gisal!" Numila yelled. The big guy was still disoriented, but there was no time to be gentle – either they were all going to come together in that moment, or the beast was going to get a belly-full of Itabayiti.

"Hard to chok!" Koyay yelled, just before the canuti dipped and they turned again. "It's trying to double-back on us!"

Numila held a spear out to the old lesini and said, "Bogula, unless Ruruga's going to die without your aid, you need to take a spear and get ready." She shook her head, no, but before the bocoani could demand an explanation, Bogula started taking off her robe. Numila looked at Koyay with a shocked expression on his face, which was probably exactly what he was seeing splashed across her face as well.

"A spear will only slow me down," the old lesini said, draped her robe over Numila's arm, dropped her tunic, and then leapt over the tailrib. As her body soared through the air, Koyay and Numila saw Bogula's arms take on a bluish-gray color and flatten out like the fins of a shark, just before she slipped into the water and disappeared.

"Tiburana to chok!" Gisal hollered.

They were both stunned by what they had just seen. Koyay watched Numila look down at Ruruga, and then Gisal, no doubt hoping the others had seen it too, but Ruruga had taken the spear from Numila and was using it to get to his feet. Koyay then remembered Madiri mentioned something odd about Bogula, and she caught his eye in time to see a smug look on his face, as if to say, *I told you so!*

"Koyay!" Numila screamed, snapping her out of her daze.

"I'm here!" she yelled back, scanning the water for the murderous beast and finding it swimming alongside them. Tiburana were unbelievably big, and they all had to admire it for a moment. Its skin was dark-gray and there were long white scratches running along the right side of its head behind its eye. Sunlight sparkled across the monstrous creature like a family of manati in the sound and... Realizing it was the perfect opportunity to spear the tiburana, Koyay shouted, "Numila, what are you waiting for?".

"Ready spears!" Numila ordered, looking back at his crew.

Gisal had the chok-line wrapped around his left arm and was holding his spear high and steady with his right hand. Behind him, Ruruga leaned against the tailrib with his bloody-mess-of-an-arm and struggled to keep his spear in the air. There was no doubt Ruruga's spear would miss. Koyay held on to the tiller with all of her might, keeping them from being rolled by the tiburana, which was repeatedly bumping against the canuti. And then Madiri stepped up next to the bocoani with his spear at the ready. Three good spears would take down the largest shark, but she wasn't sure about something as big as a tiburana.

"Let's hope we at least scare it off," Numila said, and then he shouted, "Now!"

The spears hit their marks and the beast instantly spasmed in anger, flinging its strong tail into them with so much force the canuti came clean out of the water. Numila gripped the headrib as hard as he could with both hands but was still thrown to his knees when they slammed back down hard on the water. Madiri landed on his back next to Numila who looked over in time to see Ruruga snag Koyay's ankle with his one hand, saving her from tumbling over the kona-side.

"Koyay!" Numila desperately got to his feet and raced over to help.

Ruruga was straining through his own excruciating pain but said, "She's alright."

"I'm alright," she echoed him as they pulled her back onto the canuti.

"Thank you, Ruruga," Numila said and then turned to Gisal. "Where is it?"

"About a hundred reeds off chok!" he answered.

"Fleeing, turning, charging at us, what?"

"Uh – it looks like it might have just eaten Dimgal," he said softly. "And now it's turning toward us."

There was no time to mourn.

"Madiri, how many spears do we have left?" Numila asked.

"Three!" he replied.

"Koyay..." Numila started to give the order, but she was a step ahead of him.

"I'm on it," she immediately answered, pushing the tiller away from her and bringing them head-to-head with the beast.

"Brace yourselves!" Numila shouted just before impact.

The tiburana swerved and scraped alongside the canuti, vibrating the entire vessel and making it creak and groan. She knew going head-to-head would help even out the fight. Eventually, either the beast would get tired and give up, or Koyay would make a mistake. She prayed to Mawoi that she wouldn't make a mistake. She tried to time every turn perfectly, and for quite a while they circled the tiburana, chasing each other's tails, or going head-to-head. The longer they danced, the darker the sky became. They watched in horror as the strip of gray clouds spread all around them.

Waves crashed over the ribs, dousing everything and everyone, while thunder crackled not too far away. The wind had picked up considerably, tiring Gisal and Madiri who struggled to adjust and readjust the sails with every turn. Ruruga had passed out from the blood loss and the pain and was curled up at the tail next to Koyay. She watched Numila pace back and forth on the spine, expertly syncing his steps with the dips and turns of the canuti, deep in thought and no doubt trying to come up with a plan.

Suddenly, Gisal punched a hole in the chok-side tailrib with his bare fist, fed the rope through, and then tied it off.

"What are you doing?" Numila asked, watching the big guy walk to the head.

"I need two spears," he said.

"What? Why?" Numila was startled. Koyay rarely saw her husband get startled by anything, but Gisal wasn't asking and took the two spears.

"Koyay!" he shouted at her. "On the next pass, turn into its tail!"

It suddenly dawned on them what Gisal was about to do. "Gisal," Numila yelled. "I order you to step back from the headrib and talk this through..."

"No!" he snapped, and then he reached into the pocket of his tunic, pulled out a handful of oka berries, and shoved them all into his mouth. He then climbed into the neck of the canuti with Numila tugging on his arm.

"Stop this!" Numila demanded, but the big guy was ignoring him.

Gisal was going to jump, whether Koyay followed along with his plan or not. She had to at least try to help him. The storm was nearly upon them with a thick salty mist that clung to every surface and glistened in Mawoi's afternoon glow. Gisal posed there with his right leg raised, his foot braced against the headrib, two spears in one hand, the other holding on tightly to the nose of the canuti, all while the waves of the Bocoa splashed up on either side of him.

"Here it comes!" Koyay shouted.

Gisal looked at Numila, a tear trickling down his cheek, and smiled. "Tayokun," he said.

At that moment, out of the corner of her eye, Koyay saw movement in the water on their kona-side. She only dared a quick glance in that direction for fear she would miss witnessing Gisal's attack, but in that glance she saw a bluish-gray shark's fin. And then the tiburana was there, Gisal took flight, both spears raised and pointing downward, their polished coral tips flashing in the sunlight, and he stabbed the beast as he landed squarely on its head. Numila immediately turned to grab the last remaining spear only to find Madiri had beaten him to it.

"Ahhhh!" Madiri screamed, gripping the spear tightly. He lunged over the tailrib and pierced the left eye of the tiburana. Thunder roared as the monster twisted away from the canuti, hurling Madiri out to sea and dragging Gisal below the waterline. And then Koyay and Numila both saw that bluish-gray shark dive after the tiburana.

"Koyay, let's pickup Madiri!" he shouted at her, but the canuti wouldn't move. He looked back and saw her struggle to push the tiller, offering him a confused expression.

"It won't budge!" she exclaimed.

The rudder was jammed. Madiri was about thirty reeds directly off the chok side, waving at them with one of his long arms. They knew he wouldn't be able to tread water for long, and all the blood in the water would soon attract more sharks. The wind was still blowing and getting stronger, their sails were still taut, and the canuti continued to cut through the Bocoa, quickly moving them farther away from Madiri. Koyay and Numila rushed to furl the sail, which instantly slowed their forward momentum, but they continued to drift along with the rolling waves.

"One of us has to dive down there and fix the rudder," she said.

"I'll do it," Numila replied but Koyay stopped him.

"No, my loving jellyfish," she said. "You're the bocoani and I'm a better swimmer than you." She smiled, kissed him, and then she added, "I'll be right back!"

They took a moment to search the water around the canuti for any immediate threats, and then Numila helped Koyay slip into the water at the tail. It was surprisingly not as cold as she expected, but she didn't want to waste any time enjoying the bath. She took a deep breath and dove below the waves. The saltwater stung her eyes, and the darkening skies and the shadow from the reed boat above her made visibility near zero. But she didn't need much light for what she saw. The moment she broke the surface of the water and spit out a plume of water, Numila started asking her questions, frantically reaching for her over the tailrib. He was acting like she had been gone for a mawa.

"What's wrong? What is it?" he asked.

"D-Dim-g-gal..." she said, her teeth chattering as she bobbed in the increasingly choppy water, which she realized was a bit colder than she initially thought.

"What about Dimgal?"

"P-part...his body is b-blocking the r-rudder."

Numila quickly grabbed a rope, tied one end around the tiller and the other around his own waist, and then he jumped into the water with her. They worked frantically, taking deep breaths, diving, tugging, kicking, pulling on the rope, and then they would pop back up for another breath. Each time they resurfaced, Koyay felt like the sky got darker, the wind louder, and the waves angrier. At last, they yanked on the rope, the tiller moved, and they saw the rudder working. When they climbed back onto the canuti, they found Ruruga had regained consciousness and was staring out to sea over the kona-side midrib.

"How are you?" Numila asked, panting and shielding his eyes from the rain. Koyay flopped onto the spine, trying to catch her breath as well.

"We're not going to make it," Ruruga answered, rainwater pouring off his outstretched arm pointing east.

That was when they saw the monstrous swirling, flashing, and pulsating storm about to collide with them. It was too late to retreat back to Bayamaca, and Koyay realized they simply did not have enough crew members left to wrestle with Yuraca. "Madiri!" he suddenly shouted.

They unfurled the sail, which instantly snapped taut with so much force Koyay feared the mast would break in half. Thankfully, it remained intact, and they went after Madiri. Round and round they searched the increasingly violent sea, but they found nothing. The waves had grown as tall as the mast and were getting taller, while the fierce wind blew erratically, popping the sail one way and then the other. Koyay was beyond exhausted and struggled to keep them from tipping. Thankfully, Numila decided it was time to furl the sail and attempt to ride out the storm instead of sailing around it. He called Ruruga over to hold the chok-line while he untied it, and then he glanced at Koyay.

"Thank you," she mouthed to him.

"I'm sorry," he replied, just before the Great Sea swallowed the Quest for Tizaka.

CHAPTER TWENTY-FIVE

To Move Through Spirit with Words

Holding open the worn wooden door of his bohi was an extremely old man with an understandably shocked expression carved onto his wrinkled face. Though he had aged considerably over the intervening years since she last saw him, Ennu immediately recognized Elder Sengri. There were now more lines hanging from the bags under his honey eyes than there were vines on the island of Pacca, and each gray whisker in his patchy beard stuck out crookedly. The little remaining hair on top of his balding head seemed to be receding in chunks, and reminded her of dead, ashy moss that somehow retained its sponginess. It took everything in her to control the impulse to bounce her finger off of it. Although she must have looked like a slain brocket doe that had been dragged through the forest by her hooves, Sengri's shocked expression told Ennu that he recognized her as well.

"Might I come in?" she asked in her raspy voice, sounding like a croaking frog.

"Y-Yes, of course, come in. Come in!"

Sengri shuffled to the side, allowing her to stumble through the doorway. Her left leg continued to bother her, and she had to swing it ahead of her as she moved, but it did seem to be getting better. She leaned against the cibmani wall and examined the interior of his bohi, as Sengri cautiously peeked his head out into the night, and then slowly closed the door behind him.

The bohi seemed bigger than she remembered, but then she noticed Sengri had apparently knocked down the wall separating his bohi from his neighbor's. All that was left of the original wall was a hand-wide cibmani beam running down the middle of the ceiling. Three cedar pillars were wedged into place and continued supporting the structure, successfully preventing the apartments above from crashing down on top of them. In the center of the now conjoined eastern walls sat a typical wooden table and chairs, flanked by the expected shuttered windows, which were themselves flanked by the two entrances into the structure. Bulging reed baskets appeared to have been recently moved and were now stacked and blocking the second entrance. The bottom basket partially rested on a low bench that ran along the north wall to a closed door. More baskets were stacked in the northwest corner, each one smashing down on the one below it.

In the center of the western wall opposite the table, two equally sized kitchen areas now backed up against one another and Ennu could see a small fire had been lit in each of the stone basins. She followed the smoke up to where she noticed a strange copper awning fastened to the wall and hovering an arm-length over the fires. It was definitely odd looking, but she supposed it functioned rather well as a vent for the smoke. The only other light came from two candles set into two sconces, one in the center of the north and south walls and helping to soothe the darkness of the space between them. Suddenly, she noticed she could hear a heated conversation taking place in the apartments above them, along with the soft pattering of sandaled feet. She glanced at Sengri and saw him staring at her, likely wondering what she was doing standing there and being so quiet. She doubted he could hear the fires crackling, let alone his neighbors arguing upstairs, or even the jatbays, gourd drums, and dancers outside.

"Spacious," she croaked, before limping over to a chair and sitting down.

"Uh – yes, considering..." he answered timidly. "You – uh – you look good."

"Don't patronize me, Sengri. I'm perfectly aware of my appearance," she said dismissively. But she knew, despite her matted hair, oily skin, ripped tunic and filthy robe, she likely looked exactly the same as she had the first time they met.

"Well," he smiled, "the flower's a nice touch. I believe it's a *kikuri*, if I'm not mistaken in this dismal light." He squinted at her, moving his head to avoid blocking the flickering candle attached to the wall behind him.

By the way he stood with his fists on his hips and that big, wrinkly smile on his face, Ennu could tell he was being sincere. Their friendship, though unconventional, had been a reliable constant in her often-chaotic life. She tried to recall how long they had known each other, but her mind remained in a bit of a fog after her traumatic transformation. She finally offered him a passive smirk and gestured toward the copper awning. "That's new. Is it a vent?"

"Ah, yes." He shuffled his old bare feet excitedly across the room to the fire basins, his exaggerated shadow passing over her as he went. "Bociba Simi's youngest boy Sano designed it. He's quite a clever child. You see these slits here?" He pointed to two nearly flat pieces of copper on the wall that Ennu assumed were just mounts for the awning. "They allow fresh air in from outside," he explained, "which somehow pulls the smoke up, over this bend here, and then pushes it out the other side. Ingenious!"

"Impressive," she lied, but she honestly didn't care.

"Yes, it is."

As long as she had known him, Sengri always got excited about innovations. To him, the Itabayiti were the pinnacle of Yucahu's creation, the chosen tamers of land and sea, and masters of all creatures dwelling in and on them. But it was more than just a story in the Yuki'at, and he believed, as did others, that the Great Spirit actively worked through them to continue perfecting his creation. Yucahu revealed these truths in sleeptime visions, blossoming like flower bulbs into colorful petals and feathery seeds that spread across the landscape. She and Sengri had discussed this many times, and she agreed with him, but she had since developed a concurrent belief – one which she didn't think he, nor anyone was prepared to hear.

There was a sudden scratching sound, and Sengri's eyes nearly popped out of his head. "Ranar!" he shouted, quickly shuffling from the kitchen area to the closed door on the other side of the room. "I forgot to let him out! The adulu have stopped by here four times since the start of the rainy season, banging on my door and asking questions about our friend here. Any unexpected knocking sends us into a panic."

He opened the door to let the graying old fox out to run around. Ranar briefly stopped to sniff Elder Sengri's bare feet before sprinting directly toward Ennu, his tiny little claws scraping on the stone floor for traction. He made it about halfway before leaping onto her lap and burrowing into her filthy tunic, turning himself into a fluffy pile of joyful panting and whimpering. Ennu's bright-azure eyes narrowed, but she couldn't help but smile at the adorable creature.

"He misses you," Sengri said. "H-He hasn't been the same since you left. He's quiet most days, but whimpers throughout the night. He eats well, still hunting spiny rats in the market, but he only eats their innards, kindly leaving the rest of the carcasses for me to find later. Thankfully, he now prefers filling his belly with whatever I'm having. Though I do leave dried, chopped bits of ekuki meat out for him like Tabba used to, but...well...now she's on Bahaca..." Ennu saw Sengri's wrinkled face turn sour, and his honey eyes fall to the floor. "I was making soup!" he abruptly shouted.

She let Ranar chew on her long, thin fingers as she watched the old man return to the stone counter to the left of the fire basins. He retrieved a clay pot that was charred on the bottom from frequently being set over the fire and poured freshwater into it from a gourd hanging on the wall by a thin string of brown leather. From a small basket near his left knee, he collected a handful of bones and dropped those into the pot. Ennu could smell each one, recognizing them as brocket bones. Scooting the first basket to the side with his foot, Sengri pulled a second basket forward and retrieved a handful of oycu stems mixed with bright-green grass. He plopped both ingredients into the pot and stirred it with his bent finger, passively kicking the baskets back into their original places as he did so. Though she hadn't expected Sengri to feed her, Ennu knew the invitation was quickly coming and she was prepared to gladly accept. *Anything's better than raw, baby hutia*, she thought.

She passively scratched the happy little critter behind his ears and marveled at how much gray had developed in his once fully reddish-brown fur. It looked as if his tail had been dipped in ashes, while his feet were almost entirely white.

"KAHEEP!" Ranar yelped, his voice sounding like a black bird choking on gravel.

Sengri chuckled. "He only speaks to you," he said, giving the soup one last stir before leaving it to cook. "Which is a good thing, what with the adulu coming around more regularly."

"I am the only one who understands him," Ennu suggested.

"I tried to learn," Sengri admitted.

She gave him a side-eye. "And I tried to teach you," she added, making him smile. When he did, Ennu noticed several of his bottom teeth had been threaded.

It was a common practice among the elderly, a final effort to keep their teeth from falling out. They would wrap a long thread around the loose tooth until only the tip was showing, and then they used the remaining thread to bind the loose tooth to their other teeth. Some took pride in their threading and used different colors as an adornment, but most were ashamed and tried to hide it altogether. Ennu was a bit surprised, because she didn't think Sengri was old enough to need threading.

"Oh – I saved your bracelet for you," he suddenly said, and then shuffled through the open doorway to his right, which she knew used to be his bedchamber.

Ennu didn't have the slightest idea what bracelet he was referring to. She attempted to search her vast memory, but only found blurry images spread out over the faint traces of frayed memory threads. Just then, Sengri's arm popped out of the doorway. He searched the wall blindly, using his hand to slap the flat stone until it landed on the edge of the sconce. Finding it, he snatched the lit candle and took it back into his bedchamber. Ranar heard him digging through a basket and promptly leapt off Ennu's lap to chase after the noise. She sighed and adjusted her filthy tunic. She hadn't come to Sengri for an old bracelet, or to see Ranar, or to have soup, which she had to admit was beginning to smell wonderful.

"Ah-ha!" Sengri shouted from the other room.

"KAHEEP!"

"Shh, Ranar! Keep quiet, now!" He shuffled out of the bedchamber, bringing back the candlelight. "See."

Sengri held out a shiny green-stone cuff bracelet that shimmered in the faint light as if it were under a bright midday sun. Ennu accepted it from him, just as Ranar leapt back onto her lap. The bracelet was unusual but beautiful. It was as thick as her thumb, and its sea-green coloring was even and balanced. It didn't appear to have a single noticeable flaw. As intrigued as she was, she still didn't recognize it, but the old graying fox seemed to think the bracelet belonged around his neck. Ranar shoved his pointed snout into the opening, easily squeezing his furry head and ears through, and then promptly yanked his head back out and snapped at it with his sharp little teeth.

"Ranar!" Sengri scolded him, replacing the candle in its sconce.

"It's alright," Ennu said, scratching the fox's chin. "I don't recognize this cuff anyway."

He looked at her, his head askew and his eyebrow raised. "You don't?" he asked, and she shook her head ever so slightly. "Because you gave it to me. You said, if you *ever* returned, you would be returning for this." He pointed at the bracelet in her hands.

Ennu didn't know what he was talking about, but she unfortunately couldn't trust her foggy memory to help her. Instead, she smiled and nodded, pretending to have momentarily forgotten. "Right," she said. "Thank you." She slipped the cuff over her wrist and returned her attention to the fox in her lap.

"I was tempted to trade it for a new pair of boarhide sandals," he joked, looking down at his feet, but she didn't laugh. Sengri quickly cleared his throat, "Are you staying long?"

"Why do you ask?" she answered his question with another.

When he didn't immediately respond, she looked up and found Sengri waiting for her. Ennu didn't know what to say. She only knew she needed his help in returning to Amaca where she would then summon her daughters. *Am I staying long?* Moments like this were why she hated being around the Itabayiti. They always wanted to know things – prying into her life like seagulls stabbing at a crab's shell. The constant questioning had always bothered her. They confessed details about their personal lives, seeking a similar confession from her, but they failed to understand that Ennu had abandoned the constricting structure of Itabacan long before any of them were born. *Am I staying long?* Sengri knew better than to ask her about her affairs.

"I-It's a simple question," he said softly. "There's no reason to get knotted up over it."

Hearing this, Ennu released a heavy sigh. Sengri was right. She was getting knotted. Her recently reacquired Itabayiti emotions and anxieties were becoming tangled with the frustrations of her labored transformation. She took a deep breath and looked into his honey eyes. "I'll only be staying long enough to convince you to help me," she answered him.

"Well..." he chuckled heartily, "that puts me under Chuka's hoof, doesn't it!"

"How so?" she asked.

"You don't have to convince me of anything," he said. "You should know that. I..." he started to say something else, but then suddenly sniffed the air. "Ah! The soup is ready." He spun around on his heels. "Would you like a cup?"

"KAHEEP!"

"Ranar, you're just begging the adulu to take you away from us, aren't you!" Sengri didn't turn back to the fox, but quickly continued shuffling over to the red-hot pot. He dipped his bent finger in and out of the bubbling soup faster than a scorpion's stinger, and then he sampled it in three breathy slurps. After a moment of intense contemplation, he added a second handful of grass, placed his fists on his hips, and nodded, "There."

Ennu leaned over the excitable fox and whispered into his furry ear, *"STA-UG, RANAR-AH-UN."* She watched his long whiskers twitch, and then he released a long, deep breath, just before he fell fast asleep. In an instant, Ranar was curled up into a ball on her lap and snoring softly. When Ennu looked up, she was slightly startled by Sengri setting a cup of steaming bone broth soup on the table beside her.

He paused with his fingers still wrapped around the ceramic cup, admiring the snoring fox. *"Tisk-tisk-tisk,"* he shook his wrinkled head. "Lucky fox! I haven't slept that soundly in years."

Foxes were known to live each day to the fullest, but then often died young. If they hadn't already been hunted down by the agur, they could be expected to burn through their allotted share of the Great Spirit within a decade. It was as if every last one of them believed they were in a race to see who could reach the river of Mayu first. The last of the wild foxes were now cared for by the lesini at the Temple of Osani on Amaca, while the only domesticated fox Ennu knew of was asleep on her lap.

She watched Sengri shuffle around to the other end of the table, set his own steaming cup down, and then slump into the chair. The center of the table was the darkest point in the room, which didn't bother Ennu one bit, but she was surprised to see Sengri embracing it for his evening meal.

He took a long sip of his soup, "Ahh – the right amount of kopau!"

Ennu looked into her cup and saw several strips of sweet grass the Itabayiti called kopau. The Itabayiti had brought it from their homeland a thousand years before, and commonly used it to make a tea to treat fevers. It now grew in clumps all over the islands. She took a tentative sip, thought it could have used a bit more sweet grass, but then downed the rest in one gulp.

Sengri nearly spit his next sip out, laughing, "Ha! I still got it!" He stood and reached for her cup. "Would you like some more?" She nodded and handed him her cup. "I was afraid you'd think it was underflavored."

Ennu didn't want to disappoint him, so she didn't respond, but she was interested in having some of the bones. "Could you add a few brocket bones this time?" she asked.

"Of course."

"The marrow will help clear my foggy mind."

"Oh – is that normal after one of your...um...adventures?"

Ennu glared at him. This was precisely why she avoided any exchange of private details with the Itabayiti – *if you give them a thread, they'll unravel your robe*.

"Of course, you're right. I'm sorry. Forget I asked," he pleaded, and then he quickly refilled her cup, making her feel bad.

"No. I am the one who should be apologizing," she conceded. "I'm being too defensive."

"You're being cautious," he countered. "I cannot begin to imagine what it must be like to...what it must feel like..." He paused to take another sip of his soup, clearly having trouble putting into words what he intended to say.

"I'm fine," she said. "I can hardly complain about temporary memory loss. It was my leg that wasn't functioning properly earlier, but now it seems to be nearly back to normal." She raised her steaming cup to her lips and took a more refined sip. "By evening meal tomorrow, I expect to be perfectly recovered."

Sengri nodded, drinking more of his soup. "I'm relieved."

She looked back to the copper awning. "I wonder, what could you have traded for that."

"Nothing," he replied proudly. "Simi's an old friend. I had to escort a young araco to Risca a mawa or so ago. The bociba and I took midmeal in his residence, and he had one of these hanging on his wall over their basin. Knowing how curious I can be, he called Sano in to explain it to me."

"I don't think I've ever met any of Simi's children." Ennu searched her cloudy memory.

"He and Runa have twins – Suku and Sano," he said. Ennu gave him a quizzical look, because twins were typically given the same name, and when they weren't, it was due to them either not being identical or something unfortunate had occurred. "He was born a day later," Sengri explained. "He cried incessantly, and when they finally got him to settle down, they discovered the poor child's right arm and leg were stiff."

"Stiff?"

"Bent inward, like a crab's claw. His leg too."

"Hmm."

Sengri swirled the last sip of soup around in his cup. "The brightest child I've ever had the privilege of talking to," he added, and then tossed back his cup.

"And he's crippled still?" she asked, digging the brocket bone out of her cup with her fingers.

"Mmm," he swallowed. "Deni has been treating him these past few years."

"Deni?" she asked, and he nodded. Deni was a lesini and one of Ennu's eldest daughters.

"The boy has come a long way. He walks now, but not very far."

Ennu sucked the marrow out from the end of the bone, and then dropped it into her empty cup. "I might have to look in on this boy," she said. Sengri raised his eyebrow once more, but stopped himself from asking a follow-up question, for which Ennu was grateful. "Do you mind if I help myself to a few more of these tasty bones?" she asked.

"Help yourself," he answered.

She leaned over Ranar again and whispered, "*STA-UG, RANAR-AH-UN.*" She gently lifted the sleeping critter, stood, laid him in the center of the table, and then she tossed her left leg in front of her and stumbled across the room toward the kitchen area.

"Will he be like that all night?"

Sengri's question made her smile, but she didn't let him see. "No, I don't think so, but he does need to rest," she said.

She stepped up to the fire basin, set her cup to the side, and lifted the blackened pot from the glowing-red coals with her bare hands. Sengri started to object, but then he smartly bit his tongue. The intense heat from the clay pot singed Ennu's fingertips, but it didn't hurt, it was immensely refreshing. The smell of searing flesh reminded her of the Libanu, which instantly ignited a sprawling web of memory threads in her mind, each end braided into the next and shimmering like moonlight upon the sea. Ennu wanted to remain there and marvel at the sparkling web, but she quickly realized she was being propelled forward.

An unseen force dragged her across the radiant threads and through the lifting fog in her mind. Vibrant images briefly flashed to her left and right before each dissipated into nothingness – an island of sea turtles atop a watery cliff, the trembling arms of a woman wrapped around her young children, and then a peaceful field of white beneath an angry gray sky. There was a frantic screeching sound to her left, and she turned to see a pillar of green light piercing several more threads, but then her momentum jerked hard to the right, leaving the piercing green pillar behind. She was moving faster now. The sparkling thread beneath her blurred into a mighty rushing river of light, and then she noticed something moving in the cavernous space between the river and the vast web of rivers surrounding her. It was a shadow within the darkness, a blur of black against a smooth black void, and as she watched, it began taking the form of a distorted face. Smooth, hollow eyes looked back at her, reminding her of her rapid breathing, and then an equally hollow smile split the void...

"...*BA-YI-NU!*" she suddenly heard Elder Sengri scream at her. Ennu collapsed to the hard stone floor, along with the clay pot, which smashed into a dozen pieces and spilled the remaining soup. "Are you alright?" he asked, instantly kneeling down beside her.

"I..." her tongue flopped around inside of her mouth.

"Was it my soup? I knew I should have added more kopau!"

Ennu snickered in her dazed and confused state.

"There's a laugh!" Sengri exclaimed, himself chuckling. "Come on. You just need to sit up and drink some water." He helped her lean forward, keeping a wrinkled old hand on her shoulder for support. "That's right, isn't it? Water is the most important thing after your kalu?"

Kalu? Ah, yes, she remembered, *he does know about my kalu.*

"This one seems to have strung you up the mast! Was that your first meal?" he asked, helping her get to her knees.

Ennu leaned forward over her thighs and inhaled several times in quick succession. She held the deep breath a moment before releasing all the air in her lungs in one long, slow, but continuous breath. She thought she had things under control back in the cave, but now she realized she was frighteningly wrong. Willing herself on through the pain was easy enough, but reawakening her Itabayiti mind was proving far more difficult than she anticipated.

"Here." Sengri startled her with the gourd of water to drink. She didn't realize he had left her side to retrieve it. "Go on," he insisted. She took the gourd and put it to her lips. "Now, before you curl up on the table with Ranar, tell me what you could possibly need my help with?"

"My daughters."

"The Numkalu, yes, go on."

Ennu took a hefty drink of the water, swishing it around inside of her mouth before swallowing. "Th-They've banished me," she said, as if hearing it for the first time. She looked up into his old honey eyes.

Sengri's expression turned sour again, the bags under his eyes seeming to fill with more sorrow. "I was afraid you were going to say something like that," he sighed. She gave him a confused look, to which he replied, "I mean – the day you left, the day you gave me that bracelet, I asked you where you were going, and you said..."

"To walk with Kanu," she remembered.

He nodded. "Which is an exceptionally odd thing to say, even for you. I fretted over it from sumawa to samawa, Hatoca to Niamoca. My fretting in Mayu Hall annoyed Unsari, and then Draha said I was embarrassing him, so I thought I might go annoy Boacodu Basa with my fretting in Acodun..."

"Did you mention my name to Basa?" she abruptly asked, interrupting him.

"D-Do you know him?" he asked, stammering.

"Answer the question."

"Uh..." Sengri sat on the floor beside her. "What do you mean by mention?"

"Sengri."

"Short answer; yes." He held out his hand, as if trying to stay a wild boar. "But in my defense, I didn't have a choice."

Rage filled her cheeks, as she glared into his piss-colored eyes. "I entrusted you with the truth of my kalu, and you have betrayed me!" Ennu was furious and tried to stand, but her left leg gave out and she fell against Sengri's chest. "Don't touch me!" She instantly shoved off of him, stumbled backward, her good leg conveniently bumped against the seat of the chair, and she plopped back down at the table where Ranar continued to quietly snore.

"You may not know Basa like I do. He's a recluse. He doesn't leave Acodu Hall."

"But he's the boacodu!" she shouted, silencing the old araco. Ennu watched Sengri carefully get to his feet. She could see him grimace, placing a trembling hand on one knee and the other on his lower back, as the pain from simply lifting his own body off the floor appeared excruciating. "It is you, who does not know the acodu like I do," she finally suggested.

"Possibly," he said, stretching his back, his wrinkled face contorted in pain. "But, when I said I didn't have a choice, I meant it."

She knew exactly what he meant. Ennu knew Boacodu Musaba began experimenting with spirit speak over four hundred years ago. He called it *ashmu*, to be moved through spirit with words, and the easiest application of the technique was the transference of thought. She knew all about ashmu because she had learned the technique directly from Musaba. But what Ennu couldn't immediately remember was whether or not she had already told Sengri that it was she who perfected it.

"He got into my mind, into my thoughts, and that's what I mean by I *didn't have a choice*," he said as he shuffled to his chair and sat down. "Honestly. We were discussing the kuruan around Acodu Hall when he suddenly shouted, *Who's BA-YI-NU?* So, I had to tell him something." He looked at her with his eyebrows raised and his pleading eyes. "I got out of there as quickly as I could. I mean, I haven't even told Draha or Tabba everything about you."

"Everything?"

"Well..." he hesitated. "They have met you before. And children tend to ask a lot of questions." This made Ennu smirk, as she recalled the Itabayiti obsession with asking questions. "But they only know that we are friends," Sengri clarified, and then chuckled. "Thankfully, neither of them is able to see inside of my head!"

Ennu suddenly realized she was being a bit unfair to her old friend. After all, she also had children, and they too were prone to asking a lot of questions. "I feel the same way about my own daughters," she empathized.

"They don't make it easy on us, do they?" he said with a wrinkled smile. "Speaking of... you need my help with them?" he asked and Ennu nodded. "Might I ask for a favor in exchange? Not that my help is contingent on you helping me, or anything like that!"

"No, I understand," she replied, but he gave her a confused look. "Yes, is the answer – if it is something that I am capable of doing, I will do it."

"That will do. Good," he said, relaxing considerably.

"I don't need you to interfere, but, as you have clearly witnessed here just now, I am not quite fully recovered, and I am in need of assistance in reaching Amaca."

"Is that all?" Sengri started laughing. "We could go right now, if you want!" He started to stand, but Ennu motioned for him to remain seated.

"As my memory continues to untangle itself, I am beginning to realize there is no rush in getting back to Osanum," she admitted. "So, tell me what I can do for you, and we'll start there."

Sengri sighed heavily, looked at the wall to his left, and then his honey eyes drifted up and fixed on the shuttered window above Ennu's head. "There's something happening on Bahaca," he said. "To make a long story short, I'm beginning to suspect the Mawoakin are up to something. If you could, in only the way you can, will you go look in on my Tabba for me?"

"KAHEEP!"

PART THREE
The Day of BIYAYA

CHAPTER TWENTY-SIX
ANKI

Itabaca's harbor bustled with activity under the merciless midmorning sun, appearing bigger each day of the encroaching dry season. Anki preferred it when Mawoi was smaller and seemed to be less angry all the time. He watched the countless ferries bump into one another, bobbing along in the choppy water, their ferrymen exhausted from making multiple trips already that morning. The persistent creaking and sloshing of the reed boats was only drowned out by their rambunctious passengers. Each ferry was loaded rib-to-rib with sweaty festival goers, all fanning themselves with anything at hand, and noisily complaining about the stagnant air, intense humidity, and the squawking teams of seagulls circling overhead.

Anki was told, traditionally, the Day of Biyaya was held in the final days of the rainy season when Boynay had fulfilled her duty, the soil was saturated, and Kayki could drink no more. It was cooler then. The lowaki would have finished planting their yams, gourds, and other vegetables, and turned their attention to carefully harvesting tree nuts and berries. The fishermen would return with heaping loads of shimmering whitefish, which would have provided the meat for the festival. But in those final days, the festival was postponed, the harbors were closed, and Anki felt partially responsible. His father reassured him their uncovering of the conspiracy against Yaya Amnu was something to be proud of, but Anki still felt like he and everyone were being punished.

He watched the Itabayiti slowly squeeze onto the already packed Steps of Ajan like crazy ants onto the toes of Mount Otaba's foot. Crazy ants were notorious for finding their way into the strangest of places, only to be surprised and angry when someone stumbled upon them. Anki expected the foot to raise up at any moment and shake them all off into the shallows, and he was a little disappointed when it didn't happen. At the top of the steps, he saw the agur had barricaded the entrance to the island with ramshackle huts. It had been ten days since Yaya Amnu ordered most of the agur back to Chacuca, but there was a substantial presence remaining on Itabaca for the festival. Anki could tell their huts had been refortified, expanded, and now funneled the miserable Itabayiti toward a single gate one reed wide. He wasn't bothered by the burly warriors like his brother and had actually enjoyed having a few extra people around he could talk to when they were still on Conaca, but he didn't dare talk to the rough looking men he saw at the gate aggressively searching through people's pockets.

Anki stood in the noisy gaggle alongside his brother and father, munching on a handful of bitter berries and chewy nuts he got from ferryman Haro. His father said they weren't sweet and crunchy because the lowaki were rushed to harvest them, but Anki wouldn't have known the difference and didn't care anyway. His sandals did little to save his feet from the searing hot steps, and he hopped from foot to foot to cool them off. He saw Atu was doing the same while keeping a watchful eye out for the dreaded seagulls. The evil creatures seemed to take turns diving into the crowd, stirring up the already frustrated people, only to emerge with a not-so-tasty shell or pebble, which they angrily dropped a few flaps away. Anki quickly tossed the last of the nuts into his mouth, just before a seagull swooped nearby, causing him and his brother to duck behind their father. Abensu remained firmly in place with his long legs like the roots of a strongbark tree.

Finally, the sweaty horde crammed through the agur funnel and onto the main street in front of the spirit shrine of Bitabay where they immediately spread out, taking heaving breaths and stretching their stiff arms. Anki watched Atu do the same, flapping his pale arms like gull wings, but then his brother suddenly spotted Joba next to the shrine and tucked himself back into the pack. She was standing hand-in-hand with a young araco whose perfectly angular sponge of black hair on top of his head looked like the handle of a chaak blade. They each wore traditional matching marriage belts, and Anki assumed he must be the boy Atu was so upset about. If his brother hadn't been such a jerk the past mawa, he might have felt bad for him.

Festival vendors lined the street around the east side of Badhan with their fantastically decorated carts. They spoke loud and fast, exaggerating the descriptions of their goods in between gull attacks and the sales pitches of their neighbors. The vendors were happy to haggle with anyone unfortunate enough to bump against their carts, but it looked like everyone was trying to avoid doing just that. People did commonly bring items from home they no longer needed in hopes of haggling their way up to what they wanted, but the heat was such that most people refused to carry anything they couldn't fit in their tunic pockets. Anki had a handful of shells and shark teeth in one pocket, and he had just emptied his other, but he didn't seriously think any vendor would trade with him. He knew some people might have brought gemstones, which were rare, and any vendor would gladly give up their entire store of goods for one precious stone. His father told them he once saw a woman trade an azure crystal the size of her head for a cartful of candied yams. Anki hadn't cared where the crystal had come from, but he always wondered what the woman did with all those yams.

"Did I ever tell you two about..." their father started to say.

"The woman who traded a crystal for some yams?" Atu cut him off.

"Oh..." Their father sounded slightly dejected.

Anki giggled, but he noticed his brother didn't appear to be joking. Atu was clearly looking for Demican or Hamsi over by the almec practice courts in the east field adjacent to Badhan. It's where his brother went every time they came to Itabaca and would likely be where Atu would spend the entire Day of Biyaya.

"I'll catch up with you later, baba!" Atu shouted, and then ran off toward the courts.

Their father didn't have a chance to protest, calling after him, "We'll meet you at the banquet pavilion after the game!" Atu just waved back without turning around.

Anki and his father continued walking elbow-to-elbow with the speed of the crowd around Badhan, and then up the slope toward the Grand Plaza. Sweat dripped off his brow and down his cheeks, making him involuntarily give the mean sun a dirty look – the third dirty look of the day, if he was counting. Unlike his pale older brother, Anki's cocoa skin became as hot as his temper and just as quickly. He looked for a cooling station they called a nimuru, where fresh water rained down in a mist on these blistering days. He spied one, and next to it was an oycu vendor serving the fermented drink Anki's father loved.

"Baba, can we cool off at the nimuru? There's an oycu vendor there too," he pleaded, fanning himself and sticking out his tongue.

"Of course," his father answered, guiding them in that direction.

Anki was surprised to see Luculati and Sheka running through the mist with some other children he didn't recognize. He immediately charged into them, knocking Luculati into Sheka with a squeal.

"What the..." Lucu started, but then he saw who it was. "Anki!" he exclaimed and hugged him, but then Lucu's hug turned into a headlock.

"Where have you been?" Sheka asked.

Anki broke free with a giant grin on his face. "Oh, around. Getting into trouble."

"Isn't that the truth!" his father laughed. "Taycoay, Luculati. And you must be Sheka – Anki has mentioned your...style now and then."

Sheka didn't skip a beat but looked Anki's father dead in his eyes and said coldly, "I am not stylish in any way." Then she smiled and stuck out her foot without looking, tripping Luculati onto his backside.

"Hey!" Lucu objected, rubbing his bum, and then he waved. "Taycoay, Abensu-baba."

Anki laughed and spun around in the mist. "Baga, it's hot!"

"Stop saying that!" his father scolded him. "I'm going to get an oycu and then go over to talk with the council by the Yaya's pavilion." Anki's father gave him a creepy smile, and then he added, "I see Kina Wani over there. Maybe you want to see her?"

Anki liked that idea. His eyes started to get big, but then he looked at his friends and shrugged. "Maybe," he said, making his father chuckle.

"Alright, son. See you in a moment." He winked and then left.

Clearly making sure his father was far enough away, Sheka then said, "So," She slid over to Anki, her bare feet effortlessly gliding on the wet stone. "What kind of trouble are we talking about here?"

"I heard Jokimbi got you and Biacoya banished to Yapaca," Lucu said, getting up off the ground.

"What? No!" Anki spun around some more in the cool mist.

"Yeah, that's dumb, Lucu." Sheka punched him in the arm. "I was told Yaya Amnu made you work day and night in the clay pits as punishment for the wasps."

Anki stopped spinning to look at her. She wasn't wrong, but he wondered how she could have possibly known that.

"Whoa! Is that true?" Lucu asked.

"No," Anki rolled his eyes. "But you should have been the one to get in trouble, Sheka. We knew you were the one who swapped the palm oil with vinegar."

"Vinegar?" Lucu asked.

"Can't prove it," she said haughtily, crossing her arms.

Anki smiled. "I don't care! We thought it was hilarious... until we got dragged up to the palace and questioned in front of the Yaya. I don't even know what vinegar is!"

"You got to go to the Yaya's Palace?!" Lucu almost shouted.

"Quiet down," Sheka pushed him into the nimuru. "How'd you know it was me?"

"Didn't, but now I do," he smirked.

Sheka lunged at him, but Anki dodged to the side and slid around the nimuru. "You big jerk!" She chased him, laughing all the while Lucu snuck in a jab each time they passed.

"Don't worry, I won't tell anyone about the frogs in the reed baths!" he shouted over his shoulder, passing Lucu a second time – *JAB!*

Sheka growled, "I'm gonna shave that greasy seaweed off your head!"

Anki laughed and laughed, running around the nimuru a third time. He saw Lucu was about to sneak in another jab, but Anki grabbed his arm just in time and yanked. Lucu tumbled forward directly into Sheka's path, and the two of them collided and fell hard to the ground.

"Ahh!" they both yelled.

Anki stopped running, sliding a bit on the wet stone, and turned with a big gratifying smile on his face. He saw several other people who had been watching them play were laughing and pointing. It made him feel good to have, in some small way, gotten back at Sheka, but then he felt bad for using Luculati to do it.

"Oww!" Sheka whined. "Lucu! Why do you have such a hard head!"

"He's part chacu!" Anki could hardly get the words out before he started laughing.

"Oh – you think this is funny?" She started climbing over Luculati.

"Hold it!" Anki put up his hands, still giggling. "What's fair is fair. You got me in trouble, and now we're even!"

She stopped to think it over a moment, and then she asked, "Promise you won't rat me out?"

"On Lucu's hard head, I promise!" he said, and she smiled.

"Hey! What did I ever do to you?" Lucu asked, now standing and rubbing the back of his large head.

"Hush, Lucu," Sheka told him. "You give out enough headlocks, everyone here probably owes you a kick in the shin."

Anki snorted, "Seriously!" And then he looked around at the small crowd that had gathered to watch what he suddenly realized had turned into a child-sized dispute match. "You know, Sheka, I promised that I wouldn't tell on you, and Lucu's too scared of you to say anything, but what about all of them?" he asked, pointing.

She paused to think it over for a moment, her sea-green eyes bouncing from face to face of their sweaty onlookers, and then her wide eyes narrowed, and she glared at them. "I swear by the fangs of Kanu, if any of you so much as whisper my name, I will drop a snake on each and every one of your heads!"

Most of the Itabayiti in the small crowd started laughing at her, but a few did gasp at the impropriety of such a young girl threatening them.

"She'll do it," Anki warned.

"She's not joking," Lucu added.

The crowd started to disperse, most of them clearly unimpressed by Sheka's threats, but there were a few much younger girls who remained seated and looking up at her. Anki could see they were making Sheka uncomfortable, and he stepped back under the nimuru to both cool off again and try to get Sheka to turn her back on her new fans. "How did you know about me working in the clay pits?" he asked her.

Sheka crossed her arms and took a step toward the mister. "I ran into Lewa in Ciba garden."

"Olari?" he guessed.

"Yeah, but that's not all." She took another step, allowing the mist from the nimuru to just barely graze her cheeks. "Lewa said your brother said that you and Biacoya went to Bahaca. And then she said that she asked Olari about it later, and he said that you saved his life."

The way she was looking at him made Anki feel ashamed. It was as if she knew he was responsible for the Yaya closing the harbors and cancelling the festival. He was responsible for everyone getting punished.

"You saved Olari's life?" Luculati asked, stepping up next to Sheka.

"NO! Ya scruffy headed chacu!" Sheka threatened to elbow him, making Lucu wince. "Anki saved Biacoya from drowning, along with that girl araco I saw walking up to the palace with him and Lesini Bogula."

Anki's shame instantly melted into embarrassment, and he slipped around on the wet stone, trying to put the nimuru between him and his friends.

"What? No, he didn't!" Luculati scoffed. "Did you?"

"After the harbors reopened and lessons were still cancelled," she continued, "everyone went to the springs, or to wade down Osani River, or came here to hang out in Badhan. Everyone, except you and Biacoya."

"I saw a guy swallow a snake in the Caru Market," Luculati said.

"Hush, no you didn't."

"Well...Giri did."

"Who's Giri?" she asked, but then Sheka waved her hand dismissively. "Never mind, I don't care." She slid to the other side of Luculati and peaked her head around the nimuru to find Anki's forest green eyes looking back at her.

He felt vulnerable, almost panicky, like he did that day in the damp, dark cave with the mist from the flooding rainwater dripping from his eyelids. And then she slowly laid her hand on his soaking wet arms, which he suddenly realized were wrapped around the nimuru, hugging it like he had Biacoya when he pulled his friend out of the violent waves of the shallows.

"Hey," Sheka said softly, snagging his attention away from the traumatic memory. "Where have you been?"

289

Abensu took a heaping sip of his gourd cup full of oycu and strolled briskly past the ceremonial almec court. He peered down into the submerged structure, seeing a few young men dripping with sweat and enjoying a pickup game. The court was on the near side of the Grand Plaza, longer than it was wide, ten reeds by three reeds, and each wall sloped downward at a slight angle. The angled walls helped the players scramble in and out and allowed the game ball to ricochet higher into the air. Four stone hoops were the intended targets, and two were centered on the narrower walls at either end, one above the other. When the Day of Biyaya was held during the rainy season, the court doubled as a reservoir where children could swim, but now it was just a shiny hot hole in the ground. How the sweaty young men were not passing out from the heat, Abensu did not know.

On the north side of the court was Mayu Hall. It was a grand structure with six poured cibmani columns, half-a-reed wide each, which protruded from the stone façade on either side of a towering doorway the size of a spirit shrine. The front and sides of the columns were painted deep azure, while the half-a-reed wide spaces between were pitch black. The thick frame was a reed-wide on the sides, stuck out half-an-arm's length farther than the columns, and was connected at the top by a reed-tall stone lintel. The whole enormous doorframe was painted pale orange and featured seventy-two white, six-pointed stars. Abensu had never been in Mayu Hall, but he thought if the interior was anywhere near as impressive as the exterior, it might be his favorite structure in all of Itabacan.

To the left of Mayu Hall was the attendants' quarters to the araco, a non-descript building roughly the same size as the hall, but poorly maintained and speckled with flecks of dirty white paint. He assumed the white paint was left over from when the buildings had been part of the

Yaya's palace complex hundreds of years before, but he couldn't understand why the speckles were only on the attendants' quarters. The Araco Residence beside it had recently been renovated. All of the chipped and eroded areas higher up the stone walls were filled in, the moss and vines had been removed from around the base, and the entire structure was repainted the same deep azure as the columns of Mayu Hall. It was striking, but it didn't evoke the same sense of wonder in him as the hall did. Abensu made a mental note to ask Elder Sengri the next time he saw him about the neglected state of the attendants' quarters.

Just ahead and to the south of the almec court were the banquet pavilion, the council pavilion to the right, and then the Yaya's pavilion. All three were similar in size to the buildings across the plaza, but the pavilions had no walls, which Abensu assumed was purposefully done so the wind could reach the plaza; sadly, there was no wind. The pavilion ceilings were supported by four massive square pillars in the corners and two pillars in the middle, each wrapped in bright-green vines with fat, yellowing leaves. The council and banquet pavilions each had a long stone table between the central pillars, which was flanked by equally long cedar benches. Abensu could see some workers were erecting additional wooden tables on the south side of the banquet pavilion against the backdrop of Itabacan Sound in the distance. And he saw workers had also squeezed a dozen large ceramic jugs, which he assumed were filled with oycu, between the two western pillars, obstructing his view of the council pavilion.

In stark contrast with the first two, the Yaya's pavilion was painted white like his palace, but it looked like it could use a thorough cleaning. Abensu knew there was a raised dais in place of the central table with three stone thrones on it like in the reception hall of the palace, but he could hardly see anything through the wall of adulu in their crimson tunics and shiny coral spears. He worried about Amnu. The Yaya was terrified of being poisoned and had hardly eaten anything since he first learned of the threat on his life. No amount of arguing from Unana Wana had changed his mind, which told the council there was no hope Amnu would listen to them. Abensu thought it was sadly ironic the plot to kill the Yaya might succeed after all when his old friend starved himself to death. He took another big swig of his oycu, hoping to settle the uneasiness building in his stomach, and stopped in front of the council pavilion.

His heavy eyes drifted across the Grand Plaza, and he marveled at the wave of hot air floating just above the cibmani ground. It reminded him of how the horizon looked on a windless day out on the Bocoa. To Abensu, the plaza looked just like a stone sea, stretching from the almec court all the way to the two enormous bowls of fire at the base of the Pyramid of Mayu. From there, the gray sea continued flowing up the pyramid and into the midday sky. In the rainy season, the reed-wide trenches that ran along the north and south edges of the plaza would fill with water, reflecting Ma'an during the day, and bringing the ancestors down to them at night. The trenches would then be emptied into the almec court, but there had been no rain, and at the moment the trenches were just as dry and hot as everything else.

"Taycoay, Abensu," he suddenly heard Boaraco Unsari shout behind him.

Abensu broke himself away from his concerns and stepped over the trench onto the first step leading up into the council pavilion. He saw Unsari sitting on the nearest cedar bench, his dark-azure robe folded up neatly next to him. He was eating candied yams from one of the special ceremonial plates and getting yam juice on the front of his dark-azure tunic.

"Taycoay," Abensu greeted the pavilion.

Sitting alongside, behind, or otherwise standing around the boaraco were most of their fellow council members and their families, and they all looked equally miserable. He told himself it was the heat, but Abensu knew there was more to everyone's uneasiness. Boagur Gudugu stood directly in front of Unsari in his ceremonial, boarhide tunic and fox pelt, holding his tusked headdress at his side and drinking from a water gourd, but Abensu doubted it contained a drop of water. He knew Gudugu was embarrassed to be portraying Chuka during the Tara'apti, a dramatization of the Biyaya's life, and he was likely in a bad mood. Not wanting to upset him further, Abensu simply nodded at the mountainous Chief of the Agur.

Gudugu smirked, the gourd hovering near his open mouth. "Abbsu," he slurred.

Standing to the right of the boagur was Chief of Sanitation Kasim in his sweat-stained, but otherwise pristine white tunic. "Taycoay, Kasim," Abensu greeted him, but Kasim only scoffed and turned away. When he did, he saw Gudugu's wife, Gigal, sitting on a reed mat on the floor with her daughter, Matata.

Gigal was as tall and lanky as Abensu, but in the shadow of the northwest pillar of the pavilion, she appeared small. Her column of black hair seemed to blend in with the pilar behind her, while her bright, azure-gray eyes flashed like two midday storm clouds. She had a thin face that sloped inward toward a rounded chin, which was sharply contrasted by a dozen cuyila necklaces. Each cuyila was made from a pair of carved and polished boar rib-bones that were tied together by strips of leather looped through tiny holes drilled into the tips. They were a common adornment for the wives of the boagur, which Abensu only knew because Tiam's mother had worn cuyila every day of her short life.

Matata sat in front of her mother who was in the process of putting her daughter's fuzzy-black hair into neat rows of tight braids. Matata was around the age of six, and she looked to be the mirror image of her mother. Abensu smiled at them, Gigal pensively smiled back, but Matata shyly turned away. With a soft chuckle, he continued on toward the center of the pavilion.

Chief of Gardens Tamna sat behind Unsari on the other side of the table with his back turned to them, and he wore the cleanest nut-brown tunic Abensu had ever seen him wear. Tamna was permanently hunched over from years of working in the fields, and Abensu knew he physically couldn't sit facing a table and needed a chair he could turn sideways. Being that there were only benches, Tamna sat facing Itabacan Sound. Just beyond him and sitting on a different mat on the floor were his wife, Angmu, and their son, Jumka. Abensu wasn't surprised when he didn't see Tunku with them. Their adopted son frequently caused problems around Itabacan with Kasim's boy, Kachi, and Abensu couldn't recall the last time he saw the family all together.

He knew Angmu to be a quiet, reserved woman, but when it came to Jumka, she was unrestrained in her overbearing obsessiveness. She constantly fussed over him, fixing his spiky hair, straightening the collar of his nut-brown tunic, which Abensu noticed matched both hers and his father's, and she made sure Jumka sat upright and didn't slouch. She had two long, brownish-black braids running down the sides of her smooth, dark-amber cheeks, and each braid hung perfectly straight over the front of her tunic, which was held tight at her narrow waist by a beaded belt. Brown and black feathers were interwoven into her hair and seemed to blend in like dead leaves in clay. From what Abensu had learned from Tamna, Angmu was equally the greatest woman in Itabacan, and more aggravating than a family of moles invading his gardens. Abensu had encountered moles now and then in the clay pits on Conaca, so he knew what Tamna meant all too well.

Abensu saw Bociba Simi leaning against the east-central pillar in his boarhide tunic with a plateful of assorted nuts in hand. He was scowling at each nut as he tossed them into his mouth. Behind him and just starting to lay out their own reed mat were his wife, Runa, and one of their two boys – Abensu had never met them, and he couldn't even begin to guess the boy's name. But he had learned years ago that all of the ciba wore the same style of boarhide tunics, "*Because,*" Simi told him, "*chaccus don't catch on fire like our old reed-woven loincloths.*" Abensu remembered thinking the same was probably true for the common cotton tunic, and he thought it was odd of Simi to refer to his boarhide tunic with the same word the agur used. Chaccus meant to become like a chacu, and Abensu wasn't convinced that's what Simi believed.

The boarhide tunic Simi usually wore to council meetings appeared to be extremely durable, if only a little stiff and cumbersome, but the one he was currently wearing looked to be well-oiled and lined with some sort of fur. If Abensu were to guess, he suspected the fur likely came from a maniku, but he didn't know for sure. He also didn't know Simi very well and didn't want to interrupt his intense snacking.

To the right of the bociba, Abensu saw Boyiti Macoca and the newly appointed Boadulu Konoma sitting on the other side of the table in their ceremonial tunics. Macoca's was teal and trimmed in black and gold, while Konoma wore the standard crimson of the adulu. He nodded at them with a smile. "Taycoay," he said, loud enough that they both should have heard him, but neither man acknowledged he had said anything. Abensu didn't see Macoca's wife or son anywhere, and he didn't know if Boadulu Konoma was married or not. With a shrug of his shoulders, he set his cup of oycu down and sat next to Unsari's neatly folded robe with a sigh.

The crowd around the almec court was thickening as more festival goers were making their way up the street from the harbor. Abensu thought

294

about how irritated the agur must be down at their makeshift gate, and nearly commented as much to Boagur Gudugu, but then he thought better of it. *Best to leave a peaceful boar be*, he reminded himself. Looking out over the plaza, he was actually quite surprised by how quiet the Itabayiti were. He knew the people were just as troubled by the threat on the Yaya and the raids as the council was, if not more so, and he assumed they would be happy to finally be at the festival. And then he thought the heat likely had something to do with everyone's stifled merriment. He leaned forward and craned his neck, just barely able to see Anki chasing Sheka around the nimuru – *or was Sheka chasing Anki?* And that was when the hideous slurping sound of Unsari eating his yams invaded Abensu's ear.

He looked at the rotund boaraco and raised one eyebrow. Unsari's gaze met Abensu's, and he momentarily paused his chewing, but only momentarily. He then continued even louder, smacking his lips and making sucking sounds against his teeth. Abensu closed his eyes and sighed again. He knew Unsari might just as quickly astonish him with dazzling wisdom as he was likely to compare Abensu to a simple-minded creature. *And where had Unsari gotten his hands on candied yams?* He spun around on the bench, searching the pavilion for an attendant with a basket of yams, or a table already pre-loaded with banquet snacks, but there were none. In getting his sons ready and on the ferry as early as possible, he forgot to eat morning meal and suddenly realized how hungry he was. *Did he get them from one of the vendors at the Badhan Market?*

He leaned back against the table in his silent disappointment, crossed his arms again, and let out another hot, heavy sigh. What he needed to do was relax. The ceremonial plates had been finished and delivered, his sons were safe and happy, and the Day of Biyaya was finally upon them. There was no room for despair or anxiety, despite the fact Bocoani Numila and his crew had yet to return from their quest. He felt like he needed to talk to someone about it. Maybe that would relieve a bit of his anxiety. He wasn't keen on talking to Boaraco Unsari, but Abensu knew the rotund araco's appetite for gossip was nearly as insatiable as his apparent love of candied yams. Looking around for an alternative, Abensu recognized no one else seemed interested in talking with him.

"No sign of Numila?" he whispered to Unsari.

"It appears not," Unsari replied with a little smirk and a mouthful of yams, brown juice dripping from his bottom lip.

"What are you smiling about?" he asked, apprehensive of Unsari's wry smile.

"Nothing." Unsari relaxed his face. "I sometimes forget to whom I am speaking. No, the expedition remains unaccounted for. Between you and me, I fear our Yaya is growing nervous."

"Snakes in the grass?" Abensu eyed the Yaya's pavilion only a few reeds away.

"Have you seen Hadim, Palu, or Tugdu?"

Abensu quickly looked around again, realizing Chief of Springs Hadim, Boaluk Palu, and Chief of Textiles Tugdu were missing from the gathered council. "Not since last meeting," he replied.

"That was half-a-mawa ago." Unsari shoved the last of the juicy yams into his mouth. "Maybe someone should go inquire as to what is going on." He batted his eyes at Abensu.

"Well, Tambu hasn't arrived yet either," Abensu pointed out, ignoring his attempt to get him to be the Unsari's gossip-scrounger.

"True. I'm glad we have our contingency plan in place."

Abensu knew what the boaraco was referring to, but he didn't like talking about it. He let the moment pass as Unsari continued munching on his yams. "Where did you get those?" Abensu finally asked, changing the subject.

"Yams?" Unsari asked sloppily, his mouth full, and Abensu nervously nodded. He leaned closer in order to whisper in Abensu's ear, "Angmu." He raised his legs, revealing a basket directly under the bench below him. "Shh...don't let anyone else know that I have them." He locked eyes with him and Abensu nodded, and then Unsari handed him his empty plate. "Here, load me up."

Under the smears of smushed yam on the plate, Abensu saw the juices actually improved the Yaya's image in the center. *Huh*, he thought, *maybe Ikmo was right*. He then used the plate to scoop up more candied yams but was forced to use his bare hand to keep the slippery treats from sliding off. He then gave the whole gooey plate to Unsari, plucking the fattest two yams from the top and earning a chubby, perturbed glare from the boaraco. The yams were warm, soft, sweet, and juicy, but Abensu wouldn't have cared if they had been hard as a rock and tasted like dirt. He took a large bite, chewing slowly to savor the flavor, and he almost didn't want to swallow. When he did, the relief to his hunger was instant, tempting him to devour the second yam just as quickly, but he decided it would be more satisfying if he took smaller bites.

"Thank you," he whispered to Unsari.

"Mm," Unsari mumbled in reply, his mouth full.

"I didn't have a chance to eat morning meal before we left Conaca."

"Mm-hmm."

"Had to get the boys ready and fed. I allowed our attendants to leave to spend time with their families the past couple of days – you know, since they've been trapped on Conaca for half-a-mawa. And..."

"Is there a point to any of this?" Unsari asked, abruptly interrupting him. Abensu sighed, and he tried to apologize, forgetting to whom he was speaking, but he was cut off again. "That makes four heavy sighs!" Unsari said excitedly. "I'm told, if you're able to belch out a fifth, the Great Spirit will bestow upon you a garland of kugo ears and greasy chacu butt hairs!"

Abensu chuckled, slowly shaking his head. "What made you this way?" he asked. Unsari smiled proudly but said nothing, returning to devour the gooey yams on his plate. Abensu knew it was pointless to argue with the boaraco. The best thing to do was to simply move on and away from his sarcastic abrasiveness. "I guess all of our nerves have been tested this samawa," he continued, retrieving his cup of oycu and downing the last half in one gulp. "I worry, Unsari." Abensu lowered his voice to a whisper again. "We've kicked the wasps' nest. Gudugu over there has been chasing them down, one by one, imprisoning cultists on Chacuca every day since that last meeting. Yucahu only knows how this will all end."

"For-tree," Boagur Gudugu suddenly said over his shoulder. He remained facing out toward the plaza, his headdress still tucked under his arm, and the gourd Abensu saw him drinking from earlier was now dangling near his knee by a leather string. Abensu was pretty sure Gudugu meant to say for*ty-th*ree, but it was hard to tell with his slurring. "We-gur have imprisoned for-tee-three cultists," Gudugu clarified, alleviating any confusion. He paused to burp. "Sev-kin leapt to their deaths-uh...gainst the rocks." His words tumbled over themselves, turning into a chuckle. "I can still see dumb smiles on their faces as-ay fell...shoutin' *Uansu!* Ha! To save

297

them!" He mocked the akin, calling out at the people mingling in the plaza with his cupped hand around his mouth. "*UANSU! UANSU! ŪANSU...*"

"Gudugu," his wife called to him, "Will you not? In front of our daughter?"

The boagur glanced in Gigal's direction, but then he added, "She'll learn soon 'nough. Best sh' learns about it from her baba! Fore them Yapati-kudi turn on us all!"

CRACK!

The sudden loud noise startled everyone, and they turned to see Boyiti Macoca standing up, having smashed his special ceremonial plate on the table in front of him. The look on the boyiti's face wasn't unexpected. Macoca was a sensitive man, constantly whining in the round, and getting mad when the council didn't immediately grant his requests. But Macoca had surprised everyone when he joined the council in supporting the Yaya's assault on Bahaca. It was the rooting out of the Cult of Mawoi on Yapaca that had returned Macoca to his usual whiney self. Abensu was not surprised Gudugu's mocking struck a nerve.

"You've upset Macoca," he told the boagur.

"Ha! So, wills-Orlil!" Gudugu chortled. "Ah – he's young. Like a shoat sniffin' round fur-oycu, only findin' his-own rear!" Abensu laughed, he couldn't help it, which encouraged a few others to snicker as well. But then he noticed the boagur wasn't laughing. "What's so funny, Abbsu?" The look he gave him made Abensu gulp. It was a terrifying, unwavering glare he thought might have set the table behind him on fire, if Abensu's head hadn't been in the way. "Ah-ha, ha, ha..." Gudugu suddenly burst out laughing. "Chuka's tusks! I'm only tuskin' you! Just playin...round!" He chuckled so hard, his headdress slipped from beneath his arm, and he had to quickly scramble to catch it. When he did, Gudugu let out an ear-piercing whistle of relief that echoed off the ceiling and continued ringing long after he stopped.

"Gudugu!" Unsari shouted at him. "Spare us your deafening whistle! None of us happen to be agur, you know?! We're not used to such noise! Not even me, despite my vocal, though often unappreciated opinions!"

Abensu snorted, trying to contain a chuckle. He stretched his jaw in an attempt to force a yawn and stop the wretched ringing in his ears and watched Unsari wiggle his picky finger around in his own ear. Not being the target of Unsari's sarcasm was immensely humorous.

"Hmm," the boagur grunted. "Apologies, Boaraco," he said, aggressively tucking his headdress back under his arm and fussing with the dangling gourd.

"Shouldn't you be over there with your men, prepping for your chacu dance, or whatever you'll be doing in the Tara'apti?" He pointed toward the Araco Residence diagonally across the plaza from them.

Gudugu turned to look where Unsari was pointing, but he didn't say anything. Abensu saw Gudugu's fingers drumming on his hip below the tusked headdress. He was clearly irritated by Unsari, but Abensu guessed the boagur was too proud to respond; that, or he was just intoxicated enough to not care.

"Abensu," he heard Tamna call to him.

He turned, seeing the Chief of Garden's bent and crooked back. "Yes, Tamna?" he replied. Looking past Tamna, Abensu noticed Angmu had stopped fussing with her son and was staring at him with her dark, almost black-brown eyes.

"Tell me," Tamna continued, without looking at him. "I've been meaning to ask you, why'd your boy go to Bahaca in the first place?"

They had all heard his son's story in the round from Anki himself, and Abensu could understand them being skeptical. He had actually anticipated one of the council members raising this question at some point, but no one had. What he did not expect was for Tamna to suddenly bring it up now, a samawa after the fact, and in the council pavilion right before the Day of Biyaya was to begin. Abensu let the question linger there in the stale air for a moment while he thought about how he should respond.

"Well?" Boadulu Konoma prodded him with the impatience of youth.

Abensu noticed the boadulu was now standing next to Macoca near the southeast pillar and, for some reason, his comment from earlier resurfaced – *snakes in the grass*. Turning his back to them and Tamna, Abensu looked out toward the sun-bathed plaza, crossed his arms, and sighed. "As my son told you before," he addressed everyone in the pavilion. "Anki and Biacoya had been suspended from lessons, bored out of their gourds, and their trip to Bahaca was a spontaneous, childish adventure. Anki said he happened to see his Yaali tunic at the end of the bed, and..."

"Who put it there? Did you?" Tamna asked, interrupting him.

"No, I..." he tried to reply.

"But you encouraged him to go," Macoca interjected as well, a bit more bite in his voice.

"I encouraged nothing," Abensu snapped. "Anki, my son, asked and I agreed that he could spend the day at the springs on Niamca."

"Where two segin have now drowned," Macoca said, which sounded suspiciously like an accusation.

"That has nothing...what are you trying to say, Macoca?"

"He's not trying to say anything," Bociba Simi suddenly said. Abensu guessed it was the bociba's turn to interrupt him. He wearily watched Simi set his empty plate down on the table in front of Macoca's broken one, brush his hands against themselves, and then wipe them on his slick, boarhide tunic. Simi eyed the boyiti. "*Are* you trying to say something, Macoca?" he asked. Abensu recognized Simi wasn't actually asking, and that Macoca definitely wasn't going to answer.

Bociba Simi had been a well-respected member of the council for decades, likely because he rarely spoke. Thinking back, Abensu could only think of one time where Simi had taken the round, and that was at least five or six years ago. He was a serious and intimidating man who had all of Unsari's unpleasantness, but none of the boaraco's wit.

"Of course, Macoca has nothing to say," Unsari said, sucking yam juice off of each one of his fingers. "How could he? With that tiny, warped, hutia head of his!" And then he startled chuckling loudly, eliciting a round of laughter from most of the other council members, including Tamna, Kasim, and even Simi. Abensu smiled, but he didn't want to encourage any more arguing or mockery. Unsari then leaned over to him and whispered, "By the way, that makes five sighs."

Abensu couldn't help himself and started laughing with the others. It was a welcome moment of lightheartedness, but then Boyiti Macoca huffed loudly and stomped his foot. As he turned to storm off, Abensu saw Macoca's wife, Kahila, and his son – whose name he couldn't remember – walking up the eastern steps toward him.

"What is it?" Kahila asked her husband. "Where are you going?"

"We're leaving." Macoca grabbed her shoulder roughly and spun her around.

"Oh – come now," Angmu pleaded, quietly, almost to herself. Abensu saw her glance at him briefly, but then her nearly black eyes shifted to her husband. "Tamna, make this right."

"Can I go with Amoc?" their son asked.

"Shh, not now, Jumka." Angmu placed her hand on his. "Tamna-baba?"

Tamna let out an aggravated sigh, "Great Kosa...alright! Macoca!" he shouted. "Why don't you, Kahila, and Amoc come over here and take a seat. Have some candied yams?"

"Candied yams?!" the boy called Amoc asked excitedly.

"That's right," Angmu replied. "Boaraco Unsari? Would you kick that basket back here?"

The grumbling suddenly seeping out of Unsari reminded Abensu of the gurgling sound the water made when the attendants flushed out the channels in the bath at his residence. He saw Unsari glaring up at him with weary, wrinkled, bloodshot, bark-like eyes, and then the old araco released an equally grumbly sigh. The smile on Abensu's face stretched from ear to ear. He quickly knelt down in front of Unsari. "Allow me," he said, and then shoved the basket back toward Tamna. It scraped against the stone floor and came to a stop directly beneath the Chief of Gardens.

"Thank you," Angmu said from the other side of the table.

Abensu stood and stretched his long legs, still smiling and feeling a bit better about the day. He didn't have to start counting Unsari's sighs or point out the garland-like dribble around the neckline of his tunic to let the boaraco know he had been bested. Unsari's inability to formulate a biting, sarcastic response was all Abensu needed. The two yams in his stomach had settled nicely, and the council seemed to wake up from their miserableness. Pleased they appeared distracted and less likely to ask him any more questions, Abensu felt his uneasiness lighten a little.

"Here," he heard Angmu say, the basket scraping against the floor as she pulled it closer.

"Thank you." Kahila pushed her husband forward. "We're staying, Macoca, and you would be wise to stay with us."

Amoc aggressively pushed past his father and strutted confidently into the pavilion. "It's the Day of Biyaya, baba," he said, smugly.

Abensu didn't know the young boy, but he thought he looked to be about Anki's age, or maybe a little older. He noticed Amoc and his mother wore teal tunics to match Macoca's, but Kahila's appeared to only be trimmed in gold, while Amoc's was only trimmed in black.

"Hey, Jumka," the boy said, plopping down on the mat between Angmu and her son.

"Can I go have candied yams with Jumka and Amoc, itaba?" Abensu heard Matata ask her mother. Abensu turned to see Gigal whisper something into her daughter's ear, and Matata's expression quickly turned sour.

But then Gigal told her, "Yes, of course you can go. If it's alright with Angmu..." She leaned back and stretched her long neck, apparently trying to see around the table and central pillar. "Is it alright if Matata joins you?" she asked.

"Yes – there's plenty of yams to go around!"

"Yay!" Matata shouted with glee.

"Remember what I said, kugo!"

"Yes, itaba, I will."

Abensu watched the little girl bounce across the floor of the pavilion, causing tiny, dangling boar bones set into the tips of her tight braids to click together. From where he was standing, Abensu admired Gigal's skill. Of course, he had to also acknowledge that he had never tried his hand at braiding hair, and Gigal might have a bit more experience. Like her father's whistle, the clicking bones echoed off the ceiling and continued long after Matata stopped bouncing. Abensu had to stretch his jaw out again to stop the clicking in his ears. "Now might be a good time to go speak with Yaya Amnu," he heard himself say.

"Finally!" Unsari exclaimed, wiggling his pinky finger around in his ear. When he removed his finger, he instantly heard the children giggling behind him and added, "Perhaps, I shall go with you."

"He's not well," Simi said. Abensu assumed he was referring to the Yaya and didn't turn to him, because he was too busy being thoroughly entertained watching Unsari struggle to get off the bench and onto his feet.

Afte a brief but exhausting effort, the boaraco slumped back down on the bench in a huff. "Ugh! Too many candied yams!"

"If Numila doesn't return," Simi continued, "The council may need to begin considering ...other alternatives..."

This got Abensu's attention. He spun around to face Bociba Simi. "What do you mean?"

"Well..." Simi started to answer.

But Kasim cut him off, "We replace him."

"I'm confused." Abensu looked at Unsari for clarification, but Boagur Gudugu stomped his sandaled foot. *SLAP!* The sound echoed off the ceiling and rang in his ears, again, for the third time, as well as silenced everyone in the council pavilion.

"Enough!" Gudugu shouted. "I will not tolerate any more talk of usurping the Yaya!" It was the clearest and most coherent thing he had said all morning, and Abensu was pretty sure everyone in the Grand Plaza had heard him.

Through the silence, the murmuring of the growing crowd invaded the space. Abensu could hear the sounds of children playing in the distance, the labored grunts of the sweaty young men in the almec court, and even the distinct clatter and cheers of people playing omabu-disha. Abensu looked around at his fellow council members, noting their shared nervous expressions, and then he leaned over to whisper privately to Boaraco Unsari.

"So, I should go now?" he asked, half-joking, but Unsari nodded eagerly.

In the Araco Residence on the north side of the Grand Plaza, Jokimbi sat against the warm, stone wall, surrounded by dozens of sweaty and stinky agur. He tried to focus on polishing the purple and white clam shells that made up the Biyaya's ceremonial bracelets, because he wanted them to gleam like they had never gleamed before, but it was hard to see what he was doing in the dim torchlight.

One open doorway led into the room from outside, casting a doorway-shaped pool of pale-yellow sunlight onto the floor. Unfortunately, there was no accompanying breeze. The air was motionless and filled with a thin, smoky haze from the four torches in four sconces, two of which were mounted high on each of the east and west walls. In the center of the north wall was a slightly raised dais with a single wooden chair in the center, which Jokimbi assumed must have been where the Yaya's throne originally stood. On either side of the chair were two torch basins that were thankfully unlit. He was told the residence was divided into five rooms: the araco quarters, a dining hall, the boaraco's chambers, communal baths, and the reception hall. This last room, the reception hall, was where he sat, and where he was told was as far into the residence he was allowed to go.

Jokimbi could see how the structure had once been a part of the Yaya's palace complex. The hall was surprisingly big, possibly bigger than the reception hall of the palace, but the floor wasn't nearly as well polished, and there didn't appear to be any windows or vents for the torches. Without ventilation or any airflow to speak of, all four flames added to a rippling river of smoke flowing on the ceiling. He wondered if the araco intentionally collected the smoke, but he had no idea what they would be doing with it.

The more he looked around and imagined what the Araco Residence must have looked like hundreds of years ago, the more Jokimbi saw it never would have compared to the Yaya's Palace on top of the mountain. There truly was nothing in Itabacan like the palace, and he couldn't imagine what it would have been like growing up anywhere else. For one thing, there would never have been this many agur crammed into the palace reception hall, because the adulu wouldn't have allowed it. They were extremely proud of being the sole protectors of the Yaya. He recalled Boadulu Urtulu threatening to spear Gudugu, who was a duagur at the time, for escorting a kinbet all the way up the mountain instead of waiting for her adulu escort to relieve him down at the harbor. Jokimbi couldn't remember the kinbet's name, but the girl bravely stood between the two burly men and likely saved Gudugu's life that day.

Because of the adulu's over-protectiveness, Jokimbi was rarely allowed to have friends visit him at the palace. He remembered it could get very lonely on the mountain, which might not have been the case had he grown up beside the Grand Plaza, but Jokimbi never allowed his loneliness to become boring. He recalled running around the palace alone always annoyed Urtulu, who felt he needed to send a few of his men to follow Jokimbi through the hidden passageways, down into the tunnels beneath the palace, and even into the Hall of Records. Jokimbi played his own private games with the adulu, games similar to one's children still played, like tag and Okid, but which integrated the darkness. The poor adulu didn't always know they were playing the games with him.

The memories made Jokimbi smile. In many ways, he preferred the dark. Mawoi's great light baked his delicate skin, creating more and more freckles on his arms and legs. And now the Great Spirit within him seemed to be fighting back and lightened his skin in places, especially around his ears and the tops of his hands. Jokimbi didn't want to think about how splotchy his scalp must be. Just then, his ga'an knot came undone. He grunted, set down his polishing towel, brought his coani braid back up from behind his ear, wrapped it around the thinning tuft of graying hair on the top of his head, and then tucked it under itself. To make sure it would stay this time, he wiggled his head around, and then shook it from side to side. Satisfied it wasn't going to come undone again, he picked up the towel and resumed his polishing.

"Kimbi!" he heard Duagur Addo holler at him.

Jokimbi hated not being called by his full name. *What's so hard?* he thought. *Just because Addo's parents gave him a short name, doesn't mean Addo gets to shorten his!* Jokimbi thought about how the duagur's brothers all had full, interesting names, and he wondered what ararun possessed Ahido to name her first-born son Addo. And then Jokimbi's thoughts drifted to Yaeel's drowning. *How awful!* It was so bizarre, so unheard-of for a segin to drown. When Jokimbi heard Yaeel wasn't even the first to drown that samawa, he was shocked Yaya Amnu hadn't immediately ordered an investigation. Jokimbi's father would have, but Amnu didn't. Jokimbi assumed he would see Ahido march past Badhan with Hadim on their way to demand an audience with the Yaya, but he never saw her. As he reflected more on the matter, Jokimbi realized he hadn't seen Hadim in a while either.

"Kimbi!" Addo yelled again, now walking over to him.

"What is it, Addo?" he sighed, twisting the bracelet around to begin polishing the next row of shells. They were beautiful shells and in excellent condition, but they...

"Duagur," Addu rudely interrupted his polishing again.

"What?"

Addo stopped and placed his fists on his hips. "Please, in front of my men, use my title."

Jokimbi couldn't help but roll his eyes. *His men?* "What can I do for you, *Duagur?*"

"*Addo,*" the duagur huffed.

This was getting ridiculous. "Well, which is it?" Jokimbi demanded to know, throwing his shell-polishing towel on the ground. "Are you going to be like this all day?" He was hot, the absurd boarhide tunic they insisted he wear was stabbing him in the side, and the welts on his face from the wasp attack wouldn't stop itching. Lesini Bogula had given Jokimbi an ointment, but it smelled awful, and he refused to use it.

"Hmm," Addo grunted, now standing over him and watching him scratch at his face. "You're not used to wearing a chaccus are you?"

"Since morning meal? What do you think?" He hoped his sarcasm was clear enough for the big duagur. Addo chuckled at him, but Jokimbi glared back, attempting to show Addo he was not joking. As excited as Jokimbi was to portray the Biyaya in the Tara'apti, he was just miserable enough to strip down and walk away from the festival altogether.

He saw Addo shaking his head. "It's traditionally the boadulu's role, but Urtulu refused. Said he was too old to dance." A wry little smile crept across the duagur's face, and Jokimbi thought he was about to say something else, but then Addo looked out the open doorway and just shook his head again.

Jokimbi sighed, picked up his towel, and started polishing again. Maybe he was being too hard on Addo, he thought. Maybe Duagur Addo was just as miserable as he was but doing a better job of hiding it. "I can understand that," Jokimbi finally said. "Boadulu Urtulu's not much older than me, and I can't tell you the last time I danced."

"Was."

"Was what?"

"Urtulu went to walk with Niama," Addo said. "He is a *was* now."

Jokimbi tilted his head and gave Addo a confused look. Was Duagur Addo making a joke? As he considered this, a short, involuntary chuckle escaped his pursed lips.

"Ah – so you think that's funny, do you?"

"It wasn't funny." Jokimbi quickly looked away to hide his broadening smile.

"Well, I rarely mean to be," Addo clarified, not hiding his smile at all.

Is that also a joke? Jokimbi didn't look at him, choosing to focus on polishing the last row of shells. He desperately wanted to make them shine. He looked up at the Kechet resting on the basket by the doorway. It was a cylindrical headdress made from two large, sun-bleached conch shells fastened together with strips of gold-painted leather. The sun reflected off of it and cast a beam of light on the wall over his head. The adulu kept the Kechet in a locked room in the palace with other relics from the Yayapti, and he thought it looked amazing for being almost a thousand years old. He desperately wanted his bracelets to shine equally as brilliant.

He felt as if he were a little boy again and playing in his father's bedchamber, trying on his father's clothes while their attendants dressed the Yaya for the festival. It was his father's second Day of Biyaya but Jokimbi's first. Being the only son of Yaya Shakali had afforded him an abundance of privileges, but the privilege he cherished above all others was having the best seats for festivals.

After that first Day of Biyaya, Jokimbi started having visions in sleeptime about being in the Tara'apti. He told his mother about his visions, and that he wanted to join the adulu when he was old enough, but Jokimbi's mother told him no. She said he was destined for greater things, and he remembered thinking what could possibly be greater than protecting his father. He remembered being confused, frustrated, and even angry at his mother, but she convinced his father it was a bad idea, and Jokimbi never forgave her.

He let out a relieved sigh, still unable to believe how lucky he was to be hand-picked by Yaya Amnu to portray the Biyaya, even though he wasn't the boadulu. Even though he became a coani instead, and his mother convinced his father to take that away from him too, appointing Jokimbi Itabaca's canuti instructor. Even though...

"Kimbi? Are you lost?" he heard Duagur Addo ask.

"No," he lied. "I'm right here." He then finished polishing the bracelet and started getting to his feet. "You know what?"

"What?"

"I'm kind of hoping to get a gourd of oycu in me before this thing starts."

"Well!" Addo exclaimed. "As Orlil wills! I had just come over to ask if you would like to partake in a little pre-Tara'apti imbibing with me and my men?"

"Duagur Addo, I would be honored," he replied.

"Good! Because then we have to go over everything one last time," Addo said, and Jokimbi nodded. "Excellent. May Chuka guide us!"

"Over the horizon!" all of the agur crammed into the reception hall shouted.

Jokimbi laughed, shaking his head. As he turned to follow the duagur, he glanced out through the doorway and thought he saw Chief of Wares Abensu step out from behind the Yaya's pavilion. Jokimbi squinted his wretched eyes, which didn't seem to work as well as when he was younger and watched Abensu kick at the dirt just like he had seen Anki do a hundred times. *What a weird family*, he thought.

CHAPTER TWENTY-NINE

LEWA

Lewa sat beside her brother on the hot steps leading into the attendants' quarters, fanning herself with a large green leaf. She had plucked it from a bush next to the spirit shrine of Bitabay on her walk up from the harbor, but it was already starting to wilt. Her two long braids were wound into a bowl on top of her head and away from her neck, revealing two small drill-shells poking through each of her dangling earlobes. She swiveled her head to glare up at the Great Light in the eastern sky, her earrings wobbling along the way, and then she blew out a hot puff of air. Mawoi was mercilessly beating down on the plaza, and there was nothing they could do about it. Her legs were stiff, and she stretched each one in front of her, but the movement caused her boney backside to rub against the hard stone step. With a huff, she squirmed back and forth, and then side to side, fussing with her sticky tunic and trying to relieve her discomfort.

Olari had snagged their prime seats early in the morning, having left Yapaca before dawn to beat the crowds, and he was already drenched in sweat. His freshly washed tan tunic was now dark brown and clinging to his body like seaweed, making it appear to blend in with his glistening ebony skin. Though he didn't outwardly say how miserable he was, she could tell by how dry the sponge of light-brown hair was on top of his head. Maintaining moist hair to keep his meaty head cool was an obsession of his, and when he was unable to satiate that obsession, Olari's rare but fiery temper came out. Of course, it was his own fault. No one asked him to come early.

"Hey! Why don't I go cool off at the nimuru and bring you back a cup of oycu?" Lewa asked excitedly.

"You'll lose your spot."

"No, I won't. You'll save it for me."

"No, I won't," he replied, mocking her in a high-pitched voice.

"I don't sound like that!" she huffed.

"Uh-huh," he rolled his eyes. "If you get up, I can't promise one of these people won't instantly sit down."

"Come on, O! I'll only be gone a moment – just run over to the nimuru, spin, grab an oycu, and then run right back." Lewa clenched her sweaty hands together in front of her brother's face. "Please!"

"I told you; I can't make any promises." He threw his own sweaty palms out toward the plaza. "These are prime seats, and someone is bound to take your spot. It's *way* too hot for me to fight your battles for you."

Lewa crossed her arms and huffed, "Fine." They were pretty good seats, especially for the Tara'apti, but she glared at her brother anyway.

She watched him sitting there, stubbornly dwelling in his misery, unwilling to risk losing what he had, even if it meant he could dip his big, meaty head in a giant jug of cold water. Every Itabayiti that walked by searching for an empty spot on the steps earned his sour glare, and Lewa might have been eyeing them alongside her brother if a strange thought hadn't suddenly wormed its way into her mind. *Olari is Anki*. Well, not actually, but she understood what the Great Spirit was trying to tell her. Her brother acted exactly like every young man and boy she knew. Their stubbornness was a self-inflicted punishment, which itself was just their wounded pride – *A frayed thread that chooses to unravel itself*.

There were plenty of women around them, and they were all either fanning themselves or leaning into one of the few narrow shadows provided by the front pillars of Mayu Hall. Most of the men Lewa could see were standing or sitting in the brutal heat, talking quietly to one another with miserable expressions on their downturned faces. She saw the sea of people had started seeping into the shaded alleyways between the buildings, and the majority of them appeared to be women as well. The only shaded areas where the men outnumbered the women were the council pavilion and the Yaya's pavilion, and that was only because women weren't allowed on the council or to be one of the adulu. And that was when Lewa heard a familiar voice.

She squinted past her brother, five or so people down from them, where she spotted Draha and Joba sitting hand-in-hand on the steps in front of Mayu Hall. They looked to be arguing, but Lewa couldn't hear what they were saying through her brother's big head. "Switch me spots," she suddenly told him.

"No," came his immediate response, but then he asked, "Why?"

"Just do it! Come on." She stood up. "You won't save my spot and let me go cool off. The least you can do is move over." Standing felt good, and she kicked her legs one at a time while she waited for Olari to comply. She stared at him looking up at her, neither of them blinking, until he finally grunted and scooted over. "Thank you," she said, but then she had to sit quickly before one of the circling seat-hawks sat first. The moment her backside touched the stone, it was too late as she realized she had just sat in a pool of Olari's sweat. "Gross!"

"What now?"

"It's like you peed on the step!"

"Oh – well, it's hot, and I'd been sitting there all morning."

"You could have said something!"

"You mean, like no, I don't want to switch spots?" he teased her.

Lewa let out an aggravated sigh but didn't say what she wanted to say. Instead, she accepted her fate. "Fine. It's just – fine."

"Actually," her brother said, "this spot is quite a bit cooler, and drier. So, thank you."

He started laughing, but Lewa could only roll her eyes. She quickly looked away to keep from punching him.

"Stop fidgeting," she heard Draha say. He wasn't even trying to keep his voice down. Lewa leaned forward. She could see Joba was trying to adjust her marriage belt.

"It's too tight," she told Draha.

"It's as tight as it's supposed to be," he snapped back.

"It's hot and this thing is stabbing me in the stomach!" Joba was trying not to shout but failing. Lewa saw her let go of Draha's hand and attempt to move her belt, but Draha snatched her hand back.

"We don't want to appear foolish, Joba. Ignore it! Besides, all your moving about is making me hotter than I already am." Draha appeared to stop talking to look around, realizing just how many people were quietly watching them argue. "This heat really tests the Great Spirit, doesn't it?" he asked around. "The Tara'apti better start soon, or we'll all be..."

Olari suddenly jabbed Lewa in her side with his elbow.

"Ow! What did you do that for?"

"You shouldn't be eavesdropping on them. *Itabo, goarokun Yabo*," he told her.

Lewa knew the phrase meant, *Bride, your groom comes this evening.* It was the traditional chant the Itabayiti yelled out during a nakibo, the march of the yabo to the home of his itabo. The jovial chant was intended to both alert the bride to her groom's arrival, but also warn her to flee if she no longer wanted to be his bride. Olari was telling Lewa to mind her own business because Joba had made her choice.

"They'll figure it out," he continued. "Itabo are notoriously feisty the first few mawa."

This made Lewa laugh. "And what could you possibly know about it?" she asked him. Her brother wasn't married. He had voiced his clear objection to the tradition on numerous occasions, but he never explained why he despised marriage in the first place. "Go on. Enlighten me with your waki-wisdom!"

Olari smiled. "The only reason Itabayiti get married is because their parents arrange it, and parents only arrange it so their children will have children. And then more marriages are arranged, and their children's children have children — and on and on it goes." He waved his hand in circular motion.

"Uh-huh...And what's so wrong with that?" she asked.

"Nothing," he said, emphatically. "There's nothing wrong with it, unless there are no parents to do the arranging." Olari abruptly crossed his sweaty arms and turned away from her.

Lewa was taken aback. She hadn't considered what losing their parents might mean for her marriage prospects. She knew children were promised to one another, and that it was usually arranged by their mothers, but it hadn't dawned on her that no parents meant no promises. The way Olari said it suggested to her that he was bitter about it. It was a side of him she didn't know existed. She looked at him as he quietly watched the jatbay band march up the first few steps of the Pyramid of Mayu, which signified the Tara'apti was about to begin, but Lewa wasn't ready.

"Hey," she pulled at his shoulder, trying to get him to turn around to talk to her, but he jerked away. "Draha is an araco," she said. "He doesn't have parents."

"He has Elder Sengri," Olari said with his back still turned.

"And we have ohbaba-Bolari!"

Her brother glanced at her over his shoulder and gestured with a nod toward Mount Otaba. "Up there? You think ohbaba is going to arrange anything from up there at the Yaya's Palace?" Lewa hadn't considered this either. "Why don't you ask Piddso about it the next time you two sneak off to the springs together."

"Who told you about that?" she snapped, but instantly knew the answer. "Oh – right. Atu."

"Why aren't you hanging out with him now, anyway?" he asked, finally turning around.

"Who, Piddso? Well, I..." Lewa swallowed hard. She suddenly felt dizzy, and her thoughts... She was having trouble untangling her thoughts, and her tongue kept sticking to the roof of her dry mouth. Lewa tugged at her collar and blinked several times, her vision momentarily going blurry.

"Lewa?"

She heard Olari say her name, but she couldn't respond. She was finding it hard to hold her head up, and it bobbed once, and then twice. Her bowl of hair came undone, and her braids fell over her ears and onto her shoulders. She suddenly felt Olari's hand grab hers, and then she could sort of see him looking up into her light-brown eyes.

"Lewa!" he shouted at her.

"Y-Yes?" she answered, weakly.

"Alright. Come on," he said, lifting her up off the stone step with his hands clutched around her thin arms. Her legs wobbled beneath her a moment before settling, and then she was able to stand, but she had to lean against her brother. "I'm taking you to the nimuru right now."

"But..." she swallowed again. "But you'll lose your spot?" He appeared to briefly consider this, and then he turned to the people that had been sitting on either side of them. Lewa instantly felt bad for not introducing herself earlier, but she recognized she was in no condition to do so now.

"We will be right back," Olari told them. "Please, will you try to save our seats for us?" She saw he was talking to a man in a brown tunic, but when she lifted her head to see the man's face her vision went blurry again.

"I'll try, but I can't make any promises," the man replied, which Lewa thought was just a little ironic.

"And you?"

"Same," came the gruff voice of an older man.

"That'll have to do," her brother said. "Thank you."

And then they were walking, or stumbling. Her brother was walking and Lewa was stumbling along with him. He held her up with his left arm wrapped tightly around her shoulders, and his right hand firmly gripped her elbow. As they passed Draha and Joba, Lewa caught one of Joba's fiery eyes, and it looked to be the single saddest eye Lewa had ever seen. And then her head bobbed, and her braids swung across her face, as her brother brought them up some steps, between and over several confused people, to where she suddenly recognized Tabba. The araco didn't appear to notice them because she was too busy hugging an extremely old man. But before Lewa could focus on the old man's face, they were moving again.

They passed the open doorway into Mayu Hall where, for the briefest of moments, there in the pitch-black interior, she thought she saw a tall, slender woman in a bright crimson robe staring back at her. Lewa was so startled by the woman, she momentarily arrested control of her heavy head, blinked several times, and forced herself to look again, but the woman was gone.

CHAPTER THIRTY

SENGRI

"That will do, child," Elder Sengri said, pulling Tabba's arms from around his neck. "I have to go. The Tara'apti cannot start without me."

Tabba yawned in response and shook her head wildly, whipping her long, single braid around. She had slept for nearly three days after her ordeal on Bahaca, and it took several more days for her to feel well enough to work again. It was essential the Rise of Mawoi ceremony was performed, and she was one of only a few Itabayiti that had actually witnessed it before. When Yaya Amnu asked her, Tabba agreed to return to help rehabilitate the few akin who had not thrown themselves off the cliff, and also to make sure the ritual went smoothly. Sengri insisted he be permitted to go with her, arguing his duties as Curator of Mayu Hall could temporarily be handled by Boaraco Unsari. Unsari adamantly voiced his displeasure with the situation, but Sengri didn't care. It was more important to appease Mawoi and tend to the wounded spirit than pay any attention to the grumblings of an already grumbly boaraco.

"Find a good seat and remember to enjoy yourself," he told her with a big, wrinkled smile. "The end does get quite entertaining. So, try to stay awake."

She sighed, playfully. "I will, but then I'm going straight to bed!"

"Ranar will be thrilled to have you," he said with a grin, but then Sengri saw a concerned expression wash over her face and a flicker of despair in her hazel eyes. "What it is, child?"

"What if the adulu come around again?"

"Yucahu be great — they haven't since all of this conspiracy madness began. I suspect the adulu have enough to worry about, but..." He tapped her on the tip of her nose. "Keep to the usual routine, and you'll be fine."

He smiled again, as Tabba wrinkled her nose and nodded that she understood. "Now, I must go."

"Tayaga!" She wished him luck before hugging him one last time.

Just then, Sengri caught a blur of movement over Tabba's head. It was Bolari's grandson, Olari, and he was dragging a girl alongside him who looked to be about Tabba's age. They casually moved up through the seated festival goers, the girl's head bobbing along with her two long braids dangling toward the ground like vines. Sengri assumed she had likely succumbed to the heat and, being that neither of them was yelling for help, he further assumed Olari was taking her to the nimuru to cool off. It happened at nearly every festival, especially during the dry season, and the only thing that surprised Sengri was that it didn't happen more often. A moment later, he heard a *THUMP* echo across the plaza. He didn't need to look to know it had come from the gourd drummers seated on the pyramid steps.

"And...now they're getting impatient," he chuckled. "See you soon."

Elder Sengri left Tabba on the steps and started toward the center of the plaza in his oversized gold and green robe. It was the robe of the botara, the officiant of the Tara'apti, and required twice as much fabric to make as his araco robe, even though it was sleeveless. There were all sorts of geometric shapes embroidered in gold thread on the front and back, which represented the life of the Biyaya with hundreds of strange but wonderfully unique mul. It was said to have been designed by a blind weaver who claimed she was shown the intricate pattern in a vision by the Ageless Daughter herself. Sengri believed it and he greatly admired the pattern, but the immense weight of the robe was starting to bother him.

Out of the corner of his eye, Sengri saw festival goers continuing to fill in the gaps around the Grand Plaza, noisily watching him slowly making his way to the short mound in the center. The role of botara was traditionally played by the Yaya, the embodiment of the Biyaya Spirit, but Amnu was in no condition to officiate. Being the oldest able-bodied araco, the duty fell to Elder Sengri. Oddly enough, it was his second time as botara. Fifteen years earlier, Yaya Shakali had also fallen ill and Boaraco Sengri was the oldest able-bodied araco then too. He felt a great pressure to outperform his first attempt in the position, but then wondered if the pressure he felt was instead his body giving in to the heavy robe. He grunted, scrunched his shoulders, and tried to ignore the sweat dripping down his forehead and into the wrinkles on his face. He didn't remember the robe being so burdensome the first time, but then he had to smile at his own self-delusion. *That was fifteen years ago*, he told himself, *it isn't the robe that has changed*.

Botara Sengri stepped onto the mound and raised both of his well-oiled, wrinkly arms into the air. The miserable masses instantly fell silent, their spirits showing signs of lifting. The gourd drums began beating softly, slowly growing in intensity until their raucous thumping was reverberating in the chest of everyone in and around the plaza. He lingered in that moment, enjoying the sensation rippling up through his bare feet. It was refreshing. He almost didn't notice the sweat running down his spine anymore. And then the botara smiled and brought his arms down swiftly. The drumming stopped, but their thumps continued echoing off the buildings and around the plaza like ararun searching for a vessel to embody.

"Taycoay ah'Biyaya, Itabacan!" he proclaimed, and the crowd roared to life like the swell of a great wave. He quickly raised his wrinkled arms to quiet them before the wave crested, adding, "Today we celebrate the Sixty-Fourth Day of Biyaya!" Instantly, another wave followed the first, but Sengri let this one roll back and forth and around the plaza. He felt like he was bathing in their frothy enthusiasm, and then the word *refreshing* reentered his thoughts.

Despite recent events and the suffocating heat, the people were clearly unified in their thirst for entertainment. The Tara'apti was one of their oldest traditions, a once-every-fifteen-year festival that delighted each new generation, returning like the Feast of Muwan, only without the risk of children first getting snatched away by giant hawks. But Sengri was beginning to worry the festival would be seen as a convenient distraction from the recent chaos, which Yaya Amnu explained had resulted from a Mawoakin Conspiracy. Sengri assumed most Itabayiti believed the Yaya like he did, but he heard there were some on Yapaca arguing the entire story had been made up. They likened the raids on their villages to one of Yuraca's great generational storms, which would devastate Itabacan for days, especially Yapaca. In either case, Sengri hoped to use his second appointment as botara to remind his fellow Itabayiti where they had all come from, and then maybe they could begin to heal and move forward together.

"When Yaya Obnil officiated the first Day of Biyaya to honor his baba," Botara Sengri began again, his sweaty palms resting on his hips, "there were no Yapati, or Hatti. Cibmani had not yet been invented. There wasn't a Grand Plaza, or Pyramid of Mayu." He gestured toward the pyramid, which the jatbay band mistook for the signal to begin playing. "Knock it off!" the botara shouted at them with a stomp of his left foot, eliciting laughter from the crowd. Sengri sighed. "This Day of Biyaya, we must embrace that we, like the Biyaya, are first and foremost Itabayiti!" The people responded with another roaring wave, Sengri raised his arms, the wave crested, and then his gnarled fingers shot forward toward the Araco Residence as if he were trying to squeeze the structure and pull it across the plaza.

"Oh, Great Spirit, Creator of the World, set ablaze the ovens of Ora, the Birthplace of Life!" he shouted, expecting the band to follow as planned. When they didn't immediately play, Sengri stomped his left foot again several times, rolling his eyes.

Getting the message, the jatbays suddenly rang out a single chord in unison, followed by a single thump from all the gourd drums. This time, their echoes tugged and pulled at each other, slowly fading into the air above the plaza. It was like the final gasp of a thunderstorm, followed by the momentary calm of the jungle just before the noise from croaking frogs and other assorted rustling creatures returned. As everyone seemed to settle into the silence, the agur appeared from behind the Araco Residence clad in fiery red robes and carrying golden shields. The crowd cheered while the agur raced into formation, themselves sounding like a pack of stampeding boar. Once they were all in place, they stomped their sandaled feet against the stone plaza with a mighty *SLAP!*

"Agur!" they shouted, merging their shiny shields to become the oven doors of Ora.

It was a marvelous sight, more so than the first time Sengri had seen it. He quickly offered the Great Sky an appreciative glance. Ma'an traditionally covered himself in scattered clouds and obscured the Great Light during the Day of Biyaya, but now, sunlight brilliantly reflected off the shiny agur shields as they slowly started to spin. The effect of alternating gold shields and red robes was intended to represent the flames of Ora, but everyone was more mesmerized by the swirling streams of light reflecting all over the plaza. Even Botara Sengri was momentarily distracted, but he quickly reminded himself that he was the botara, and it was his responsibility to keep the festival moving along. He snapped to face the oven, raised his hands again, and continued his officiating duties.

"Yucahu, breathe your Great Spirit into Ora, the Genesis of the Ancient One!"

He threw his hands forward and the jatbays rang, the drums thumped, and then the golden shields opened to let in the Biyaya Spirit, closing rapidly afterward with a *THUD!* Out of the corner of his eye, he could see the festivalgoers getting to their feet in defiance of the heat. They leaned forward and shuffled around to get a better view of what was going to happen next, and Botara Sengri was more than happy to oblige them. With his hands still outstretched toward the agur, he continued.

"Oh, Lord of All, bring into your creation the Biyaya!"

He tugged at the air as if pulling on an invisible rope. The audience started cheering, the drums began thumping, and then the cheers transformed into claps in rhythm with the drums. The sound grew louder and louder, reverberating throughout the Grand Plaza until their raucous noise seemed capable of splitting the island in two. When it seemed as if the ground beneath his feet might actually split, the Biyaya suddenly burst through the swirling golden shields, knocking several of the agur to the ground and landing on one knee in the plaza. The Itabayiti went wild. They were hollering, whistling, and applauding with tears streaming down their glistening cheeks, which Sengri acknowledged could just have easily been sweat. His own sweaty, oily, and wrinkly arms trembled at his sides as a supreme sense of elation washed over him; one which he had not felt since he was a child in Mayu Hall, having just passed his first test of the araco. Sengri smiled, *Yes, you're exceeding your own expectations.*

The Biyaya stood in a boarhide tunic with gold stitching around the armholes and along the bottom edge. The symbol of Yucahu was branded into his chest piece, and a golden boarhide belt, shining as bright as the agur shields, held it all together. Bracelets and armbands made of gleaming white and purple shells adorned his wrists and biceps, and anklets of green grass and colorful flowers were strapped tightly just above his bare feet. On top of his head was the Kechet, which shone in Mawoi's great light like the Yaya's Palace on top of Mount Otaba. It was a spectacle for the generations, and Sengri was glad to see nearly all of Itabacan had turned out for the festival to witness it.

Botara Sengri raised his arms again, silencing the crowd, but also relishing in the power at his fingertips. But then something seemed wrong. The Biyaya was snapping his head back and forth like Ranar trying to break the neck of a spiny rat. The Biyaya then started violently slapping his own face, neck, and chest, before spinning around in circles as if dancing with an invisible partner. This was not part of the Tara'apti, and Sengri didn't know what to do but look around at the shocked masses. He offered them his own confused expression and noticed a murmur erupting in pockets throughout. The concerned whispers quickly intensified into a cacophony of chatter until a frightening hush suddenly fell on the plaza.

He turned from them in time to see the Biyaya throw off the Kechet, sending it tumbling through the air like the big, shiny pair of white conch shells it was. Sengri tried to chase after it in the hopes of catching it before it hit the ground, but the robe of the botara was simply too long and heavy. Instead, he stumbled off the mound and fell to his knees, just before the Kechet smashed into a dozen pieces on the stone plaza a reed away. Several people screamed, there was shouting from the adulu behind him, and Botara Sengri heard himself say, "Baga!" He scrambled the short distance on his hands and knees to pick up the destroyed ancient relic and saw Jokimbi was still writhing about on the ground not too far away. Fortunately, the moment he stretched his hand out to grab the first piece, Sengri saw what had happened.

"Crazy ants!" he shouted, awkwardly recoiling his hand and crawling backward.

There were more gasps in the crowd, followed by hushed whispers, but then Sengri saw one of the agur suddenly appear from inside the Araco Residence with a large water-gourd. The man ran over to Jokimbi, doused him in the face with the water, and then immediately ran away as if he were putting out a small fire. Sengri couldn't believe it. And then, several young men near the almec court started cheering, setting off a wave of applause and laughter throughout the plaza. Sengri frantically checked his own wrinkly arms and legs for the dreaded ants. When he was certain he didn't see or feel any, he released an exhausted but relieved sigh. He looked back over his shoulder at the Yaya's pavilion where the adulu had formed a wall around the Yaya and his family with their spears at the ready.

A few moments later, Jokimbi shakily got to his feet, sweat and water dripping from his chin, and Sengri was surprised to see a half-smile forming within Jokimbi's blotchy red face. Though he was clearly embarrassed, Jokimbi still waved at the crowd who responded with another round of cheers, instantly converting his half-smile into a full ear-to-ear grin. It was then that Sengri's body seized, and a breathless gasp escaped his lips as a sudden cool breeze struck the sweat on his neck and flowed down through the collar of his robe. It was both shocking and immensely refreshing at the same time. Taking the cue from the Great Wind, he quickly scrambled to his feet, dusted off his robe, and addressed the relieved and rowdy crowd.

"Maroha, we welcome you to the Tara'apti!" he shouted, earning a roar of applause from the masses. He looked at Jokimbi, "Is the Biyaya ready to continue?" Jokimbi nodded, weakly, as a beaten wrestler might. Satisfied, Sengri then turned to the Yaya's pavilion. "With the Yaya's blessing, we will continue the Tara'apti!" He bowed to both show his respect but to also let the breeze once again blow across his sweaty back. The festivalgoers seemed to remain quiet in anticipation of the Yaya's response. Hearing movement, Sengri looked up over his thinning eyebrows and saw Yaya Amnu trying to force the adulu out of the way with his wahas.

"Get out of the way!" the Yaya grumbled. "There, finally!" He took several labored breaths, locked eyes with Sengri, and said, "Please, proceed, Botara Sengri." But then, surprising Sengri, Yaya Amnu stood shakily with the help of his wahas and hollered with all of his frail might, "It's hot and we're all getting hungry!"

Sengri chuckled, everyone laughed and cheered, and then the band spontaneously played several beats of delightfully bouncy music. Botara Sengri stood up, spun around on his heel, and took a long, deep, and welcomed breath. Feeling ready to continue, he raised his sweaty, oily, wrinkly arms back into the air, and silence once again followed.

Down the sloping street from the Grand Plaza, Atu tried to ignore the echoing jatbays, thumping drums, and the mass of people cheering and applauding. It wasn't that he disliked festivals, he loved festivals and had been excited to be at his first Day of Biyaya, but he hadn't prepared himself for seeing Joba and Draha so soon into the day. Nearly running into her had ruined his morning, and if he hadn't immediately spotted Demican by the almec courts, Atu might have turned around and asked ferryman Haro to take him back to Conaca. The worst part was that she appeared to be happy. She had been smiling at everyone as she proudly showed off her marriage belt, rubbing on it like Anki when he first got his yaali tunic. While Demican had always wanted to be an almec player, Atu had wanted to be with Joba. Now he was just glad to be anywhere but within eyesight of her.

He sat beside Demican watching the almec players practice. The courts were surrounded by a lush green field of thick-bladed sweet grass, which Atu and Demican were plucking and using to make whistles. He heard the field was supposed to be trimmed by the Cult of Almec, but it looked like they had been neglecting their duties. In front of them, just beyond the edge of the grass, were four practice courts. Two of them were identical to the ceremonial court up at the plaza, while the other two were at ground level, their stone hoops affixed to pillars at either end. Piddso told them the wall-less courts improved a team's passing and aim. Atu had nodded along as if agreeing completely, but he never heard of a team winning without bouncing the ball off the walls.

"Here, try this one," he said, handing Demican an extra-thick blade of grass. Dem had big hands, which made it hard to make any sound but farting noises.

"They keep splitting!" Dem said in his newly developed, extremely deep voice. He then flicked the split blade of grass off his finger before taking the one Atu offered him.

"I guess you've got too much spirit in you." Atu blew over the piece of grass and through the space between his thumbs, creating the whistling sound of a cuckoo.

Dem chuckled, aligning the blade of grass between his large thumbs. "Not enough spirit to join the team, evidently."

"What?" Atu looked at him skeptically, and then he yanked a handful of grass out of the ground between his legs. "They're just practicing for the ceremonial match, that's all. Can't have a tree like you fumbling around out there and messing up their choreography."

"Choreography?"

"Ya know, for the match." Atu held the torn grass on his flat palm out in front of his mouth, and he was about to blow it away when a sudden breeze came up from the harbor and stole his fun. "Aww, man!" He watched the torn grass float away to his left, but he couldn't be mad at Maroha for trying to cool off the day. He turned back to feel the wind on his face and noticed Demican staring at him. "What?"

Demican tilted his head. "Are you saying the match will be planned out like the Tara'apti? Like a play?"

"Yeah, why?"

Demican shook his head as he brought his thumbs up to his mouth. "That's disappointing," he said, and then he blew on the blade of grass, but nothing happened. After a few adjustments, he blew again and this time his thumbs instantly farted. Atu nearly fell over laughing. "Baga! Why am I so bad at this?"

"I told you; you got too much spirit in you. You're blowing too hard!"

Demican flicked the blade of grass away like he did the others and watched the wind take it. "Well, at least we're trimming the grass."

"Which is ridiculous," Atu scoffed. "I thought the Cult of Almec was supposed to be taking care of this?"

"They were, but Piddso said so many of them had been detained by the agur that the few who were left just couldn't keep up."

Atu rolled his eyes, "Couldn't keep up? That's the dumbest thing I've ever heard."

Demican shrugged, "Piddso said it."

Atu huffed. Now he had another reason to hate the cults. He spit on the ground, thinking about all of them – the Cult of Mayu, the Cult of Mawoi, and even the Cult of Almec. There were dozens of cults throughout Itabacan, and every cultist was as useless as the next. At least the Cult of Almec devoted their lives to something interesting, even if it was only because they believed the game ball embodied the Great Spirit and the hoops were the Birthplace of Life. Atu suddenly realized the Day of Biyaya ceremonial match was probably going to reenact the cult's idiotic beliefs, and the realization made him feel just as disappointed as his friend.

"Why does the Cult of Almec trim the grass?" Dem asked.

"Baba told us, a long time ago, a handful of council members were angry that players weren't contributing to Itabacan – except for playing almec," Atu explained, tugging on another handful of grass. "Evidently, they proposed that players at least be responsible for something else. Somebody suggested the beautification of Itabaca and, well, that's what happened."

"Beautification?"

"A bunch of sweaty, dirty, rowdy man-boys expected to make things look pretty."

Demican laughed, "And that's why the Cult of Almec stepped in."

"Yup." Atu tossed the grass into the wind and watched it blow away.

"Well," Dem started, pausing to stretch his long arms over his head. "Even a little overgrown, it is the best-looking patch of grass in all of Itabacan."

Atu snickered, "Sure. Hey, where's Hamsi?" He had been meaning to ask about their friend, but his thoughts kept getting invaded with images of Joba. He felt more distracted now not being anywhere near her than he had out on the canuti working the lines alongside her.

"My brother said..." Dem began, but Atu cut him off.

"Addo?"

"Yeah, he said the family members of the coani who went on that quest are being held on Chacuca for some reason."

"What?" Atu nearly screamed.

"I guess it was a council decision."

"What?!" he did scream. "Baba didn't say anything about that!" Demican only shrugged in response. "Will they be allowed to come to the festival?" he asked, and his friend shrugged again. "They should have detained my brother too," he joked, but Demican didn't laugh. Atu guessed he was probably thinking about Yaeel, which kind of made Atu feel bad. "Hey, I'm sorry. Wouldn't it be nice if Yaeel was still alive to..." He tried to make up for his bad joke, but Demican just stared at him with watery eyes.

"They arrested by baba too," Dem said, his deep voice squeaking for the first time that day. He then wiped his nose on the collar of his tunic, cleared his throat, and then continued watching the almec players practice.

Atu wasn't sure how to respond. First his father rushed them out of the residence and onto the ferry, which he just now realized had caused him to forget his tunic belt. He yanked out another handful of grass and tossed it aside. And then Joba just had to be right there at the top of the Steps of Ajan, greeting all of Itabacan with Draha and their ugly, matching marriage belts. It was ridiculous! Atu wanted to enjoy his first Day of Biyaya at the council pavilion with everyone else, not be stuck there with Dem making farting noises, and not knowing when he might unharness another sad story into his lap. He yanked out another handful of grass and tossed it to the side as well. It was too much drama for one day, and Atu was including the Tara'apti. He needed to think about something else — anything that didn't make him want to crawl around the field and yank out every last blade of sweet grass.

He brought his boney knees up to his chest, draped his arms over them, and looked down at his slightly less pale skin. Sailing lessons had been canceled indefinitely as the Yaya's investigations began targeting the coani, or so Atu's father told him. He thought it was just a little convenient, his father needed his help in the clay pits, but it turned out to be a nice change of pace. The only downside was having to scrape bits of clay out from under his fingernails every evening, but he had to admit, his skin was noticeably tanner somehow, and it seemed smoother too. Atu had tried moisturizing with coconut oil like he remembered his mother doing, but it always ended up making him look like a polished conch shell, which made him grimace. He may be destined to vomit over midribs or dig mud out from under his fingernails for the rest of his life, but at least he knew, no matter what, he could always count on himself.

There was a sudden commotion down at the harbor, interrupting Atu's rambling thoughts. He noticed Demican was on his feet with a hand to his forehead, blocking out the sun. The almec players down in the sunken court hadn't heard a thing and continued practicing.

"Whoa!" Dem exclaimed.

"What is it?" Atu squinted as he stood, but he still couldn't see that far.

"That is one beat up canuti!" he replied, but then he quickly dropped his hand.

"Numila!" they shouted to each other at the same time.

Demican instantly took off at a sprint, his long sturdy legs pounding the cibmani street. Atu followed as best he could, zipping past the vendors who were too busy fending off their goods from the persistent birds to notice anything else. Demican reached the agur huts first where a lone, startled warrior stood pointing toward the harbor. Atu watched him fling himself around the edge of the gate by grabbing the inner support beam, nearly bringing the entire ramshackle structure crashing to the ground. Atu had to dance over and around palm fronds and pieces of wood that had broken free in his friend's wake, but then he charged down the Steps of Ajan two steps at a time.

When he stepped onto the stone dock, he saw a tattooed man lying on his back near the mooring post. The man was missing half of his left arm and had what looked like a torn piece of a tunic wrapped around his bloody stump. Then he saw half-a-dozen random people attempting to lift the mast off the spine of the canuti, aided by Demican who had jumped on to help. Some of them were clearly vendors, there were a couple agur, and then Atu recognized old Haro and his frantically twitching cheek. As soon as the mast was in the air, Atu noticed Bocoani Numila, and he was pulling on something. Atu stepped closer and saw he was pulling on an arm, and then Numila dragged the attached body farther out from underneath a blood-stained sail. As the mast splashed into the harbor, teams of seagulls overhead squawked their approval.

Numila dropped to his knees and placed his ear to the chest of the person lying on the spine. Atu saw it was a woman, but he couldn't see her face. Numila didn't appear to like what he heard, or maybe what he didn't hear, and there were tears streaming down his cheeks. He suddenly slammed his fist on the reed boat and shouted, "No! Please, Yucahu, no!"

Atu guessed the woman had to be Koyay, Bocoani Numila's wife. "What can we do, Bocoani?" he heard himself ask.

Numila looked up with his exhausted red eyes and seemed to recognize him and Demican for the first time. "Boys," he sighed and got to his feet. He pointed to the tattooed man. "Ruruga needs a lesini immediately." And then he pointed to a strange looking jungle-green bag tied at the top with sail line. "Please, run that to the Yaya."

"Everyone is at the Grand Plaza," Atu said, a little unsure why the bocoani was telling them what needed to be done instead of the agur. "I bet there's a lesini is up there somewhere."

"Good, and..." Numila started to say something else but looked down at his wife's lifeless body and began crying again. He stood there with his bloody hands on his soaking wet hips and sobbed so hard no more words would out.

Atu hadn't noticed Demican retrieve the bag until he leapt onto the dock and handed it to him. "I'll stay here and help them," he said. "You run as fast as your little bird legs can carry you!"

Atu rolled his eyes and started to respond, but he found he didn't have anything witty to say. Instead, he nodded, "Right." He then turned and started running with all of his might.

CHAPTER THIRTY-TWO

KINA

Up at the Grand Plaza, Kina Wani reminded herself she was actually enjoying her first Day of Biyaya, even though it had started so awkwardly. She couldn't remember ever seeing anyone writhe about on the ground twice in one mawa before, especially not the same grown man and both times due to pranks involving insect attacks. Kina thought it was funny, even if it did almost ruin the Tara'apti entirely. She was beginning to understand why someone like Sheka would be tempted to pull these kinds of pranks. Of course, she only assumed Sheka had been responsible. Anki and Biacoya both told her how clever the girl was, which also made Kina smile – *girls should not be underestimated*.

Her soft black hair was braided into three tight braids that began at her hairline and ran all the way over her head and down to the middle of her shoulders. Coincidently, her mother's hair was done in the exact same wani style, which Kina knew was not coincidental at all. At least she was allowed to keep a few dark-red flowers tucked into her braids here and there. Additionally, they also shared matching white tunics trimmed in gold thread and held tight with matching gold belts. Her father's outfit was likewise coordinated, but he added a long, sleeveless boarhide robe because he was the Yaya and expected to wear the most uncomfortable looking things – especially on extremely hot days like today. Fortunately, when the Kechet got smashed, her father wisely offered his own conch-shell headdress to replace it, which completed the Biyaya's outfit and relieved the Yaya of the burden.

Kina fanned herself with a piece of palm-bark Bolari had shaved thin and attached to a wooden handle with leather string. He even helped her paint the outline of her hand on the front in dark-red paint, but she didn't tell him she was inspired by the many hands in the cave on the cliffs. The fan worked extremely well; much better than the large leaves she saw other girls using. Her mother had a similar fan that Bolari had also made, but her mother's was quite a bit bigger and had the symbol of Yucahu burned into the front. Kina had asked Bolari how he made the design without setting the whole fan on fire, but he didn't tell her, which she thought was fair.

On the mound in the center of the plaza, Chuka held hands with the Biyaya and danced in circles to a sweet melody performed by a single jatbay. The soloist was a girl not much older than Kina, but she was somehow able to make her stringed-gourd instrument resonate with beautiful swooping tones. Kina loved it, especially in contrast with the silly dance taking place. She saw the swelling of Jokimbi's face had gone down a bit, leaving behind dozens of little, red, painful-looking ant bites. To his credit, he continued smiling through his humiliation, while Boagur Gudugu played the Great Boar ancestor with an open-mouthed scowl. He looked like he was going to get sick at any moment. His head bobbed about like a coconut in the shallows, and his sandaled feet flopped around like they had forgotten how to be feet. To add to the spectacle, agur warriors pretended to be the waves of the Bocoa, wiggling up and down on their bellies all around the dancing men like beached fish.

Kina glanced at her father, hoping to see him enjoying the festivities, but he appeared to be asleep. He always appeared to be sleeping lately. His sweaty head rested on his fist, his dusty elbow on the armrest of the throne, and his thin, sunken cheeks looked like pieces of raw boarhide someone had stretched over a gourd drum but forgot to tighten. She inhaled quickly and looked away, successfully stemming the flow of tears. She and her mother had hardly slept the past several days, each of them worrying in their own ways. Kina understood why her father avoided eating and believed the threat on his life was very real, but she didn't understand why he would resort to starving himself to death. The only times she had seen him eat were when he made her cry during evening meals, which had become a near-nightly occurrence. But then he started taking his uneaten meals into his bedchamber alone where he wouldn't be bothered by her tears.

She could not understand why anyone would want to harm her father. He was the nicest, most sincere man she had ever known. Of course, she didn't know a lot of men. She was only ten, after all, and had lived on top of a mountain her entire young life. There was Bolari, and Boacodu Basa gave her scribe lessons, and there were the various adult male attendants and guards wandering around the palace, but that was about the extent of her interaction with men. Boys, on the other hand, were another matter entirely.

Kina was only beginning to understand the often-frustrating nature of boys. Her mother made sure to give her daily reminders of how dumb and impressionable they were, but Kina was also actively learning on her own. From what she had gathered, she didn't think boys were all that simple. Sure, they usually wanted to avoid responsibility and have fun, but she had a sneaking suspicion there might be something deeper going on. After all, her father had once been a boy and he now lived for responsibility. He was rarely distracted by games like Biacoya, or silly stories like Anki, or shiny objects like Amoc. Her father was a man and in Kina's eyes he was the best of them. It didn't make sense for anyone to want to poison him, especially not with the fruit from a strange old tree no one had ever heard of. But now, even without being poisoned, he became confused and quietly complained to her and her mother about severe pains inside his head.

Just the day before, her parents were arguing over postponing the Day of Biyaya. Her mother wanted to wait another mawa and put more distance between the festival and the recent traumatic events, but her father hoped the distraction of the festival would help cool the rising tensions. Kina had listened to them from across the hall in her room, and though she agreed with her mother, she had been relieved to hear her father's determination win out. Shortly afterward, her mother yelled for their attendants to send for Lesini Gigal, and then her father collapsed on their chamber balcony. The more she thought about it, the more concerned she became he might have already been poisoned. *Could they have gotten to him some other way?* she wondered, not noticing that she had stopped fanning herself and was picking at her fingernails again.

A sudden commotion snapped Kina's attention back to the Tara'apti. One of the agur waves had stopped wiggling and was standing, bringing the whole production to another unexpected halt. A moment later, he pointed and then she and everyone else gathered in the Grand Plaza followed his outstretched finger to a strange sight over by the almec court. There they saw a pale-skinned boy ducking and dodging between, under, and over spectators, and he appeared to be followed by a flock of shrieking seagulls. The horrid creatures dove after him, and he frantically batted at them with one flailing arm over his head. The entire plaza had fallen silent, except for the solo jatbay player who humorously didn't know what to do and continued playing. When the boy was only a few reeds away from the Yaya's pavilion, Kina recognized him as Anki's brother, Atu. And then the adulu surrounded her and her family again with their spears, and annoyingly blocked her view.

"Yaya Amnu!" Atu shouted, hunching over and out of breath. Kina peered at him through a gap between two adulu and saw he carried what looked like a green bag – a bag that appeared to be the target of the squawking beasts. "Yaya Amnu?"

"My love," Kina's mother nudged her father awake.

"Yes?" her father grumbled.

"Another one of Abensu's sons is here – I'm sure to ruin your day," her mother whispered but Kina heard every word. She had involuntarily become quite sensitive to her mother's condescending whispers, to the extent Kina was confident she could pick her mother's hushed voice out of a pack of howlers on the far side of the mountain in the middle of a downpour.

"Abensu?" her father asked, still waking up from his nap and a little confused.

"Yes, his son..."

"Anki?"

"No, Atura. He appears to..."

"He doesn't like it when people use his full name," Kina blurted out, though she wasn't sure why.

"Don't interrupt," her mother told her, causing Kina to shrink in her seat.

She looked down at her fingers. Over the past mawa she had picked at and peeled off strips of her fingernails to prevent them from chipping. Some Itabayiti were chewers, others were pickers, and those with attendants could order them to use a chaak to cut their nails cleanly for them. Her mother had told her they needed trimming, but Kina forgot, and then her pointer finger got chipped in the cave on the cliffs. To keep it from snagging on her tunic, she picked at it until there were no pointy edges left and the tip of her finger felt smooth. She didn't like biting her nails, and she didn't want to bother their attendants, and it just seemed more convenient to pick at them herself. The problem was, no matter how much picking and peeling she did, they just kept growing and it was hard to keep her fingernails smooth and matching.

"Move aside!" Yaya Amnu yelled at the guards. He tried to push them with his frail arms but then he gave up, grabbed his wahas, and poked at them until they moved. "And what is that horrendous sound?"

"Seabirds, my love."

"Birds?" he asked and Unana nodded. "Well, get rid of them!" He tapped Boadulu Konoma on his shin with the wahas. "Now!" he shouted.

"Yes, my Yaya!" the boadulu said, bowing. Konoma immediately ordered the two men standing in front of Kina to go after the birds, which she hoped might give her a better view of what was going to happen. She caught Konoma rubbing his shin where her father had tapped him, which made her smile.

The two adulu clumsily stumbled down the stairs in their crimson tunics, the butts of their spear shafts clacking against the stone, and then each one stopped to look back at the boadulu. After he nervously encouraged them to continue, they did, but Kina thought it was just a little silly. It reminded her of when Jokimbi had to corral the boys in the reed bog. To her amusement, just like how the boys recklessly slashed at the reeds, the two adulu started thrusting their coral-tipped spears wildly into the air. The squawking gulls easily avoided getting stabbed by the poorly placed jabs, all while the jatbay soloist continued playing. Kina couldn't see the jatbay girl anymore because Konoma was annoyingly in her way, but she had to wonder what the girl was thinking.

Once again, the contrast between the sweet melody and what she was witnessing was amusing and Kina started to giggle, which made her mother snicker, which then made her father let out a weak little chuckle. She wondered if the other jatbay players were encouraging the girl to keep playing, or if she just thought it would be funny on her own. Either way, Kina was grateful, because it was the first time her family had laughed together in days. That is, until Atu managed to ruin it by finally catching his breath.

"Numila – harbor – lesini..." he gasped, continuing to duck away from the wild spears and psychotic seagulls. At the mention of Numila, her father's chuckle instantly vanished, followed by her mother's snicker, and then Kina reluctantly let her giggle fade as well. "It's bad," Atu continued. "Bocoani Numila said to give you this."

He held up the green bag, but it was instantly covered in half-a-dozen noisily flapping, screeching birds, forcing him to drop it. The seagulls went for the contents of the bag, clawing, pecking, and tearing bits of fabric away. White feathers flew everywhere, and bits of green string floated through the air with puffs of white dander. A crowd started to form around the scene, while hushed murmuring spread across the plaza like wind rustling the leaves in the trees.

WHAM-WHAM-WHAM!

Yaya Amnu slammed his wahas on the stone floor of the pavilion, quieting the murmurs, but the birds remained undeterred. "Yucahu, forgive!" he shouted. "Urtulu? What are you waiting for?"

"Konoma, my love," her mother whispered, correcting him.

"Yes – yes..." her father grumbled, "...Konoma!"

"Uh – Adulu!" Konoma gulped as loud as he could. He was clearly not used to his new position.

"Adulu!" his men responded, stomping their feet.

Konoma pointed at the gaggle of birds, "*Kotedu!*"

At the order to attack, the rest of the adulu charged down the steps with their spears, while the first two merely shifted from jabbing their spears into the air to landing killing blows on the frantic birds on the ground. There were a few shocked screams from the crowd, intermixed with several enthusiastic cheers as the dreaded seabirds finally faced their destiny. After the first few gulls were skewered, the survivors got the hint and took flight, squawking angrily at the adulu before joining the rest of their flock on the roof of the pavilion. It was simultaneously the most absurd but also terrifying experience of Kina's young life. What remained at the foot of the pavilion was a bloody mess of dead but still twitching gulls, feathers, and shredded green fabric.

"Finally!" her father exclaimed, twisting his pinky finger around in his ear. "Now, did I hear you say something about Numila?"

Kina heard Anki's brother repeat what he said before, adding additional details about Ruruga or something, but she was no longer listening to him. She was horrified by the violence, but also strangely captivated by the mess left behind.

Having seen the agur slaughter a massive boar with huge, pointy tusks, she was no stranger to gruesome sights. Kina guessed she was probably six or seven at the time and recalled watching them hang the beast by its hind hooves. The boagur carefully pierced the base of its throat with a long thin blade to drain the blood, which they collected in a large ceramic bowl. Once that was done, the agur skinned and disemboweled the creature with their chaak blades. She remembered not being grossed out or scared at all but fascinated by how each cut appeared to be made with great skill and care, as if each slice was part of a ritual. In fact, she recalled the boagur muttering a chant, which she remembered thinking was similar to one the Yucakin performed. Unfortunately, she didn't understand the chants then and couldn't remember either one now.

The agur separated each piece of the boar, whispering those ancient words, and she was told that every little bit of the creature would be used by someone somewhere in Itabacan, which she thought made a lot of sense. The Itabayiti didn't like to waste food and generally preferred to keep things clean and tidy. The final step of the ritual had been the matter of the tusks. If they were larger than those on the boagur's current headdress, a ceremonial bonefire was lit, the boar's head was placed on it, the Great Spirit was released, and a new headdress was made from the skull. Kina would never forget as long as she lived watching Boagur Gudugu take off his old headdress, dip it into the bowl of thick, gooey blood, and then whisper to it before tossing the bloody leather-wrapped jawbone into the blazing flames. When she asked him what he had whispered, the boagur said, "Sutak'balo." It was the first time she heard anyone utter the phrase and, for some reason, it just now popped into her head again.

She admired the contrast between the dead birds, bloody feathers, and the torn and lifeless green fabric. The idea that Sutak may have had a hand in creating the mess enticed her. *Or had it been Karun?* Karun was Sutak's sister and the Withering Spirit of Decay. Both were said to be the children of the Great Spirit, the younger siblings of Orlil, the Ageless Daughter. Bolari told her the Great Spirit passed these responsibilities down to his children as he became busy breathing life into new and wonderous creatures far away from Itabacan. He said the Gusiti were one of Yucahu's creatures, but Kina wasn't sure she believed that. She also didn't know that she believed any of the Yuki'at, but it was something distracting to think about instead of the violent assault she had just witnessed.

Kina looked up from the mess to see Gudugu joining the small crowd forming around the Yaya's pavilion. He had removed his headdress and tucked it up under his arm. A look of relief had replaced his scowl, but Kina saw that he still appeared to be on the verge of getting sick. She wondered if Karun might be at work on him too, which made her wonder the same about her father. She turned to look at the Yaya and suddenly became aware he was talking. It took a moment to focus on his words through the tangle of invasive thoughts running wild through her mind.

"...collect everyone on the island and bring them to the plaza."

"Yes, my Yaya," Gudugu bowed, but then he suddenly vomited. His chunky, gray spew splattered everywhere, sending the adulu leaping away as if trying to avoid a pool of lava. The boagur just grumbled and casually wiped his mouth on his sweaty forearm. "Baga."

"Aww, man!" Kina heard Atu shout from behind the scrambling guards. Her mother gasped, but Kina couldn't help but smile. It was disgusting, of course, but not as bad as the slaughter of the gulls, and she had also been anticipating Gudugu getting sick all morning.

"If I had actually eaten anything in days, seeing that might have just killed me," her father commented quietly.

"My apol-logies." Gudugu bowed again, and then he raised one glaring eye up to the sun. "Muhwo-ee's not pleased wit-me. I'll leave a kanbati behind to clean-this, an keep'em here in the plaza." He nodded over his shoulder to the gathered masses.

"Good idea," her father agreed, but then added, "and get yourself some water, Gudugu."

"Yes, my Yaya."

Her father looked around as if searching for someone. "Sengri? You there?"

"I am," came the meager reply. "Excuse me," Sengri mumbled, peaking around Gudugu's boulder-like shoulders. Kina noticed he was keeping his long robe hiked up and off the ground, even though he was a reed away from the vomit.

"You're the botara. Tell everyone to remain in the plaza, and..." Yaya Amnu suddenly snapped his head to look at the pyramid. "And tell that girl she can stop playing now!"

"Yes, my Yaya," Sengri bowed and then immediately gestured for the jatbay girl to stop, which she did. He bowed again to the Yaya as he backed away, lifting his enormous robe just above the ground, and then he spun around and shuffled his old feet over toward the mound.

Kina passively watched him, twirling the handle of her fan with the tips of her fingers and wondering if her father would have been a better botara. Botara Sengri raised his wrinkly arms to get the crowd's attention and began relaying the Yaya's instructions, "My fellow Itabayiti..." But Kina didn't care to hear the same message again and looked down at her twirling fan.

"The inside of my head keeps pounding," her father said, pinching the bridge of his nose. "It's like a hundred ciba tampers smashing the dirt at the same time. And why do I smell omaki?" Kina instantly became alarmed, recognizing his complaints were the same as the day before.

"Gudugu," the Yaya called for the boagur again, a twinge of pain lingering there in his voice at the end of the boagur's name. Kina looked and saw the boagur had begun giving orders to his men and had his back turned. "Gudugu!"

"Yes, my Yaya?" he spun around on his heels, appearing confused why he had been called upon again.

Kina twirled her fan faster.

"No!" her father quickly corrected himself, pinching the bridge of his nose again. "No...I-I meant...Konoma."

"My Yaya?" Gudugu asked, understandably wanting to be sure.

Yaya Amnu waved his frail hand at him. "You have your orders, Gudugu. I need Konoma!" he demanded.

Konoma first cleared his throat before he asked, "My Yaya?"

Kina watched the boagur roll his eyes and slowly turn back to his men, and then she saw him take a big swig from a strange-looking water gourd attached to his hip by a long leather string. When she returned her attention to her father, she found him vigorously rubbing at his dry, pale cheeks and jaw with his sweaty palms.

Her fan twirled even faster.

"Numila..." her father tried to say, but then he abruptly slumped over in his throne.

Kina instantly knew what was happening, but nobody else did, and she didn't know how to handle it. Her father made her and her mother swear to secrecy about his earlier collapse, and he had released their attendants for the festival. She quickly looked to her mother for guidance, but her mother's eyes were closed as if in prayer. Kina was about to look away when she noticed her mother's mouth was moving ever so slightly. She squinted, hoping narrowing her eyelids might improve her hearing, but all she could hear was the gentle breeze blowing in her ear.

She twirled faster.

"Agur!"

The warriors startled Kina, causing her to lose her grip on the neck of the fan and send it twirling out of her hands and down the pavilion steps, to where it broke into two pieces on the hard stone ground beside Atu's bloody green bag. The agur loudly stomped their sandaled feet before marching across the plaza with their orders; Gudugu half-walked, half-stumbled behind them taking another drag from his strange-looking gourd.

"Unana Wani?" Konoma tried to get her mother's attention.

"Itaba?" Kina immediately followed the boadulu's lead. She poked her mother's forearm with a timid finger and waited for a response, but when nothing happened, Kina started to worry she might have to assume the role of interim ruler and felt the well of tears forming in her eyes.

With both of her parents seemingly incapacitated, it would be her right as eldest wani, but she wasn't ready for that much responsibility. She was still a child. Children were supposed to be having fun and avoiding responsibility. She had seen some children playing around the nimuru earlier, and that was where she should have been. She should be laughing and chasing her friends while cool, refreshing water splashed on her face. The tears came streaming down her ebony cheeks, and Kina snatched her mother's arm with both hands and yelled, "ITABA-WANI!" Just then, her mother's right eye popped open like a yellow fish's mouth, and Kina nearly died.

"Patience, child," her mother calmly whispered.

Kina released a heavy sigh of tearful relief but didn't let go of her mother's arm. "But baba..." She looked around cautiously before whispering, "It's happening again, and I...I-I don't think...I can keep our secret any longer." She was sobbing. Atu was staring at them, waving at floating gull dander in front of his pink face. Boadulu Konoma's wide eyes bounced from her to her mother, and then to her slumped-over father and back again. There were the adulu with their coral spears shimmering in the midday sun, and the small-but-growing crowd of strangers just behind them. And then she realized the cacophony of squawking seagulls had replaced the jatbay girl's sweet melody, and...

"This is Bogula's robe!" came a smooth but firm voice Kina instantly recognized as belonging to her ditaba, Lesini Gigal. She quickly wiped off her tear-streaked cheeks and watched Gigal prod at the green bag with her bare foot. As she did, Kina noticed the horrid birds had mysteriously fallen silent.

"Took you long enough," her mother said, snapping Kina's turquoise eyes back and forth. She felt as if she were trying to follow an invisible almec ball bouncing between teams.

"Yes, well..." Gigal paused to smile at Kina, but then glowered at the people standing around her. "There seems to be an inordinate amount of Itabayiti between the council pavilion and here."

"Unavoidable," her mother replied, dismissively. "Now, our Yaya needs your attention."

"I see that, and I see Bogula's robe here at my feet." She pointed at the robe insistently. "Why is she not in it?"

"Answers will come in due course. You have my word."

"Hmm..." Gigal knelt down, picked up the broken handle of Kina's palm-bark fan, and began rummaging through Bogula's bloody robe with it.

"Boadulu Konoma."

"Uh..."

"If you don't mind," her mother gestured with both of her upturned hands to the lack of privacy around their pavilion, to which the boadulu acknowledged with a nod of his head.

"Adulu!" he shouted.

"Adulu!" they responded, stomping.

"*Lu'wani!*"

With the order to protect them, the adulu charged back up the pavilion steps, their sandaled feet slapping against the stone and exciting the seagulls as they surrounded Kina and her family. Shoulder to shoulder with their spears at their sides, they also blocked her view again, but she didn't mind it this time. She had quickly become irritated with all of the staring people and was glad to be rid of them.

Her mother suddenly jumped up off her chair and turned to her father. Kina was still trying to keep from sobbing but managed to ask, "How can I help?"

"Here," her mother handed her the large fan. "We need to cool him down."

Kina nodded and took the fan, along with a deep, calming breath. She climbed over the armrests and stood on her mother's now-empty seat, positioned herself over her father, and then she started fanning him. She watched her mother carefully peel his boarhide robe from off his thin shoulders, and then she wiggled it out from behind and beneath him. Once the heavy-looking thing was free, she let it crumple into a pile on the dais floor. Then she tore a strip of fabric from the bottom of her father's white tunic, snatched a water gourd out from underneath his throne, un-stoppered the top, poured a bit onto the torn fabric, rung it out, and then started blotting at his face with the now-damp cloth. Kina was amazed by her mother's effortless, swift, and calculated movements.

"Found it!" Kina heard Gigal shout from the other side of the wall of adulu.

"Great! Konoma, let Lesini Gigal through!"

"Yes, Unana Wani," came the snappy reply.

To Kina, her mother sounded slightly panicked like when Kina had been stung by all those wasps, but less angry and more urgent. A moment later, a gap appeared between two of the guards and Gigal's long legs strolled through.

"Do you have a..." she started to ask but Unana cut her off.

"There are cups beneath my seat."

"Taycoay, Kina," Gigal greeted her in a hurried voice.

"Taycoay, Gigal-ditaba," Kina replied, watching Gigal glide down into a kneeling position in front of the chair she was standing on. Kina continued fanning her father and looked out through the gap in the wall of adulu to the still-growing crowd. They seemed to be pushing toward the bottom steps of the pavilion, which Kina thought was just a little threatening. She was once again relieved when the gap closed.

"There was something else in Bogula's robe," Gigal said, retrieving and arranging the gourd cups on the floor next to her knees. "I have to be honest, I'm not entirely sure I know what it is." Kina watched her pull a wooden vial from somewhere inside of her robe and pour its contents into one of the cups. Next, she dumped a handful of browning leaves she had retrieved from somewhere else and dropped those into the cup. Lastly, the handle from Kina's broken fan appeared, and Gigal used it to smush the ingredients together into a chunky, dead-moss green slime that smelled horrible.

"Yaya Amnu?" Kina heard Atu call out to her unconscious father again.

"Who's that?" Gigal asked.

"Tiam's boy, Atur..." her mother started to answer, but then stopped herself and looked at Kina. "Atu," she finished with a roll of her eyes; Kina smiled back at her.

"And what does he want?"

"He brought the green bag," Kina explained.

"Bogula's robe," her mother corrected her. "Brought it up from the harbor."

"I see. And is that where our Bogula..."

"Unana Wani?" Atu cut her off, sounding closer and a bit more desperate.

"Thank you for your service to your Yaya," Unana replied. "You may go now."

There was a moment of silence, but then Atu asked, "What about lesini for Numila?"

Unana sighed. "I have already sent lesini to the harbor," she said, which was news to Kina, but then she recalled that she had been quite distracted by the slaughter of the gulls.

"Oh."

"Amnu, is there anything I can do?" This time it was Atu's father, Abensu. Kina recognized his deep voice because he had come by their pavilion earlier to talk with her father. And then Kina's face lit up as she suddenly realized Anki might be with him. He hadn't been with Abensu

340

before, but her father asked him to bring Anki the next time he came by. She looked at her mother to find her mother already staring right back at her.

"Abensu, is Anki with you?" her mother asked.

There was another moment of silence, and then he answered, "Unana Wani?"

"I am."

Another brief silence passed, allowing the sound of the continuous breeze, the seagulls, and the incoherent murmuring from the crowd to enter the pavilion. Abensu finally answered, "Yes. Both of my boys are standing next to me."

Her mother knelt down to add more cool water to the strip of fabric in her hands, and then she hollered at the boadulu again, "Konoma!"

"Yes, Unana Wani?"

"You may allow Abensu and his son Anki through!"

"Yes, Unana Wani."

"Here," Gigal handed Unana the gourd cup half-full of light-green liquid. "It's the best we can do without being able to boil it."

"I'm sure it will be fine." She added a splash of fresh water to the mixture and stirred it with her finger.

"Also, do you know what this is?" Gigal held out a handful of bright-red berries she pulled from somewhere inside of her robe. Kina was a little surprised her ditaba would be asking anyone anything because Gigal always seemed to know more about everything than everyone.

Just then, another gap appeared and Abensu and Anki stepped through. Out of the corner of her eye, Kina saw her mother drop the damp strip of fabric over the berries. It seemed intentional, but she could never tell with her mother.

"Is that..." Abensu started to ask but was distracted by the swiftly closing gap behind him.

"Tizaka? Yes," her mother quickly answered, handing Gigal the cup of green juice. She stood to face Anki's father, who was easily two hands taller than her, placed her fists on her hips, and then pushed her shoulders back with confidence. "Abensu, I need you to gather any coani you can find and take them down to the harbor." Kina saw his eyes jump from her mother to her unconscious father and back again, clearly concerned about the Yaya, but then she wondered if he was actually confirming whether or not he needed to follow her mother's orders. "If what Atu says is true," Unana continued, "we must move Numila's canuti before anyone is allowed to leave the plaza."

Abensu nodded slowly. "Not wanting to spark another controversy," he guessed. "Very wise, Unana Wani. But — if I may — why not call for one of the coani?"

"Because you're already here," she snapped, but then her mother sighed. Kina noticed her weight shift from one foot to the other as she popped her hip out to the side, which was how Kina could tell her mother's patience was wearing thin. "But also, because they are not you."

Her mother's comment appeared to make Abensu nervous, though he was clearly pretending it hadn't, which made Kina snicker. She had never seen Anki's father so squirmy. She followed his speckled-brown and green eyes as they wandered up to the ceiling, around to the right, and then out to the council pavilion. She pursed her lips and turned back to see where else Abensu's eyes might have wandered only to find him staring right back at her. She immediately looked down, but doing so brought her startled eyes in line with Anki's, which then made him shy away behind his father. The instant embarrassment she felt seemed enough to loosen every tight braid on her head, and Kina quickly turned her whole body to hide the big dumb smile on her face.

Abensu chuckled and said, "I can do that, Unana Wani — for Amnu."

"That will be enough. Thank you, Abii."

"Can I leave Anki here with you?" he asked.

"But baba..." Anki tried to protest, but Unana spoke over him.

"Of course," she said, and then hollered, "Konoma!" This time, the boadulu didn't even get a chance to respond as his men understood the drill and opened the gap on their own.

"Tayaga," Abensu said. "May the Great Healer smile upon you."

"Go!" she shouted at him.

Abensu left, the gap closed, and Kina continued fanning her father. Gigal stood next to her, blocking her view of Anki with her pillar of hair, which was just fine with Kina — though she was curious what he might be thinking. She bet it was the first time Anki had ever been left alone with three women while also surrounded by over a dozen armed adulu. The thought made her smile, which she found comforting as she looked down on her withering father.

Gigal dabbed at his chapped lips with the damp cloth until she seemed satisfied, and then she brought the gourd cup of foul-smelling slurry up to his mouth.

"Not yet," Unana stopped her. "Where did you put those berries?"

"Back in my robe, why?"

"Give them to me," she said, but Gigal hesitated. "Now, sister!"

"Fine!" Gigal pulled them out from within her robe and handed them over.

"Anki, come here," Unana demanded. Kina peaked around Gigal's hair again and saw the shocked expression on his face.

"M-Me?" He pointed to himself, and her mother nodded adamantly.

"Yes. Take these berries and crush them as best you can." She looked down and saw the broken fan handle on the floor, picked it up, and handed it to him as well. "Here, use this."

"But I don't..."

"Do it, and I will allow you to sit with Kina for the remainder of the festival." When he heard this, Anki's eyebrows nearly raised off the top of his head, making Kina snicker. "I will assume your silence is compliance. Now, do as I ask, and quickly!"

Anki immediately dropped down onto his backside right where he stood and began crushing the berries. Her mother turned back to Gigal, who Kina could tell was just as puzzled as she was about the berries.

"What is..." Gigal started to ask, but Unana held up her hand, apparently determined to not let any more questions be asked for the rest of the day.

"All that matters now is for you to know it will help. Once the boy is finished, we will combine them and..."

"Finished!" Anki shouted, holding the gourd cup in the air and rapidly tapping the broken handle on the stone floor – *click-click-click*. Kina was a little shocked and saw that her mother and Gigal were equally surprised. Gigal snatched the cup from his hand and examined the contents in disbelief. "Baba had to remake some of the ceremonial plates," he explained. "Me and Atu spent the past samawa breaking up the bad batches. So, I've had a lot of practice crushing them into a powder."

"Thank you, Anki, son of Abensu," Unana told him with a smile. "Gigal, let's have it." She held out her hand and Gigal gently placed the cup on her palm, clearly still in disbelief. "And the other." She held out her other hand, and Gigal gave her the first cup too. "Now, sister, these combined will not only give our Yaya the peace of mind to eat, but the necessary strength as well. I'll need you to go to the banquet pavilion and bring back a plate of yatak and honey."

Gigal scoffed, "That's what attendants are for!"

"My husband released our attendants for the day!" Unana snapped, stomping her tiny foot. "We are on our own! I've suffered all the stress and disrespect I am willing to endure this Day of Biyaya. Now, please, don't tempt me to force you."

"Unana, I..." Gigal began, clearly wanting to argue with her, but she stopped herself. "Alright, Unana Wani." She adjusted her robe and clasped her hands proudly together at her stomach. "As you wish." She then stepped up to within a hair of the back of the nearest adulu, a skinny, tree-like man named Atriska who was easily a hand taller than Gigal. "Move!" she shouted, startling him and causing him to lose his grip on his spear, which he then had to chase after. Kina heard Gigal laughing as she casually strolled through the opening.

"Kina," her mother reclaimed her attention. "Fan."

"Oh!" She didn't realize she had stopped fanning and instantly started back up. "Sorry, itaba."

"Anki, come over here and stand beside Yaya Amnu."

Anki cautiously got to his feet. "Is he going to be alright?"

"Yes, but he will be very grumpy," she said, and Anki feigned a smile. "Now, what I need you to do is hold his arm down on the armrest." She lifted the Yaya's seemingly lifeless left arm by the wrist and gently placed it on the armrest. "I will hold his other wrist, while I pour the juice into his mouth." She paused to gently place the Yaya's right arm on the armrest. "He is not going to like being forced to drink this, but we must be certain that he does. Understand?"

Kina's mother was talking to Anki, but he was looking up at her, so she nodded for him, trying to encourage him to help. At least she hoped what they were about to do would help. She quietly begged the Great Spirit within her to let the tizaka help. The quest to retrieve the plant was all her

344

father could talk about. Every meal those first few days started and ended with, *"Don't worry. Numila will return soon with the tizaka, and this entire ordeal will be behind us."* A few days later he added, *"Besides, I'm as thin now as I was when I was a boy!"* Kina's mother confirmed that her father was in fact as scrawny as when they first met, but then came the dizziness, the daily exhaustion, and then the collapse. She squeezed her eyes tight against the encroaching despair and took several deep breaths.

"Alright," she heard Anki say. "Let's do it." Kina opened her eyes and saw him smiling at her, but then his expression turned serious, and he grabbed her father's wrist with both hands.

"Good. Konoma!" Unana hollered.

"Yes, Unana Wani?"

"It seems awfully quiet in the plaza. Would you mind making some noise with your adulu?"

"Uh – what kind of noise?"

"You adulu have a wonderfully exciting chant you do when you run your drills. While we wait for the Tara'apti to resume, why don't you entertain us?"

He was quiet for a moment, as if considering whether or not to comply with her order, but then Boadulu Konoma said, "Of course, Unana Wani."

The three of them waited in silence for the chant to begin, Kina waving her fan, Anki and her mother holding on to her father's wrists, and the stinky cup of tizaka hovering in front of her father's open mouth. The whooshing of the breeze remained steady, the murmuring of the crowd just below it, and then, at a near whisper, almost inaudibly, came the soft chanting voice of Boadulu Konoma.

"Adulu, asacu iYucahu."

"Isati iYucahu, isati adulu!" they shouted in response, and then stomped their feet and slammed the butts of their spears against the ground – *STOMP-CLACK!*

"Adulu, lu'Yaya, lu'cudu, a'Itabacan!"

"Iluti'Yaya, iluti'cudu, a'iluti Itabacan!"

STOMP-CLACK!

"Un'adulu..."

Boadulu Konoma grew more confident as the chant continued, which Kina thought was an important development for him in his new position. After the first time through their call and response, the gathered masses started cheering for the adulu, and before they knew it, nearly everyone in the plaza was stomping and clapping with them.

"Ready?" her mother asked, reminding Kina and Anki that they had an important job to do. After they both nodded that they were ready, she said, "Here we go!"

STOMP-CLACK!

A short stream of chunky, greenish-brown juice flowed between Yaya Amnu's lips and down his throat, causing him to cough and choke before he reflexively swallowed it. Kina's mother made sure he took every last drop, and then she set the cup in his lap and braced his chest with her hand. A moment later, his entire body spasmed and he started to struggle.

STOMP-CLACK!

His eyes popped wide open and looked directly up into Kina's tear-flooded eyes. She mouthed, *I love you, baba*, as she choked on her own emotions, unable to force any words to come out. Through it all, she never stopped fanning, and no matter how badly she wanted to, Kina never looked away or closed her eyes.

STOMP-CLACK!

CHAPTER THIRTY-THREE

ANKI KAREB

It all happened so fast. Anki was still processing his father abandoning him at the Yaya's pavilion when he was suddenly having to restrain Yaya Amnu and keep him from squirming off of his throne. It reminded him of when he and his brother would sneak over to Amaca to spy on Mugan Galo while he cleared his brocket traps. Whether fawn, doe, or buck, every terrified brocket reacted the same to one of Galo's simple snares and would inevitably tighten the palm rope around their skinny legs and often hurt themselves. Of course, in this scenario, Anki and Unana were the snare, and Yaya Amnu was the familiar panicked buck with his huge eyes, skinny legs, and inevitable submission to his fate.

Unlike Mugan Galo, Anki was pretty sure Unana Wani had no intention of slaughtering the Yaya or making a tunic out of his skin, but there was a moment when she was muttering a strange prayer that Anki became concerned. It sounded like Itabayitian but harsher and throatier. He was only able to recognize two words – Osani and tizaka. He wasn't sure what the rest of it meant, but he was relieved when he noticed her muttering helped drown out Yaya Amnu's muffled demands that the boadulu arrest them. Anki also thought it was extremely clever of her to suggest the adulu begin chanting, further adding to the confused noise, without which Anki feared his first Day of Biyaya might become his last.

Once Yaya Amnu started to calm down, Unana explained what was happening, which he seemed to understand, but it was hard to tell because he could hardly say anything. Like when Biacoya had inhaled that green powder, the Yaya coughed a lot and seemed in great pain when he did try to speak. It wasn't until Lesini Gigal returned with yatak and honey that the Yaya's expression changed from one of anguish to appreciation. He instantly devoured the first plate of food, but Unana had to warn him to slow down or risk becoming sick. If he threw up the tizaka, they would have to do everything all over again. Unsurprisingly, Yaya Amnu immediately started to chew a little slower.

Gigal brought a second helping of yatak and honey, along with a gourd of hot water and a handful of green leaves. They looked like ordinary strongbark leaves but much less shiny. When Kina asked what they were, Unana said they came from a special shrub called oka, and that a tea made with oka leaves would give the Yaya the vitality of youth. Anki wasn't sure what that meant, but neither Kina nor Yaya Amnu asked her to explain, and Anki decided he shouldn't either.

As Gigal finished preparing the tea, Anki noticed the adulu's chant fading away and the quiet murmuring of the gathered masses return. The light breeze from earlier intensified and whipped across the plaza in sporadic bursts, kicking up sand and dust and reminding everyone in attendance that there hadn't been a single drop of rain in several days. Anki sat uncomfortably on the armrest of Kina Wani's small throne, shifting his backside from left cheek to right cheek and back again. He did his best to be subtle about it and not bother Kina. Unana Wani told him she would send for another seat, but then the Yaya needed her attention and Anki guessed she must have forgotten.

He sighed and shifted his backside again, wondering if his brother had gone with their father to the harbor or if Atu was still standing there on the other side of the adulu. He guessed his brother was probably sitting on the stone steps of the pavilion and was likely just as uncomfortable as he was, especially considering Atu had a very boney butt. Anki would prefer sitting on just about anything but a cibmani chair. He was even including the giant boulders along the shoreline of Conaca. At least those giant rocks had dips and grooves where his backside could fit snugly. He and Biacoya had made a game out of testing different positions on all the various angles and curves to find the perfect spot to sit. Cibmani offered only one boring position, and it was flat and unforgiving, and made Anki's backside numb.

"Has the Tara'apti finished?" Yaya Amnu abruptly asked, his voice weak and gravelly, but Anki noticed his words were surprisingly coherent for the first time. "I can't see anything with them in the way." He gestured with a floppy hand toward the adulu.

"Not yet, my love," Unana answered him. "Now, drink your tea." She took the gourd cup from Gigal and held it in front of her husband.

The lesini cleared her throat. "Unless you think he might be able to eat a *third* helping of yatak and honey," she said, "I need to go help our sisters. I'm worried about Bogula."

"Of course," Unana quickly replied. "And thank you, Gigal."

Lesini Gigal didn't say anything else in response, bowed to both Unana and the Yaya, and then stepped up behind the same adulu she had scared earlier. Before she could startle him again, the guard immediately stepped aside and motioned for her to come through. Anki heard her laughing again as she left the pavilion. Once she was gone, the guard quickly scrambled back into position and Anki had a chance to see his face for the first time, instantly recognizing him as one of Demican's many brothers.

"We must finish the Tara'apti by midmeal," Yaya Amnu said, but Unana forced him to take another sip of his tea.

"Must we?" she asked.

"And Coaynam has to conquer Okungur before the Great Light passes beyond the wall."

"Uh-huh," she indulged him and nodded along.

Unlike the Canutaloc, the almec match during the Day of Biyaya represented the Biyaya's internal struggle between the darkness of loss, Okungur, and the light of destiny, Coaynam. Team Okungur had black tunics and painted bands of black and gray around their arms and legs, while team Coaynam wore white and were adorned in shell anklets and wristbands. The game ball was painted gold to represent the Biyaya Spirit, which was passed through the stone hoops representing courage and doubt. Of course, Coaynam always won. Each team understood their place in the ceremonial match, as did the spectators, but it was the action they craved.

Kina leaned over to Anki and whispered, "I don't think he remembers what happened."

Anki was beginning to wonder about that himself and nodded in response, offering her a forced frown. He worried Yaya Amnu would start feeling better and change his mind about not arresting him. He was almost glad the Yaya had no memory of what just happened. Of course, he would never let Kina hear him admit it out loud. He thought if only he could say something that wouldn't upset her, then maybe he could distract her from all of this unpleasantness. Whatever he came up with had to be good enough to make up for the last time he tried to talk to her and she got stung by all those wasps.

"Boadulu Konoma!" Yaya Amnu tried to shout, sounding stronger and more like himself.

"My Yaya!" Konoma squeezed his head through the wall of adulu like a curious baby monkey through a bunch of hanging vines.

The Yaya started to say something, but Unana Wani made him take another sip of the tea, which he did reluctantly. "This tastes awful!" he protested.

"I know, my love, but you'll get used to it."

"When?" he asked, skeptically; Unana only snickered in response. "Oh – you find this humorous, do you?" When she didn't say anything, he turned to the boadulu. "Is this funny to you, Konoma?"

"M-My Yaya?" Konoma stammered uncomfortably, trying to squeeze the rest of the way onto the dais, but then he stumbled and fell flat on his face.

The boadulu's clumsiness made Unana's snicker turn into a full-throated chuckle. Konoma instantly popped right back up, brushed himself off, adjusted his belt, and then bowed, but Yaya Amnu was no longer paying any attention to him. Instead, he was smiling from ear-to-ear at his wife with one suspicious eyebrow raised. The way he was looking at her reminded Anki of when she and Kina had surprised them in the palace reception hall. He followed the memory thread to when she tackled him on the Yaya's throne. Her hug had been exactly what he needed and the thought of it now started to make him giggle, which Anki tried to stifle, but a single snort squeaked out of his dumb nose. He quickly covered his face with both hands.

"Oh – so it is funny!" the Yaya shouted but he discreetly offered Anki a little mischievous wink. The playful exchange brought a cool wave of relief over him, and a much-needed bit of lightheartedness to their seriously bizarre morning. "I say we tell Sengri to skip to the end of the Tara'apti," he said, looking up at Mawoi in the midday sky. "Agreed?" he asked all of them, though Anki wasn't sure why.

Unana shook her head, chasing the Yaya's mouth with the gourd cup, "Not until you finish your tea!"

She sounded serious, but Anki could see she was also having trouble suppressing a smile. He turned to look at Kina and was surprised to see her shyly scrunching down in her seat. Yaya Amnu noticed her too, quickly ducked beneath the cup of tea, and reached a frail hand across his wife to his daughter.

"Don't worry, my little obsidian gem," he said. "Your baba is feeling much better now – honestly!" A single tear trickled down her soft, ebony cheek.

"She's not going to believe you," Unana told him, holding the gourd cup over his head and covering the top with her other hand. "You've teased her one too many times."

"Enough," Kina shakily mumbled.

It seemed like an odd thing to say in the moment and Anki didn't have a clue what she meant by it, but then he saw a sparkle of understanding in Yaya Amnu's deep-brown eyes. To his surprise, the Yaya swiftly stood and knelt down at Kina's feet, sending his wahas clattering to the floor and making Unana have to swing the cup of tea out of the way.

"Kayki be merciful!" Unana hollered at him.

Yaya Amnu laid his forehead on Kina's knee. "I'm sorry for the pain I've caused you. You and your itaba," he said, placing a frail hand on Unana's knee. "I've acted selfishly and, yes...enough is enough." A moment passed, the Yaya holding his breath and waiting for her response, and then Kina threw her arms around his neck and squeezed him tightly.

"Easy, Kina," Unana told her as she laid a hand on the Yaya's, and then she took a deep breath. "You could have warned me you were going to leap into the air like Okid escaping Maboti's pot!" Anki noticed the cup in her other hand was as far away from the Yaya as she could stretch.

"I'm..." Yaya Amnu started to say something, but then he looked up into Unana's dark-azure eyes.

They were rare and penetrating eyes, and a color which Anki only ever remembered seeing in the clothing of the araco, or maybe the feathers of an echo bird. There was something about her eyes that made him very nervous, and he quickly looked away, deciding it might be best to avoid eye contact with Unana altogether.

"The Biyaya Spirit simply lifted me off my throne," Yaya Amnu explained. "There wasn't much I could do about it."

"That's the oka, my love," she said, matter-of-factly, while adjusting her tunic. "Now, what is it you wanted to say to Konoma? He's been bowing over there and waiting patiently."

"Right." Yaya Amnu pushed himself to his feet and turned to the boadulu. "Konoma, you may move your men aside now, and then I will need you to escort Bocoani Numila up to the palace and have him wait for me there. Understood?"

"Yes, my Yaya," Konoma said with a half-bow, and then he spun around and relayed the orders to his adulu.

As much as Anki was in awe of the crimson guards, he kept his eyes on Yaya Amnu whose sudden nimble and lively movements astounded him. *The Great Spirit is clearly at work*, he silently concluded. The Yaya had so quickly gone from ensnared brocket fawn to full-grown buck chewing through its palm-rope snare that Anki half-expected him to go prancing around the plaza. It was as if Yucahu had blessed him with...*the vitality of youth*. The instant he remembered Unana's words, he heard himself whisper, "So that's what she meant."

"What who meant?" Kina asked softly.

He turned and saw her rubbing her eyes. "Unana Wani," he whispered back.

"About what?"

Anki wasn't sure if he had heard Unana correctly, but he guessed, "Orka?"

Kina stopped rubbing her bloodshot eyes to correct him, "*Oka*."

"Oka?" he asked, and she nodded. "Alright, oka. The vitality of youth."

"What?"

"That's what your itaba said and now look at your baba."

"Oh," she nodded, seeming to understand.

"I wonder what it is."

Kina appeared to consider whether or not she should respond, but then she scooted across her small throne and pressed herself up against Anki's hip. "Um..." she began at a whisper, looking up at him with her big turquoise eyes. "I'm not exactly sure." Anki liked looking into her eyes because, unlike her mother's, Kina's eyes were bright and reminded him of the insides of clam shells. "I've heard itaba mention it once before when

352

talking with Lesini Bogula. She said oka used to grow in Itabacan somewhere, but I don't know where, or even when that was, or even why it no longer grows – wherever."

Another sudden burst of wind from the south shoved the rear guards against the backs of the thrones, causing a grumbling clatter of wooden spears, bodies, and stone, and also interrupting Anki and Kina's conversation.

"Baga," he muttered to himself, but then Anki snapped to see if his father had heard him, momentarily forgetting his father had gone down to the harbor.

The strong southerly intensified and tore through the pavilion, rushed down the steps, and kicked up a swirling column of sand known as a Hand of Maroha. They were common occurrences later in the dry season but were almost unheard of so soon after the rainy season. Anki, Kina, and everyone else quietly watched the Wind Spirit playfully twirl the sand like rainwater spiraling into a rat burrow. The Hand of Maroha danced across the plaza until it decided to chase Botara Sengri off the mound, making him scurry toward the Araco Residence.

"At least the wind feels nice," Kina said with a cute little giggle. "And it's not as bad as the sand storms the Wind Spirit stirs up during the Canutaloc."

"I bet Elder Sengri would disagree!" Anki added, making her giggle louder.

They watched in amusement as Sengri fled the swirling column of sand. He almost made it to the steps of the residence, but then he tripped over his long robe and tumbled forward onto the hard-stone ground. The crowd oohed at first, but then they cheered him on. With the eyes of the gathered masses upon him, Sengri scrambled forward again, crawling up the steps to where Jokimbi stood leaning against the wall. Just when it seemed like the Hand of Maroha was about to smack both of them, the column lifted off the ground and vanished into a dissipating cloud of sandy mist.

"Aah..." the crowd playfully whined before offering the men a spattering of applause.

"Sengri!" Yaya Amnu shouted, his hands on his narrow hips.

The elder araco searched the crowd for the voice with his squinted eyes, gradually coming around the plaza until he found the Yaya. "My Yaya?" he shouted back.

"The Tara'apti – skip to the end!" Yaya Amnu told him, but Sengri didn't respond right away. He appeared to be making sure the Hand of Maroha had truly vanished. "Sengri?!"

"Yes, my Yaya! I am trying to – uh – remember the..."

"Risca!" someone shouted from the crowd, interrupting Sengri's response, which was followed by a spattering of laughter.

"I was getting to that!" Sengri snapped, but Anki could see he was smiling. "Yes, my Yaya – *Orisa, Orisa*..." He started telling the story to the delight of everyone, but he briefly stopped to grab Jokimbi by the collar of his chaccus, yanking the Biyaya with him down the steps of the Araco Residence toward the center of the plaza. "...*Fire as water, the Biyaya Spirit calms your fury...*"

From the north side of the Pyramid of Mayu, the Hurassakin came running in their strange loincloths and rock skirts. Anki's father had taken him and Atu to the island of Risca to visit the Temple of Hurassa once when they were very young. He remembered, even while standing on the tips of his toes, he couldn't reach his father's belt, but he could reach the rocks of the Hurassakin skirts. They were long, thin, rough rocks attached by strips of copper, dangling and clacking together as they ran. His father said the rocks were given to the akin by the Fire Spirit to protect them, but Anki was never sure how they worked.

When the Hurassakin reached the mound, each of them immediately fell to their hands and knees and started arranging themselves into rows. Botara Sengri continued the story, circling them, followed closely by the Biyaya. Out of the corner of his eye, Anki caught the blur of someone running and turned in time to see Bociba Simi emerge from the crowd onto the open, sand-strewn plaza. One of his attendants chased after him with one of the ciba skirts trying to untangle the dangling rocks. The day just continued to surprise Anki, and he looked to see if Kina was seeing what he was seeing but found her pointing at the loinclothed men who were now climbing over one another to form tiered levels like a miniature pyramid.

"Aren't they supposed to be wearing red tunics?" she asked her mother.

"Yes, and no. They are Hurassakin," Unana answered her. "They aren't supposed to be doing anything until..." She stopped short when she also noticed the bociba. "Well, there's something you don't see every day," she remarked.

"Yes, and no?" Kina asked.

"It appears that skipping ahead in the Tara'apti might have confused some of our performers," Yaya Amnu observed with a smirk. "Ah, I see. Because the agur are gone, the akin have taken the role upon themselves."

Anki gently nudged Kina with his elbow, "Look!"

Just as Kina turned her head, Bociba Simi's attendant caught up with him, holding out the rock skirt and trying to get it around Simi's waist, but then the bociba abruptly stopped running. He slammed into Simi's back, sending both men tumbling to the ground.

The Yaya coughed as he burst out laughing. "First Jokimbi, then Sengri, and now Simi?" He closed his eyes, brought his hands up to his face, blew a puff of air into his palms, and then swept his breath down and out toward the plaza. "Oh, Great Spirit, may all council members suffer the same humiliation this Day of Biyaya!" he joked, continuing to sweep his breath down and out again and again.

"Stop it!" Unana playfully slapped his chest with the backside of her hand, trying not to smile.

Anki thought it was funny, but not just in a stomach-grabbing, roll-on-the-ground-laughing kind of way. Though it was a pretty good joke, and he was definitely going to tell Sheka and Luculati all about it later, he was unexpectedly becoming aware of how normal the Yaya and Unana were.

He had always been taught the Yaya and his family were destined to rule over the Itabayiti, and for their part, the Itabayiti were expected to revere them. Anki's father told him they were *Inkuyu*, which he explained was an ancient Itabayiti word for a sacred vessel that once contained Yucahu. But his father warned him to never repeat the word because it was forbidden to be heard by more than three pairs of ears. When Anki asked his father why he was being told the word in the first place, his father said, *"As your baba, it's my duty to teach you to speak and read our tongue. One day the Yaya will die, we'll hold a Yamayu – a bonefire for the Yaya – and you, as yaali, might have to drink oyma and prepare yourself to become the next vessel."*

Anki remembered having a lot more questions, but his father had told him they would talk about it in the morning, tucked him into bed, and then he blew out his bedside candle. He couldn't remember if he slept at all that night or not, but how could he have? Sacred vessels for Yucahu? What did that mean? *Weren't they all filled with the Great Spirit?* Thinking about it now, what really bothered him was that they never talked about Inkuyu again. He hadn't even thought about their conversation until just now, sitting there, watching the Biyaya be carried into the Araco Residence on a brightly painted cano. There was a roar of applause from the crowd as Botara Sengri returned to the mound in the center of the plaza, waving his old, wrinkly arms to quiet them down before he spoke. Anki got the feeling the elder araco was just as relieved the Tara'apti was over as everyone else.

"Coay ah'Biyaya continues with the ceremonial almec match!" he shouted.

Though the crowd was applauding, Anki thought they sounded about as enthusiastic as he and his friends were to meet Instructor Jokimbi in the reed bog. Even their sad, shuffling feet across the sand-strewn plaza kind of reminded him of students sloshing through the shallows. He watched in fascination as the women fanned themselves with large, browning leaves, and the men rested their interlocked fingers on top of their heads, exposing their underarms to the gently cooling breeze. Their discolored and sweat-stained tunics appeared stiff and uncomfortable, and Anki didn't envy them at all. But most of the children didn't appear to be bothered by the heat and chased each other around and between the slow-moving masses. He did see a few had to be dragged along by the hand or carried on shoulders, but it mostly seemed like the adults were desperately trying to keep some distance between themselves, their children, and each other.

Seeing the children made him miss his friends all the more, so he stood on the tips of his toes and searched the eastern edge of the Grand Plaza for them.

"Konoma!" Yaya Amnu coughed again.

"You sent him away. Remember?" Unana reminded him.

Noticeably irritated, he shouted, "Adulu!"

"Adulu!" they responded in unison, stomping their feet.

"Where's Atriska?"

"Here, my Yaya!" the immensely tall and skinny guard spun around.

Hearing the name, Anki quietly congratulated himself. He knew he recognized Atriska, even if he hadn't initially remembered his name. Demican and all of his brothers had nearly identical foreheads, similar chunky eyebrows, and they all had slightly varying shades of the same toad-brown and yellow eyes.

"Young man," the Yaya said, "being that one boadulu has been sent to walk with Niama, sadly taking a couple of your friends with him, and his successor is currently not here, I need someone I can trust to follow my orders promptly and accurately. Do you think you can do that?"

"Y-Yes, my Yaya," Atriska stammered, appearing just as shocked by the Yaya's question as the rest of his fellow adulu.

Anki was a bit more confused than shocked. He knew Boadulu Urtulu had been condemned to the deeps because Anki had been there to witness it himself. He also knew Konoma was promoted to replace Urtulu, but he was unaware more adulu had been sent to walk with Niama. It was as if Yaya Amnu went through his adulu the same way Anki's father had gone through the rows of drying clay plates, identifying defects and discarding the bad ones. His father said it was a necessary step to achieve the most consistent and desirable final product, and he had likened it to the field workers de-weeding their fields, or sanitation workers cleaning out Itabacan's drainage ditches. As the words of his father popped into his head, Anki suddenly realized they sounded familiar, but not because his father had said them.

And then he heard Yaya Amnu exclaim, "Great! You're now Duadulu Atriska."

"My Yaya!" Atriska bowed excitedly.

Anki couldn't believe it. Had he just witnessed an adulu getting promoted? His father told him adulu promotions took place at the palace, involved an elaborate ceremony with rituals and a feast, and they were always officiated by the boadulu. He looked at Kina for confirmation, but she just gave him half-a-smile and shrugged her shoulders.

"Now, Duadulu Atriska, clear us a path to the court," he ordered with a wave of his wahas.

"My Yaya?" he replied, his excitement quickly fading to confused panic.

"Two rows – or columns – about a reed or so apart?" The Yaya seemed to be getting tired again and wiped a sweaty palm across his sweety forehead. "A path, Atriska. It's not that complicated."

"Yes – of course, my Yaya!" he answered nervously, and then he spun around on his heels. "Adulu!"

After a moment, the rest of them responded, "Adulu!" – *STOMP!*

"Form two – uh – columns from here to the almec court!"

"Adulu!" Their response and stomp came quicker, and then they scrambled from around the pavilion and lined up into two even columns with their spears pointing outward, forming a protected path for the Yaya and his family.

"In keeping my word, you may remain with us, Anki," Unana Wani told him. "At least until your baba returns." Anki smiled back at her, appreciatively, but without making eye contact.

"Baba?" he heard Yaya Amnu quietly ask her. "Where is Abensu?"

"I sent him to the harbor with the coani to move Numila's canuti."

"Oh." The Yaya sounded as confused as any normal Itabayiti might after having lost consciousness for half the morning. "Well, Abensu was the best navigator I ever saw," Yaya Amnu added, his wahas clacking on the stone steps between each of his delicate footfalls.

His comment caught Anki by surprise, causing him to lose his balance and the tips of his toes slipped off the top step. He immediately kicked out one of his big feet, flung his long arms out wide, and landed awkwardly on the next step down. Bent over at the waist with his arms stretched out like gull wings, he looked over at the Yaya who acknowledged Anki's clumsiness with a grin. "My baba was a coani?" he asked.

"Briefly," Yaya Amnu answered. "Your baba even saved my life a few times while out on our many excursions around the great wall." He gestured with a swirl of his finger.

"More than a few," Unana corrected him, grabbing the Yaya's finger as she effortlessly glided down the steps to stand by his side.

"Well...the number of times isn't what's important, my love," he said dismissively.

Anki was amazed to hear it had even happened at all. His father didn't tell him he used to be a coani. Come to think of it, Anki suddenly realized he knew next to nothing about his father. From his earliest memories to now, they had always lived on Conaca and his father had always been the Chief of Wares. He was fully aware his family used to live on Yapaca, but the idea that his father had lived a completely different life before Anki was born seemed as fantastic as the Yayapti.

"In fact," the Yaya continued, "your baba might have become bocoani, if your ohbaba hadn't..."

"Hush, my love," Unana shushed him. "What the boy knows and what he does not know is for his baba to decide." Anki almost protested, but he thought better of it and kept his mouth shut.

"Of course, you're right," Yaya Amnu conceded, offering Anki another mischievous wink.

Anki watched the Yaya take several increasingly labored steps forward on the guarded path before turning to Unana and whispering in her ear. He tried to hear what the Yaya was saying, but the crowd started cheering for the almec players who were jumping into the sunken ceremonial court.

"He's asking for more tea," Kina Wani said, startling him and nearly making Anki slip off another step.

"Baga! You shouldn't sneak up on people like that!"

She laughed, "I was definitely not sneaking."

"Right." He nervously rolled his eyes and tried to compose himself.

"You and Biacoya. Both jumpy boys," she said, shaking her head and poking his shoulder with her thin finger.

"I am?" he asked, honestly. "I mean, no we're not!"

With all that had happened since the reed baths, Anki had started to feel slightly on edge. It was as if he had somehow accidentally outsmarted a ferocious beast that was still angry at him and continued to linger in the shadows. Every time he closed his eyes, he saw Biacoya's face slip beneath the dark, choppy waters of the sound. Every night, he had to get himself good and worn out just so he could fall asleep, otherwise he would lie awake with his eyes wide open until exhaustion finally caught up to him, or Mawoi's great light poured in through his window and he was forced to get up and pretend everything was normal.

"Have you gotten to see Biacoya?" she asked politely, as if listening to his thoughts.

Anki hopped from the bottom step to the ground in one big leap. "Yeah, a few times," he answered, not really wanting to talk about it. He had just explained everything to Sheka and Lucu, and talking about Biacoya made him sad, especially since his best friend probably wouldn't be allowed to come to the festival.

"Itaba told me he's lucky to be breathing at all. She said kincham was once the deadliest plant in Itabacan – more deadly than even pufferfish or jujo."

"What's a jujo?" He had never heard of such a thing.

"It's an extremely dangerous snake that lives in the Niknob," she said, hopping down the steps like he had done, but it took her three big hops in her perfectly white, spotless and flowy tunic. "Baba says they used to be found on every island, but we gradually killed them off. Now, only the Niknob jujo remain."

When she landed in the sunlight, Kina twirled on the balls of her feet, making the length of tunic below her shiny gold belt puff up like a sail. Anki thought she looked like one of the flowers of the kapok tree that would gently float to the ground during heavy rains. She was beautiful and he was instantly compelled to look away and try to quickly think of anything else. He stared down at the sand and dirt slowly drifting across the plaza, getting between his toes and sticking to his sweaty shins. *Nope, that isn't working.* He could still see her stubby little ebony toes, which looked like giant click-bugs. He watched them walk past him, heading toward Kina's parents, and with his head still down, Anki followed behind her.

"Boys are so weird," she commented over her shoulder.

"What makes them so deadly?" he asked, ignoring her comment and trying to steer the conversation back to the snakes he had never heard of and was pretty sure Kina had made up.

"Baba says one bite from a jujo can turn your leg to rock and make blood come out of your eyes."

Now he was positive she was making it up. "No way!" Anki shouted, daring to lift his head and racing up next to her.

Kina glared at him, "Shh. That's why baba won't let me visit Yapaca without an escort, even though he also said jujo keep to the swamp and only slither out to eat spiny rats."

"Huh." Anki was perplexed. She didn't act like she was lying, though he still felt like he would have heard about a creature like the jujo by now. He was ten years old after all, and there wasn't much mystery to Itabacan anymore. At least, Anki didn't think there was.

"Maybe you and Biacoya can take me with you on one of your adventures?" she asked him in her sweet, honey-like voice. Anki's stomach suddenly felt like it was being tickled from the inside again like he was stuffed full of bees. "Maybe we can visit the Niknob together," she suggested, and then abruptly stopped walking a reed away from reaching her parents.

Anki stopped too, but before he turned to face her, he noticed the adulu had placed four wooden chairs along the edge of the almec court, which he assumed meant he would get to watch the ceremonial match from the best seat imaginable. It was almost too good to be true! No more elbowing his way to the front of the council pavilion or having to stand the whole time to see over those seated on the pavilion steps. But beyond that, he'd also get to watch the match with Kina. Anki looked down into her mesmerizing turquoise eyes only to find them filled with sadness. "What is it?" he squeaked, the buzzing in his stomach moving up into his throat.

"I..." she started to say something but stopped herself to pick at her fingernails, which Anki just noticed had been nearly peeled off entirely.

He grabbed her hands. "Why are you doing that?!" he asked, examining her fingers.

"I don't know," she admitted, sounding on the verge of tears.

Anki bit his nails too when they got long. His brother trimmed his with a chaak he stole from the reed yard, and people like Bogula preferred to let their nails grow until they broke off on their own. But Anki had never seen anyone peel them off entirely.

"They look like baby rats," he observed, twisting her hands this way and that.

"Gross!" She yanked her hands back angrily and glanced over at her parents.

"You're gonna pick your fingers to the bone!"

"Shh! Will not!"

"Well, that's what it looks like you're doing. Why don't you have your attendants trim them for you?"

Kina crossed her arms and tucked her fingers into her armpits. "Why don't *you* leave me alone?"

As she glared at him from under her furrowed brow, her bright-turquoise eyes deepened to the extent that Anki thought they looked just like her mother's. The resemblance was remarkable, but there was no accompanying urge to look away. Her penetrating eyes didn't make him feel the least bit nervous. All he felt was sorrow for having upset her, which was the one thing he told himself not to do. She continued to glare at him, and Anki wanted to tell her he was sorry, but he could only offer her an apologetic smile. As he did, the edges of his vision seemed to darken, creating a pool of light just over her sweaty face. It was as if Mawoi had suddenly applied a thin layer of Ikmo's ashen glaze to Kina's soft cheeks and wrinkled forehead, and Anki wondered if the peculiar moment might be a sign.

Most Itabayiti believed Yucahu spoke to them through visions in their sleep, but when they were awake, the Great Spirit might come to them in these peculiar moments. If there was a message for him, or even for both of them, Anki had no idea what it could mean. He watched Kina's frustrated expression begin to fade, as if she was wondering the same thing, and he was about to ask her about it when they were both startled by a raucous cheering from the direction of the almec court. He assumed the match had started and turned to confirm his suspicion, but he was surprised by a vast shadow covering the Grand Plaza.

"Ma'an has blessed this Day of Biyaya," Kina observed, looking up.

Above them, a fluffy white cloud the size of the entire island of Itabaca seemed to have stopped purposefully to block the midday sun and relieve them of Mawoi's torturous heat.

"Kina! Anki!" Unana Wani hollered. "Come and take your seats, the match is about to begin!"

"We should go," Kina told him, taking a step toward the court.

"Wait," Anki stopped her, grabbing her hand. "I'm sorry about what I said. You're right, your gross fingernails are none of my business." He was only half-joking, but she thankfully giggled.

"Come on, Anki, son of Abensu," she said and poked him in the arm again.

Kina led the way to their seats on opposite sides of her parents. It was a little annoying to not be sitting by her, but Anki was definitely not disappointed by the view. After the chaotic beginning to the Day of Biyaya, the excitement of the ceremonial almec match rejuvenated the crowd. They cheered as the grunting men slapped the heavy ball with their equally heavy clay mitts, and oohed and aahed when the players collided with their sweaty bodies in the shiny hot hole in the ground. Almec was a spectacle of the highest proportions, and the match was mesmerizing. The Great Sky had cooled any concern for the heat and allowed the match to distract them from whatever was happening down at the harbor.

It wasn't until midway through the match that Anki allowed his eyes to wander away from the action to search the packed rim of the court for his father and brother. After the second pass, he spotted them crammed between the southern edge of the court and the steps of the council pavilion. His father appeared to have been waiting for Anki to see him and waved enthusiastically, while Atu pretended to not notice Anki at all. He didn't blame him. If he had been dragged down to the harbor during the festival and missed the end of the Tara'apti and half of the almec match, Anki would be pouting about it too.

The match continued and the crowd cheered and roared with delight. They shoved the events of the past mawa far back into the dark recesses of their minds and lifted the traumatic fog that threatened to divide them. When the final point was scored, the Itabayiti applauded and whistled so loud, thousands of birds replied in a chorus from the base of Mount Otaba, throughout the dense jungle, and then the sound rippled up into the still-hovering cloud overhead. Just then, Mawoi reappeared from behind the western edge of the cloud as if being chased out of his hiding place by the birdsong. The final point had been scored by Milag, one of Anki's favorite players, and once the roar of the crowd settled, Botara Sengri invited everyone to join Milag and the other players in the banquet pavilion for the feast.

While the masses filed into the pavilion like giant ants returning to their nest, Anki found his father and brother were waiting for him in the council pavilion where a separate buffet had been arranged for council members and their families. Together, they devoured roasted manati and juicy giant hutia meat. There were pineapples, coconuts, gourds, yams, and berries, as well as gooey yatak bread with honey and delicious chunks of honeycomb. Luculati was there, along with Amoc, Jumka, and a few of Atu's friends, but there was no sign of Sheka, which wasn't surprising at all. They were also missing Biacoya, but Anki wasn't surprised by that either. Even without his best friend, the enormous feast was another massive success. Oycu filled every adult's cup, while all of the children enjoyed their fill of coconut milk and honey.

When he couldn't eat one more piece of dried peach palm fruit, Anki made his way to the front steps with Luculati. They talked about the almec match and how Milag, though having not scored a single point for team Coaynam the entire match, miraculously came through in the end. Piddso had actually been more aggressive and scored more points, but Anki didn't want to mention it to Lucu. If he did, Lucu would accuse him of echoing Atu again, and then his friend would never stop teasing him. They both wondered where Sheka had gone and if she had even seen the match. Recognizing Lucu had a lot to say on the matter, Anki let him while he secretly spied on Kina in the Yaya's pavilion. He hadn't been able to see her through the wall of adulu, but now he realized he had an unobstructed view.

He watched Unana Wani hand an empty plate to one of the adulu, but she kept her open hand out to receive another plate covered in food. Yaya Amnu seemed to have eaten a bit more and was enjoying another cup of oka tea. And then Anki spotted Kina on the far side of the dais sitting on the floor beside her father's throne. She had her legs crossed and was eating from a plate in her lap. He wondered what she was thinking about. Was she also thinking about the almec match? Was she thinking about him and their peculiar moment? What was she about to say before he upset her by stupidly joking about her gnarled fingernails?

"Hey!" Lucu suddenly punched him in the shoulder.

"Oww! What did you do that for?"

"I said, look, ya dope!"

Anki rubbed his shoulder, following Luculati's outstretched finger across the plaza to a blur of motion that disappeared behind the attendants' quarters of the araco. "What?"

"Wait for it..." he said, slowly moving his finger across the vine-covered building to the Araco Residence beside it. "Almost there..."

"Lucu, I..."

"Have some patience, Anki – baga! No wonder the yaduka is always trying to take control. You never focus on anything long enough to let it figure out what's going on!"

He was about to punch Lucu right in the mouth for that comment, but then Anki saw something emerge from behind the Araco Residence. It was a boar-drawn cart with two men standing in it. One of the men he could tell was Boadulu Konoma, but the other had his back turned. "I don't..." he started to say, but then it dawned on him, "Numila."

"That's what I was trying to tell you while you were staring over there at that girl!"

"I wasn't staring!" Anki stretched his arm over his head. Lucu had really punched him hard – so hard it made his fingers go numb.

"Your eyes were stuck on her like bitumen on the ribs of a canuti!" Lucu poked him in his side.

"Were not!" he laughed, swiftly bringing his sore arm down to cover his side.

"Like a chacu snout deep in the mud pit searching for oycu!" Lucu continued poking his ribs, hip, back, belly, and then he circled back to repeat sequence.

Anki thought it was unfair. He couldn't fight when he was being tickled so badly. "Stop it!" he shouted, hardly able to breathe through his laughter.

"*LUCU!*" Boagur Gudugu growled at his son like an approaching storm. Luculati immediately stopped and looked up at the towering, boulder-like, beast-of-a-man standing over them. "Get up and go help your itaba with your sister. The bonefire is about to begin."

"Yes, Boagur!" Luculati scrambled to his feet and ran up the steps and into the council pavilion.

The Day of Biyaya bonefire was held toward the end of the festival as Mawoi passed behind the Pyramid of Mayu. Anki's father told him the chaccus worn by Jokimbi would be put in a reed basket and placed on top of a stack of cedar logs fifteen rows high, and then the whole thing would be set ablaze.

"Anki?" he heard his father calling and looked up to see him peeking over Gudugu's enormous shoulders.

"Yeah, baba?" Anki stood and shook out his arm, his shoulder starting to feel better.

"Abensu, your help today was invaluable," the boagur said without turning around, and then his weary gaze fell to Anki. "Listen to your baba, boy. He's as scrapy as the scrappiest agur, even without any tusks. One day, Chuka willing, you'll grow up to be just as tough as he is." With a nod of his big, sweaty head, Boagur Gudugu stomped the rest of the way down the steps and over to where Anki saw the agur had started stacking logs at the base of the pyramid.

"Come on, son, let's go," his father told him, following the boagur with Atu trailing several steps behind.

"Where are we going?" Anki asked, hopping off the pavilion steps.

"To the bonefire, of course!" his father joyfully exclaimed.

By the time they reached the front of the gathering crowd, Anki noticed Yaya Amnu was already climbing the steps of the Pyramid of Mayu and had been adorned with a long, flowing, red and gold ceremonial robe. He took the tall pyramid steps with the strength and energy of a younger man. Anki didn't know if anyone else was truly appreciating how miraculous the Yaya's recovery was, and then he wondered if he would even be allowed to tell his own father about oka or him restraining the Yaya.

He looked back at Atu still trailing behind them and weaving through the crowd like a nimble reed blowing in the wind. Would his brother believe him? *Sure, he would*, Anki told himself. Atu was the one who brought the green bag up from the harbor. He had to know the importance of his own involvement and would surely recognize, and maybe even be proud of what his little brother had done to save their Yaya. Anki would give just about anything to have his older brother's approval, despite how big of a jerk he could be at times. When he turned back around, Anki had to squint against the sun directly over the top of the pyramid. He saw Yaya Amnu had raised his arms high into the air like Sengri had done on the mound, and the mass of Itabayiti surrounding them instantly fell silent.

"For nine hundred and eighty-four years," Yaya Amnu began. "Itabacan has been resilient and thrived despite the efforts of Yuraca to tear down our walls." He spoke from halfway up the pyramid, his long robe cascading down the steps like the molten rivers of Mount Orisa. "We overcame the wicked Musu, when the Maboti spirit possessed him to murder Yaya Tano right here on these steps! Generations after that, Yaya Gahun rightly relocated the citizens of Niamca and Amaca to new accommodations in order to keep our water clean. And recently, as some of you now know, a conspiracy was thwarted that would have sliced through Itabacan like a dull chaak through reeds." There was a buzz of chatter throughout the crowd, but Yaya Amnu shouted over them, "The Great Spirit will never forsake this place!"

Everyone cheered as Yaya Amnu started down the steps. Anki wasn't sure why he was changing positions, but the Yaya was doing so with that same vitality of youth. Just before he reached the row of adulu guarding the base of the pyramid, he paused to once again look out at the crowd. Anki saw that the agur were almost finished stacking the cedar logs of the bonefire, and more people were coming forward to fill in around it. They spilled over onto the green grass to the south and the cibmani street to the north, squeezing in together to be nearer to the bonefire and the Yaya. Anki looked up toward the top of the pyramid and the western sky beyond it. Chuka had finally pulled Mawoi's cart behind the pyramid, casting a shadow over the plaza once again and relieving them of the heat. Where they had all been squinting before, the smiling faces surrounding Anki stirred up a swarm of emotions from the pit of his full stomach. It was more than just anticipation for the conclusion of the Yaya's speech, or the lighting of the bonefire, or the dancing that would follow. It was reverence, the recognition of the sacred, the Inkuyu, and in that moment, Anki thought he was starting to understand.

"This day is evidence of our commitment to the Biyaya legacy," Yaya Amnu continued. "Part of that legacy is to honor those among us who have embodied the fundamental spirit of the Itabayiti. Those whom we can trust to carry the Biyaya legacy forward for generations to come. To that end, it is now that I award Anki, son of Abensu, and Biacoya, son of Tambu, the Order of the Kareb!"

The announcement took Anki by surprise, almost as much as the resounding applause from his fellow Itabayiti. Slightly embarrassed, he instinctively tried to hide behind his father, but it was no use, he was surrounded by admiration. Strangers patted him on the back, their shadowy faces leaning uncomfortably close and smiling with their big white teeth and stinky breath. Anki felt himself starting to get upset. He could feel the tears of panic mixing in with his already-stirred-up emotions and begin to build along the bottom edge of his eyes. He was tempted to run away, but a familiar voice made him pause. He peeked out from behind his father and there, leaning on a twisted walking stick wrapped in dried vines, was Biacoya. Anki laughed through his tears and ran to hug his friend, but Tambu stopped him with one of his massive hands.

"Take it easy, Anki," Tambu said in his gravelly voice. "Biacoya's not ready for wrestling just yet."

"Yes, Tambu-baba," he said. Instead of tackling his friend, Anki greeted him with an exaggerated bow, and Biacoya graciously returned the greeting. Suddenly, from out of nowhere, Kina slammed into Anki and almost knocked him off his feet.

"Congratulations!" she shouted, pinning Anki's arms against his sides and squeezing the Yucahu out of him.

"Thanks," he gasped.

"In addition!" Yaya Amnu shouted over the applauding crowd, trying to settle them down. "In addition, it is time that I announce the promise of our daughter, Kina Wani, to Anki, son of Abensu."

The crowd once again erupted with applause and congratulations, and Anki was once again embarrassed beyond belief. He shyly looked at Kina, expecting her to meet his gaze, but she wasn't looking at him but at Biacoya. Her lips were moving but the noise of the crowd was too much for Anki to hear what she was saying. He didn't know what to do. He felt his father's large hand on his shoulders and was tempted to hide in his shadow, but then his father pushed him toward Kina. As he stumbled forward, she turned to him with her bright turquoise eyes, smiled, and took his hand.

"Without this young man's courage and determination..."

Anki could barely hear the Yaya continuing to speak. His tangled thoughts raced around themselves into confused knots, while all of the excitement flooding his ears collided with the tumultuous waves of emotions rocking him back and forth from within.

"...this Day of Biyaya may not have been possible..."

He knew how he wanted to feel. He wanted to be able to enjoy the admiration and not be so conflicted all of the time, but that seemed harder to achieve than spotting a whitefish in Itabacan Sound. One right after the next, his brother's mocking voice popped into his head, followed by his father's disappointed voice. He heard Jokimbi accusing him, his friends teasing him, and he felt like he might drown at any moment and be unable to suppress the yaduka any longer.

"...I, your Yaya, might have been murdered like Tano, but..."

Anki suddenly felt Kina squeeze his hands and he saw that she was saying something to him. Strangely, the voice he heard didn't seem to come from her. It was the voice of a woman, warm but firm, and her words didn't appear to match the movement of Kina's lips.

"...*unraveling is not destroying*," he heard the woman say.

Her words floated there on the surface of his mind, calming the choppy waves and allowing Anki to breathe more easily. With each peaceful breath, the noise of his surroundings trickled back in, and he braced himself for a deluge of tears. To his surprise, the deluge didn't come. His breathing remained steady, and he didn't feel the least bit overwhelmed. How long he had been looking into Kina's eyes, Anki didn't know, but he thought they appeared to be brighter than ever before.

"...Thank you, Anki Kareb!" the Yaya concluded, met by a third wave of applause.

Yaya Amnu brought the crowd's attention back to his final blessings as Mawoi finally dipped below the western wall and dusk fell on Itabacan. This was the sign for the Hurassakin to ignite the bonefire and for the musicians to start playing. It didn't take long for the wood to crackle and pop, and soon the humongous fire roared to life. An abundance of flickering light washed over the Grand Plaza, bathing everyone in red and orange, accompanied by an immense amount of heat. The flames quickly reached the reed basket at the top, there was a hissing sound, and then a plume of black smoke billowed upward. Anki watched Yaya Amnu eagerly waft the smoke toward himself, reversing the prayer gesture Anki had seen him make earlier when he was joking around. For some reason, Anki couldn't help himself and he started laughing, which spread first to Kina Wani, before infecting Biacoya Kareb as well.

At first, the Itabayiti had backed away from the bonefire, but the thumping rhythm of the gourd drums and the chorus of jatbays became too enticing. The music echoed off the surrounding structures, crisscrossing this way and that around the plaza before striking each and every one of them and coursing through their veins. They couldn't help it. Once again, the Itabayiti ignored the heat and danced far into the night.

The Last YAALI

Atu glared at his brother, but then he noticed Unana Wani watching him and he quickly smiled before looking away into the darkening sky. Since he was a little boy, he had a vague distrust of the Yaya and his wife. He could remember back when his family lived on Yapaca and he would play in the flowers of the public gardens. His mother helped him learn to swim in the shallows, and he would later sit in her lap to hear her tell him stories about their ancestors. She called him her little moon and Atu distinctly remembered praying to Kuraka with his mother every night before bed. They were happy memories, and Amnu and Unana were often in them.

But then he was on Conaca, they were expected to pray to Kayki instead, and it wasn't long after that his mother gave up her spirit to his baby brother. He could feel the tears welling up in his eyes as he remembered her bonefire, but the tears dried up the instant he recalled Yaya Amnu and Unana Wani hadn't been there. The more he thought about it, the more he realized they were absent from his memories from then on. Atu's father worked every day for the Yaya while an attendant was sent to raise him and Anki. *An attendant!* Not his mother or father, but an attendant. The more he remembered, the angrier Atu became until he felt his father's calloused hand on his shoulder.

"It's time," his father told him.

Atu sniffled but played it off as a cough, "Hopefully to get away from this smoke!" he said, and his father chuckled.

"You'll see, son. Now, follow me."

Atu shrugged his shoulders and did as he was told, thinking anything would be better than having to endure more praise for his stupid little brother. He followed his father through the sweaty crowd to the other end of the plaza and up the few steps into the council pavilion. Once inside, Atu was shocked to be greeted by the rest of the Yaya's council standing shoulder to shoulder in a circle.

"W–What's going on?" he asked.

"Step into the center, Atu," his father instructed him, and Atu hesitantly did as he was told. "In Boadulu Konoma's absence, Boagur Gudugu will be officiating."

Atu nodded, as if he understood what was happening, even though he didn't have a clue. Attendants were lighting torches and hanging them from hooks high up on the pillars of the pavilion above the winding green vines and yellow flowers. With each lit torch, new shadows formed in the circle, which were sharply contrasted by the brightly illuminated faces staring back at him. He knew most of the council members, but some of them had been replaced since the last time he cared to listen to his father complain about them. Now there appeared to be several members he didn't recognize at all. Atu noticed Boagur Gudugu had stepped into the circle behind him, blocking the only exit and holding a neatly folded white yaali tunic. It was then that Atu realized exactly what was about to happen.

"Place your hands beneath mine and repeat these words as they are spoken to the Great Spirit..."

"If this is the yaali ceremony, where is the Yaya?" Atu asked, nervously interrupting the boagur.

"The Yaya is not permitted to know who his yaali are," Atu's father explained. "There can be no interference in a yaali appointment, and there can be no influence in the Yaya's succession."

"Oh."

"All will be explained to you later by the Order of the Yaali," Gudugu added. "Now, place your hands beneath mine and repeat these words as if they are spoken to the Great Spirit: I have awoken from sleeptime, but I am still asleep."

Atu did as he was told and slid his pale hands beneath the boagur's thick and wet hands. He took a deep breath before repeating, "Great Spirit, I have..."

"Oh, Great Spirit," Gudugu corrected him.

Atu sighed, "Oh, Great Spirit, I have awoken from sleeptime, but I am still asleep."

"Good. Now, I have eaten from the earth and sea, but my tongue has never tasted."

"Oh, Great Spirit, I have eaten from the earth and sea, but my tongue has never tasted." He thought being asleep kind of made sense, but Atu wasn't quite sure what his ability to taste had to do with becoming a yaali.

"I have learned to hear and speak, but my thoughts remain empty."

"Oh, Great Spirit, I have learned to hear and speak, but my thoughts remain empty." *Am I supposed to be both asleep and ignorant?* he wondered.

"I have seen both light and dark, but my eyes have never opened."

"Oh, Great Spirit, I have seen both light and dark, but my eyes have never opened," Atu repeated the line, but he was starting to find them to be just a bit ridiculous.

"I have lived for many years, but living is unknown to me."

Alright, this is getting stupid, he thought. He looked up at the boagur skeptically, and Gudugu looked back down at Atu with tired and annoyed eyes. "Oh, Great Spirit, I have lived for many years, but living is unknown to me?"

A wave of relief washed over Boagur Gudugu's face and he sighed "Now, Atu, son of Abensu, this council recognizes you this day as one of the yaali," he said, stepping aside. "You may put on your yaali tunic and be seen."

First his father started clapping, but then the rest of the council joined in – some of whom even patted Atu on the back and told him "Congratulations." Boagur Gudugu helped him quickly change out of his faded green tunic and into the beautiful white yaali tunic with its gold stitching. The crisp fabric felt cool against his warm skin, and it smelled as if it had been pressed with red-heart flowers. Then his father came forward to fit the gold-colored boarhide belt around Atu's waist and tighten it for him. When he was finished, his father stood and Atu watched his long legs push his balding head up until his father loomed over him like a strongbark tree once again. The tree then leaned forward, and his father pressed his forehead against Atu's.

"I am very proud of you, Atura, my little moon," he told him. "This is a great honor."

Atu forced a smile, though he was having a tough time not laughing at how absurd he thought the whole ceremony had been. His father smiled back, honestly and proudly, and then gave Atu the biggest hug his father had ever given him.

Atu returned his father's hug, but for some reason, and he wasn't immediately sure why, the smile on his face turned crooked and ugly.

CAST OF CHARACTERS

ABENSU [ah-bin-soo]: current Chief of Wares, husband of Tiam, and father of Atu and Anki

ADDO [ah-do]: a brother of Demican and a duagur

AMNU [ah-m-new]: the twenty-fourth Yaya of Itabacan, husband of Unana, and father of Kina

AMOC [ay-mahk]: son of Boyiti Macoca and Kahila

ANGMU [ang-moo]: wife of Tamna and mother of Jumka; adopted mother of Tunku

ANIKNA [ah-neek-nah]: the brother of the Biyaya and second Yaya; one of the springs on the island of Niamca

ANKI [ah-n-kee]: second son of Abensu and Tiam, and brother of Atu

ATRISKA [uh-tris-kah]: a brother of Demican and an adulu

ATU [ah-too]: firstborn son of Abensu and Tiam, and brother of Anki.

BAYOM [bay-ohm]: one of the thread vendors

BELANGAS [beh-lawn-guhs]: twin sons of Chief of Textiles Tugdu and Gilo, and brothers of Nawuni

BIAM THE STRONG: a former wrestler who became the first Boyiti of Yapaca

BIACOYA [by-ah-co-ya]: son of Tambu and friend of Anki

BOGULA [bo-goo-la]: one of the lesini

BOLARI [bo-la-ree]: grandfather of Olari and Lewa, elder attendant to the Yaya

COKI [co-kee]: the former boyiti and a well-respected wrestler

DEMICAN [dim-ee-kahn]: son of Chief of Springs Hadim and Ahido, brother of Yaeel, Atriska, Macu, and Addo; best friend of Atu

DENI [din-ee]: one of the lesini

DIMGAL [dim-gahl]: one of the coani; scrounger during Quest for Tizaka

DRAHA [drah-ha]: adopted son of Sengri, brother of Tabba, and boaraco in training

ELAYA [ee-lay-uh]: one of the lesini, former wife of Yaya Shakali, and mother of Jokimbi

ENNU [in-new]: friend of Sengri

GABENI [guh-bin-ee]: the former bocoani

GALO [gah-lo]: current mugan, husband of Suga and father of Joba

GIGAL [gih-gahl]: wife of Boagur Gudugu and mother of Luculati and Matata

GIRI [gee-ree]: one of the duagur in training

GISAL [gih-sahl]: one of the coani on the Quest for Tizaka

GOACOLO [go-uh-co-lo]: one of the Mawoakin and guardian of Tanoc

GUDUGU [goo-doo-goo]: current boagur, husband of Gigal, and father of Luculati and Matata

HADIM [ha-dim]: current Chief of Springs, husband of Ahido, father of Yaeel, Atriska, Macu, Addo, and Demican

HAMSI [ha-em-see]: son of Madiri and friend of Atu

HARO [hay-row]: an elder ferryman

JOBA [jo-buh]: daughter of Mugan Galo and Suga, and love interest of Atu

JOKIMBI [jo-kim-bee]: son of Yaya Shakali and Elaya, brother of Yahuba, Kahila, and Turan, husband of Matia, and father of Sheka

JUMKA [joom-kah]: son of Chief of Gardens Tamna and Angmu; brother of Tunku

KACHI [ka-chee]: son of Chief of Sanitation Kasim

KAHILA [ka-he-la]: wife of Boyiti Macoca and mother of Amoc

KASEO [kah-say-oh]: infant son of Numila and Koyay

KASIM [kah-sim]: current Chief of Sanitation and father of Kachi

KINA [kee-nah]: daughter of Yaya Amnu and Unana, and friend of Anki and Biacoya

KONOMA [ko-no-ma]: one of the adulu

KOYAY [koy-ay]: current Harbor Chief, wife of Numila, and mother of Kaseo

LEWA [lu-wuh]: granddaughter of Bolari, sister of Olari, and assistant to Jokimbi

LUCULATI [loo-coo-la-tee]: son of Boagur Gudugu and Gigal, brother of Matata, and friend of Anki and Biacoya

MACOCA [ma-co-ca]: current boyiti, husband of Kahila, and father of Amoc

MACU [ma-coo]: a brother of Demican and a segin

MADIRI [muh-deer-ee]: one of the coani, brother of Chief of Gardens Tamna, and father of Hamsi; linesmen on the Quest for Tizaka

MATAS THE WHITE [ma-tas]: a famous wrestler

MULAK [moo-lahk]: brother of Koyay

NAWUNI [na-woo-nee]: daughter off Chief of Textiles Tugdu and Gilo, sister of Belangas, and friend of Kina

NUMILA [new-me-la]: current bocoani, husband of Koyay, and father of Kaseo

NUN [noon]: a lesini

OBNIL [ohb-nill]: son of Biyaya, the third Yaya, and originator of the Day of Biyaya; one of the springs on Niamca

OBOCO [oh-bo-co]: one of the ferryman

OLARI [oh-la-ree]: grandson of Bolari, brother of Lewa, and a Waki

PIDDSO [pid-sew]: an Almec player and friend of Lewa

RANAR [ruh-nar]: pet fox belonging to Sengri

RURUGA [roo-roo-guh]: one of the coani

SENGRI [sang-ree]: current Elder Araco and curator of Mayu Hall; adopted father of Draha and Tabba and friend of Ennu

SHEKA [sh-eh-kah]: daughter of Jokimbi and Matia, friend of Anki and Biacoya

SOCI [sew-chee]: one of the Mawoakin and closest confidant of Tanoc

TABAY [ta-bay]: mother of the Biyaya

TABBA [ta-buh]: adopted daughter of Sengri, sister of Draha, and araco to the Mawoakin

TAMBU [tahm-boo]: Chief of Vines and father of Biacoya

TAMNA [tahm-nuh]: Chief of Gardens, husband of Angmu, father of Jumka, and adopted father of Tunku

TANOC [tuh-nahk]: child boakin to the Mawoakin; parents unknown

TIAM [tee-ahm]: wife of Abensu and mother of Atu and Anki

TIKTALI [tik-tah-lee]: former bocoani and discoverer of the Gusiti

TUGDU [tug-doo]: current Chief of Textiles, husband of Gilo, father of Nawuni and Belangas

TUNKU [ton-koo]: son of former Chief of Gardens, mother unknown, adopted by new Chief of Gardens Tamna brother of

TURAN [to-rahn]: one of the lesini

UNANA [oo-na-na]: daughter of Nun, wife of Yaya Amnu, and mother of Kina

UNSARI [oon-sah-ree]: current boaraco and friend of Abensu

URTULU [ur-too-loo]: next boadulu

YAEEL [ya-eel]: a brother of Demican and a segin

ITABAYITI GLOSSARY

ACODU [ah-co-do]: scribes who taught reading and writing

ADULU [ah-do-loo]: the Yaya's personal guards

AGURAKIN [ah-goor-ah-kin]: Warrior-Priests

AGUR [ah-goor]: warriors trained to guard the Grand Gateways

AKIN [ah-kin]: Itabayiti priests who maintained the various temples

ALMEC [all-mehk]: a ball game created by Yaya Almec

ALUK [ah-look]: crab trappers on the island of Hatca

AMACA [ah-ma-ka]: the most forested island of Itabacan; home of the Lesini

AMUNTI [ah-moon-tee]: a rival tribe long ago back in the Itabayiti homeland

ARACO [ay-ra-co]: stargazers and intercessors to the ancestors

ARARUN [ay-ra-roon]: wandering spirit

ASHMU [ah-sh-moo]: to be moved through spirit with words

BABA [bah-bah]: father

BADHAN [bahd-hahn]: the largest village in Itabacan

BAGA [bah-gah]: an exasperated exclamation the Itabayiti used to convey anger

BAHACA [ba-ha-ca]: the easternmost island of Itabacan; home of the Mawoakin

BAYAMACA [by-ya-ma-ca]: also known as Hurassa's Palace, Bayamaca was an uninhabited, volcanic island southwest of Itabacan

BITABAY [by-ta-bay]: the First Mother of the Itabayiti; see Tabay

BIYAYA [by-ya-ya]: first Yaya

BOACODU [bo-ah-co-doo]: chief of the acodu scribes

BOAGUR [bo-ah-goor]: chief of the agur warriors

BOAKIN [bo-ah-kin]: chief of the akin priests (different for each temple)

BOARACO [bo-air-ah-co]: chief of the araco stargazers

BOCOA [bo-co-ah]: also known as the Great Sea, the Bocoa surrounded the Itabacan archipelago

BOCOANI [bo-co-ah-nee]: chief of the coani, lead navigator of the Yaya's fleet, and primary instructor to the children of the Yaya's council

BOHI [bo-he]: homes converted from reed huts to cibmani structures with stone floors, walls, and a roof

BONEFIRES: funeral pyres

BOTARA [bo-ta-ra]: officiant of the Tara'apti and the overall Day of Biyaya festival; traditionally taken by the Yaya

BOYITI [bo-yee-tee]: elected chief of the Yapati

BOYNAY [boy-nay]: the Rain Spirit

BUKU MARKET: southernmost market in the village of Badhan

BUKUN [boo-koon]: one of the original villages on the island of Itabaca; later became the Buku Market.

BUKUPU [boo-koo-poo]: what the Buku Market converted to at night

CAGES: either left or right side of the hull of canuti and made of ribs

CANO [ca-no]: part of fishing canuti which extended outward for stabilization

CANUTI [ca-noo-tee]: reed boats in the image of Kanu

CARU MARKET [ca-roo]: northernmost market in Badhan

CARUPU [ca-roo-poo]: what the Caru Market converted to at night

CHAAK [cha-ahk]: a small, curved stone blade used for harvesting reeds

CHACU [cha-coo]: boar

CHACUCA [cha-coo-ca]: southernmost island of Itabacan; home of the agur

CHEST: hull of canuti

CHOK [cha-ahk]: port side of canuti

CHUKA [choo-ka]: also known as the Great Boar; pulls Yucahu's cart

CHUKAKIN [choo-ka-kin]: priests for the Temple Pyramid of Chuka

CIBA VILLAGE [see-bah]: where the workers on Risca live

CIBMANI [sib-man-nee]: liquid stone used for building

COANI [co-ah-ni]: Itabayiti navigators

COAYNAM [co-ay-nahm]: the Light of Destiny

CONACA [co-nah-ca]: northernmost island of Itabacan with a large clay deposit

CUYILA [coo-yee-lah]: a necklace made from polished boar ribs

DITABA [die-tah-buh]: second mother

DUAGUR [doo-ah-goor]: an agur lieutenant

DUKYA [dook-ya]: vizier to the Yaya or second in command

DURALI [doo-ra-lee]: the Land Asleep where Mawoi goes at sunset

DWAMU [dwah-moo]: holes in the walls of the observatory; star ports

EKUKI [eh-koo-kee]: small field mice

GA'AN [gah-ahn]: hair knot worn by coani

GOSU [goh-soo]: a weasel-like creature with short but strong claws; sometimes called kugosu

GUSITI [goo-see-tee]: also called Golden People; only other civilization known to the Itabayiti

HAMACA [ha-ma-ca]: island where the Itabayiti grow their cotton

HATCA [ha-aht-ca]: island where the Itabayiti harvest and process crabs

HEKURA [heh-koo-ra]: when the moon is least visible in the sky; also called the Sleeping Moon

IKADUN [ih-ka-doon]: Biacoya's personal training canuti

ITABA [ee-ta-ba]: mother

ITABACA [ee-ta-ba-ca]: the largest island in Itabacan and original settlement of the Itabayiti

ITABACAN [ee-ta-ba-cahn]: an archipelago of twelve islands discovered by the Itabayiti and made into their new home

ITABATI [ee-ta-ba-tee]: Many Mothers

ITABAYITI [ee-ta-ba-yee-tee]: Children of the Many Mothers and founders of Itabacan, having fled their homeland of the Land of Many Rivers

ITABO [ee-ta-boh]: bride

JARA [jah-ra]: vine workers and rope makers

JUJO [joo-jo]: pufferfish

KANBATI [kahn-ba-tee]: formation of warriors

KANU [kah-noo]: the Great Serpent, said to have taught the Itabayiti how to build reed boats called canuti

KANUAKIN [kah-noo-ah-kin]: priests of Kanu

KAODONITI [ka-oh-doh-nee-tee]: the Itabayiti ancestral homeland; also known as the Land of Many Rivers.

KAPOK [kah-pahk]: a large tree with winding roots and white flowers

KARUN'KALU [kah-roon-kah-loo]: Ennu's threat guardian; a gift from Karun

KARUN [kah-roon]: the Withering Spirit of Decay, sister of Sutak

KAYAKIN [kay-ah-kin]: priests of Kayki

KAYKI [kay-kee]: the Earth Spirit

KECHET [keh-cheht]: a ceremonial headdress made from two conch shells

KIKURI [kee-koo-ree]: red-heart flowers often used in bathing and decoration

KIOSAY [kee-oh-say]: an ancient tree from the Itabayiti homeland

KOKI [koh-kee]: a type of tree frog with bulging eyes

KONA [koh-nah]: starboard side of the canuti

KOPAU [koh-pow]: sweet grass

KOTEDU [koh-teh-doo]: attack

KUDI [koo-dee]: a hateful term for anyone thought dirty or lesser, especially beggars and sanitation workers

KUGO [koo-goh]: howler monkeys

KURAKA [koo-ra-kah]: the Moon Spirit

KURANAN [koo-ra-nan]: Itabayiti months, composed of twenty-nine days divided into fourteen-day weeks called mawa, and a final day where Kuraka sleeps and is called Hekura

LESINI [leh-see-nee]: healers

LIBANU [lee-ba-noo]: a place or process referred to by Ennu

LOWAKI [lo-wa-kee]: field worker

MA'AN [mah-ahn]: the Great Sky

MABOTAKIN [ma-bo-tah-kin]: priests of Maboti

MABOTI [ma-bo-tee]: an ancient evil force that once ruled the nighttime; also called the Dark Shadow

MANATI [man-ah-tee]: manatee

MANIKU [man-ih-koo]: nearly hairless rodent-like creatures with long noses and tails

MAROHA [ma-row-ha]: the Wind Spirit

MAWA [ma-wa]: a period of fourteen days

MAWOAKIN [ma-wo-ah-kin]: priests of Mawoi in the Temple of the Sun

MAWOI [ma-wo-ee]: the sun; also known as the Sun Spirit or the Great Light.

MAWOI-COAY [ma-wo-ee-coh-ay]: a variation of the common greeting, Taycoay, only used by the Mawoakin

MAYU [mah-yoo]: the Milky Way, also called a smoldering river; where Yucahu resides and where Itabayiti ancestors return after death

MIDRIB [midrib]: middle part of the rib or side railing of a canuti

MUL [muhl]: constellation

MUWAN [moo-wahn]: giant hawks that once thrived throughout Itabacan

NAKIBO [nah-kee-bo]: march of the groom to the bride's residence

NANI [nah-nee]: large hairy beasts that once roamed the Land of Many Rivers

NIAMA [nee-ah-ma]: the Water Spirit

NIAMCA [nee-ahm-ca]: island in Itabacan with several freshwater springs

NIMURU [nee-moo-roo]: a water sprinkler or mister used during hot days

NITABA RIVER [nee-ta-ba]: flows down Mount Otaba on the island of Itabaca

NUMKALU [noom-ka-loo]: Ennu's daughters

NUM-NUM [numb-numb]: a tart and slightly sweet-tasting fruit

OBYA [ohb-ya-ta-bay]: the ancestral mother of all Itabayiti mothers

OKA [oh-kah]: a shrub on the island of Bayamaca with small and extremely bitter berries, which are said to possess the vitality of youth

OKANBATI [oh-kahn-ba-tee]: the second kanbati

OKUNGUR [oh-koon-goor]: the darkness of loss portrayed in the almec match during the Day of Biyaya festival

OLLULI [oh-loo-lee]: rubber tree

OMABU [oh-ma-boo]: a colorful shrub that often blows away and rolls around during the dry season

OMABU-DISHA [oh-ma-boo-dee-sha]: a miniaturized and portable game using marked sticks and any small object to represent a rolling omabu shrub

OMAKI [oh-ma-kee]: fertilizer

ORA [oh-ra]: the Birthplace of Life

ORISA [oh-ris-ah]: volcano on the island of Risca

ORLIL [or-lil]: the Ageless Daughter of Yucahu and sister of Sutak

OSANI [oh-sa-nee]: the Great Healer

OSANUM [oh-sa-noom]: towering plateau on the island of Amaca

OTABA [oh-ta-ba]: a mountain on the island of Itabaca

OUBAYOCA [oy-bay-oh-ca]: one of the few islands discovered beyond the walls of Itabacan; also called the Island of Blood

OYCU [oy-coo]: a plant that grows in darkness and is made into a fermented drink

OYMA [oy-mah]: a drink prepared from oycu reserved for the Yaya

PACCA [pah-ca]: island of vines and rope production

PAGASHLA [pa-gah-sh-la]: underwater creature, also called toe pinchers

RIB [rib]: multiple bundles of reeds bound together

RISCA [rih-ska]: most volcanic of all of Itabacan's islands

ROUND [round]: circular area in the center of the Council Rotunda

RUDU [roo-doo]: alarm

SAKIMI [sah-kee-mee]: a star in the Urgoca-mul and one of the springs on Niamca

SAMAWA [sa-ma-wa]: the second mawa of each kuranan when the moon shrinks to become Hekura

SANACA [sa-na-ca]: one of the few islands discovered beyond the walls of Itabacan

SCROUNGER [scrounger]: sailor responsible for distributing items to the other sailors on the canuti

SEGIN [say-gin]: water purifiers

SEKOM [she-kum]: a tool used in the observatory

SHIYITI [she-yee-tee]: the movement of the people

SHOATS [show-tz]: sailing students, also baby boar

SIKULKA [see-kul-ka]: the Frost Spirit who is thought to be responsible for the Cooling Wind.

SPARKER [sparker]: tool to start fires

STUG [stoog]: to be still or silent

SUMAWA [soo-ma-wa]: the first mawa of each kuranan when the moon grows

SUTAK [soo-tahk]: also known as the Great Preparer, son of Yucahu and brother of Karun

SUTAK'BALO [soo-tahk-ba-low]: the hand of the Great Preparer

TAYCOAY [tay-coh-ay]: a good day greeting; hello

TAYOKUN [tay-oh-koon]: a good night greeting; goodbye

TIBURANA [tih-boo-ra-nah]: a giant shark

TULU [too-loo]: what the Gusiti call the furry creature they skin to make their minimal clothing

UANSU [ooh-an-sue]: the Great Hawk

UCA [ooh-ca]: large owl-like creature

URGOCA-MUL [oor-go-ca-muhl]: the Echo Bird constellation

UTUCHU [ooh-too-choo]: the Wicked Weaver

WAHAS [wah-hass]: the Yaya's staff made from woven vines which signified the Yaya's authority

WAKI [wah-kee]: clay diggers and workers

WANI [wah-nee]: a title bestowed upon the family members of the Yaya

WOIGIR [wo-ih-gear]: warrior's cart

YAALI [ya-ah-lee]: candidates to become the successor to the Yaya

YABO [ya-bo]: groom

YADUKA [ya-doo-kah]: a child who is thought to have stolen the Great Spirit from their mother during birth; also known as a Spirit Thief

YAKANBATI [ya-kahn-ba-tee]: a third kanbati or formation of warriors

YAMAYU [ya-ma-yoo]: a bonefire for the Yaya

YAPACA [ya-pah-ca]: the flattest and most populated island in Itabacan

YATAK [ya-tahk]: a flatbread made from yuca roots

YAYA [ya-ya]: name of the hero of the Yayapti, first ruler of Itabacan, and the title passed down to every ruler of Itabacan since

YAYAPTI [ya-yahp-tee]: the story of Yaya and the Itabayiti escape from the Amunti and the founding of Itabacan

YUCA [yoo-ca]: a plant with many medicinal qualities and roots made into flour

YUCAAKIN [yoo-ca-ah-kin]: priests of Yucahu

YUCAHU [yoo-ca-hoo]: the Great Spirit

YURACA [yoo-ra-ca]: the Storm Spirit

FEBRUARY 2026

MARCH 2027